Dust and Ashes

By Anatoli Rybakov

HEAVY SAND
CHILDREN OF THE ARBAT
FEAR
DUST AND ASHES

DUST AND ASHES

Concluding Volume of the
Children of the Arbat
Trilogy

ANATOLI RYBAKOV

Translated by Antonina W. Bouis

LITTLE, BROWN AND COMPANY
BOSTON NEW YORK TORONTO LONDON

First Edition

This novel is a work of fiction. Names, characters,
places, and incidents are either the product of the
author's imagination or, if real, are used fictitiously.

Library of Congress Cataloging-in-Publication Data

Rybakov, Anatoliĭ Naumovich.
    [Prakh i pepel. English]
    Dust and ashes / Anatoli Rybakov; translated by Antonina W.
Bouis.
        p.   cm. — ([The Arbat trilogy ; v. 3])
    "Concluding volume of the Children of Arbat Trilogy."
    ISBN 0-316-76379-9
    1. World War, 1939–1945 — Soviet Union — Fiction.   I. Bouis,
Antonina W.   II. Title.   III. Series: Rybakov, Anatoliĭ Naumovich.
Arbat trilogy ; v. 3.
PG3476.R87P713 1996
891.73'44 — dc20   95-36018

10   9   8   7   6   5   4   3   2   1

HAD

Published simultaneously in Canada
by Little, Brown & Company (Canada) Limited

Printed in the United States of America

The Story so Far

Dust and Ashes completes the trilogy begun by *Children of the Arbat* and *Fear*. The story begins in 1933 and ends in 1943, the most tragic decade in the history of the Soviet state: the peak of the Stalinist Terror and the first defeats in the war with Nazi Germany.

The main characters of the epic are Sasha Pankratov, a Moscow student, and Josef Stalin, the dictator who unleashed an unprecedented reign of terror against his own people.

Sasha grew up on the Arbat, a central and ancient neighborhood in Moscow. On a trifling excuse — an innocent, if flippant, poem written in the school newspaper — he was arrested and exiled for three years deep in remote Siberia. After his term was over, he was not allowed to return to Moscow or to live in any major city; he traveled around the country and ended up in Ufa, where his comrade Gleb then lived. This is where the reader of *Dust and Ashes* encounters Sasha.

Still back in Moscow are Sasha's classmates, the generation of the "children of the Revolution," who grew up in the Stalin era and whose lives are affected in various ways by the tragedy of their time. The fate of this generation is the subject of the trilogy.

Yuri Sharok serves in the secret police (NKVD). The novel finds him in Paris, where he is a Soviet spy. Before leaving the Soviet Union, he had an affair with Lena Budyagina, the daughter of a famous Soviet diplomat. Lena's parents were shot in 1937 and she has been left alone with her baby by Sharok, with whom she has broken off her relationship. Yet another former classmate lives in Paris, Vika Marasevich, the daughter of an esteemed professor. A famous Moscow playgirl, Vika married a French journalist and was recruited to be an informer by the NKVD in Paris. Her brother, Vadim Marasevich, is also an NKVD informant and serves the regime with his pen as a literary critic.

Another young man from Sasha's old circle is Maxim Kostin, a Red

Army commander, who is doing his military service in the Far East. He is in love with Nina Ivanova, a fervent Communist, who, despite her loyalty to the Party, has fallen under political suspicion. In order to protect Nina from arrest, her sister Varya sends her to Maxim in the Far East. Varya is the youngest in the Arbat crowd, and she rejects the Communist ideals of her older friends.

She likes Sasha Pankratov, his boldness and honesty, and she helps Sasha's mother by standing in the long lines at the prison to pass Sasha food and clothing. After Sasha's exile to Siberia, she fell into a flashy crowd, spending her time in nightclubs, and made an unfortunate alliance with a billiards player. But this empty life disillusioned her and she got a divorce and a job as a draftsman. Her old feelings for Sasha have returned and she and Sasha begin corresponding. She falls in love with him and dreams of their being together. But upon his release from exile, Sasha had learned of her marriage. The news stunned him and he broke off with Varya. They separated, still loving each other. Some Russian critics have called Sasha and Varya the "Russian Romeo and Juliet." Their love story is a central plot element throughout the trilogy, and the reader will learn how it ends in *Dust and Ashes*.

All these stories and passions are told against the background of the tragic events of the period: the harsh transformations in society, the diplomatic games on the eve of war by two tyrants — Stalin and Hitler — and the war itself.

PART I

1

YOU'RE IN LUCK, DEARIE! The first time I went to the post office, bang, there was your telegram! I headed straight for the train station."

Gleb was smiling, showing his white teeth, and looking at Sasha.

"Leave your things in the baggage room for now. My landlady won't let me bring in a second person. We'll find you your own apartment."

They accepted his suitcase at the baggage room, but not his rucksack. "We don't take things without locks." Gleb gave the attendant a ruble. "All right, boss, today we do." He put the pack next to the suitcase and gave them a receipt for two articles.

"Let's walk," Gleb proposed. "I'll show you the city."

The city was like any other, a regional center. Grocery store, hardware store, stationery, bakery, pharmacy. . . . Like Kalinin, like everywhere. Dreary. Old one- and two-story wooden houses. The occasional stone buildings had signs with the names of institutions written in Russian and then in Russian letters in the Bashkir language. That was the only reminder that this was the capital of the Bashkir Autonomous Soviet Socialist Republic. Otherwise it was the sticks, with cobblestone streets, wooden sidewalks here and there, and sometimes no sidewalks at all. Dust. The dreariness of Russian cities. Or maybe, it was his own depression. Starting over, yet again.

"It's a nice town," Gleb said. "Russians, Tatars, Bashkirs. The Tatars try to pass themselves off as Bashkirs. . . . You can't tell them apart — thin, scrawny beards and mustaches, no hair at all on their cheeks and they don't shave. But the Bashkirs don't confuse themselves with the Tats. You're Turkic, they say, and we're like Hungarians, Magyars."

"The Bashkirs are also Turkic," Sasha said.

"Probably. . . . They're peaceful and hospitable. But touchy. Don't pick a fight with them, dearie."

"Of course not!"

"Just recently we were in a small group and one intellectual from Leningrad, a young fellow, said to a young Bashkir, something like, 'I agree with you, old man.' Understand, dearie? He used the expression 'old man' the way they do in Leningrad. But the Bashkir took offense and smacked him in the face! 'How dare you call me an old man?' If there had been girls at the table, then he would have been humiliated in front of the women. At least it was an all-male group."

He laughed and then pointed at the pavilion with a sign that read "Koumyss."

"See, they sell *koumyss,* mare's milk. It's very healthful. It helps with tuberculosis. There's a TB spa nearby — Shafrakovo, where they treat you with *koumyss.* And incidentally, the Bashkirs use it to make *araka,* a fermented drink. They even distill it. They drink like horses, and pay no attention to the Koran at all. 'Gots money, party in Ufa. No gots money, stay in Chishma.' That's their motto."

"What's Chishma?"

"A station near Ufa. Didn't you notice it coming in?"

"I didn't pay attention."

"They like to eat even more than they like to drink. They eat mostly horse meat and mutton. The *bish-barmak* is not bad, edible."

They were walking through the center of town, along Egor Sazonov Street, named for a Socialist revolutionary, a terrorist, who killed the Tsarist minister Pleve. Could he have been from Ufa?

They were coming across more and more people in the NKVD uniform, in polished boots and jodhpurs, their faces square and immobile. Why were there so many of them here? The headquarters of the NKVD of the Bashkir Autonomous Soviet Socialist Republic was on Egor Sazonov Street. A long, two-story brick building, its windows were covered with thick metal bars; four entrances reached the middle of the sidewalk — windowless boxes, heavy doors without glass shut tight.

Gleb squinted at Sasha. "This is where the exiles from Leningrad come to report."

"Gleb," Sasha asked. "Did you know that they were introducing a passport regimen in Kalinin?"

"Yes."

"Why didn't you tell me?"

Gleb stopped in his tracks.

"What do you mean I didn't tell you? I remember my words exactly: 'Today Kalinin is not a closed city, tomorrow it will be.' What do you call that?"

"Well, a hint . . ."

"That's not enough? Did you want the date and the number of the resolution? I don't know that." He shook his head. "Even a child can understand a hint like that. Especially since I asked you to leave the city with me."

"You're right," Sasha said. "But I didn't get the hint until I was in police headquarters."

"You got it." Gleb chuckled. "In your position, dearie, you have to be quicker on the uptake. And quicker to split."

"It came out for the best. I have my documents, got fired from work, was registered out of my apartment."

"If that's better, then fine."

"You don't think so?"

"You know best," Gleb said evasively. "My job was to warn you."

"All right, then. Tell me, have you started your hackwork?"

"Dearie! How dare you! 'Hackwork'! What do you mean? Our troupe is under the direction of Semyon Grigoryevich Zinoviev himself."

"Any relation to that Zinoviev?"

"That one is a Jew, and our Semyon is Russian. A former soloist of the Maryinsky Theater, author of the book *Contemporary Ballroom Dancing* — a mighty personality, a major figure. He rented the Palace of Labor, and he's signing contracts with the factories and plants here. Thirty rubles a person and you learn the fox-trot, rumba, tango, and Boston waltz. You came just in time. He's desperate for an assistant. Nonna isn't enough to help him with all the classes."

Gleb slowed down and looked Sasha over. "Do you have another suit?"

"What's wrong with this one?"

"It's old, it's worn, it's old-fashioned. And your shoes. . . . Shoes are the most important thing, dearie! Some English lord can wear the shabbiest tweeds, but his shoes! They have to sparkle! You'll be showing them how to move their feet, and what will they be looking at? Your gorgeous hair, your enchanting eyes? No, dearie, they'll be looking at your feet. And if they see worn or dirty shoes, they're not going to be thrilled by your dancing, are they? It's not aesthetic! And Semyon Grigoryevich cares about aesthetics, dearie. Men show up for their classes wearing polished shoes and a tie. Do you have a tie?"

"Never wore one in my life."

"You'll have to start now. And you must buy a pair of shoes today. Black ones. Black goes with any suit. And you'll get a tie to match. The tie has to harmonize with the shoes."

"Did Semyon Grigoryevich teach you that?"

"I knew it without him. You're underestimating him. He's organized this in a major way. It's not just some fancy-pants dance class. This is ideology, dearie, and don't you forget it."

"You don't say."

"If a group of thirty people gets together, what do you think — that *no one* is going to take an interest? And there's more than one group. Everyone in Ufa is coming for lessons — Russians, Bashkirs, they all want to learn the Western European dances. And that means that the people whose job it is have to keep an eye on us. Which means we have to be careful. And don't worry about the rest. Semyon will take care of himself and he won't forget about you either. The main question now for you is housing."

"Is it hard to get a room here?"

"That's not the problem."

"What is then?"

"Don't worry, we'll manage."

"You're not telling me something. Is my arrival a problem for you? Tell me straight and I won't be a burden. I'll find a job."

"And you'll be better off than in Kalinin?"

"You speak in riddles and hints."

Gleb stopped again and said seriously, "You have to understand hints, dearie. The times call for it. All right, let's go, you'll see our office."

They turned off Sazonov Street into an alley. A crowd of people had gathered in front of a small house with a sign that announced "Booking Agency."

"Wait here," Gleb said and went inside.

Sasha stood a bit down the alley. Many of the people in the crowd seemed to know one another, and they hailed each other, moving from group to group, hugging, kissing, exclaiming, "How many moons!" There was something overly theatrical about it. They were playing to a crowd. It was *phony*. How could Sasha live and work with people like that? They were alien to him, their lifestyle was alien to him. Should he drop the whole thing? Go look for a job in a garage?

Gleb came out. "Let's go."

And he showed Sasha a slip of paper with an address on it. "It's right in the center of town. There's only one hotel in the city and they only take big shots, people's artists and honored artists. Everyone else is billeted in apartments. Did you take a look at this crowd? Magicians, hypnotists, readers, dancers, reciters. Who else? Oh, yes, Bashkirs with their *kurais*. Do you know what a *kurai* is?"

"No."

"It's a pipe, like reeds. The Bashkirs have melancholy music, rather dreary, but it's listenable. They all hang around the agency and form troupes. It's important to have a good manager — a key figure who goes ahead, does the advertising, rents the hall. It's a lucrative business to bring a real live actor to the sticks! You need at least one famous name on the poster. And we've got loads of them here — Kachalov, Ktorov, Tseretelli, Ulanova! No complaints. Smirnov-Kachalov, isn't that something?" He squinted at Sasha again. "Why so quiet, dearie?"

"What do you need all this for? You and Semyon don't give concerts. And you've been sent here from Kalinin."

"You know what they say? 'Oh, so you're from Kalinin? Well then, teach your stupid dances there. But if you want to be here, then work for us.' Our boss is Marya Konstantinovna. You'll meet her soon. A tough woman from the intelligentsia. Bear that in mind. You can come to terms with her. And also remember that you have to pay for your own apartment."

"I understand."

It was a corner house, one side on Aksakov Street, the other on Chernyshevsky. A tiny room in a small apartment. But it was separate, not simply behind a curtain, the way Sasha's place had been in Kalinin.

That was an improvement. The landlady was befuddled and distracted. She couldn't find her glasses and blamed the children, who must have hidden them someplace. The girl and boy, around twelve or thirteen, went off to the kitchen to look for them. The boy was coughing. "Don't croak!" his mother shouted at him. "Look for my glasses."

They found the glasses at last.

"And where's the directive?" the landlady asked.

Gleb gave her a charming smile. "Maria Konstantinovna was in a hurry. She gave us the address and will write out the directive on Monday. She wrote the address in her own hand. You know her handwriting."

The landlady examined the slip of paper suspiciously.

"Do you have doubts?" Sasha reached into his pocket. "Here's my passport."

"I don't need your passport. I'm not going to register you."

No need to register! Marvelous! Sasha's recalled all his suffering and humiliation registering in Kalinin. He wouldn't have that problem here. And he could see why — a traveling performer lives in many cities in a year's time. It's silly to register in each one. There wouldn't be enough pages in his passport. Great, he'd take up dancing!

"Maria Konstantinovna will take care of all the paperwork," Gleb promised.

"Do you have your luggage?"

"I'll go get it at the train station right now."

"Just remember one thing," she said, hurrying the children into the next room and shutting the door. "I must ask you not to bring women for the night."

Sasha's eyes widened. "Of course not! Who would do that?"

"Lots of people," the landlady said. "The actor Tsvetkov lived here before you. It was bad enough that he was a drunkard, but no, he also brought in women. He looked reasonably decent, but he behaved terribly. I have children, you know."

"Everything will be fine," Gleb assured her.

"When you move in," she went on, "I'll give you the key to the apartment. You'll be coming back late from the theater, and we go to bed early."

"I'll try not to disturb you," Sasha said.

∾ 2 ∾

ON AUGUST 24, 1937, a reception was held in St. George's Hall of the Kremlin in honor of the pilots Gromov and Yumashev and the navigator Danilin, who made a nonstop flight over the North Pole from Moscow to America. In 62 hours 17 minutes in a Soviet ANT-25, they covered 10,148 kilometers — a world record for distance.

At tables set perpendicularly to the stage sat major Party and Soviet workers, higher military ranks, leading aviation engineers, celebrated pilots, and famous people from the arts and sciences. The people responsible for the guest list knew the position of each guest, Comrade Stalin's attitude toward him, his reliability in terms of behavior at the reception and in every other sense too. These special people decided whom to invite with his wife, whom without, and how to seat them all: closer to the head table, in the middle of the room, or by the entrance. This depended on the degree to which Comrade Stalin knew the person. Comrade Stalin found it more pleasant and more peaceful to see familiar faces at surrounding tables. Comrade Stalin did not like asking, "Who is that?" Comrade Stalin knew for himself who that was!

The tables were set with wines and *zakuski,* hors d'oeuvres, but no one touched anything. The head table, parallel to the stage and perpendicular to the other tables but at a distance from them, was also set with wines and *zakuski,* but beyond the bottles, decanters, wineglasses, and bowls of fruit could be seen a neat row of empty chairs. The Party and government big shots had not yet arrived. They would arrive precisely at seven. In expectation of that exciting moment, the guests talked among themselves in low, controlled voices. No one looked at the clock. Checking the time would be an expression of impatience, which would be tactless and disloyal to Comrade Stalin.

The significance of the moment was emphasized by the waiters, young, sturdy, and grim fellows in black suits and white shirts, with napkins folded over their arms, who stood with impassive faces at each table above the seated guests. There were pairs of waiters at each door. Everyone knew that the waiters were civilian employees of the NKVD, who were there in addition to the guards at every passageway, landing, and staircase of the palace, and in addition to the freelancers for the NKVD who were sprinkled among the guests at each table.

At exactly seven o'clock the side doors opened and Stalin, accompanied by the Politburo members, appeared in the hall. Everybody rose, pushing back their chairs, and the hall erupted in stormy applause. The ovation continued while the leaders approached their table, found their seats, and then, standing by their chairs facing the guests, applauded them in turn. The guests applauded the leaders, the leaders applauded the guests. Then the Politburo members turned to Stalin and applauded him. The guests also applauded Stalin, extending their clapping hands toward the place where he stood, as if trying to reach Comrade Stalin, hoping that he would hear their individual claps. Only the grim waiters, still standing immobile by the table, but no longer rising high above the guests, did not applaud. The guests had risen and many of them turned out to be taller, larger, and more impressive-looking than the waiters.

Stalin applauded, his hands barely touching as he held them above the table, his elbows almost straight, and beneath his lowered eyelids, he slowly regarded the people near him with his heavy gaze. Once he recognized those nearest him, he looked deeper into the hall, but he could not discern anyone through the flutter of applauding hands. Then he stopped applauding and sank into his chair. Molotov and Voroshilov, who were standing next to him, followed suit, and then the other members of the Politburo sat down. But the guests were still standing and applauding. Then Stalin raised and lowered his hand slightly two times, inviting his guests to be seated. But the guests could not cease their expressions of rapture. They had come not to drink vodka and cognac, champagne and Mukuzani, not to eat caviar, salmon, pâté, mushroom julienne, and Kiev cutlets. They had come to see Comrade Stalin and to express their love and loyalty.

Stalin said something to Molotov, who rose and, unlike Stalin, raised not only one hand but two, palms out, as if to say, "Enough, comrades, enough! Sit down!! Comrade Stalin remembers and values your feelings, but everything in its time. We have gathered here for a particular reason and let's begin. And so please stop the ovation. Sit down."

The first to stop clapping were the people closest to the presidium. The faces of the members of the Politburo called on them to allow the program to start. And, aware and disciplined, they sat down in their seats. The waiters immediately bustled around their tables, pouring vodka and wine as requested.

But the rest of the guests were still standing and applauding. Now, when the front tables were seated, the people in the middle of the hall were visible. They wanted Comrade Stalin to see them and to read their unlimited love and adoration in their faces and their eyes. Molotov raised his hands higher, waving them, letting the guests in the middle of the hall know that Comrade Stalin, and Molotov, and the other members of the Politburo saw them, understood and appreciated everything, but still asked them to sit down. Applauding for a few more seconds in gratitude for his waves, the middle tables sat down. And the waiters began working around them, pouring their wines.

It was only the guests at the most distant tables that continued to applaud. Now when everyone between them and Stalin was seated, they hoped that Stalin would see them, too. Molotov gave someone standing at the side door a look, who signalled someone else, and at that moment the waiters started moving at the last table, politely but persistently saying, "Comrades, comrades, sit down, please. Comrades! You are being asked to sit down! Come on, come on, comrades, let's not hold things up." They even started pushing in the chairs at the guests' knees, and the honored guests quickly took their seats. And just as at the other tables, waiters filled shot glasses and wineglasses. Molotov rose and at that exact second the waiters finished their work and froze at their stations.

In his introductory remarks Molotov mentioned the illustrious achievements of the Soviet people in all areas of life: economics, science, and culture. These historic successes were particularly evident in the work of our mighty aviation, in the development of which the Soviet Union was leading the entire world. The USSR had become a mighty aviation power. These achievements were due to the brilliant leadership of Comrade Stalin, who personally expended enormous attention to the development of the aviation industry, who was a fatherly mentor and adviser of the pilots, the glorious eagles of our country.

The hall erupted in another ovation, the guests moved their chairs, stood up, and applauded, reaching with their hands for Comrade Stalin because now this ovation was intended personally for him; his name had at last been mentioned.

Stalin rose and lifted his hand. Silence reigned in the hall.

"Go on, Comrade Molotov," Stalin said and sat down.

Everyone smiled and laughed and applauded Stalin's joke.

Molotov wanted to continue, but at the front row, where the pilots were seated, Chkalov stood up, spread his broad shoulders, filled his lungs, and shouted, "For our beloved Stalin, Hurrah! Hurrah! Hurrah!"

And the room echoed the three cheers.

Stalin chuckled to himself. It was improper to interrupt the head of the government. But it was Chkalov, his favorite, the man who personified Russian daring, boldness, and impertinence. Chkalov, the greatest pilot of *his* era, *his* time. There was nothing Molotov could do. He'd have to accept the fact that the reckless pilot knew little of etiquette.

Molotov was an experienced chairman and he quieted the audience. He continued, "Evidence of the might of our aviation is the achievement, unprecedented in world history, of our illustrious fliers Gromov, Yumashev, and Danilin. In flying across the North Pole to America, to the city of " (and Molotov looked at his speech) "San Jacinto in California, they set a world record for distance of nonstop flight."

Stalin chuckled again. Molotov got back at Chkalov for interrupting him. He did not even mention his flight. Yet it was Chkalov who blazed the way, for he was the first to fly to America across the North Pole. Molotov was vain and touchy. Stupid people are always touchy.

Molotov concluded with a toast in honor of Gromov, Yumashev, and Danilin.

More applause, shouts of "Hurrah to Soviet fliers!" But no one stood up. People stood only in honor of Comrade Stalin. They stood when Comrade Stalin stood to touch glasses with Gromov, Yumashev, and Danilin, who were invited up to the head table. But as soon as Comrade Stalin sat down, everyone else sat down quickly and tucked into the *zakuski*. They had grown hungry listening to Molotov's long speech, and then probably they had not eaten too much at home in anticipation of this luxurious feast.

As usual, the concert program was opened by the Red Army Chorus and Dance Group, under the leadership of Alexandrov, and as usual, with a cantata about Stalin, written by Alexandrov. They listened reverently, without eating. But as soon as the ensemble moved onto the next number, they returned to their consumption — men drank vodka, the ladies took wine, and they all ate the food.

The ensemble was followed by several singers: Kozlovsky, Maksakova, and Mikhailov. And then by the puppeteer Obraztsov. The leaders watched, turning toward the stage, while the guests tucked into the food — the leaders had seen it all a hundred times before.

In between the acts, toasts were raised, all, of course, to Comrade Stalin. A leading aviation engineer said, "The Soviet aviation industry was created by the solicitude of Comrade Stalin. Comrade Stalin knows the people working in the industry well, and he suggests the solutions for complex technical problems, and he teaches us engineers to look far into the future."

And they ate and drank to Comrade Stalin. And Stalin also drank, eating little, as was his custom. *He* liked receptions like this and *he* understood their significance. No wonder the tsars held grand balls and Peter the Great had instituted his assemblies. This lends the leader's rule an aura of festiveness, it gives his entourage the opportunity to feel *his* disposition, to mark *his* achievements, *his* victories.

The Russian people like victories and do not like defeats; they remember only the former and do not wish to remember the latter. They remember the victory of Dmitri Donskoi, or Alexander Nevsky, or Ermak, the taking of Kazan and Astrakhan, the victories at Poltava and over Napoleon. But they do not want to remember the Tatar Yoke, or how Khan Devlet-Girei burned Moscow, or the defeats at Sevastopol and Port Arthur. The Russians sweep that from their historical memory and leave only the victories. A Russian likes to show off; it's in his blood, a compensation for ages of backwardness, poverty, and servitude. *He* had learned that in exile, he saw it among the peasants in the village, and *he* had observed it among the Russian master craftsmen in Baku. A temperamental, hot-blooded Georgian drinks wine and then sings Georgian songs with other Georgians, dances and has fun. But the quiet, docile Russian peasant drinks and gets belligerent, picks a fight, tries to prove his strength. That bravado is an important component of the Russian character. It urges the Russian to do desperate things. It is the reason the people love their heroes so much and the reason pilots are so popular. Pilots show the whole world how strong their nation is, how valorous and bold are its sons.

And the people are thankful to *him* for bringing them up that way. And *he* can be proud that *he* turned this backward, browbeaten, illiterate nation into a nation of heroes. *He* will go down in history for the greatness that the people achieved under *his* rule. Everything else would be forgotten. The deprivation and troubles, the *excesses* that are inevitable in creating a vigorous, centralized power. Who would remember the pathetic pygmies that he tossed overboard the ship of history, these carrion that called itself "the old Lenin guard"? They sensed mortal danger!

Even his "faithful friend" Klim Voroshilov crapped in his pants and called *him*. "Koba, what should I do if they come for me, too?" *He* said nothing then, dragged it out, tormented the poor soul, and then said, "Just don't open the door." Voroshilov calmed down and there he was, the pink little fool, drinking and smiling, and sitting next to *him*. These were military pilots, his people. Let him be happy, the coward. But the other bastards might not get scared. They might be capable of anything. They had to be dealt with swiftly and decisively. Everyone would forget about them. But they would remember Chkalov and glorify him. And *his* time will remain in the national memory as a heroic time.

That is what Stalin thought as he sat next to Molotov and Voroshilov, sipping his wine, nibbling at his food, turning toward the stage when the performers were on, and not listening to the orators' toasts. He applauded them all, raising his glass. Then he said to Molotov, "Give me the floor."

Molotov struck his glass with a knife, which no one heard, but the waiters instantly froze in their places, the room quieted down, and everyone turned toward the presidium.

"Comrade Stalin has the floor," Molotov announced.

Stalin rose and everyone else rose. More applause, more ovations.

Stalin raised his hand and everyone stopped. Stalin lowered his hand and everyone sat down.

"Fill your glasses, comrades," Stalin said.

A flurry crossed the room. People hurriedly filled their glasses. It didn't matter with what. They couldn't make Comrade Stalin wait.

Silence was restored.

"I want to raise this glass," Stalin said, "to our courageous pilots, our present and future Heroes of the Soviet Union. I want to tell them, the current and especially the future Heroes of the Soviet Union, the following. Bravery and daring are inseparable qualities of a Hero of the Soviet Union. A pilot has concentrated willpower, character, the ability to take risks. But bravery and daring are only one side of heroism. The other side, no less important, is ability. Boldness, they say, can take cities. But that is only when boldness and bravery and readiness to take risks are combined with excellent knowledge. And that is what I wish for our courageous pilots, the glorious sons and daughters of our people. I raise this glass to the current and the future Heroes of the Soviet Union. For pilots small and great — it is too soon to know who is small and who is great; that is still to be seen. To Kokkinaki, who accidentally did not become a Hero of the Soviet Union but who will be soon, I predict that for him. We have already drunk to the health of Comrades Gromov, Yumashev, and Danilin. But let us not forget that their heroic flight was prepared by the accomplishments of other pilots. The outstanding fliers of our times, Heroes of the Soviet Union Chkalov, Baidukov, and Belyakov, who made the *first* nonstop flight across the North Pole. From Moscow to Vancouver in British Columbia." Stalin pointed to the table where the men were seated. "It is these men, Chkalov, Baidukov, and Belyakov, who blazed the first path across the North Pole to America. Let us drink, comrades, to our glorious pilots, Heroes of the Soviet Union, current and future."

Stalin drank. And everyone drank, then put down their glasses and applauded. Stalin himself was talking to them. They all applauded and shouted, "Long live Comrade Stalin!" "Hurrah for Comrade Stalin!" The pilots tried harder than the rest, clapping in rhythm and shouting out hurrahs in unison. Chkalov, Baidukov, and Belyakov left their table and headed for the presidium. They had been called, naturally. No one dared to cross the space between the table of the presidium and the other tables without a special invitation. Stalin had shaken the hands of the pilots. He had shaken hands with Gromov, Yumashev, and Danilin, and now it was the favorite pilots' turn. But Chkalov,

Baidukov, and Belyakov came to the presidium with their glasses in their hands.

"Comrade Stalin," Chkalov said, "may I address you?"

"Please."

"Allow me to clink glasses with you and drink to your health."

"Well, why not have a drink?"

Stalin poured wine into his glass, clinked his glass with the pilots' glasses, and everyone drank.

Stalin set down his glass. "Are there any other requests?"

"Comrade Stalin," Chkalov said, looking boldly into his eyes. "In the name of all the fliers. The next act is Leonid Utesov's jazz orchestra. In the name of all the fliers . . . Please . . . Let Leonid Utesov sing 'From the Odessa Jail.' "

"And what is this song?" Stalin asked, even though he knew the song. Vaska was always humming it at home. *He* was not pleased that *his* son was singing thieves' songs.

"A marvelous song, Comrade Stalin. The words, Comrade Stalin, may be prison words, in thieves' jargon, but the tune is just the best, Comrade Stalin, it's got the right stuff."

"All right," Stalin agreed. "Let him sing it. We'll listen."

In the green room, where the performers waited for their entrance (the ones who had performed already were in the next room at dinner tables set especially for them), there appeared an officer with three rhomboids on his shoulder. He called Utesov over to one side and demanded, "What are you planning to sing, Comrade Utesov?"

Utesov listed his repertoire.

"You will sing 'From the Odessa Jail,' " the officer ordered.

"No, no," gasped Utesov. "I've been forbidden to sing it."

"Who forbids it?"

"Comrade Mlechin."

"And who's that?"

"What do you mean, who? He's head of the repertoire committee."

"I don't give a shit about your rep committee. You will sing 'From the Odessa Jail.' "

"But Comrade Mlechin — "

The officer's eyes bugged out. "Have I not spoken clearly, Citizen Weisbein? You will sing 'From the Odessa Jail' as your first number.

That" — and he paused and then added in a vicious whisper — "is the wish of Comrade Stalin."

And so Leonid Utesov began his appearance by singing "From the Odessa Jail" accompanied by his tea-jazz orchestra.

> *From the Odessa jail two lags escaped,*
> *two lags ran for free-ee-dom.*
> *They stopped with the Abnyarskaya gang,*
> *They stopped there to rest.*

He sang with great spirit, inspired by Comrade Stalin's wish, aware that just then he had to fear no repertoire committee. He would sing "Jail" and "The Hop" and "Murka" and other banned songs.

The band played enthusiastically. The percussionist performed miracles on his drums and cymbals, the saxophonist and the brass were hot. The final chord came, ending on the same bravura note that they had started with.

No one could understand what was happening. At a reception like this, in the presence of Comrade Stalin, in the presence of the members of the Politburo, Utesov dared to sing a thieves' song. What did it mean? Was this ideological diversion? They were afraid to move, much less clap. Even Chkalov, Baidukov, and Belyakov were still, not knowing how Comrade Stalin would react. The confused musicians lowered their instruments, and Utesov, pale and clutching the edge of the piano, discouraged by the deadly silence, wondered in horror if this could have been a provocation. Had the officer played a cruel trick on him? How could he prove that he had been ordered to play the song? He didn't know who the officer was, he didn't know his name, all he remembered was his rank.

And suddenly he heard soft clapping. It was Comrade Stalin himself. And the hall picked up his applause rapturously. If Comrade Stalin was applauding, that meant he liked it, that meant he approved. And rightly so! If you're going to have fun, then have fun! Right! Bravo! Encore! Encore! Bravo!

Utesov, sweaty and barely able to catch his breath, turned to the band and with a practiced movement brought them to their feet. The musicians banged their instruments on the music stands, their way of applauding the audience. The hall continued shouting "Bravo!" and

"Encore!" Stalin looked at Utesov and shrugged, as if to say, What can you do, the people want it, you can't let the people down.

Utesov sang it again.

> *Comrade, comrade, my wounds hurt,*
> *my wounds hurt deep inside.*
> *One is healing, the other is infected,*
> *and the third is in my side.*

The pilots sang along, tapping their feet, beating their knives and forks on their plates and glasses. Other tables were also singing along, and when Utesov finished there was a roar of "Encores!" Comrade Stalin applauded, and the Politburo members applauded, and Comrade Stalin shrugged once again, and Utesov sang it a third time.

> *Comrade, comrade, tell my mother*
> *That her son died at his post.*
> *With rifle in one hand and saber in the other*
> *And a merry song on his lips.*

The pilots were not only singing along and tapping their feet, they were screaming out the words, and some of them had climbed up on the tables to dance, kicking over the wineglasses and platters. Even Alexei Tolstoy, the writer, fat, respectable-looking, with a sweet girlish face, climbed up on a table and clumped around, breaking dishes. A count acting up.

The song was a thieves' song, of course, but there was something about it. The words were sentimental; criminals like that. "My wounds hurt. . . . Tell my mother. . . ." but the melody was sharp and catchy. *He* remembered well the convicts *he* had met in prisons and transport gangs. Of course they were criminals. And now, when they tried to steal Socialist property, they had to be persecuted severely, punished severely. Socialist property was inviolable. But back then, in tsarist times, the line between crime and protest was sometimes vague. Protest against injustice, oppression, and poverty. The poor illiterate people could not always rise to the higher social interests. They wanted justice for themselves, they wanted a redistribution of wealth on their own level. In Baku, in Bailovo Prison, *he* talked with convicts. He enjoyed their company much more than that of *his* "colleagues," the political prisoners. The "colleagues" were constantly arguing and debating, theorizing, settling scores, intriguing, each one trying to prove that he was smarter, better educated, and more decent than the rest. Life among the criminals was simple and clear. The laws, rules, and customs were also simple, clear, and inviolable. And they had order and discipline. Unquestioning subordination to the gang leader, loyalty to the organization. Betrayal was ruthlessly punished. The most universal punishment was death. They did not have other means of punishment. The slightest suspicion meant death. They had no means of investigation. Unquestioning subordination to the leader, loyalty to your organization.

The criminal principle, the atavistic principle, exists in every person. In the interests of state discipline and order it must be suppressed. But when the criminal principle manifests itself in such an innocent form as it did today here in the Kremlin palace, in that boisterous song about a thief who escaped from prison, in dancing on tables . . . Well, that sort of manifestation of the criminal principle can be acceptable. *He* punished severely for the slightest infraction, but when people come to *his* party, people should feel happiness and pleasure.

Comrade Stalin was pleased by this conceit. People were sincerely happy, wholeheartedly having fun. And if people are having fun, then things are going well. If people in the country are having fun, then things in the country are also going well.

3

THE GROUP formed a line (when crowded, two lines), with Semyon Grigoryevich in front, commanding: "Start with the right foot. Step forward — one! Left — two! Right foot to the right, bring the left to join — three! Right foot forward again — four! Which foot is free? The left! We do it all again, starting with the left foot. Forward — one, two! To the side — three, four! Which foot is free? The right! Now we do the same steps backward: right, left — one, two! Right, left — three, four! We're back to the starting position."

This box step was the basis of the fox-trot, rumba, and tango, and they repeated it many times. Then all this was done to music, to the clear, percussive beat of the fox-trot or rumba. Right forward — one, two, glissade to the right — three, four! *"Fiesta, shut the door, Fiesta, turn off the light...."* One, two, three, four! ... *"Higher and higher, we soar like the birds...."* One, two, three, four! ... *"And each propeller protects our shores."* ... One, two, three, four!

Once he was convinced that the movements had been mastered, Semyon Grigoryevich had them do it in couples — gentleman forward, ladies back, ladies forward, gentlemen back.

Semyon Grigoryevich was impressive-looking. Solid, even on the heavy side, middle-aged, with a clean-shaven actor's face and thick head of silvery hair, he would show up at class in a dark suit, white shirt, bow tie, and highly polished patent leather shoes. He used a black lacquered walking stick with a massive round knob. During class he put his stick in a far corner to protect it. Semyon Grigoryevich's voice was pleasantly pitched, with an actor's control, intelligent. He made everything he said sound significant, and in his introduction, as Gleb had warned Sasha, he referred to Socrates and Aristotle, who had maintained that dancing was beneficial to the health and developed artistic taste and musicality. Western dances, he maintained, usually interpreted as being bourgeois, were actually based on folk dances. The tango is the national dance of Argentina. The rumba came from Mexico. The slow fox-trot is usually danced to the blues — sad melodies of the American Negro. Semyon Grigoryevich asked Gleb to play a few bars of the blues and pointed out their hopeless sadness. It was the sadness of the Negro population of the U.S.A., enslaved for centuries and now still oppressed in that bourgeois society.

Sasha was cool toward Semyon Grigoryevich: a beetle, that's what he thought of him. He hustled around the Party committees and factory committees with his fancy walking stick, signing contracts, paying under the table, using his respectable appearance to make deals. It made Sasha sick. You could expect anything from a man like that. Actually, that held for everybody nowadays — they were all like that. And Sasha himself, having raised his hand to vote for the execution of Tukhachevsky, now shared the responsibility with them for the death of innocent people. Memories of that rally, the fear that had engulfed him, oppressed him. He disgusted himself. He tried to persuade himself that was the way the world was, but he knew that was the way he was.

No one believed anyone, and he did not believe anyone. He didn't talk about politics, not even about what was in the papers. "Really? No, I didn't see it. . . . I must have missed it." Sasha read very few papers. He sometimes stopped when he passed the stand with the daily display of *Pravda* and looked through it. It was always the same — victorious relations, labor records, greetings to the great Stalin, Stalin's pictures, the exposure of spies, saboteurs, and Trotskyites, and now Bukharinites were added as well as "lurking" unknown spies, who were gouged out of their nests. There was information on executions, trials, decorations of KGB officers for "special achievements in the struggle with the enemies of the people." In one list of medal recipients Sasha saw the name Yuri Denisovich Sharok, awarded the Order of the Red Star.

Budyagin and Mark had been shot. The leaders of the Party that created the October Revolution, the heroes of the Civil War, were destroyed, and the counterrevolutionaries and anti-Soviets were being given medals in the name of the very Party that they had destroyed, in the name of the workers' and peasants' regime that no longer existed. Whose dictatorship had Stalin brought into being? The proletariat had no rights. The peasants who were not destroyed had been turned into serfs called "collective farm workers." The state apparatus lived in fear. The dictatorship was Stalin's, only Stalin's, and no one but Stalin's. Stalin did not represent any class, he represented only himself. Lenin's assertion that a dictator can express the will of a class was not correct. A dictator expresses only his own will. Otherwise he is not a dictator.

Sasha also read an article by Vadim Marasevich. So Vadim was published in *Pravda* now, too, attacking some novel, accusing the author of being an apologist for the kulaks, so-called "exploiter peasants." "Whether the author intends it or not," Vadim wrote, "his novel does a great service for international imperialism, helping to corrupt Soviet people, undermining their faith in the great work of Lenin and Stalin." A fine accusation: subject to arrest under Article 58 of the Criminal Code, that's for sure. Nice boy the professor's son turned out to be.

They've all sold out, they all turned into whores. Universal fear had given birth to universal roguery. Everyone was under the bell jar. Their eyes and ears were everywhere. There were personnel departments everywhere, questionnaires, forms, demands to see your passport, which indicates your nationality.

So his decision had been a good one. Dancing! There were eyes and ears here, too, but they didn't need your biography, you didn't have to fill out their forms. The landlady hadn't even asked for the official directive from the agency to house him, which Gleb had promised. She must have forgotten. Sasha came home late and got up late; sometimes he wasn't home at all. He lived quietly, no one visited him, he paid the rent on time. That suited the landlady. Gleb did mention that he should drop by the booking agency and show his passport to Marya Konstantinovna, but he only mentioned it in passing. Sasha pushed the thought aside. They aren't asking for my passport, fine.

The first Sunday after he had arrived in Ufa, he called his mother. Her voice was agitated. The operator had said, "Ufa calling," and when she heard Sasha's voice, she asked in fright, "Sasha, dear, why are you in Ufa? What's in Ufa?"

He tried to calm her down. "I'm in Ufa with a truck brigade, we'll be here two or three months, transporting grain, so I'm not sure if I'll be able to call regularly. But I'll try. As usual, on Sundays. Write to me at the Ufa Central Post Office, hold for pickup."

But his mother sensed that something was wrong and she was worrying about him again. "Why are you so far away?? Why did you go to Bashkiria from Kalinin?"

"Mama, it's not up to you and me to decide how to run the harvest. We had orders to come here, and here we are. There's nothing to worry about."

"Visit the brother of Vera's husband. I gave you his address."

"If I have time, I will."

He called his mother the following Sunday, too, then skipped a week, and then called again. She seemed to have calmed down.

But what would happen to her if he were arrested here or wherever the fates took him? In 1934 he was arrested at home, and his mother searched all the prisons in Moscow until she found him. But if they picked him up in Ufa or somewhere else, how would she look for him? She wouldn't know whether he was alive or dead, arrested or not. She wouldn't know where to start — which prison, which hospital, which cemetery. It would kill her.

He did not go to see Vera's relatives. He didn't know how they might react. It was dangerous to entertain people with a record. And there was no need. He had a job, he was used to this life, peaceful and even easy. In Kalinin, as he rolled off the kilometers in his truck, he kept going over the same old thoughts, and he pounded on the newspapers, falling into despair, especially at night, in his lonely, depressing evenings. Here the evenings were fun — music, pretty girls whose eyes were radiant and who forgot about their bosses, the Party committees and the unions, and the boredom of their jobs. They hung on his every word.

"Left foot forward — one! Right foot forward — two! Right forward — one, two! Glissade to the right — three, four! . . . "*Masha pours the tea, and her eyes are full of promise*." . . . One, two, three four! . . . "*Masha and I by the samovar, drinking tea till the dawn*." . . . They tried hard. And they forgot their lousy life and the fact that their cash wouldn't last until the next payday. . . . It was a good job, it made people happy.

In each group Sasha would pick out two or three talented girls and use them to illustrate the steps. They became his assistants. He found one girl, her name was Gulya, in the first group. She was slender and flexible, around sixteen, with a childlike face, tender and trusting. She had a good sense of rhythm, a light step, and strong hands. She could hold her partner firmly and move him in the right direction. She worked without giving up on even the dullest students, ones other assistants had given up on. "He just doesn't get it," they'd say. "Whichever way you turn him, he goes the other way." Sometimes, Sasha had to work with such inept students himself, taking the lady's part.

"Our motto," Semyon Grigoryevich pompously reminded everyone, "is that we get one hundred percent success. Everyone can learn to dance. People are born with the ability."

Sasha often caught Gulya looking at him, and she would blush and turn away. She must have a crush on him; at that age, girls often fall for young teachers. Once, as they were dancing, Gulya overcame her shyness and said, "Would you like to go to the theater after class? It's right here, upstairs at the Palace of Labor."

Gulya took out two tickets from her breast pocket. "I have the tickets."

"Thank you, Gulya, but we have a meeting at the booking agency after class today. Why don't you go with a girlfriend?"

He didn't have a meeting, but he wasn't about to start an affair with this girl.

He remembered Varya's invitation to the skating rink at the Arbat Cellar. Another primitive move. He could think about Varya now without jealousy, without hurt. It was all over. Forgotten. She had the charm and attractiveness of youth and he had been lonely in Siberia. Her postscripts to his mother's letters meant a great deal because he got mail from no one else. Therefore his expectation of freedom got mixed up with her. Varya became his Moscow, his Arbat, his future. It was all his own invention. But the wound hurt when you touched it. So he tried not to think too much about Varya. But one time when he was on the phone with his mother, he asked who came to see her. He hadn't planned on asking that, but he suddenly wanted to hear Varya's name.

"Who visits?" his mother repeated. "Varya drops by, sometimes my sisters. Why?"

"Nothing," he replied. "I just wanted to picture how you live."

So, Varya dropped by. That news gladdened him. Although, if you thought about it, it didn't say much. He had wanted to hear Varya's name. He heard it. Period.

4

AFTER SHAROK'S FIRST TRIP TO PARIS, there was another, and then they left him there with the passport of a Russian émigré, Yuri Alexandrovich Privalov, which was obtained in Spain. It was a stroke of luck that both Sharok and the dead man had the same first name: Yuri. His cover story was well developed. As a boy, he had ended up in Shanghai, fleeing the Revolution in Russia, and his parents died there. He made his way to Paris, where he got a job in an advertising agency owned by a Frenchman. Back in Russia, in Nalchik, he had some distant relatives, but naturally, he did not communicate with them and did not even know if they were still alive. The cover was reliable, albeit not a diplomatic one. Speigelglass entrusted him with two agents — General Skoblin ("Farmer") and Tretyakov ("Ivanov"). Sharok had met "Farmer" previously, with Speigelglass, when they were preparing the case against Tukhachevsky. He did not see the dossier on "Ivanov" until he got to Paris.

Sergei Nikolayevich Tretyakov, a major industrialist before the revolution, a minister of the Provisional Government in 1917 and then a minister in the kolchak government, was recruited in 1930 for two hundred dollars a month. He had a good reputation in the émigré community. But his greatest value as an agent lay elsewhere.

The ground floor of Tretyakov's house at rue Colisee 29 was the headquarters of ROVS, the Russian Military Union. The Tretyakov family lived on the third floor, and he on the second, right over the office of General Miller, chief of ROVS. They placed a bug in the office ceiling and Tretyakov stayed home all day, listening and recording. He gave his notes to Sharok. Thus, Soviet intelligence had access to top-secret information in the White Guards émigré organizations.

Sharok preferred dealing with Tretyakov to dealing with Skoblin. Skoblin was patronizing and the meetings were dangerous. The émigrés suspected him of collaborating with the NKVD, he could be followed, and they had to change the time and place of their meetings frequently. Tretyakov was beyond suspicion, he was not under surveillance, and they usually met on Wednesdays around five at the Henri IV Café on the corner of the Place de la Bastille and boulevard Henri IV. They sat in the small café, uncrowded at that hour, but never talked about business. They set their magazines on the table. When they left, Tretyakov took Sharok's magazine, and Sharok took Tretyakov's, which contained the texts of the recorded conversations. Speigelglass had warned him once, "Tretyakov is disillusioned with the émigré community, but he's far from charmed by us. I think that he might even be hostile and he is not giving us everything he has. You have to keep expressing your dissatisfaction and demanding more from him. He is working solely for the money, and he will always be begging and wheedling. Don't give in. Two hundred dollars a month and not a penny more. If he works poorly for you, give him a hundred and the rest when he gives you something better. Receipts are obligatory. Be very careful of his excursions into the past — he likes recalling the olden days, and he'll keep you for hours."

But Sharok was pleased with Tretyakov. Unlike the short, fragmented, and not always substantial reports from Skoblin, Tretyakov's information was full, elaborate, and significant. Tall, handsome, and dignified, a Russian nobleman to the hilt, he sipped his coffee and talked about prerevolutionary Russia, about old Moscow. Sharok recalled his father's stories of the same period, and against Speigelglass's advice, did not interrupt Tretyakov. Why not listen? But at the same time, he observed the old man and drew conclusions. His moods changed quickly. The blissful smile left his face as quickly as it appeared, and he would turn red and berate the émigrés. "They've lost all significance in terms of the struggle against the Soviets. Foreign powers have stopped betting on them. You don't bet on corpses, you know."

Sharok allowed about forty minutes for his meetings with Tretyakov, not suspecting that soon he would spend almost two days with him. It happened during the kidnapping of General Miller.

They should have gotten rid of Miller long ago. Miller knew about

Skoblin's ties with the Gestapo, which was not a threat, but Miller also knew Skoblin's role in the case of Tukhachevsky and other Soviet military commanders. That was why Speigelglass considered him an unwanted witness. He and Skoblin worked out the kidnapping plan, set for September 22. It was that operation that finished Skoblin.

Before leaving headquarters, Miller left a sealed envelope with orders to open it if he did not return by evening.

Miller did not return. They opened the envelope and found this note:

> Today at 12:30 P.M. I have an appointment with General Skoblin at the corner of rues Jasmin and Raffet. He is supposed to take me to a rendezvous with two German officers: Colonel Stroman and Werner, who works with the German embassy here. Both speak Russian well. The meeting is taking place on Skoblin's initiative. It may be a trap, so I am leaving this message.

Miller's co-workers showed the note to Skoblin and tried to take him to the police. But Skoblin managed to escape and get in touch with Speigelglass. Sharok was ordered to hide Skoblin at Tretyakov's house, that is, in the same building as ROVS headquarters, where no one would think to look for him. After two days, Speigelglass moved Skoblin to Spain and left for Moscow.

The sight of Skoblin frightened Tretyakov, and when he learned in the newspapers the next day that Skoblin had taken part in the kidnapping of Miller, he was terrified — by hiding Skoblin in his apartment, he became an accessory in the crime. For two days Sharok kept him under sleepless watch, calming the old man down, and when Skoblin was moved to Spain, he paid him five hundred dollars for his services. Those had been Speigelglass's orders. Tretyakov quieted down once he saw Skoblin leave his apartment safely and had gotten his payment, especially since his name was never mentioned in connection with the case and he remained above suspicion as usual.

Sharok learned the details of Miller's kidnapping from the newspapers. Skoblin brought Miller to boulevard Montmorncy, where two men at the entrance to a villa shoved him into a car and sped off to Le Havre. They put him in a crate on board the *Maria Ulyanova,* a Soviet ship, which immediately raised anchor and headed for Leningrad. Sharok could only guess at the fate of General Miller — they must have shot him.

Reading the newspapers closely, Sharok chuckled — all the hulla-baloo. Bolsheviks on French territory kidnapping people in broad daylight! They had gotten General Kuryopov and now General Miller! The truck that had delivered Miller to Le Havre belonged to the Soviet embassy. The famous Burtsev, who had exposed the provocateur Azef, joined the campaign. Burtsev felt that the main agent of Moscow was not Skoblin but his wife, the celebrated Russian singer Plevitskaya. Skoblin was just second fiddle to her. Plevitskaya was arrested and awaiting trial in jail. And then, in September, the former Soviet spy Ignatii Raiss, who broke with the Soviet Union, was killed in Lausanne. The situation was heating up and Speigelglass and a few of the other Soviet residents were waiting it out in Moscow. Sharok, who had a good cover, remained in Paris. He was studying German, among other things.

Speigelglass had told him, "A spy must know at least two languages. You had French at school and German in college — if my memory serves me, that's what your application says."

"Yes, we had German in college."

"So work on it. Your landlord is from Alsace, his wife is German, they speak the language. Practice with them."

He added, in a joking tone, but significantly, "Study hard, we'll be testing you. And one more thing: develop ties with the émigrés on a regular basis. It can be business, commerce, too, if necessary. You must have a circle of acquaintances who can vouch for you. 'Ah, Yuri Alexandrovich. We know him.' They can be ordinary people, not necessarily titled ones."

"There are princes among the ordinary émigrés," Sharok responded with a joke of his own.

"That will do, too," Speigelglass said seriously.

5

SEMYON GRIGORYEVICH hired two more accompanists — a pianist and a bayan player, Lyonya, a huge, good-natured fellow, placid and willing to drag his bayan wherever he was told. He played by ear and had a primitive repertoire. He drank quite a bit and in that sense was good company for Gleb and for Sasha, who had started hitting the bottle, sometimes quite hard. The other musician, Misha Kanevsky, was a professional pianist, thin, with a nervous face, gray restless eyes, and long elegant fingers. He had studied at Leningrad Conservatory, but did not graduate and ended up in Ufa. There wasn't much work at the booking agency because the singers usually came with their own accompanists, and so he took the job with Semyon Grigoryevich. He had turned down a job playing in a nightclub band. "They won't turn me into a nightclub lackey," he had said.

And he smiled a crooked, scornful smile, grimacing and squinting.

It was clear who "They" were: Misha had been exiled from Leningrad after Kirov's murder, one of the thousands of "representatives of the bourgeoisie and nobility." His father, a lawyer, had owned a house in St. Petersburg before the Revolution. After the Revolution the house had been requisitioned and the lawyer was considered a "former major homeowner" while Misha became "the son of a former major homeowner." There were many young men like him in Ufa, their position unclear. They were allowed to keep their passports, but the Leningrad residency permit had been removed.

Kanevsky had pictured quite a different future for himself and resented being stuck in Ufa doing a menial musical job, thanks to Them. He hated everything about the town — Their clubs, Their uprights and grands, which needed tuning although the rubes did not realize it, Their slogans on the walls, Their banal modern tunes that he was forced to play. He despised Gleb and Lyonya, who were no musicians, and Semyon Grigoryevich, Nonna, and Sasha, who were hacks in it for the money. He kept to himself, did not join their conversations, even took smoke breaks off to one side. He didn't go to the restaurant or the House of the Red Army dances with them. As soon as the lessons were over, he disappeared.

Gleb didn't like him and treated him coolly.

"I can't stand that Jewish haughtiness," he said to Sasha.

"Jewish? So, you're an anti-Semite? I hadn't thought that of you."

"I'm not an anti-Semite, dearie, all my best friends at school and college were Jewish. And my neighbors in the apartment, wonderful people! And many of my teachers were Jewish, and they were among the best. But every nation has its flaws, and Jewish intellectuals are haughty. Kanevsky thinks very highly of himself, considers himself a genius."

"I hate it when people stress someone's nationality — 'that Armenian,' 'that Ukrainian,' 'that Georgian.' If Ivanov steals something, you'll say, 'Ivanov is a thief.' But if Rabinovich steals something, you'll say, 'The Jew is a thief.' "

"Don't get so upset. I may be wrong about Jews. But he's an unpleasant character."

"You're the character! He's just a miserable, persecuted man."

During the lesson, Gleb looked over at Sasha and felt guilty about what he had said. Later, he stopped thinking about it and played the piano, nodding in rhythm, his face softer and his gaze vacant. He had obviously remembered something. He was still at the piano when the lesson was over, hands in his lap. He nodded to Sasha to come over.

"Have you ever noticed, dearie, that the simplest tunes and most simple-minded words can create a mood? It doesn't have to be anything fancy, but using the word 'remember' really helps. No one can resist it."

"For instance?"

"Here's one with your name in it — '*Sasha, do you remember how we met on the shore,*' " he sang, accompanying himself with one hand. People lingered in the doorway to listen. Gleb sang beautifully. " '*Sasha, do you remember the quiet evening, I asked for more?*' That was Isabella Yuryeva. Here's one by Leshchenko: '*Remember in the olden days in Moscow, they baked blini. You loved me then and made blini for me. Dunya, give me one from the pan, Dunya kiss me right where I am, your kisses are as hot as fresh blini from the pot.'* And so on."

Sasha was running classes by himself now and giving the introductory speeches. He didn't repeat Semyon Grigoryevich's lines, he didn't quote Socrates and Aristotle, but he did say that people had always danced everywhere and always would because dancing brings joy. He did quote Pushkin.

> *Alas, I killed a lot of time*
> *On various pleasures!*
> *But if it weren't for the morals,*
> *I would love balls to this very day.*
> *I love the wild youthfulness,*
> *The crowds, and life, and joy,*
> *And the ladies' planned outfits;*
> *I love their legs, although I doubt*
> *That in all of Russia you will find*
> *Three pairs of elegant legs.*

"But here, I think, Pushkin and I must disagree. If he were to come to one of our classes, he would see that there are many lovely legs in Russia."

Everyone smiled and Sasha started the lesson.

"That's great, using Pushkin for the introduction," Gleb said.

Kanevsky, who usually did not get involved in conversations, snorted. "It's contemporary and timely. They recently celebrated the centennial of Pushkin's death in the duel and now all Soviet people know his name. I read a statement by some milkmaid or swineherd, I don't remember, but she said, 'Good for Tatyana. She let Onegin have it. When she was a simple gal living in the country, he turned her down. But when she was a big shot's wife, all of a sudden he wanted her.'"

He stopped, twisting his lips into a bitter and scornful grimace. Sasha was the only one with whom he had a more or less normal relationship. Sasha pitied him, embittered and impotent, pathetic in his pride. Kanevsky felt Sasha's compassion and exchanged a few words with him now and then, and he preferred accompanying Sasha's class to the others. But nevertheless, he couldn't control his sarcasm. This reminded him too much of the official and officious Pushkin ceremonies, pompous and false. How could he use Russia's greatest poet for this hackwork? Sasha himself knew that he was playing the same tune as everyone else. But he hated to lose such a charming and pleasant introduction. He didn't want to dispute the bourgeois origins of the dances. Or make speeches about capitalist exploitation of the Negro population of America. No, Pushkin's verses about the ball, the crowds and the joy, were much more appropriate.

"Kanevsky jabbed you hard today," Gleb noted.

"What do you mean?"

"With Pushkin. . . . Trying to say that the authorities were exploiting Pushkin and so were you."

"Well, it could seem that way."

"Not to everyone, dearie. I, for instance, didn't think so. I liked it. It's just that Kanevsky hates everyone and despises everyone. . . . Milkmaids, swineherds . . . has he ever met one? I'll bet he drinks milk, but he despises milkmaids. He should see their hands. The fingers are gnarled and swollen. You can't tickle the ivories with them. Go try milking a cow, you'll see how much strength it takes."

"You're fixated on Kanevsky! First, he's a Jew, now, he says the wrong thing. Maybe you don't like the fact that his piano playing isn't worse than yours?"

"He should play better than me. He studied at the conservatory, and I didn't study anywhere. And I'm not a musician, I'm an artist. I don't like something else about him. I don't like that we're going to end up in prison because of him. That's what I don't like about him."

Sasha shrugged.

"Oh, yes, dearie! What he meant about Pushkin was that all the boors are talking Pushkin now."

"Why assume that's what he meant? You're twisting his words."

"No, I'm not. But be vigilant, as they like to say nowadays. I have to be, I have to think about who's next to me and what I can expect from them. The times are like that, dearie. And you, especially, should have to be vigilant!"

"Why especially?"

"You know why. In Kalinin you still felt like an ex-con, you were cautious. But you've forgotten about it here and you're going to land in a mess. Actually, you lost your vigilance back in Kalinin."

"How?"

"I warned you at the Seliger about the change in the city's regime.

You should have quit your shitty job at the motor pool the very next day. That idiot director, what's his name, Proshkim, he would have let you go in a second, and you could have left there with me. But you stayed."

"We've talked about that. So I quit a few days later."

"Oh, no, dearie, not at all. You didn't quit, you were fired. That's a big difference. 'Due to leaving the city' and 'of his own volition' are quite different. 'Due to leaving' means either you were sent up river or thrown out of town. You were lucky. Instead of depriving you of your residence permit, they could have exiled you. But I guess they were given such a tight deadline to clear out the city that they didn't bother with details, who goes where. They just got rid of everybody and that was that. Assignment completed! You were lucky. But luck can run out."

"Who knows what would have happened if I had left with you. This way everything is legal with me. I left work legally and I was unregistered from my place of residence legally."

"Unregistered, yes! But are you registered anywhere? Hah? You're just living quietly and peacefully, without thinking. But if you were to get into a fight with these Bashkirs here and the police were to get involved, they would ask for your documents. 'Wait a minute, where are you registered? Nowhere? But it's not allowed to live anywhere for more than three days without registering. Are you hiding out? Are you a criminal?' You've already gone by for several months without registration and before you know it, it'll be half a year and then a year. You'll come to some other city and go to register, and they'll ask you where you spent that year? And what will you answer? At the next place you might not have a friend in the passport office. And even here Marya Konstantinovna at the booking agency will take a look at your passport and say, 'I'm taking you off the books, you don't have a residency permit.' By the way, dearie, didn't I tell you that you have to go see Marya Konstantinovna with your passport? Didn't I?"

"Yes, you did, but just in passing."

Gleb slammed both hands on the table. "Don't pull that nonsense with me. What do you mean 'in passing'? Nothing is unimportant or in passing for you. Everything is significant. You have to catch on instantly and move it!"

"There's no point in talking about it now," Sasha said grumpily. "I'm not going to go back to Kalinin, and no one's ever going to annul my unregistration. We have to figure out something for here."

"Why didn't you figure something out yourself before now? It's a dog-eat-dog world, dearie. You've been in tough situations but apparently you've lucked out each time. But your luck can run out, you can have big trouble, dearie, so keep your eyes open."

~ 6 ~

GLEB'S WARNING came true the very next day. Was he clairvoyant, or had he known ahead of time?

In the morning when Sasha was washing, his landlady came to see him. "Alexander Pavlovich, people came by yesterday from the electoral district. The passport woman from the building was with them. They're compiling electoral lists for the Supreme Soviet elections. You must have read about it in the papers. National elections in December."

"I've read about it, of course, I know."

Once again, he had that unpleasant ache in his heart.

"They're compiling lists of residents." The landlady's voice was boring and monotonous. "Everybody has to vote, one hundred percent. I wrote you down, Pankratov, Alexander Pavlovich, performer, sent by the booking agency. And the passport woman cut in, 'You never gave me any instructions from the booking agency.' Alexander Pavlovich, don't I remember your giving me that paper?"

Sasha started mumbling. "I don't remember. . . . We did bring you some paper from there when my friend and I came here the first day."

"Maybe I put it away somewhere. I keep forgetting things. But it's easily fixed. I've lost these instructions before or my lodgers have, just crumpled them up in their pockets. Marya Konstantinovna always gave us a copy. And she'll give you one, too, but make sure she puts the right date on it, like on the original. They want you to come by with your passport at the electoral district office. It's not far, at the school, between six and eight in the evening."

"What if I move before the elections?"

"They'll explain all that, and they'll give you a coupon."

All he had wanted was a little peace — without having to go

anywhere or do any explaining, without being humiliated. And now he had to pay for it. The newspapers wrote about the coming elections as a triumph of Soviet democracy. Rallies were held for candidates — "worthy sons and daughters of the Soviet people" — to be elected Deputies of the Supreme Soviet "from the bloc of Communists and non-Party members." Of course, everywhere, people nominated Comrade Stalin as their first choice. Sasha read that every day and in the back of his mind was the nagging thought that the elections could mean trouble for him, but he kept pushing the thought away. And this is what it got him. How stupid not to have listened to Gleb then. If he had left Kalinin with him, he would still have the Kalinin residency permit on his passport. Now they would start questioning him at the electoral district office and he'd get his landlady in trouble. She kept him for three months without registering him. And Marya Konstantinovna would get it, too. What should he do? Should he go see Vera's brother-in-law? He had lived in Ufa a long time; maybe he could provide some advice.

He was met at the door by a woman with frightened eyes, wearing an old house dress.

Sasha introduced himself and added, "Vera Alexandrovna has written to you about me and she called Sergei Petrovich."

"No, no, Sergei Petrovich is gone. He went away for a long time. I don't know when he'll be back."

She shook her head. She didn't offer him a seat. All she wanted was to slam the door on Sasha as quickly as possible.

Sasha left. She must have been afraid to let a man with a record into her place.

But that Sunday when he called his mother in Moscow, she said, "Don't go visiting at the address Vera gave you. Her brother-in-law is in the hospital, for a long time."

Sasha realized that Vera's relative had been arrested, and that was why his wife was terrified. An ordinary engineer, father of three, and they put him away.

That Sunday evening, he told Gleb, "You were right."

"What happened, dearie?"

Sasha told him about his conversation with the landlady.

"You're in it now, dearie." Gleb smiled. "You know the Bashkir saying: 'Made a mistake, meant to yell hurrah and yelled fire instead'? What are you going to do?"

"I'm leaving Ufa tomorrow. Otherwise they'll have me by the throat. Of course, it's my fault and I'm letting down the landlady, and Marya Konstantinovna, and Semyon, but what else can I do?"

"How are you letting them down?" Gleb regarded him with a mocking smirk.

"I'm leaving, and they'll have to take the heat."

"You keep worrying about others." Gleb was still mocking him. "About humanity, about how not to let people down. Humanity will take care of itself. It's not asking for your advice."

"I don't understand what you're talking about."

"I'm still on the same subject. 'They'll have to take the heat.' What heat is there? Big deal, some dancer on a tour was here for a while, didn't register, and left. So what? There are dozens of those rolling stones around. Who's going to investigate the case, who cares about you? It's the building administration's fault for allowing you to live there for three months without registering. Marya Konstantinovna? So, she'll say to Semyon, 'A fine bunch of people you have working for you!' After all, she's at fault too. And that's it. If you leave, you won't be letting anyone down. Except yourself, of course. What are you going to do in the new place? All right, girls fall all over you, but you're not necessarily going to meet one right away who can help you out. Oh, no, dearie, if you leave, they won't have any heat to take. But if you stay, then they'll have to put their minds to it. Semyon and our pretty Marya Konstantinovna will have to do something with you, they'll have to fix up their mistake."

"That's unacceptable. It's blackmail."

"Tsk-tsk, that's your naughty, corrupt intelligentsia streak talking again. You're so squeaky clean! You can always leave, but you should try to make the best of it here first. Semyon needs you, you're a celebrity in Ufa. When Semyon signs a contract with some factory, they say, 'Send us that dark-haired one who runs the classes at the Palace of Labor.' You're that famous. . . . I'll tell you the truth, I never expected it myself! When you take that first step and drawl 'And a one!' your 'and' draws everyone with you. With your talent and figure, dearie, Mother Nature meant you to be a dancer, not a truck driver. If you had gone to ballet school, you'd be a star by now.

"So why would Semyon let you go? So that he can run all those classes by himself? Do you think he uses a walking stick just for show? His legs hurt. He can manage the first class and impress people, but then he needs two days in bed to recover. Do you think he'd be able to handle six hours a day? And there's no replacement for you. So, he has to take care of your case. He'll figure something out with Marya Konstantinovna, don't worry! They're in this together and she can do anything. Just the other day she got this hobo an apartment with a registration, temporary, but still, what do you care? You just have to cover up those three months. They'll stamp it at the police and you can do whatever you want. Talk to Semyon, make a clean breast of it. He's been around, he'll know what to do."

And things did go the way Gleb said. Semyon Grigoryevich took Sasha's passport and returned it the next day with two residence instructions. The copy for Sasha's landlady and the other, for a new address, with the request to register him temporarily. Sasha went over to look at the apartment. It was in a pathetic little house on the outskirts of Ufa, with vegetable fields and endless autumn mud. Sasha was sorry he hadn't worn his boots. The landlady was a sharp-eyed old woman who showed him a cubbyhole with a wooden couch instead of a bed, and a nail in the door instead of a closet. She took his passport, the registration instructions, and a month's rent in advance. This lousy place was twice as expensive as the room in the middle of town — the cost of being registered.

Sasha had no intention of living in that hole and coming all the way out here through the mud every night after class. He had a residency permit now and he could live wherever he wanted. He hung his old suit and raincoat, which he wouldn't need in the winter, on the nail, stuck an old pair of shoes under the couch, and placed a toothbrush on the stool near the window, to give the place an appearance of being inhabited. He went down to the electoral district office, which his landlady demanded, stood before the members of the electoral commission, three of them, and they checked his passport, entered him on the rolls, gave him an invitation to vote, and without any good reason drilled their hostile gazes into Sasha and spoke officiously to him.

And Sasha remembered how they handed out passports in their building on the Arbat in early 1933. The worried residents huddled in the building office. He was particularly struck by two old ladies, who trembled in fear, afraid to approach the desk with the militiaman, a passport woman, and a skinny, elderly man — a representative of the public. Each resident held a completed application, which was put down on the desk along with a birth certificate and a work certificate. Many of the old people did not have birth certificates and they had to prove their identity, place and time of birth, with other documents. The policeman examined them, asked questions if there were problems, and demanded other papers. If the documents were in order, he would open the desk drawer, check against a list in it, write an approval on the application, and hand it on to the passport woman.

Sasha did not understand then why that procedure had caused anxiety in anyone. There were no criminals there. Everyone in line had been living in the building all his or her life. Sasha had known them since he was a child.

Gurtsev was ahead of him in line, a polite, intelligent man, husband of a famous ballerina who had died the previous year. Sasha remembered the pomp of her funeral, with Gurtsev in a black coat following the coffin. They were not close friends, but they greeted each other like people who ran into each other frequently in the courtyard, on the stairs, and in the elevator. Gurtsev handed over his documents. The policeman looked them over, checked his list in the desk drawer, and set Gurtsev's documents aside.

"Be at the eighth division of the militia tomorrow morning at eleven."

"But — " began Gurtsev.

"Citizen, I have explained everything to you. Next!"

"But I would like to know — "

"You'll find out everything there. Next!"

As Sasha's mother later told him, Gurtsev did not get a passport. He was ordered out of Moscow because his father had been a factory owner before the Revolution. Several other families in the building were refused passports. The two old ladies were refused. They said that the people without passports had to move at least one and one-half kilometers outside Moscow.

Why hadn't he spoken out then? But now, when it was a problem for him, he was thinking about it.

Sasha moved in with Gleb. They set up a folding cot and added thirty rubles to the rent. Sasha went to his place on the outskirts of Ufa once a week, usually on Sunday mornings. He brought his landlady a cake on November 7, the anniversary of the Revolution. The old lady was pleased with the present. She didn't ask why he never spent the night in his room; she was used to her lodgers not staying overnight. But as December drew near, she reminded him every time he appeared that he had to vote. Otherwise there would be a lot of trouble. She had been strictly warned about it. He had better come early, too, because they threatened to start going around all the apartments after twelve to get everyone who hadn't shown up by then.

Gleb also warned him about voting. "Don't even think of crossing out anyone on the ballot. They're all marked. They'll know it was you right away."

Sasha, naturally, did not cross out the sole candidate's name, he didn't even notice what it was. He didn't go into the booth, either. It was way at the other end of the room, and they would suspect that you were crossing things out if you went in there. He walked past all the "volunteers" in every corner straight up to the urn and dropped in his ballot.

Everyone did that. There was nothing surprising in the fact that 98.6 percent of the voters had voted for the "bloc of Communists and non-Party members." Nor was Sasha surprised by Stalin's words at the election eve meeting. "Never in the world have there ever been such truly free and truly democratic elections, never! History has never seen such an example." The only thing that did surprise him was the 1.4 percent voting against the official slate.

～ 7 ～

BEFORE LEAVING, Speigelglass turned over another agent to Sharok — Mark Grigoryevich Zborovsky, code name "Mak," a.k.a. "Tulip." Speigelglass was in a hurry, but "Mak" was so important that Speigelglass felt it necessary to bind their contract in his own presence. Zborovsky worked in the Trotskyite International Secretariat, as personal secretary and trusted friend of Trotsky's son, Lev Sedov, who published the *Bulletin of the Opposition* in Paris and was working on the creation of the Fourth International.

Sharok had no doubt that Speigelglass had been "hunting" Trotsky for a long time. At one time Speigelglass counted on Skoblin and his close friend in Bulgaria, General Tukrul, for that assignment. Trotsky's murder by white émigrés would have looked like an act of revenge for losing the Civil War. People working for Miller and Dragomirov tried it when Trotsky moved from Turkey to Europe. But they failed.

But there were no White émigrés in Mexico, where Trotsky settled in January 1937. That left Mark Zborovsky as the only man who could get into Trotsky's inner circle, through his son. And in the meantime he was a valuable source of information. Lev Sedov trusted him with everything, including his personal correspondence with his father. They called Zborovsky "Étienne" in their letters. The level of Sedov's trust can be seen from this letter to his father: "During my absence, Étienne will take my place, he and I have the closest ties and he deserves absolute trust in all respects." Zborovsky gave a copy of this letter, like all the letters between father and son, to Sharok. Thus Moscow knew what the International Secretariat was doing as well as every step Trotsky and his allies took. In the files, Lev Sedov was called "sonny" and Trotsky "the old man."

Sharok liked Zborovsky, who was an intelligent, taciturn Jew with a clear, open gaze and unhurried movements. It turned out they were almost the same age. Zborovsky was born in 1908 in Umani in the Ukraine and later lived in Poland, where he had been a member of the Polish Communist Party. He spent a year in a Polish prison and then moved with his wife to Berlin and then to Paris. He fell on hard times financially and in 1933 he was recruited. He had a sister and two brothers back in the Soviet Union.

At their next meeting Zborovsky gave Sharok materials on the preparations by the Trotskyites for the Fourth International Congress and the addresses of the delegates they expected. He also gave him copies of the latest letters from Sedov to Trotsky and from Trotsky to Sedov. Zborovsky's movements were relaxed, his gaze open and clear. This was not gabby Tretyakov or haughty Skoblin. He did not have that self-assurance that Sharok found so annoying in Poles in general and in Polish Jews in particular. He gave the impression of a man who was gentle on the outside but hard on the inside, who knew his worth but did not emphasize it. There was no extraneous talk. Zborovsky said that Sedov's relations with his common-law wife, Jeanne Martin, were still strained. Jeanne was a woman of exalted enthusiasm and she wanted to boss both her ex-husband, Raymond Molyneux, and Sedov. But Molyneux had left the political arena, and besides their work in the Trotskyite International Secretariat, Jeanne had nothing in common with Sedov except the upbringing of Seva Volkov, Trotsky's grandson and Sedov's nephew, whom he adopted after his sister, Elizaveta, committed suicide. Zborovsky talked about it with restraint and even with a certain sympathy for Sedov.

Sharok could see why Sedov trusted Zborovsky. It would be difficult not to trust a man like that. That is, if you didn't know that Zborovsky returned that trust with treachery and was paid for it. But by now, in his fifth year working for Soviet intelligence, Sharok was no longer surprised by anything. There were no heroes, no saints. Everyone could be bought, sold, betrayed, broken, frightened. From soldier to marshal, from laborer to minister.

In a Paris newspaper Sharok read an article by a former colonel of the gendarmes claiming that Comrade Stalin, when he was still Josef Dzhugashvili, had been a paid informer for the Tsarist secret police with the code name "Ficus." The article even quoted documents showing that Dzhugashvili had worked for the gendarmes. Gurtsev, that great exposer of provocateurs, had said that the Central Committee of Bolsheviks had two agents of the Tsarist secret police. Gurtsev had named one — Malinovsky — and could not name the other, but insisted that he existed. Now Gurtsev's claims were corroborated by the gendarmes colonel who named the man — Stalin. And the Paris papers also wrote that former Soviet military leaders had gotten hold of documents from the Tsarist secret police showing that Stalin had worked for them. Tukhachevsky had not had time to make them public because Stalin had him shot first.

Did Sharok believe this? Why not? He was working for the Soviet secret police; why couldn't Stalin have worked for the Tsarist secret police? Intelligence, counterintelligence, spies, informers — they all existed and always would. No one is guaranteed not to do that kind of work. But Sharok did not discuss those articles with anyone. He didn't read them, see them, even hear of them. Just mentioning them could cost you your life. He was cautious about everything. As he handed over the latest *Bulletin of the Opposition* to Speigelglass, he said, "I don't even want to read this thing." Speigelglass replied, "You should. You should know your enemy." Sharok said nothing, but he thought to himself that Speigelglass would not last long with that attitude. Nor would Trotsky. His son's best friend was our agent. Both son and father trust him, consider him a loyal friend. You can't trust anyone. Trotsky does not understand that and as a consequence he will die. Comrade Stalin understands that. He trusts no one, he destroys everyone around him. Traitors die in his meat grinder, but of course so do his loyal friends.

In late January Zborovsky informed Sharok that Sedov was not well and complained of stomach pains. Naturally, anyone could have a stomachache, but something flickered in Zborovsky's eyes as he talked about it. There was something in his voice. Sharok understood that this was extremely important, that this was a situation that had been discussed previously, and he informed Speigelglass in Moscow by a coded message. Speigelglass demanded daily bulletins on "sonny's" health and told Sharok that "Nikolai" would arrive in Paris the very next day. Sharok was to set up a meeting between "Nikolai" and "Mak," but would not be participating in it himself.

Sharok had seen "Nikolai" once in Moscow, at Lubyanka. He had been surprised then to see that a man who looked like an ex-boxer spoke

French so fluently. Sharok understood why when he heard that Nikolai was part of the group led by Yakov Isakovich Serebryansky.

Sharok was sent on an errand by his then-supervisor to Serebryansky's house, a mansion on Gogolevsky Boulevard, where he met his wife, Polina Natanovna, who had just arrived from the dacha with her little boy and had brought him into his father's study. She had a significant face. Intelligent eyes. "The lady's got a past," Sharok thought respectfully and felt nervous for some reason. He didn't linger. Back out on the street, going over his impressions, he decided that Serebryansky looked like a Roman patrician. Medium height, solid build, large features. Much later Sharok learned that Serebryansky, a former Socialist Revolutionary, ran their special task group, that is, he handled kidnappings and murders. The other Chekists called members of his group "Yasha's gang" behind their backs. "Nikolai" was one of the group, so that it wasn't hard to guess the reason for his arrival in Paris.

After his meeting with Zborovsky, "Nikolai" vanished. Zborovsky remained in contact with Sharok and soon informed him that Sedov was very sick and that Zborovsky and Jeanne Martin had checked him into a hospital on rue Narcisse Dias as Monsieur Martin (using Jeanne's surname). Only Jeanne and Zborovsky were allowed to see him. Now Zborovsky reported daily to Sharok, and Sharok passed it on to Moscow. On February eighth, Sedov had an appendectomy. The operation was a success. On the ninth, tenth, eleventh, twelfth, and thirteenth, his condition was good and he walked around his room. On the fourteenth, new information. The night before, Sedov suddenly developed hallucinations. He ran around the hospital, shouting in Russian, and fell on the couch in the director's office. He was given a second transfusion, but they could not save him. On February sixteenth, Sedov died while in a coma. The autopsy revealed nothing. Nor could it have. The poison "Nikolai" gave to Zborovsky was unknown to French doctors. It caused death only on the tenth day. It had been sprinkled on his body before Sedov was moved to the hospital.

8

HE HAD a scratchy throat and a cold, and his doctors had suggested that he stay home. Stalin obeyed and did not go to the Kremlin.

It was an overcast day. There was snow on the veranda, and on his orders the snow had not been removed. If there were no tracks in the snow, it meant that no one had approached. And as usual, the sight of the untouched white snow soothed him. Snow lay on the tree branches and on the roof of the guardhouse. They removed snow from the roofs only when he was in the Kremlin. But while he was at the dacha, no one was allowed up on the rooftops to shovel. He did not like scraping overhead and he did not like people walking above him. Even the road from the gate to the house was not cleared because they did not want to waken him accidentally.

It was dusky in the room, but Stalin did not turn on the light. That would ruin the coziness that he usually felt on gray wintery days, in the peace and quiet of his house. He washed. He did not shave because no one would be seeing him today.

Valechka brought in his breakfast tray.

"How do you feel, Josef Vissarionovich? How's your health?"

"All right. I'll go to the library later."

She gave him a meek look.

"What are you staring at? Don't recognize me?"

"But you were going to stay at home, Josef Vissarionovich. And the doctors — "

"The doctors gave permission for the library," Stalin interrupted.

"Then that's just wonderful."

Her "wonderful" meant that when Stalin came outside in his thick felt boots, fur coat, and fur hat, the path from the house to the library would have been cleared and the porch of the library, a wooden house one story below ground, swept. And the library would have been aired out and heated. When had they had time?

The books were set up properly on the shelves, by section and in alphabetical order. He found whatever he needed quickly, he couldn't waste time looking. Karl Marx said that his favorite pastime was rummaging in books. Marx did not run a state and he had time to rummage. Lenin used the State Public Library, from which books could not be removed, and asked to keep books through Sunday to return Monday morning. Was he trying to set an example as the head of the government? No. It was simply that old intellectual habit of following library rules. Lenin was essentially a bookish man and that was the source of his major miscalculations. But for *him,* a book was merely a tool in *his* work, nothing more.

A book lay on the desk — *Tales from the Childhood of Stalin.* They had printed up one copy for him and were waiting for his permission to do a full print run. They would not get it. It was a bad book. An unnecessary book. Everything in it was treacly, perfect, with kindly parents, a friendly, hardworking family. Lies! The "fellow countrymen" particularly annoyed him. The author kept quoting them. Those sons-of-bitches tried so hard! They were exploiting a childhood friendship that had never existed. He did not remember these childhood friends, and if he did recall one or two, it was as snotty, cruel boys who had either despised him or ignored him. Now they were full of stories, trying to show off a relationship that would save them a place in history.

It was written by a Russian woman, but the book was totally Georgiafied. The stupid fool had been trying to please him! It was full of Georgian names, and baby nicknames at that: Zuriko, Besiko, Temriko, Otariko, Gogi. . . . How would Russian children read that? They'd laugh at it and the silly names like Soso and Sosiko.

There already was one child, little Volodya Ulyanov, baby Lenin. With blond curls and rosy cheeks, a little Russian aristocrat, his picture was on all the badges and banners, a sweet Russian son of the nobility. Why did they need yet another one? And with the strange and funny name Sosiko? For Soviet children *he* must be an all-powerful leader, Comrade Stalin, in uniform and boots, not a peer. Children are impressed by military uniforms. Lenin was something from the distant past, but *he* was alive. And for Soviet children, *he* must be alive, a living father, a living God. The dead Jesus can be an infant, and even then only when depicted with the Madonna. Jesus and Lenin had done their historical work and now could be charming tots. But *he, he* could not be little!

They were digging around! Some idiot Ossetian scholar did some research and wrote that Comrade Stalin allegedly came from the Ossetian Dzugat clan. There's this village in Ossetia, Dzugata, and everyone who comes from there is a Dzugata. Those who were baptized in the north were given Russian endings to the surname and became Dzugaev or Dzugatov. In the south, a Georgian priest added a *dze* or a *shvili*. And so *his* ancestors were first "Dzugashvili" and finally "Dzhugashvili." Everyone wants to claim *him* now, the Ossetians and the Georgians.

Hitler does not allow anyone to write about his ancestors. And he's right! Hitler's father, Alois, was the illegitimate son of a peasant woman named Schicklgruber. He had his mother's name until his father, Hitler, showed up and officially recognized Alois as his son. Ever since Alois was called Hitler and his son, Adolf, was also Hitler. And Führer Hitler was right. Why should the German people know all this? So that they can gossip and mock? And how would "Heil, Schicklgruber!" sound?

Some idiots were digging around in Lenin's biography. Lenin's ancestors on his father's side were Russian and Kalmyk, and on his mother's, Swedish and Jewish. Why should the Soviet people know that? Hitler wants racial purity, but *he* does not. *His* own children have a Georgian father and a Russian mother with a bit of German blood. So what? The Russian nation is a mixture of Slavs and Finno-Ugrics, Turks and Mongols. Mixed marriages inside the U.S.S.R. should be encouraged because they will create a unified Soviet nation. But marriage to foreigners must be stopped. They lead to espionage and treachery. Where did marriage to foreign princesses lead the Romanovs? To the last tsar, Nicholas II, being German in fact, since all his ancestors had been married to Germans and there was no Russian blood left in Nicholas II. And the people rejected him. The tsar was a German and his tsaritsa was a German. How could he fight his own Germans in the war?

He was not the scion of a royal dynasty and *he* did not need a genealogy. *His* mother was Georgian. *His* father was registered as a Georgian. Therefore *he* was Georgian by origin, but in fact, *he* was Russian. He belonged first of all to the Russian people. *His* entire life and all *his* work were tied to the Russian people. And that idiot scholar had dug as far as the record book of the Gori Cathedral for 1878, where allegedly it was recorded that on December 6, the Gori residents Vissarion Ivanovich Dzhugashvili, a peasant, and his legal wife, Ikaterina Gabrielovna, had a son, Josef. The newborn was baptized by Father Khakhanov and deacon Kvinikdze. The rite took place on December 17. So, it looked as if *he* had made himself a year younger. What for? To start school later? To enter the army later? They wouldn't get away with trying to cast a shadow on *him*.

His role as leader in the Revolution, in the Civil War, and in Socialist construction — serious studies like that should be encouraged. But digging around in his personal biography had to be stopped once and for all.

On a sheet of paper, Stalin wrote in blue pencil,

> To the Central Committee of the Komsomol Children's Publishing House:
> I am categorically against *Tales from the Childhood of Stalin.*
> The book is rife with factual errors, distortions, exaggerations, and undeserved praise. The author was misled by fanciers of fairy tales, fibbers (perhaps even "honest" fibbers), and toadies. I feel sorry for the author, but the fact remains.
> But that is not the most important thing. The main point is that the book has the tendency to inculcate in the consciousness of Soviet children (and people in general) the cult of personality, of leaders as sinless heroes. This is dangerous, harmful. The theory of "hero" and "crowd" is not a Bolshevik theory but a Socialist Revolutionary theory. Heroes create nations, turning the crowd into a nation, say the SRs. The nation creates heroes, is the Bolshevik response to the SRs. The book adds grist to the mill of the SRs. Any book like that will add grist to the mill of the SRs. It will harm our common Bolshevik cause. I suggest you burn this book.
> 16 February 1938
>
> J. Stalin

He put the letter in a folder, set it aside, and picked up another file. Reports on Trotsky with his Fourth International and the *Bulletin of the Opposition.* He looked through it daily. "Stalinism and fascism are symmetrical phenomena. In many of their traits they are incredibly alike." Trotskyite demagoguery! What was the real similarity between Bolshevism and Nazism? In hatred toward Western bourgeois democracies, particularly of conceited England that had enslaved half the world. *He* and Hitler had common enemies, and those enemies would unite them at the right time, and the right time was coming. And in the meantime *he* carried on *his* game with the Western democracies, scaring them with Hitler, and Hitler played his game, scaring them with Stalin. But to actually fight against the U.S.S.R., with England and France in his rear guard? To exhaust himself in a war like that? No, Hitler wouldn't do that, he was too smart. Trotsky knew that very well and he predicted *his* union with Hitler in order to appear a prophet. Trotsky just wouldn't let up. "Stalin is destroying the Bolshevik Party. Stalin will go down in history as the most despised and most disgusting Cain of all time. The monuments he had erected to himself will be destroyed or placed in museums of totalitarian horrors. And the victorious working class will erect monuments on the squares of the liberated Soviet Union to the miserable victims of Stalinist hatred and vileness. . . . Stalinism will be crushed, destroyed, and covered with dishonor forever."

Planning to crush and destroy *him!* The bastard! We'll see who gets crushed! If Slutsky and Speigelglass can't manage, *he* will find others who can fulfill the Party's assignments. That family has to be cut down at the roots; no one must survive.

From the same file Stalin removed a list of the Trotsky family members. Once again, for the umpteenth time, he read it:

Alexander Davidovich Bronstein, Trotsky's older brother — shot in 1937, in a prison in Kursk.
Boris Alexandrovich Bronstein, Trotsky's nephew — shot in October 1937.
Olga Davidovna, Trotsky's sister — sentenced to ten years in prison.
Nina Lvovna, Trotsky's oldest daughter by his first marriage — died of tuberculosis in 1928.
Her husband, Nevelson — shot in 1937.
Their daughter, Valya, born in 1925 — lost in an NKVD orphanage center and they still can't find her, the sluggards!
Zinaida Lvovna Volkova, Trotsky's younger daughter — committed suicide.
Her husband, Platon Volkov — shot in 1937.
Their son, Vsevolod Volkov, born in 1926 — lives in Paris with his uncle Lev Sedov, Trotsky's older son.
Sergei Lvovich Sedov, Trotsky's younger son — shot October 29, 1937.
Alexander and Yuri, Trotsky's nephews — shot.

Alive: the villain Trotsky; his second wife, Natalya Sedova; his older son, Lev Sedov; and, his eleven-year-old grandson, Vsevolod Volkov. First, Trotsky had to be liquidated. Lev Sedov should not be touched yet. Our agent Mark Zborovsky has his confidence and we get complete information through him. Sonny will come later, after his father.

It had been a mistake to let Trotsky go abroad when he did. *He* should have dragged him into court like all the other bastards. After they made him stand on one leg for ten hours, he would have signed anything. Those bastards Rykov and Bukharin turned out to be shit just like Zinoviev and Kamenev. Naturally, they pretend to have "ideals" — "I am obeying the Party's orders and will confirm my statements in court." Liars! They couldn't take the investigation and signed whatever they were given. Vanya Budyagin didn't "obey the Party's orders." And how they worked him over! *He* had sent Andreyev to the prison to watch. Andreyev took a look and fainted. What a weak-nerved Politburo member he turned out to be. The man watching faints while the man to whom things were being done does not. That means, he is a strong man. And the ones who sign are weak. Yagoda broke others, but when his turn came, he signed immediately. And so would Trotsky. And if they had interrogated his wife, sons, and grandchildren in front of him, he would have signed everything. And if he didn't, he would have rotted to death in jail. Of course, they would have made a fuss in the West. So what? What harm can that bring to the Soviet Union? None. If it's profitable, the capitalists are ready to trade with the devil. Love of humanity is one thing; gold is another. They will swallow the Bukharin-Rykov trial, too.

The trial will start March second. An open trial, with defense counsel, with representatives of the press, the diplomatic corps, the intelligentsia, particularly writers. They considered Bukharin a poetry specialist, so let them listen to their favorite.

His thoughts were interrupted by a short, low whistle. He listened. A pause and then another short, low whistle. A cricket? Yes, it seemed to be. How could a cricket get in here? *He* hadn't heard one in a long time. Not since *his* childhood probably. No, *he* couldn't remember a cricket in Gori. It was in the village when *he* was in exile. It used to chirp at night. It didn't bother *him*. *He* liked it, it was peaceful and it made the silence more obvious. *He* would lie there thinking while the cricket chirped quietly behind the stove, meekly, not arrogantly. . . . But there was no stove here, they had central heating. Probably, crickets could live anywhere, not just around stoves. *He* remembered that Nadya used to take the children to the Art Theater to see *Cricket on the Stove*. That's why *he* thought that crickets had to be around stoves, but obviously this isn't so. Should *he* tell Vlasik? What for? He'll just look for it, stomping around in his boots and it would make the books shift. The cricket wasn't bothering anyone. It wasn't nasty like a roach or a bedbug. It was just singing to itself. Let it sing, let it chirp, the lonely little creature!

Stalin got up, put on his fur coat and his fur hat, and listened. The cricket had stopped. He waited. . . . No, the cricket was silent. It must have fallen asleep.

Stalin went out on the porch. The night was dark, even though it was just barely evening, around seven probably. The lights were burning brightly in the house, on top of the house, in the guardhouse, and in other buildings. And the path from the library to the house was illuminated by lanterns suspended on posts. And he could see guards at the gate and in huts along the fence. Stalin stood and breathed the cold February-moist air. Then he went to the house.

He dined alone. Yezhov was waiting for him in the guardhouse. Valechka cleared his dishes. Stalin sent for Yezhov.

He appeared with his files. A tiny man, a midget, with violet eyes. An illiterate, stupid bone-breaker. He couldn't make the *right* decisions on his own. He had to turn to *him* for the slightest thing, demanding sanctions for every action. It wasn't clear who the Commissar of Internal Affairs was — Yezhov or Stalin. After Yezhov was removed, *he* would release several dozen people, military men, to show that Yezhov had put them away unjustly. The people would react positively, the people would be happy. Both *he* and the people had been deceived by Yezhov. A terrible drunkard. An alcoholic. And that meant he talked. And what he said was unpredictable. *He* didn't need a witness like that. Beria would replace him. Beria was not a fool, but a decisive man. *He* could talk to Beria. Beria understood *him*.

Stalin indicated a chair and warned him: "I'm a bit under the weather, I have a cold. So keep your distance. What do you have?"

Yezhov placed the transcripts of recent interrogations on the desk. Stalin looked through them. Everything was correct. All the things *he* had ordered them to add to the statements yesterday had been signed by the accused.

Stalin closed the file. "How's Budyagin?"

"He still refuses to make a statement, Comrade Stalin. I interrogated him myself. Experienced people ran the investigation, and eyewitness confrontations showed him up, and . . . He won't confess, Comrade Stalin."

Stalin raised his heavy eyes. "Will you manage with Budyagin?"

"Definitely, Comrade Stalin."

"No," Stalin said grimly. "You won't. I know Budyagin back from exile. Don't bother with him. Shoot Budyagin."

"Yessir, Comrade Stalin," Yezhov replied.

"What is happening with Trotsky?"

"There is important information, Comrade Stalin. Last night in Paris, Trotsky's son, Lev Sedov, died at the hospital."

Stalin regarded Yezhov with his heavy, immobile eyes. "What for?"

"I had informed you, Comrade Stalin. We have our man near him — "

"I asked you, why did he die?" Stalin interrupted.

"The orders came from Comrades Slutsky and Speigelglass."

"I am not asking them, I am asking you — *why?*"

"It was assumed that after Sedov's death, Trotsky would take Zborovsky to Mexico."

Stalin slammed his fist on the desk. "Idiots! Bastards! After his son's death, Trotsky will never take Zborovsky to be with him. On the contrary, he will be even more careful. Idiots! This was a vile act of sabotage! Speigelglass is sabotaging the main assignment. Slutsky is Yagoda's man. I had warned you about that long ago. Why is he still working for you?"

"I had informed you, Comrade Stalin. His arrest would frighten our agents abroad. To start with, he has been removed from the central apparat. He is being transferred to Uzbekistan. He's leaving in a few days."

Stalin pondered and then looked up at Yezhov again. "Leaving, is he? . . . Make sure he has a good send-off."

9

VADIM WOKE UP in a marvelous mood. He jumped out of bed, swung his arms around a bit to loosen up, and then headed for the bathroom.

"Put on the kettle!" he called to Fenya in the kitchen. She had the radio on as usual and was listening to songs by Soviet composers.

He usually told her to turn off the organ-grinder immediately, but this time, on the contrary, he tapped his feet to the music and sang along in the shower:

> Oh, it's good to live in the Soviet land,
> Oh, it's good to be loved by the country,
> Oh, it's good to be useful to the country. . . .

What a glorious day, a remarkable day. And still humming, he came out to the kitchen. The delicious aroma of toast filled the air. Fenya sat down at the table and, regarding Vadim with radiant eyes, said, "So, Kalinin himself signed your medal?"

"Kalinin signed the decree on my commendation."

"What joy, what joy . . ."

Fenya was sincerely pleased for him. But his father responded indifferently to the news, glancing through the newspaper article casually. Too bad. There were several thousand writers in the country, but only 172 of them were given decorations! Sholokhov, Fadeyev, Tvardovsky, Katayev, Mikhalkov, Gladkov — and next to these idols is the name of your son, Daddy, here take a look! Look how they appreciate him! . . . Just ask Fenya, she'll tell you about the dozens of telegrams of congratulations from newspapers, magazines, publishing houses, theaters, film studios, and all kinds of committees and departments.

"You're way ahead of all your friends, all that useless trash," Fenya said, referring primarily to Ershilov. She didn't like him. She always tightened her lips into a straight line when he came by. She was illiterate, but her female intuition was on target. Ershilov was supposedly Vadim's best friend, but he only mumbled a few platitudes of congratulations. He was envious: Why did Marasevich get a decoration and not me?

"You're the smartest of the lot," Fenya added and patted him on the head, the way she used to when he was a child.

And then the phone rang. It was Zhenka Dolmatovsky. "Well, Vadim, how's the drill?"

He meant that he'd have to drill a hole in his lapel for the decoration. Not the funniest of jokes. Zhenka Dolmatovsky had gone to the same school in Krivoarbat Alley, but three years behind Vadim. His poetry was published in the *Pioneer Pravda* when he was still at school, and eventually he graduated to the *Komsomol Pravda*. He was talented, but arrogant. All those home-grown jokes, the stupid puns, he had to make everything into a jingle. . . .

One day at the Writers' Club he asked Vadim, "Whom are you going to Ermilize tomorrow?" That is, since Ermilov is your mentor, you criticize our brethren on his orders. He ought to pay for saying that about Ermilov. One word to Altman, one little sentence in his report — and there'd be a puddle where Zhenka used to be. But he was small fry. Let him live. However, he would definitely put Zhenka in his place.

He'd have to put the poet Vasilyev in his place, too. He had said, "Congratulations on your Happy Kids." That's how everyone jokingly referred to the Badge of Honor, which depicted figures of two young workers, one male and one female.

Another phone call. Klavdya Filippovna, an editor at the State Literary Publishing House. "Well-deserved, congratulations."

The whole day went like that. Vadim sat in the armchair by the telephone, accepting congratulations, and in the breaks between calls looked over the issue of *Pravda* with the honors lists. He bought ten copies. Nine he put away in his desk, and he used the tenth to make his calculations — how many Muscovites got awards, how many people from Leningrad, Kiev, how many critics, how many people his age. It turned out that of the young critics in major cities, he was the only one to be decorated.

In the evening Vadim went to the Writers' Union for a rally. The more celebrated writers spoke, thanking the Party, the government, and Comrade Stalin personally for his paternal care for Soviet literature. When Comrade Stalin was mentioned, everyone rose and applauded. The resolution of gratitude to the Party, government, and Comrade Stalin personally was passed unanimously to stormy applause.

Wherever Vadim went now, he was met with joyous greetings. Vadim went to various editorial offices, walking from room to room, from section to section, as if on an errand, but actually to be seen and to receive his share of smiles and congratulations. And if he did not get enough attention in some department, he was hurt — not for himself of course, but on behalf of Soviet literature. The idiots don't read the papers, yet they work on the ideological front!

But whether he was congratulated or not, his fondest wish had come true. The important people had accepted him as one of their own. Distinguished by a high government order, he was now one of them, the masters and rulers of life. Now he would be on the list for the Kremlin hospital. After all, how many order-bearers were there among writers? It was a good word, order-bearer, it had a solid sound. In France, they called them Chevaliers of the Legion of Honor. But chevalier, or cavalier, was too lightweight, too flippant, too French, too womanizing somehow. In contrast, order-bearer was a powerful Soviet word, like gun-bearer, armor-bearer, or standard-bearer — it meant being part of a brotherhood of knights, it had a masculine, courageous sound. Of course, there was the Russian word for rhinoceros, "horn-bearer." The word came to mind, but he didn't see what it had to do with anything.

They said that Comrade Stalin himself went through the list of honorees with the members of the presidium of the Writers' Union and that he was not pleased by Katayev for his not-very-flattering opinion of Mikhalkov's work. Angry with Katayev, Stalin demanded that Mikhalkov get a higher award than originally indicated. Now Seryozha Mikhalkov was on his way up. And why not? He was talented and a beloved children's poet. But things would be tough for Katayev now. Good. He was a typical Odessa boor, pushy and shameless. . . . Vadim wondered what had been said about him? After all, they had gone over the list name by name. He got the award, so it must have been good. But what exactly, and who said it? Maybe Comrade Stalin? "I've seen Marasevich's articles. . . . Is this that Marasevich?" "Yes, Comrade Stalin, it is." "Well, he's a gifted man and he had the right positions. We must encourage young talent."

Of course, there may have been nothing of the kind. Comrade Stalin might have asked simply who this Marasevich was, they told him, and Stalin left Vadim on the list. But he would love to know the details. Whom could he ask? He couldn't very well go to Fadeyev, the head of the Writers' Union, and ask, "Alexander Alexandrovich, what did Comrade Stalin say about me?"

Fadeyev would just look at him with his red, hungover eyes and say, "You're not acquainted, are you? He didn't even mention your name."

And another thing. When he was approving the list, did Comrade Stalin know that Vadim was also "Vaclav"? The list was clearly vetted at Lubyanka, where they crossed off the unreliable names. They left his. That meant they were sure of him, and Comrade Stalin was sure of him.

When would they hand out the decorations? He knew it would be at the Kremlin, and he knew that President Kalinin would do the honors, but when, when would they pin it to his jacket, when would everyone see at last that he was an order-bearer?

At the Vakhtangov Theater, for instance, the manager and the artistic director congratulated him, but the actors said nothing. They didn't read the papers, the jerks, they were busy memorizing their lines and didn't deal with any other written forms. Even Veronika Pirozhkova, who always said something nice to him, did not mention his order. She didn't know. Too bad. Pirozhkova, like everyone else at the theater, treated him respectfully but without the usual sucking up that actors do to a critic. She was a skinny blonde of indeterminate age — eighteen or pushing thirty — with a capricious mouth and big blue eyes that always smiled at Vadim. Pirozhkova did not call him Vadim Andreyevich, like everyone else. She called him Marasevich, and her smile was teasing, either mocking the importance of his persona or mocking his lack of response to her attention. But at twenty-eight, Vadim was still a virgin and he was shy around the possibility of that kind of a relationship, even though he was attracted by Pirozhkova — her eyes, and her mocking smile, and that familiar "Marasevich."

She played minor roles, but once Vadim paid notice to her in a

review: "V. Pirozhkova was convincing in the episodic but charac-
teristic role of Anna." Veronika kissed him at the theater in front
of everyone. "Thanks, Marasevich!" Actors and actresses liked kissing and it didn't necessarily mean anything, but Pirozhkova's kiss
burned him. After that night, he imagined their meetings, her em-
braces and kisses, he pictured her naked, and then would get up and
pace the room, to keep from returning to the practice that he had
enjoyed when he was a teenager and from which his father had broken him.

At last, the ceremony! In the Kremlin. And it was Mikhail Ivanovich
Kalinin who bestowed Vadim's order.

They called out Vadim's name. He came up. Mikhail Ivanovich
handed him a box which contained the order and the award certificate,
shook his hand, and smiled. It wasn't an ordinary smile, like the one
he gave to the others, but a confidential smile, to a good friend, which
conveyed that he could not speak to him, setting him apart, here at an
official occasion. And he shook his hand warmly, not matter-of-factly.
When they moved to another room and were being seated for the group
portrait, Kalinin, who was in the front row center, looked around for
someone, but did not find him. Vadim was sure that he was looking for
him. He may not have read his articles, but he knew Vadim's father. He
was Kalinin's doctor. Too bad that no one noticed Kalinin looking for
Vadim. Everyone was too busy with his own decoration, too wrapped up
in his own glory and certain that Kalinin had given him special attention
and that he was the truly important person here.

At home Fenya made a hole in the lapel of his jacket, embroidered it
with button-hole stitching, and Vadim inserted the order. He put on his
jacket and looked in the mirror. Fantastic! Fenya stood in the doorway
and admired him.

"It looks good, Vadimushka, so beautiful. You're like a people's
commissar of something, I swear to God!" Her voice trembled. "I wish
Sergei Alexeyevich could see you. He'd have been so happy for you,
Vadimushka. He loved you ever since you were a little boy."

Stupid woman! Idiot! A fine time to bring up that ridiculous barber.
She ruined the moment.

But then again, why worry about him? She didn't ruin anything.

The incident with the barber was over. He couldn't torment himself over that his whole life, now could he? It was his own fault. Heads were rolling of much better people, and much better people were confessing — but the barber wouldn't confess. And enough thinking about that. Episode closed.

The next day Vadim made the rounds of the editorial offices again, leaving his coat in the cloakroom and wandering around the rooms with the decoration in his lapel. And once again everyone greeted him and hailed him and admired the order. And the ones who had not known about the award last time joined the chorus this time. Vadim accepted their congratulations modestly and with dignity. Their congratulations had nothing to do with him personally. It was not him, but Soviet literature that had been rewarded, and he was genuinely happy and proud for Soviet literature.

That evening Vadim went to the Vakhtangov Theater and took off his coat, as usual, in the manager's office, the way all the important guests did. He hurried backstage, as if looking for someone and opened the door to the dressing room, where among the other extras, Pirozhkova was getting ready for the performance. He saw half-dressed women in front of their mirrors. . . . Oh, pardon me, so sorry. . . . But Veronika Pirozhkova saw him, jumped up, and dragged him into the room.

"Girls, look! Our Marasevich has been decorated!"

She threw her arms around him and gave him a big kiss and the rest of the women also hurried to embrace him.

"I'm sorry," Vadim mumbled, "I'm looking for Komarov — "

"Komarov?" Veronika asked. "He's right here, I'll get him for you."

They went out into the hallway and she whispered, "Are you free tonight?"

Vadim's heart stopped. "Yes."

"Let's celebrate your decoration. I'm through after the first act."

"With pleasure. Let's go to a restaurant."

She shook her head. "No, no, I can't. All those gossips will say that I'm trying to seduce you or some other nasty thing."

Her voice trembled and tears came to her eyes.

"What's the matter! Why are you crying? Don't cry, please."

She wiped her eyes with a hankie. "I don't like it when people say bad things about me. I'm so happy that you received this honor. It's like a holiday for me. Why don't we go to my place? We'll listen to music and talk. I live alone. All right?"

"All right," Vadim managed to say.

"I'll be waiting for you outside by the stage door after the first act." She kissed his cheek and ran off.

Vadim suffered through the first act without seeing a thing that happened on stage. A date with a woman, alone in her room. . . . "I live alone." Why? She must have moved here from the sticks and rented a room. Or maybe she was married and her husband was on a business trip. What if he came home? But he wouldn't dare strike an order-bearer. And Veronika would not take the risk, she knew with whom she was dealing. What scared him was something else. What if he couldn't do it. He had failed twice before. What if it happened again?

But there was no way out. Pirozhkova would be waiting on the street in the cold.

And how could he leave after the first act? They would think he didn't like the play and that would cause a real stir in the theater. They would think he had become uppity now that he was an order-bearer. Whether he likes a play or not, a critic has to stay to the end. He would have to make up a good excuse.

In the intermission Vadim went to the manager's office, picked up the phone, dialed some numbers, and pretended to have a conversation. He even asked people to keep it down in the room so he could hear better.

"Yes, yes. . . . When? I see. . . . All right. . . . All right, I said. I'll leave right away. Yes, this minute. Please call and tell them I'll be there in twenty minutes."

He hung up and looked around portentously. "Unfortunately, I must leave immediately."

"Has something happened, Vadim Andreyevich?"

"I've been summoned!" Vadim said in a way that suggested it was a call from way up high, maybe even the Central Committee.

Vadim and Veronika stopped at the gastronome on Gorky Street.

Vadim bought some fortified wine, sausage, cheese, butter, a jar of marinated mushrooms, and some dried fish. He bought generously, showing off, because he knew how poor a struggling actress could be. She shook her head and said, "Marasevich, Marasevich, why so much?" but she kept checking the shelves for other goodies.

Veronika lived in Stoleshnikov Alley ("Right in the center of town," she said proudly) in a large communal flat. As she went down the hallway, she pointed things out. "Here's the toilet, this is the bathroom. Don't pay any attention to anyone. They're all bourgeois!"

She spoke loudly, not caring whether her neighbors heard or not.

She had a medium-sized room, skimpily furnished.

Veronika led Vadim to the window. "Look, Marasevich, what a lovely view."

"Beautiful," Vadim concurred, even though it was dark and he couldn't see a thing.

Something creaked behind him and Vadim turned in fright.

The mirrored door of the chiffonier was half open and a crumpled dress fell to the floor. Veronika pushed it back inside and stuffed a twist of newspaper in the door to hold it shut.

"There. Now I'll give you some slippers."

Vadim removed his shoes and put on the slippers.

"That's better, isn't it, Marasevich?"

"Very comfortable."

"And your jacket. Off with it, Marasevich! It's warm in here, they give us heat."

She helped him off with the jacket, which he hung on the back of a chair, and then laid out the food. She only had two plates, so she put the cheese, sausage, and butter on one, and the fish on the other. She sliced bread on a newspaper.

"Let's eat like students. You're probably not used to this kind of service, are you?"

He shrugged his fat shoulders in protest. "Why do you say that?"

"I'm having temporary difficulties," Veronika said mysteriously. "Open the bottle, Marasevich. An opener? No, sorry. This is the first time I'm drinking wine in this house, in honor of your award. Do you appreciate that, Marasevich?"

"Yes, yes, of course."

"Just give the bottle a hard smack on the bottom. . . . Have you seen peasants do that?"

Vadim twirled the bottle in his hands and gave it an ineffectual slap.

"Let's try something else." Veronika took the bottle from him. "We'll push the cork inside, and we can drink. By the way, I do have a screwdriver."

And she started working with it. "The cork will go down to the bottom, there's nothing harmful in it."

When she had the bottle opened, she poured wine into two water glasses, and raised hers. "To the high and deserved — please note that, Marasevich, 'deserved' — government award!"

They clinked glasses and she downed her wine.

Vadim sipped half.

She shook her blond curls. "Oh, no, Marasevich. None of that. You have to drink to your decoration, otherwise you can't wear it."

Vadim drained his glass.

She handed him a pickle on a fork. "Eat. Have some of the fish, too, while I make you a sandwich."

She made one with butter, sausage, and cheese. "Try a triple-decker."

Vadim liked it, and he ate everything heartily. Besides, he was afraid of getting drunk. Then he wouldn't be able to do it for sure.

In the meantime, Veronika had poured more wine into their glasses.

"Let's drink to you, now," Vadim said. "To your successes in the theater, may your talent be appreciated."

A grimace crossed her face. "Talent isn't enough at our theater. The actors are always backbiting and trying to keep anyone else from advancing. No more about that. Today is your day. . . . Oh, Marasevich, I've started using the informal 'you' with you."

"Fine. I'll use it with you, too."

She grew more lively. "Let's drink to it, let's do the Bruderschaft toast." She said, "Bruderschaft, O Bruderschaft . . ."

They linked arms, drank from each other's glass, and kissed. Veronika put her glass down on the table. "No! There's more to it than that."

She moved her chair closer to Vadim's, took his head in her hands, and gave him a long kiss, then she looked deep into his eyes, a serious, even suffering look, and suddenly said, "Would you like an omelette? I have eggs. You know, a sausage omelette is so delicious!"

She cut up the sausage, put four eggs and a chunk of butter on the plate, and went to the kitchen.

Vadim was left alone. The fear of failure overwhelmed him. And it would be just like the last time, a poorly disguised, or not even disguised, scorn, yawns, averted eyes, an indifferent parting. And then she'd tell her friends at the theater, "Marasevich is impotent." He shouldn't have come, he shouldn't have gotten involved with an actress, with any woman from circles where he was known as a critic. But maybe he would manage. There was something very confident about Pirozhkova. He needed to be more confident, too. The doctor told him, "Everything is in working order, just don't lose your nerve. Everyone goes through this sometimes." Maybe today it would work. And if it didn't, he'd pretend to be drunk. "It's your own fault, you got me drunk." Right. That's what he would do.

Veronika came back with a frying pan. She divided the omelette and poured out more wine.

"Let's drink to happiness. To happiness, Marasevich?"

"To your happiness! To your success!"

Her eyes filled with tears again, as they had at the theater.

"What's the matter?" Vadim asked anxiously.

She wiped the tears. "Nothing, I just remembered something. Forget it! Let's drink!"

As they ate the omelette, she said, "They'll be even more afraid of you at the theater now, you'll see! They only pretend to respect you. Actually, they fear you. The women there — all those honored and people's artists — are whores. Anyone of them would lie under you to get a good review. They pretend to be proper, but they never say no. The hell with them! Let's dance!"

"I'm not very good at it. Besides," he said, pointing at the bottle, "I've had too much."

"Too much? Nonsense! But all right, if you don't want to dance, let's play cards."

A deck of soiled cards appeared in her hands. Vadim had no idea where it came from.

"It's a simple game. Watch. I'll take the top card off the deck, and you guess if it's red or black. If you guess, I take something off. If you don't, you take something off. Well, come on, Marasevich! Red or black?"

"Red," Vadim babbled. He had never heard of this game.

She took the top card from the deck — a seven of diamonds.

"Ladies and gentlemen, Marasevich is right! I lose, I'll take off my belt."

She removed it. "Guess again!"

"Red," Vadim whispered.

She turned over the card — ace of hearts.

"Right again. You're a magician, Marasevich."

She got up and pulled her dress over her head, revealing a white silk slip on thin shoulder straps, low cut, so that her breasts were visible.

Vadim was afraid to look up.

Veronika picked up the deck again. "Color?"

"Red," Vadim repeated.

She turned it over. Queen of clubs!

"Wrong, Marasevich, wrong," Veronika crooned happily. "God is just, you can't win all the time. Take something off!"

"I'll take off my tie," Vadim muttered.

She untied it and put it on the table. "Let's go!"

"Black."

It was a ten of diamonds.

"I'll take off my watch."

"Sneaky Marasevich! A watch isn't clothing. Take off your sweater! Take it off, come on, don't cheat." Suddenly, she tossed the deck on the table. "Listen, Marasevich, why are we playing games, losing time? Do you find me attractive?"

"Of course," he mumbled.

"And I find you attractive. Let's lie down in bed. We're adults, conscious, rational adults. Get undressed, darling." She raised her slip, and undid the garter, releasing a stocking. "Do you want me to put out the light?"

In the dark he could hear her moving, pulling down the covers, and then the bedsprings, and her voice, "We'll warm up the bed for Marasevich. It'll be so warm and cozy. Come on, Marasevich, come to me. Don't be afraid, everything will be all right."

Vadim worked on his fly buttons, but his fingers had trouble obeying his command.

"Hurry up, slowpoke."

Vadim was in his underwear, and in a trembling voice asked, "Should I take everything off?"

"Of course, everything! It's nice and warm in bed. . . . Come on, come on, my little slowpoke, give me your hand." She found his hand, felt around his body, and helped him remove his underpants. "It's lonely and boring here in bed without you, it's no good here without

Marasevich. . . . Get in, honey, get in and don't be afraid. I'll do it all, you'll be so happy. You'll see!"

And it did work out. She was experienced and knowledgeable. For the first time Vadim experienced satisfaction and he was proud — a real man! And he managed it a second time, too! Veronika whispered hotly in his ear, "Right, honey, right, good, don't hurry, take it easy, there, there, that's good!"

She had a flexible, hot body, with small breasts. He put his hand on one. She pushed down on his hand with her own.

"The broads in our theater are superwhores. But they all pretend to be virgin queens. They'll screw, but first they have to play the innocent. But I like you and I don't see anything wrong with that at all. Why pretend? Am I right? Marasevich!"

"Of course you're right," Vadim said.

He lay in bed, facing Veronika, inhaling the arousing scent of her body, and he was happy, smiling in the dark.

∾ 10 ∾

NONNA HANDED OUT THE PAY. Everyone signed a receipt, everything was on the up-and-up, legal.

One day, they all got paid at the same time. "This calls for a celebration," Gleb announced.

"Exactly," concurred Lyonya. "Stakanov in the morning, Busygin in the afternoon, Krivonos at night." He was making a drinking joke out of the names of three of the most famous shock-workers, who had surpassed all quotas, in the land. He turned Stakhanov into Stakanov, from *stakan,* or glass; Busygin's name sounded like *busoi,* or drunk; and when he said Krivonos's name, which literally meant "crooked nose," Lyonya twisted his own, to look like a drunkard after a brawl.

Kanevsky was quiet.

"Well?" Gleb said. "Come on."

"I don't know," he replied indecisively. "I usually eat with the landlords at my place."

"We work together, we all got paid, the right thing to do is to go out drinking!"

"Well in that case, let's go!" Kanevsky said with a grimace.

"Don't do me any favors," Gleb warned. "We all work in the same place and we should stick together."

Kanevsky smiled mockingly in reply.

They took their usual table at the restaurant, in a corner far from the band. Gleb said that he had enough music at work.

They ordered a bottle of vodka, a mug of beer each, some herring with boiled potatoes, and a meat salad with mayonnaise.

Gleb held the bottle over Kanevsky's shot glass, but Kanevsky covered the glass with his hand. "No thanks, I don't drink vodka."

"Shall I order some champagne for you perhaps? Which kind? Domestic or French?"

"I try not to drink at all."

"Don't spoil the party, Kanevsky."

"All right," Kanevsky said unexpectedly and raised his glass.

"That's better!" Gleb smiled, revealing his white teeth. "That's being one of the boys."

They drank, ate, and had another round. Gleb ordered a second bottle and more beer all around and pork chops for everyone.

Sasha watched Kanevsky. The man wasn't accustomed to drinking. He'd get loaded and then they'd have to take care of him and get him home — and who knew where the hell he lived?

Sasha signaled Gleb, by nodding toward Kanevsky, to stop giving him liquor.

But Gleb said, "This is nice! Let's drink to the success of West European dancing in the city of Ufa and the entire Bashkir Republic! Am I right, Sasha?"

"Right, right, but I think Misha's had enough." Sasha moved Kanevsky's glass over to his own. "You don't mind, do you?"

"Not at all," Kanevsky said, twisting his mouth. "I can drink or not, I don't care."

"Eat! See what a nice chop you have? With fat on it. An old driver once taught me to eat fatty food when you drink — that way you'll never get drunk."

"That's true," Lyonya chimed in. "The fat absorbs the alcohol before it gets into your system."

"Fine." Kanevsky bent over his plate. "If you want me to eat, I'll eat. If you want me to eat fat, I'll eat fat."

Thank God! He didn't seem drunk, he held on to his knife and fork, dealing handily with the pork chop.

"I want to continue my toast," Gleb said, raising a glass once again. "So, to the development of West European dancing among all the peoples of the Bashkir Republic — Bashkirs, Tatars, Russians, Ukrainians, Jews, Cheremises, Mordovans, Chuvash, Germans, Estonians, and so on. . . . Some give us dirty looks and think we do hackwork. There are people sweating in factories, and all we do is jiggle our legs and make money. No, no, friends! We are men of the arts, of Socialist culture. You cannot have socialism without culture!" He turned to Sasha once more. "Am I right or not, dearie!"

"Right, you're right, but much too long-winded."

"I don't understand what socialism you're talking about," Kanevsky suddenly said.

"What do you mean?" Gleb was stunned. "I'm talking about our socialism, which is victorious in our country."

"You can't have your socialism or not yours," Kanevsky said, staring into his plate. "It is an absolute concept. German fascists also call themselves socialists. But as long as there are armies, militia, and other means of force — there can be no socialism in its true meaning."

Gleb stared in bewilderment and then smiled and said, "Look at that. Turns out Kanevsky is a theoretically versed comrade, and I had no idea."

He was in a hurry all of a sudden. "Right, boys, let's have a final drink."

Everyone except Kanevsky drank up.

Gleb got the bill, figured it out, and told everyone his share.

They went outside. It was around ten o'clock. It was drizzling and Kanevsky hunched down into his coat and raised the collar.

"Well, which way?" Gleb said, either asking or merely saying goodbye, and walked off with Sasha.

After a few steps, he asked, "What do you have to say to that, dearie?"

"What are you talking about?"

"Kanevsky. It's impossible to build socialism in one country. That's Trotsky's theory, you know. Remember?"

Gleb was right, but he didn't want to put down Kanevsky. "He was talking about the German fascist state. Not about us."

"No, dearie, you can't fool me! What did he say? 'There is no socialism as long as there are the army and the militia.' Note, he said militia, not police. Dearie! He was talking about the Soviet Union."

"Militia, police, big deal! Don't make a mountain out of molehill."

"And if *they* find out about those words tomorrow?" He nodded his head toward Egor Sazonov Street, where the NKVD headquarters were.

"How would they?"

"How? Anyhow? From me, say."

"Is that how it is?"

"Yes, yes! What do you really know about me? Or maybe from you!"

"It's like that, huh?"

"Yes, dearie, like that. I don't really know everything about you either. Or maybe it will be Lyonya. We don't know him at all. Or Kanevsky himself. We don't know who he is. We'll be hauled in and asked, 'Did he say that?' 'Yes.' 'Then why didn't you report it?' And we'll be arrested under the article for not reporting crimes. At best. The worst case would be as a Trotskyite group."

Gleb stopped in his tracks and turned a beet-red face to Sasha. He shook his fists and practically shouted, "It makes me want to bawl like a hungry cow! If you're invited to go out for fun, you should sit quietly and behave like a normal person, surrounded by friends. . . . No, he had to gab the devil knows what, showing off. Getting people into trouble!"

Sasha had never seen him like this. "Calm down," Sasha said. "I don't see any reason for hysterics. What are you afraid of, for God's sake! Get hold of yourself. People blow things like this out of proportion when they're scared, and then they pay for it later."

They got to the corner. "I turn here," Gleb said, suddenly calm.

"You should think about what I said."

"Certainly, dearie, certainly."

"Get some sleep, and think about it with a clear head."

"That's what I'll do, dearie. I'll have some hair-of-the-dog-that-bit-me and think about it."

What a stupid business. Kanevsky was a fool, a lunatic. He'd get into trouble someday and take others with him. But today's conversation was nothing. And if Gleb didn't do anything, the incident would end quietly.

But it didn't.

About two days later Sasha had a new accompanist. Stasik played both piano and the bayan and he was a cheerful, quick fellow. He managed the work readily, picking it up fast. Like Lyonya, he played by ear. He couldn't read music. Naturally, he didn't come close to Kanevsky in musicianship.

That evening over dinner in the restaurant, Sasha asked Gleb, "What happened to Kanevsky?"

"He won't be working with us anymore. Semyon fired him."

"What for?"

"We're moving out to the outskirts, dearie, to all those macaroni factories. There's no piano there and that means we need a third bayan player. Stasik is like me, a double threat."

Sasha put down his glass. "You're lying."

"Drop it, dearie. I swear, why are you getting so pesky about it?"

"What did you tell Semyon?"

Gleb gave him a piercing look. "Do you want to know everything?"

"Yes, I do."

Gleb poured himself another shot. "Why aren't you drinking?"

"I'll drink later."

Gleb drank and speared a piece of herring on his fork. "Well, I said, 'Get rid of Kanevsky. He talks too much.'"

"Did you tell Semyon what he says?"

"Why should Semyon know what he talks about? You have to answer for what you know, too. Maybe Kanevsky was saying that he wasn't paid enough? Semyon is no fool. If a man talks too much, it's better to get rid of him."

He poured himself another drink and looked at Sasha's glass. "This is no good. You think I can drink the whole bottle by myself?"

They drank. "You've killed the man," Sasha said.

"Me? What are you talking about?"

"He's been thrown out on the street, left without bread."

"Don't worry, he'll have his bread." Gleb nodded toward the band. "There's the bread, with butter, too. 'What does a poor Jew need? A piece of white bread. The caviar can be black.' But, please, no more accusations of anti-Semitism."

"Why did you tell Semyon that Kanevsky talks too much? To make sure he got fired?"

"Yes, dearie. That's exactly why. I do not want to work with a jerk who says things in public that can get me arrested the next day."

Sasha said nothing.

"You condemn me for it?" Gleb asked.

"Yes, I do."

"I see." Gleb chuckled. "All right."

He poured another drink, which he had without any food. He hiccuped. The drink was getting to him. "I'll tell you a story about my friend. Would you like to hear it?"

"I can listen."

11

GLEB PICKED UP THE BOTTLE and saw it was empty.

"All right, dearie, I'll tell you the story, and then we'll have another drink. So, I had a friend, my best friend, a true friend in Leningrad. We lived in the same building, on the same staircase, on the same floor. We went to the same school. He was first in literature, and math, even gym. He came from simple peasant stock in Novgorod, but he was a genius. He got the highest grade on the entrance exam to the Physics and Mathematics Institute. He had ideas! He had read Karl Marx's *Capital* back in ninth grade. He didn't drink or whore, but he did smoke. He had reddish blond hair, blue eyes, he was tall and handsome! And most important, he had soul. Everyone came to him for help, and he always helped as much as he could. And then, you see, it happened. . . . My friend had joined the Trotskyite opposition while still in college. He had always spoken out openly and he had never hidden his views. You may ask why he was friends with me, someone without a party and without ideals? I may be a lightweight, dearie, but I'm loyal. And he knew that. I think that's why he liked me. He told me everything. Of course, he didn't fill me in on real secrets, and he didn't name names. They had started arresting and exiling people by then. But he did share his views."

Gleb beckoned to the waiter and pointed to the vodka decanter. "Bring some more!"

"Maybe we've had enough?" Sasha said.

"One more drink won't hurt."

Gleb poured Sasha a drink and one for himself. "There was one man he simply couldn't stand." He squinted. Sasha knew he meant Stalin.

"He called him the gravedigger of the Revolution. I don't remember everything he said, but I clearly remember what he said about socialism in a single country. That's why Kanevsky bothered me so much, dearie. I used to hear that from a friend I trusted. I don't know Kanevsky. My friend used to say that it was impossible to build socialism in a single country. And the ones who said it was possible simply wanted to turn our country into a 'besieged fortress,' a 'citadel surrounded by enemies,' which spies and saboteurs would keep trying to enter. What they wanted to create, he said, was a military situation, the conditions for a personal dictatorship of one man, for terror and repression. And to maintain that we had already built socialism in our country was to compromise the very idea of socialism and, in the final analysis, to bury it." He stopped and stared at Sasha, with a murky gaze.

"Why don't you finish your story another time?" Sasha said.

Gleb looked up at him from beneath his lowered brow. "Do you think I'm saying too much? Don't worry, I'll never do that. I never, ever will."

He pushed himself up from the table. "Gotta take a leak. . . . You order some tea. Very strong. Like *chifir*. You know what *chifir* is?"

"I do. But the waiter may not."

"Explain it to him."

And he headed for the toilet, without clutching onto the tables, but not walking too steadily, either.

Sasha ordered two strong teas.

What a curious picture. And unexpected. It turned out that it hadn't been just debauchery, just a bohemian life, however provincial, for Gleb, as Sasha had thought. He was always so careful, and now he was talking with sympathy about a Trotskyite, at a time when you could only attack and curse Trotskyites. Back in Kalinin Oblast, Sasha had heard the story of a young woman on a collective farm who sang an old ditty when it was her turn to be in the middle of the circle dance — *"I'm so pretty and of my beauty I'm so certain, if I don't marry Trotsky, I'll marry Chicherin."* And she got ten years in the camps for it. Some man said, "Trotsky was a world-class orator," and he got ten years. "Trotsky is an enemy, of course, but before, he was number two after Lenin" — that meant ten years. That was the situation now. And here was Gleb with his confidences. . . .

The waiter set down two glasses of tea. The tea was dark brown, almost black. You had to add something to the tea, burnt sugar or something, Sasha couldn't remember what, to get that color.

Gleb came back, all his white teeth showing in a smile, his hair wet and combed. He must have put his head under cold water. He took a big sip of tea.

"Good! Where were we, dearie?"

"I suggested finishing up your story another time."

"No way. You'll have to listen to the end, dearie."

Sasha was always amazed by Gleb's capacity to drink and sober up fast when he needed to. He drank before class and even during the lessons (he brought it with him), but he never lost the beat or played a false note.

"So this was the kind of man my friend was," Gleb resumed his tale, "and naturally, he was sent up in the late twenties. He wasn't in a long time. Major Trotskyites began making their statements. 'We have no disagreements with the Party anymore, we submit to its decisions, and we ask to be reinstated in its ranks.' They were brought back from exile, and my friend also returned to Leningrad. He would drop by. We would sit and talk, and I realized that he was disillusioned and was going to devote himself to his science. He had been given his place back at the institute, he married a good girl, who bore him a son. He was crazy about the boy. They didn't have much money and he tutored in physics and math. Everything was fine. He was still listed formally in the Party. He had been reinstated automatically but Party membership was a real burden for him. He skipped meetings and didn't do his assignments. He kept hoping that he would be expelled for his passivity and then he could live a peaceful life. But he didn't get to live a peaceful life at all, dearie."

Gleb's voice broke and he stopped. He put his elbows on the table and clutched his head. "Let's have another drink. . . . I can't talk about this."

The waiter brought more vodka and a plate of sausages. Gleb drank and ate.

"Yes. . . . So, then some old comrades from exile dropped in to see him and they began talking about stuff. Hitler had just come to power and they kept saying, 'Hitler and Stalin, they're the same thing, can't you see it?' They talked about all kinds of things among themselves. He should have stopped them, the idiot. He should have said, 'I don't take an interest in politics and stop talking about this' or simply, 'Don't come to my place anymore.' I guess he didn't have the willpower. He was a gentle man, or maybe you make such good friends in exile that you can't break it off, or maybe he was afraid they'd think he turned into a coward, or maybe he trusted them and thought they were as decent as he was. Maybe they were decent, but they had big mouths. Prison and exile hadn't taught them a thing. And they gabbed in other places, not just at my friend's house.

"But anyway, when they came a second time, he let them know, tactfully, of course, he belonged to the intelligentsia after all and that he could not receive them. They had only a small room in a communal flat and the baby needed its sleep and he did work in the evenings. They didn't come after that. And he thought that this was the end. However, it wasn't. One fine day, a pleasant-looking young man came up to him at the institute, took him aside, showed him his red document case, and said, 'You'll have to accompany me. It's not far.'

"They went to the Big House, that's what we call the NKVD. He was taken in to see some man in an office, who sat him down in an armchair and asked how he was doing after exile. Was anyone being mean to him?

"My friend replied, 'Everything is fine, no one is being mean.'

" 'And what about your comrades from exile?'

"My friend sensed a trap, but he wasn't quick enough. 'I don't know. I don't see any of them.'

"The man took out a sheet of paper from his desk and read off the names of the people who had come to see my friend. 'Have you seen these people?'

" 'Yes, they came to see me twice.'

" 'And what did you talk about?'

" 'Nothing much.'

" 'Did you reminisce about Siberia and exile?'

" 'We did.'

" 'Recalled it in a romantic haze?'

" 'There's not much romance in Siberia.'

" 'Did you talk about politics, then?'

" 'I'm not interested in politics. I study physics and mathematics.'

"The NKVD man took out another piece of paper. 'Here's something that so-and-so said.' And he read word-for-word the musings of one of the assholes. 'Did he say that?' What could my friend do? 'Yes, he did.'

" 'How did you react?'

" 'I didn't listen. I went on with my work.'

" 'Let me get this straight. People are carrying on anti-Soviet conversations in front of you, and you didn't listen? Of course you listened. Otherwise you could not have confirmed what I just read to you.'

"My friend was silent. There was nothing he could say. Clearly, one of the people who had come to his place had been an informer. Maybe more than one.

"The man kept pushing. 'Nothing to say? Let me answer for you. You capitulated so that you could be reinstated in the Party and destroy it from within. You headed an underground Trotskyite group, which met at your place. I have all I need to arrest you and your group and to turn you over to the courts.'

"My friend replied, 'I took part in no Trotskyite activity and I took part in no conversations. But informing is against my moral convictions. My mistake was in not refusing them my house the minute they came there.'

"The man kept up his steamroller. 'We will arrest you and your group. During the investigation you will all admit your guilt because you are guilty. The article under which you will be charged is 'creation of a counterrevolutionary organization,' which calls for five years up to the death penalty. If you want to live and to save your family, think about how to save them. You say that you have no differences with the Party. Prove it.' And he openly proposed that my friend collaborate with them. 'And if you refuse, you have only yourself to blame.'

"Of course, my friend rejected that proposal. But refusal meant they would immediately send him to a cell and he would have to face the camps or the firing squad. And he did not want the camps or the squad. Not because he was afraid — he was a brave man. But why was he going to die? Because some idiots chattered in his presence? He did not want to die for them. For an idea? The idea had been betrayed by his leaders, who were swearing up and down on every corner. My friend was not willing to die for that and he did not want his wife and son to die for it either. So he signed. But he had no intention of becoming a stoolie. He hoped to get out of it, you see."

The people at the next table finished their meal. One stayed behind to pay, the other three got up and stood between the tables. Gleb stopped talking. The restaurant wasn't crowded, since it was a weeknight. A singer, rolling her eyes and pressing her hands to her breast, sang Gypsy love songs. *"Only once are there meetings like this, only once does Fate cut the thread."* She was bad, but Sasha loved Gypsy love songs.

The people who had been standing near them moved on to the coatroom. Gleb went on.

"And so he went to Moscow, to the very top, to see Comrade Solts. Have you ever heard of him?"

"Of course. In fact, I know him. A good man."

"Really? A good man? You know better, dearie. He was called 'the Party's conscience.' And so he went to see the conscience. Solts actually received him. And so my friend said, 'They want to recruit me. How can it be acceptable in Party ethics and morality for one Communist to secretly inform about other Communists?'

"And Solts replied, 'The Communist organs do not approach everyone. For instance, they never approached me. But they came to you. That means it is your personal business, so you solve it yourself.' "

"Solts said that to him?"

"That's what my friend told me. And he always spoke only the truth."

Could Solts have been so heartless? Too bad. He had remembered him with a halo. "Well, and then what happened?"

"After Moscow, after Solts, my friend came to me and told me everything that you've just heard. We sat up the whole night, and talked about that and many other things. He despised Zinoviev, Kamenev, and Radek, and Bukharin and Rykov, too. Their eloquence helped Stalin and they paved their own path to the gallows. Here's what he said about Trotsky — a major figure, no equal to him, and his line was right — 'You can't build socialism in a single country, you have to give freedom to factions and groups. And that is the way to freedom of views and opinions, and that means democracy.' "

"I don't think Trotsky was such a democrat."

"Dearie, I'm telling you what my friend said. Naturally, not a bourgeois democracy, but a socialist, proletarian one. I don't know these things. In general, he approved of Trotsky — a genius, but one who regarded himself in the mirror of history. He didn't want to become a new Bonaparte, and so he lost the game. He had a loyal army, and back in nineteen twenty-three he could have arrested and executed the three of them: Stalin, Zinoviev, and Kamenev."

"Execute? What kind of democracy is that?"

"Dearie! In our country, everything depends on executions — dictatorship and democracy."

"Turns out you're a philosopher, too."

"Whatever. My friend talked on about many things — everything was lost, the October Revolution was dead, and the country was headed for fascism. And his own life was over. He was calm, as if reading a lecture, I swear! He must have taken a decision. He stood up and said, 'Anything could happen to me and I want at least one person in the world to know my true story. That person is you. And I hope you won't repeat our conversation to anyone for a while. Learn to keep quiet!' Understand, dearie? 'Learn to keep quiet.' Golden words."

Gleb looked around the table glumly and leaned back in his chair.

"Why are we just sitting here like dopes at a birthday party? Let's have another drink. Look, there's still sausage to be eaten. Let's not let it go to waste."

He ate and drank. And then he said, "I didn't see him for the next two days, and on the third night our doorbell rang. What happened? There was a police detective, the local cop, and the janitor.

" 'Get dressed. We need you to be a witness.'

"They brought me to the neighboring apartment, to his room, where they were doing a search. My friend was not there, only his wife, all upset, and the baby in his bed. They searched until morning, without finding anything. So they wrote up some old books, pro forma. Otherwise, what had they been doing all night, right? They left, and I stayed. I asked his wife where he was. I thought he was in jail. But she said, 'He's in the morgue now.'

"What it was, dearie, was that he committed suicide. He poisoned himself at the institute. He waited for everyone to leave for the night and took poison. He had talked with old Comrade Solts, the Party's conscience, and killed himself afterward. That's the kind of conscience the Party has! When people came in the next morning, they found him in a lecture hall.

"We buried him at Volkovo Cemetery, next to his parents. His mother and father were already there. And I'll tell you something, dearie, he did the right thing. If he had lived, he would have been executed twenty times over and his family would have been destroyed. This way, it was a private matter — he wasn't the first or the last to commit suicide. His family is fine, the boy is at school. And I'm the only one who knows his whole story, all his suffering. They know at the Big House, too, but that doesn't count. He's one in thousands for them, but for me, he's the only one.

"He was a great man, dearie! And he's gone! And because some assholes wanted to shoot the breeze. And now you tell me, dearie, after that how am I supposed to treat jerks like Kanevsky? What right does he have to speak the words that get you arrested, that get you shot, in front of me, in front of you, in front of Lyonya? To show off his education? I don't give a shit about his education. I've forgotten more than he knows. How can I trust some Kanevsky when my friend signed what the NKVD wanted? And that signed paper is in their archives and a hundred years from now someone will read it and say, 'And this one was a stoolie, too.' He was the most honest and decent man who never spoke an untrue word in his life."

Gleb leaned toward Sasha. "I didn't tell you this story because I'm drunk, dearie. I don't want you to consider me a bastard because of Kanevsky. I got rid of Kanevsky tactfully so there wouldn't be any troublemakers among us who could be our downfall. And incidentally, that was something you should have done."

"Why me?"

"Because of your background. While you were driving trucks in Kalinin, their personnel department, that bitch Kirpicheva had started a whole file on you, even though you were only a simple driver. You can thank our dear workers and peasants militia for making you move away from Kalinin. So when Kanevsky started his bullshit, I thought, why isn't Sasha saying something? I mean, just imagine that they hauled us in for his conversation. Hah? Lyonya and I are nothing, bayan players, but you? You've done time, you're a contra. And so on . . . one contra was developing Trotsky's theories in front of another contra. An organization! And you're the head man. You'd get ten years in the camps, minimum.

"And you feel sorry for him. 'Oh, gosh, he's out in the street, oh dear, how will he make a living?' My friend felt sorry for everyone, too. You know, I'll tell you something. That first time when you showed up in Kalinin with Lyuda, I took a look at you and guessed right off that you had been behind bars."

"How perceptive."

"It was written all over your face, your sweater, your boots, the whole picture, so to speak. I'm an artist, dearie, and I have a good eye. I could tell right off that you were a *zek*. And not an ordinary one, but an intellectual, unsuited for this world's life, just like my late friend. I'll tell you something else." He moved closer and put his hand on Sasha's shoulder. "The minute you walked in, it was like a knife went into my heart, you're so much like him. He had reddish hair, and yours is black, and he was bigger than you, but still, you're alike. Yes, yes, you have the same facial expressions, you're of the same breed. You're looking for justice. You're too delicate. And nevertheless, I liked you right away in Kaliningrad. I thought another real human being has appeared in my brutish life. Even though I also sensed deep inside that my friend had died because of his delicacy and you would too."

"I'm afraid that you'll die before me," Sasha said.

"Oh really? Why is that?"

"About three months ago, what did you tell me about Kanevsky?"

"Something about Pushkin's anniversary, I don't remember exactly."

"I'll remind you. You said, 'We're going to end up in jail because of Kanevsky. I have to be on the lookout, I have to think about the people around me.' Didn't you say that?"

"I guess I did," Gleb agreed reluctantly.

"Then why did you invite Kanevsky to join us at the restaurant? Why did you seat him next to you? Why did you make him drink vodka? He didn't want to go with us."

"Well, we're working in the same collective, we got paid at the same time. If I invite some of you out and not him, it's not nice."

"Oh, it's not nice," Sasha repeated mockingly. "You criticize your friend for not chasing out the people he had served time with, had been in exile with, and you drag a guy to the restaurant who you know could land us in jail. What do you have to say to that?"

Gleb was silent.

"Nothing to say? Then I'll tell you something else. He didn't start the conversation about socialism and all that other nonsense, you did. You started it and he told you what he thought. You provoked him. Why?"

Gleb looked up at him. "Are you serious?"

"Absolutely serious. You provoked him and then hurried off to Semyon. 'Fire Kanevsky, he talks too much.' "

Gleb shrugged. "Well, if you consider me a provocateur. . . ."

Sasha finished his drink and bit a crust of bread. "If I considered you a provocateur, I wouldn't be sitting at this table with you. I'll tell you why you dragged Kanevsky to the restaurant. You hate his 'haughtiness.' So, you think you're a genius. You keep away from the rest. You don't want to be in our company. Well, then, dearie, I'll show you that you're a hack like the rest of us, playing fox-trots in all these clubs. And so you have to hang out with us. We're celebrating payday, and so will you. We're drinking vodka, and so will you. We're bullshitting about socialism, and so will you. It's a question of honor!

"I'm telling you, Gleb, you can't control yourself, and you'll end up in trouble before me."

"Thank God," Gleb said. "I thought you were going to call me a stoolie."

"Your friend's story is tragic and sad," Sasha continued. "But he was doomed. I saw Trotskyites when I was in exile — they were strong. That's why they had to be eradicated, every last one of them. Strong people are dangerous nowadays. They need weaklings, who can be molded any way they want. And to keep from being molded, we have to be careful, we have to be in control. Do you think I enjoy dancing the fox-trot? Do you think that's all I'm good for? But I'm lying low, I'm in the rushes in the marsh. It's not a very heroic position for a man, but I want to remain a decent person in these vile times, and maybe when the time comes, I'll be able to surface again. But you're blowing bubbles, and those bubbles will lead them to you.

"Semyon's going to go to them tomorrow and say, 'My colleague Dubinin reported to me that the pianist Kanevsky talks too much.' They'll call you in and say, 'Thank you, Gleb Vasilyevich, for acting like a real Soviet man. So keep it up and report all anti-Soviet conversations to us.' And they'll have you on the hook. You wanted to show off before Kanevsky. And now you'll get what's coming to you."

The lights were dimmed at the restaurant.

"Time to go home." Sasha called the waiter and paid.

"I'm sorry about what happened," Gleb said. "You can do what you want. But I'm your friend, Sasha!"

"I know that." Sasha stood up. "All right. Let's go."

12

VARYA RAN INTO LENA BUDYAGINA by accident. Varya had been to the Udarnik cinema with Igor Vladimirovich, and when they came outside, the street was filled with people, it was warm and lively and the windows of the gastronome were filled with bright lights. The crowd from the cinema moved toward Polyanka. The Stone Bridge was humming with activity, jackhammers ripping, lights flickering. The bridge was being expanded and work went on around the clock. Igor Vladimirovich suggested taking a stroll along the embankment. They turned left, and Varya saw Lena Budyagina at one of the entrances to the huge apartment building.

Lena was opening the door and turned around for some reason. Varya could see by the tension in her face that Lena had recognized her. Though her straight black hair still hung down to her collar and she still had bangs, it was not easy to recognize Lena in an old baggy coat and worn shoes. And a lot of time had gone by. . . . How much? They had welcomed in the New Year right before Sasha's arrest. That made it four years ago. Lena had been with Yuri Sharok then, and Sharok had openly flirted with Vika Marasevich. Lena made a fuss, and yet had left obediently with Sharok. As they went out, Sasha had said to her, "Couldn't you find yourself a bigger shit?"

Lena stood in the open doorway, uncertain whether she should go inside or take a step toward Varya. Varya often saw such indecision nowadays on the faces of people who were no longer sure yesterday's friends would greet them.

Varya smiled and offered her hand. "Hello, Lena!"

A gentle, shy smile appeared on Lena's face. She bent her head down and looked up. Varya remembered that look and the last time she saw it. It hadn't been at that New Year's party. It was later, at the Club of Workers in the Arts on Staropimenovsky Alley. Varya was there with Kostya, Lena with Sharok and Vadim Marasevich. Lena had given Varya a gentle, shy smile and looked up at her, inclining her head because she was so tall. Lena was gorgeous then, and everyone had stared.

"Hello, Varya." Lena walked toward Varya and shook her hand. "I'm happy to see you. How are you, how's Nina?"

"Everything's fine with me. Working hard. As a matter of fact, I'd like you to meet my boss. . . . Igor Vladimirovich, Lena."

Varya did not use Lena's surname, not because she was afraid to say it out loud, but because she did not know whether Lena was still using it.

"Nina lives far away now," Varya continued. "She got married almost a year ago."

"I've been wondering about her. She hasn't been around at all."

"Do you live here?" Varya interrupted because she did not want to talk about Nina. No one must know that Nina was with Max.

"Yes, here, with my son and brother."

She didn't mention her mother, which meant she as well as Lena's father must have been arrested.

Then Lena held out her hand. "Well, I don't want to keep you. When you write to Nina, send her my best."

"May I come by to see you sometime?"

Lena looked at her in surprise. "Of course. . . ."

"Give me your telephone number. I'll call to make a date."

Lena shook her head. "We haven't had a phone in a long time."

"Is this your entrance?"

"Yes. First floor, the apartment on the right. Three rings. I'm usually home until four every day."

"You're not working?"

"Not yet. Actually, not anymore."

"I'll tell Nina I saw you. And I'll come visit very soon. You don't mind?"

"My situation is such that it might be better for you if you didn't visit."

"I know your situation. What of it?" Varya shook her head. "We're old friends, we were at school together, and I can't come to see you?"

"Well, then, I'll be happy to see you."

Varya and Igor Vladimirovich continued down the embankment.

Varya glanced over at him. "Ready, Igor Vladimirovich?"

"Ready."

"You're about to find out whom you just met."

"I have a good guess. Family of someone arrested."

"But what a someone! Budyagin. Ivan Grigoryevich. Do you know the name?"

"Yes. He used to be Ordzhonikidze's deputy. And an ambassador before that."

"He was arrested last year. And shot. Lena said, 'I'm living with my son and brother.' That means the mother was shot, too. She was an old Bolshevik herself."

"I had the impression," Igor Vladimirovich said carefully, "she wasn't very eager to have you come."

"Absolutely. The way she sees it, she should not have visitors."

The natural question here would have been, "And how do you see it?" But asking that would have also been giving advice: "You shouldn't go see her." So Igor Vladimirovich said nothing.

Varya did not attend the meetings convened to condemn "spies, saboteurs, and killers." She would go instead to the institute where she had evening classes. If the meetings were held in the daytime during working hours, she would go to the Moscow City Council or the Moscow Construction Committee. Igor Vladimirovich would confirm that he had in fact sent her there on business. How she found out ahead of time that these political meetings were going to be held, he did not know. Once, she was caught unawares by a rally, and so she simply said as she walked out, "So I'm off to the bureau, Igor Vladimirovich!" And he replied, "Hurry, they're waiting for you." Varya acknowledged his help. She stopped at the doorway, looked straight at him, and nodded.

He went back to his office and looked out the window to see her cross the street. What could he do? He was in love with her. He had fallen in love long ago — the moment he met her at the National Hotel. She had come to the nightclub with Vika, which did not say much for her. But when she took off her broad-brimmed hat and he saw her eyes, he realized that it did not matter with whom she had come. What mattered was that she leave with him. Then he lost track of her. Vika told him that she had married some Greek pool hustler but the marriage was failing. When Lyova brought Varya to work as a draftsman at their office, Igor Vladimirovich took it as a sign.

Two years ago he had sent her a letter because he wanted her to know how he felt. The next day she came into his office, in a sleeveless dress, and stopped in the doorway. He asked her to sit down and complimented her on her tan.

"I've been to the beach," she replied. "In Serebryanny Bor. But I'm here about your letter." And, after a pause, Varya announced that she loved another, a man who was far away and would be back in a year, and that she would wait for him. He found the strength to smile. "Well then, Varya, I'll wait, too."

Naturally, he wanted to know the identity of the man she loved, but he did not consider it possible to ask her. But from what Vika said and what Lyova let slip, he gathered it was probably a friend and classmate of Varya's sister who was in exile in Siberia, and that Varya had been renting a room with her husband from the man's mother. However, two years had passed since then, and there were no changes in Varya's life, which led Igor Vladimirovich to believe that something had gone wrong. He saw that Varya was depressed, that she did not take her vacation time but stayed in Moscow, waiting for something. His chances were getting better, but he was afraid to hope too much. He would be happy if things stayed as they were. They worked together, he saw her every day, and he could not live without that. He would settle for this, if only things would not get worse — these were difficult times and Varya was not behaving cautiously.

What worried him most was that Varya skipped out from the holiday demonstrations. All the staff members were in place by nine o'clock in the morning, dressed up, forming columns, carrying flowers and banners across Red Square. Ivanova was the only one missing. One time he let her know that she should not behave this way. "Why annoy the geese?" as he put it. People will notice. She replied that she went to these demonstrations with her institute — wasn't that a convincing conclusion?

"No," he said. "Evening institutes do not organize groups for the demonstrations."

She was getting away with it now, Igor Vladimirovich realized, because no one at work other than himself took her seriously — just a pretty draftsman and nothing more. And the ones who were in charge of keeping an eye on such things never even suspected that any dissent could be possible in these times, especially from a slip of a girl. People who were world famous stood at attention. Varya may have missed a few meetings and that wasn't right, but she took evening classes and she had official permission. And then Ivanova never permitted herself anything out of line. She never spoke a superfluous word at work. When they were alone, Varya laughed, was outraged and sarcastic, but only when they were alone.

"Why so quiet, Igor Vladimirovich?"

"Nothing. Just thinking."

"I know what you're thinking about. You didn't like the way I said, 'Ready, Igor Vladimirovich?' You thought that I was trying to get you. Everyone is so afraid of everything all the time. But I do that only out of a sense of balance. Lyova and Rina idolize you. 'Ah, our Igor Vladimirovich, he's so handsome! Ah, our Igor Vladimirovich is a genius, he's Stalin's chief adviser on rebuilding Moscow.' If I join that chorus, you'll turn into an icon."

"You're always quick to find the right answer."

"What do you mean?"

He meant a conversation he had overheard in the canteen. The staff usually lunched in small groups, chatting in line and at the tables, talking about fashions, shopping, marriages and divorces, but primarily, the latest news — the trials. Everyone expressed outrage over the crimes of the defendants. Varya alone sat in silence over her plate.

"Ivanova, what are you thinking about? Don't you agree?"

A disgusting creep asked her the question, a new draftsman called Kostolomov — literally "Bone Breaker" — who had been sent to their group by the personnel department. Igor Vladimirovich did not want to hire him because he did not have any experience. Igor Vladimirovich's department did not need any more draftsmen anyway, but personnel insisted. Igor Vladimirovich even asked some of his friends for advice on what to do. "Don't worry about it," they said. "If personnel is sending this man to you, it means that you don't have enough informers in your group."

Varya looked up at Kostolomov. "I didn't hear what you were talking about. I have a math exam tonight, and I was doing problems in my head."

Naturally, Varya remembered the occasion, too. "You turned pale, Igor Vladimirovich, when you saw me open my mouth to answer that bastard." She smiled. "You shouldn't worry. I'm an adult, you know."

"You may be an adult, but you're not very careful."

"Say, where do you think his surname came from? Do you think his ancestors worked for Ivan the Terrible's secret police? They must have been torturers who broke people's bones."

"Maybe. But he may have come from a line of folk healers, people who set bones."

They were crossing the Krymsky Bridge toward Zubovskaya Square. The steel girders of the bridge loomed grimly in the dark.

"I once proposed stringing lights along the top," Igor Vladimirovich said. "It would have brightened the bridge and enlivened the Moskva River. They turned it down — not enough electricity, they said. But I really wanted it done. I had just been in New York, where at night the bridges sparkle with lights which make them seem airy and light. An enchanting picture. It made me envious."

"We'll never see it," Varya sighed. "And how I'd love to go to India, to Africa. But I might as well dream of going to Mars. We're serfs, and our master won't let us go beyond our village."

He was always amazed how this girl, raised in a Soviet family, educated in Soviet schools, could develop such intransigence. Everything was bad, everything was ugly, everything was unfair. Was it just youth? When she graduated from the institute, he would help her secure an interesting job, where she could find herself. She was gifted, talented even, and she would realize that work was the most important aspect of life.

"What does your friend do?" Igor Vladimirovich asked as they approached Varya's house on the Arbat.

"I don't know. Why do you ask?"

"She doesn't have a job, and apparently she can't find one."

"You should have seen her two years ago. I don't think there was a more beautiful woman in all of Moscow. She dressed so well, she had lived abroad for many years. And now she's in worn shoes and a used coat. She must have sold all her things to feed her baby and her brother."

"Find out what she knows how to do. I'll try to help."

Varya looked at him. And for the first time he saw something more than the usual friendly interest in her eyes.

❧ 13 ❧

W HEN HE GOT THE ORDERS to return to Moscow, Sharok
hesitated.

The evening of February 17 Yezhov held a banquet for Slutsky, who
was going to Uzbekistan. That same night, Slutsky died. And even
though *Pravda* ran a brief but warm obituary, Sharok was not deceived.
Moscow was not Paris and you didn't need a drug that took ten days
to act when you could use an instantaneous one. And then Speigelglass
vanished, too. There was a new man in his place, Pavel Anatolyevich
Sudoplatov.

Slutsky had been doomed. But the fact that Speigelglass had been
arrested too made Sharok think it had to do with the murder of Lev
Sedov. With Sedov's death, Zborovsky lost access to Trotsky's correspondence and the chance to get into his inner circle. Serebryansky was
arrested, and all his men, including "Alexei." So much for being a boxer
with excellent French.

Speigelglass gave the orders, "Alexei" passed along the drug, and
Zborovsky did the work. Sharok had had nothing to do with it and had
regarded it an ill-considered operation. But Sharok knew the institution for which he worked. No arguments worked there. If they had "to
purge Speigelglass's people," that's what they would do. Shoot them all,
and that was that.

What should Sharok do now? Not go back, just slip away? Where?
Ask for asylum, become a defector? They'd find him. The way they
found and killed Ignatii Raiss. On the other hand, he couldn't be considered one of Speigelglass's people. Yezhov himself had sent him to work
for Speigelglass. Maybe in order to replace him when the time came.

Maybe that's why he was being recalled. Yezhov had said, "Take a good look" back then.

However, at the present time Yezhov was also People's Commissar of Water Transport. A more than strange appointment. Water transport! Who cared about river shipping? Yezhov's predecessor, Yagoda, had not been executed right away. First he was made People's Commissar of Communications, and only then arrested. But Yagoda had been removed from the NKVD right away. While Yezhov was still there, and Sharok was Yezhov's man, and a Russian, not some Pole or Jew, like those Slutskys and Speigelglasses. He had to go back, come what may!

As Sharok had expected, they wanted to talk to him about Sedov. He was not interrogated. It was just a chat. They asked him to write a memo. Sharok described what had happened. And what had happened? Sedov was sick, Speigelglass sent "Alexei" and ordered Sharok to set him up with Zborovsky but not to be present at the meeting. He got them together. Was not present. And ten days later, Sedov died. That was it. Sharok thought about it for a long time and added cautiously, "Sedov's death in many ways devalued Tulip's significance as a source of extremely important information and deprived him of the opportunity to infiltrate L. D. Trotsky's circle."

He turned in the memo, and then there were more days of waiting. He hung around the department. He met Pavel Anatolyevich Sudoplatov and told him about Tretyakov and Zborovsky. Sudoplatov, naturally, knew all about them, but he listened attentively as he sipped hot tea from a glass. He was getting the flu, he had chills and his eyes watered, his nose was red, and he didn't look his best. Nevertheless, he made a strong impression on Sharok — a cold, ruthless man, a real intelligence officer. He told Sharok to familiarize himself with Zborovsky's current reports on the preparations in Paris for the Founding Congress of the Trotskyite Fourth International.

On July 20, Lavrenti Pavlovich Beria was named Yezhov's deputy and head of the Main Directorate of State Security. It was clear to everyone. Yezhov's days at the NKVD were numbered and Beria, one of Stalin's closest associates, was here to replace Yezhov. Sharok felt even greater anxiety. He had placed all his hopes on Yezhov. And now what? There was no one to cling to, no one to ask for help, no more familiar faces. Everyone had been put away — Molchanov, Vutkovsky,

Stein, Dyakov. It was dangerous to mention you had worked with these convicted enemies of the people.

The only old acquaintance left was Viktor Semyonovich Abakumov. He was very important now — head of the Rostov Regional NKVD, one of the largest branches. And he had started out as a clerk in their division. His career took an upward turn under Yezhov. He set up cupboards in his office for confiscated books, and he probably never read a single book in his life. Ignorant, uneducated, foulmouthed, he was a ladies' man and a fox-trot aficionado. He was a lumbering bear, but thought he could dance well. And if Sharok had not protected him that time, he would be freezing his rear end off up north as some camp supervisor. But there was no way to remind him about it. He would take offense — "You mean I owe my career not to my abilities, not to my limitless loyalty to the work of Lenin and Stalin, but to you, you little shit?" That would turn him into an enemy. People don't like to be reminded of favors they owe. Perhaps Abakumov did not want to remember that period at all. After all, it was he who had to interrogate his former bosses and colleagues. Better to keep away from him. Abakumov came to Moscow often, but Sharok made no attempts to meet with him. They ran into each other accidentally in the hallway. Abakumov was proceeding noisily, the way big bosses do. He didn't shout and stomp, but it was clear that this was a boss because he didn't make way for anyone, but pushed along like a tank down the center of the hallway, nodded to people he knew and didn't know, and nodded to the guards who didn't ask for his pass because they knew his face.

He nodded to Sharok, the way he did to everyone as he passed, but then he stopped.

"Yuri, is that you?"

"It's me, Viktor Semyonovich."

"Glad to see you. I thought you were over there." Abakumov nodded his head to one side, in the direction beyond the border.

"Sort of."

"Are you staying or going back?"

"I can't say for sure, Viktor Semyonovich, that's what our work is like. Here today, tomorrow there." Sharok also nodded in the direction abroad.

Abakumov laughed loudly. "We used to sing that in the Komsomol,

'Over seas, everywhere, here today, tomorrow there.' " And he asked unexpectedly, "Married?"

"Not yet."

"Not settled down?"

"So far."

"Listen, are you still in that apartment by yourself? I remember we had a housewarming there."

"Yes, I'm still there."

"Do you know the difference between a comedy, a drama, and a tragedy?"

"Well," Sharok began. "A comedy is —"

"Let me explain," Abakumov interrupted. "When you have what to do it with and who to do it to, but not where to do it, it's a comedy. When you have the 'what' and the 'where' but not the 'who,' it's a drama. But when you've got who to do it to and where to do it, but not what to do it with, it's a tragedy." He burst out laughing again.

"Understand what I'm getting at? Got any heifers?"

"Always."

"Let's get together tomorrow evening, at night. You collect the quorum, I'll bring the champagne. Just give me the address, I don't quite remember it."

Sharok wrote it down and refused the champagne. "No need, Viktor Semyonovich. I've got everything at home."

The coming party inspired some hope in Sharok. If Abakumov wanted to spend the night with a girl in his apartment, that meant Sharok was all right. Abakumov knew with whom he could get drunk and with whom he should not. He knew that Yezhov's days were numbered, but he seemed confident. That meant he had support from somewhere else as well.

Sharok called Kalya and told her to show up the next evening with a girlfriend. "Just make sure she's not a prude! This is for an important man! This could mean something big for me."

Kalya promised to take care of everything. She must have thought that this big shot could help Sharok stay in Moscow and then he would marry her. She was dumb, of course, but she was a good broad, a loyal one.

The next day Sharok felt much more cheerful. He put together a summary on Zborovsky's reports about the coming Congress of the

Trotskyite Fourth International. The official announcement stated that the Congress would take place in Lausanne, but it would actually be convened in a Paris suburb in the villa belonging to the Rosmers, friends of Trotsky. They were expecting thirty to forty people from fifteen or sixteen countries. Zborovsky appended a list of the countries and delegates. The goal of the Congress was to approve the "World Party of Social Revolution." Sharok handed in his report to Sudoplatov at the end of the day. Sudoplatov ordered him to ask Zborovsky for a list of all the clerical staff of the Congress.

"Pavel Anatolyevich," Sharok said, "I have some personal business this evening. Permission to leave at seven."

"Fine, as you like. I won't be needing you this evening."

Sharok had gone back to his office, locked his desk, and turned off the desk lamp, when the internal telephone rang. Sharok was ordered to come immediately to the office of People's Commissar Comrade Yezhov.

And once again, the way he had two years earlier, Sharok went down the long corridor to the left wing of the NKVD, going up stairs and down others and then up again, showing his pass to guards at every landing, and once again, he wondered why Yezhov wanted to see him. Had Abakumov said something? Unlikely. Sharok had not asked him to do anything. Paris? He had reported to Sudoplatov. And another thing, the foreign division now reported to Beria. Was Yezhov going around him then? Then Beria would make Sharok pay for it. In general, this talk did not promise anything good.

Together with the secretary, Sharok crossed the familiar office. The same enormous desk, the glassed-in bookshelves along the walls, drapes on the windows, the same expensive furniture and the portrait of Comrade Stalin over the armchair. The secretary knocked on the door in the far wall, and a hoarse voice shouted, "Enter!" The secretary opened the door, let Sharok pass, and went away.

Yezhov sat on a couch in the small room, shirtsleeves rolled up, hair unkempt, a battery of bottles and dishes arrayed on the table in front of him. He focused his eyes on Sharok. The telephone rang. Yezhov picked it up, listened, and replied rudely, "I explained it all in simple Russian. You didn't understand? Then, fuck you!"

He hung up. He was not only drunk, but also agitated and excited. His murky eyes regarded Sharok suspiciously. "Finished reporting?"

"Yes sir, Comrade People's Commissar, I have," Sharok responded, standing at attention.

Yezhov did not offer him a seat. "Gotten sick of living far from the Homeland?"

"It's my job, Comrade People's Commissar."

"Job. . . . Jobs can be changed."

"As you wish, Comrade People's Commissar."

"And if I order you to move to the People's Commissariat of Water Transport. What would you think of that?"

"An order is an order, Comrade People's Commissar."

"Stop talking about orders. Orders, orders. . . . I'm asking you, do you want to move with me to the Water Transport Commissariat?"

Sharok's brain was working feverishly. It was dangerous now in the NKVD. It would be a good idea to move into civilian work, but getting involved with Yezhov was even more dangerous.

"Why the silence?"

"I don't know what kind of work it would be, Comrade People's Commissar."

"There's plenty of work, not enough workers, just saboteurs and big talkers. Understand?"

"Yes. But I am a lawyer by training. That's the reason I was hired here. But river transport. . . . I don't even know what it is."

Yezhov took another drink, looked around the table, but didn't pick up any food. Without looking at Sharok, he said, "We'll find you suitable work. There's a legal section and personnel and a special section."

"Permission to think about it, Comrade People's Commissar."

Yezhov tried to focus on him. It was a mean look. Sharok's heart contracted with fear.

"You don't want to do it!" Yezhov concluded viciously.

"I want to think about it, Comrade —"

"Everything's clear!" Yezhov interrupted. "Go!"

~ 14 ~

AT THE NKVD STORE on Bolshaya Lubyanka, Sharok bought vodka, wine, and enough *zakuski,* hors d'oeuvres, to fill his briefcase. His apartment was on Ostozhenka, in Zachatyevsky Alley. In the twenties some NEPman, that is, an entrepreneur under the short-lived New Economic Policy, carved it out of a former mansion. The NEPman had kicked the bucket a long time ago in the camps on Naryma or the Solovetsky Islands, and he had been replaced by a professor, who dropped dead in the camps in Kolyma or in Vorkuta, and Sharok was given the apartment. Two rooms, kitchen, bath, toilet, a couple of cupboards, a balcony — the works. It was convenient for Sharok — not far from the Arbat and his mother and father — and it suited the NKVD because when he was abroad, his apartment was there for secret meetings with informers. They had a set of keys. His parents had another set. They went there on Sundays when there were no secret meetings — that was the arrangement. Kalya once offered to keep an eye on the apartment. He chuckled. "Honey, you think there's no one to keep an eye on things where I work? Don't even come near here without me." The only concession Kalya managed to get was permission to keep her robe hanging in the bathroom.

But whenever Sharok was in Moscow, she played the role of hostess with all her heart, cleaning, washing, cooking, showing off her household skills. They had been together for three years and it was time to make decisions. So now she was setting the table, pretty, cheerful, with strong, large hands. She had brought a friend, a tall, dark-haired girl who looked like a Gypsy, with long, slender legs and gilt earrings.

"My friend Aza."

Blowing smoke from her cigarette, the girl friend added, "Gypsy Aza."

And that's how she introduced herself to Abakumov, "Gypsy Aza."

"Really?" Abakumov wondered.

"Don't I look it?" Aza shook her shoulders in the classic Gypsy dance.

"I can do that, too." To Sharok's amazement, Abakumov shook his fat shoulders, not like Aza, of course, but a fair imitation.

"You're from our camp," Aza said with approval.

"And we'll sleep in the same tent," Abakumov rejoined.

He acted as if he had known the girls a long time. He had been with so many in his life that he couldn't tell them apart anymore. He had made a grand entrance. His chauffeur brought up a package and left once he got his instructions when to return.

Abakumov ordered Sharok to open the package.

"Viktor Semyonovich. You shouldn't have! See, the table is full of things."

"Reinforcements never hurt. What did Napoleon say? What do you need for victory? To concentrate the main forces in the main direction. So, girls, was Napoleon Bonaparte right or not? Do you know who he is? Have you read Tar-lee?"

What a hick, thought Sharok, he can't even pronounce the name correctly. Abakumov had never read Tarle, Sharok was sure. Probably when Stalin had Tarle reinstated as an academician, Abakumov rushed out to buy his book on Napoleon and put it on his shelf.

"We know Napoleon, and we read it." Aza sat with her legs crossed, smoking away.

"We'll check later," Abakumov said with a laugh. "But now, children, let's eat. I'm starved. Hungry as a wolf."

Kalya had unwrapped the package and set out the Armenian cognac, the caviar, smoked salmon, smoked beef, and grapes.

"Where do we start?" Abakumov asked, reaching for the vodka.

"With what you've got in your hand," Aza said, shaking her earrings for emphasis.

"Right," Abakumov said, looking at her. "If you're going to drink, drink vodka, if you're going to love, love a beautiful woman, and if you're going to steal, steal a million."

He drank glass after glass, and made everyone join him. They drank to their meeting, to the women, Kalya and Aza, to Yuri, to the families and friends. . . . And he ate like a pig. He even snorted.

Yuri drank carefully. They had to have a talk. He was betting his life. If they threw together an SP case, they would need participants. Yezhov tried to help him out by transferring him to another commissariat. I'm saving you, you know! Oh, you don't want my help — then burn on your own! They could come for him tonight. And they would find Abakumov in bed with a girl. As a comrade, he should warn him. But would he appreciate it? He would just run off now. And he wouldn't get him out of prison, either. Better he should get pulled in by the same noose. If they didn't come tonight, tomorrow Abakumov would do what was necessary to save him. He would have to. Otherwise, if they arrested Sharok, Abakumov would be involved. "Who are your acquaintances?" "Comrade Abakumov. We drank and wenched in my apartment." Try to get out of that!

In the meantime Abakumov took off his jacket — he had come in civilian clothes — and unbuttoned his shirt, showing his hairy chest. He was feeling around under Aza's skirt with his hairy hand. She wriggled and feigned passion. She was pretty drunk herself, and Kalya's eyes were shining as she laughed and giggled. He had to keep his head clear. Even though Abakumov was high up, you didn't need great brains to break bones. Someone like that wouldn't be sent to Paris. They needed Speigelglasses, Sudoplatovs, and Sharoks there — the people who were the backbone of Soviet intelligence — professionals. He had handled General Skoblin and Minister Tretyakov. He could handle a boor like Abakumov, he would force him to take on this work. As long as he didn't get drunk. Sharok was drinking Narzan mineral water instead of vodka. The glasses were made of thick green glass, so the bubbles were not visible, and anyway, Abakumov wasn't watching Sharok drink. He was busy drinking and eating, feeling up Aza, and making passes at Kalya. He poked her in the chest and said, "That's a fine chest of drawers there. You're a fine woman, you've got everything you need." If Sharok hadn't been there, he would have taken both women to bed.

Then Abakumov had Sharok start up the gramophone and danced with Aza. He might have been drunk, but he stayed on his feet, fat and hearty. He even did intricate steps, though you couldn't tell if he was dancing a tango or a jig. He undressed Aza as they danced, unbuttoning everything on her, and got under her panties. She put up with it, merely looking over at Kalya and Sharok, shaking her head as if to say, Just look at this character!

The record came to an end.

"Where can I get some rest?" Abakumov asked hoarsely.

Sharok pointed to the bedroom door.

Abakumov pulled Aza by the hand. "Let's go into the tent, Gypsy girl!"

Aza gave Kalya and Sharok another look and shrugged. See what's happening to me now? But she followed Abakumov without a murmur.

Sharok and Kalya lay down on the couch. "In the morning, go to the bathroom with her," Sharok told her, "and stay in there while I talk with Viktor Semyonovich."

He did not have to wait for morning. He had no sooner drifted off than he heard Abakumov's voice. Sharok reached for the light switch. Abakumov was in the middle of the room, fat and naked except for his shorts, with his belly hanging over them. Aza was seated at the table in her slip.

"No more sleep, little man, it's springtime." Abakumov sat down next to Aza and poured himself some Narzan. "Get up, get up, let's party."

Sharok slipped into his shorts under the sheet and went over to the table.

"Get up, Kalya!" Abakumov ordered.

"Turn your back, Viktor Semyonovich. I'm not dressed."

"So what! As if I haven't ever seen a naked broad."

Kalya covered herself with her hands and dashed to the bathroom. She came back in her robe.

With a nod at Aza, Sharok said, "Go wash up. I'll call you."

The women left. Soon they could hear water splashing in the bathroom.

Abakumov poured himself some vodka and a glass for Sharok. "Bottoms up."

They drank.

"Viktor Semyonovich, I'd like your advice."

Sharok related his conversation with Yezhov as if he were reading a transcript. He also told him that Yezhov was not pleased.

Abakumov poked his fork in the food, chewing this and that, and watched Yuri.

"Have you reported to Sudoplatov?"

"When? Yezhov didn't release me until very late. I was afraid to be late for our meeting. Do you think Sudoplatov can help me?"

"He can't," Abakumov replied with unexpected sobriety and conviction. "But he should know. He'll be called in by Comrade Beria, who will say, 'Do you know that your workers are being lured over to a different commissariat?'

" 'No, I don't,' Sudoplatov will reply.

" 'Ah, so Comrade Sharok is negotiating behind your back. Playing a double game. Is that it?'

"Do you see my point?"

"You're right, Viktor Semyonovich."

"When you get to work today, go straight to Sudoplatov. Tell him everything, just as you told it to me. Stress this — 'I did not give my consent. I feel duty bound to tell you about it.' And then just sit quietly. Wait. I'll take care of the rest."

He leaned forward and looked up at Sharok. "Abakumov does not forget loyal friends. Understand?"

"I understand. Thank you, Viktor Semyonovich."

"Then let's drink to that. You've been putting away mineral water all night instead of vodka. I saw. I understand. You were preparing for a conversation. I'm not condemning you. But now, let's drink."

He threw back his head and emptied the glass. "We've finished with your business," Abakumov said. "Now let's have fun. Like the song, 'We'll drink and make sport, live it up, life is short.' Aza is all right, she knows what she's doing. How about Kalya?"

Sharok sobered up instantly. He understood where Abakumov was leading. "This isn't my first time with Kalya, Viktor Semyonovich. We're even thinking of —"

Abakumov interrupted. "That's why you need some fresh meat. Let's trade!"

There was no way out, he was in this swine's hands. He could go to Yezhov today and report, "I dropped by Sharok's place last night, he's an old work comrade. And the son of a bitch was sitting there, drunk, and running you down. He said that you were trying to get him to leave the service. What a bastard!" And then they would take Sharok out of the office and shoot him, no questions asked.

"How can I follow you with Aza?" Sharok said with a smile.

"You'll manage, you're a young man! Where are the girls, anyway?"
He stood up and opened the door to the bathroom. "Done splashing?
Like the old song, 'Girls in tub, titties bouncing . . .' "

"We'll be dressed in a minute, Viktor Semyonovich," Kalya said.

"What for? You'll just have to get undressed again."

"We'd rather, anyway."

Kalya came out in her robe and Aza was wearing the slip. Abakumov
poured vodka for everyone. "Come on, girls, down the hatch."

Sharok went to the kitchen and called Kalya. He said to her, unhappy
and grim, "I talked to him. He promised to help. Not just my fate, but
my very life depends on him. Do you understand that?"

"Yes, yes, of course I do," she said in fright.

"He didn't like Aza, she's too demanding. I told you to bring someone easy. You'll have to work in her place."

She didn't understand what he meant at first and then, when she did,
she exploded in rage. "Are you crazy? I'll leave right now! What are you
saying?"

"Just what you're hearing. For my sake. For my life." He grabbed her
wrist and squeezed as hard as he could. "I'm asking you. I swear, we'll
never bring this up again. It will be as if it never happened. But you have
to do it! Don't even think of resisting! I'm warning you. If you don't do
it, it'll be the death of me. But it will be your death, too!"

They came back to the table.

"Now let's dance!" shouted Abakumov, polishing off the ham. "Get
the music going, Yuri. Come on, Kalya, we'll cut the rug."

He put his paws all over her, pressed her close to his naked, hairy belly
and moved around the room, trying to put her hand down his shorts.
When they reached the bedroom, he opened the door and pushed Kalya
inside.

She looked back beseechingly at Sharok.

He waved her on — go!

In the morning Sharok went to see Sudoplatov and told him about his
conversation with Yezhov.

"It's your own personal business," Sudoplatov noted dryly.

That evening, Sharok was told to report to Lavrenti Pavlovich
Beria.

Sharok had only seen portraits of Beria. The artists flattered him, of course, but Beria's face turned out to be unnaturally smooth in real life, too, as if it had been pumped full of air and the pince-nez stuck on.

There were two other men in the office — Sudoplatov and an officer who resembled Serebryansky, but had refined features and lively eyes that made him seem handsome and attractive.

Sharok stood at attention and presented himself.

"Sit down." Drilling Sharok with his beady eyes, Beria asked, "What is the situation with Zborovsky?"

"With the death of Lev Sedov, all he has left is access to the files of the Trotskyite International Secretariat," Sharok replied succinctly.

"Is there a possibility of getting him into Trotsky's inner circle?"

"Very small. They suspected Zborovsky of Sedov's death. The suspicions are gone. Sedov's wife, Jeanne Martin, was constantly with him and Zborovsky did not touch Sedov's food. But they still do not trust him. Zborovsky asked Trotsky for permission to come to Mexico, and Trotsky refused."

The officer sitting next to Sudoplatov studied Sharok.

"What prospects do you see?" Beria asked.

Sharok knew that they were discussing the assassination of Trotsky, but he was supposed to talk only within the framework of this discussion, about getting their own man into Trotsky's circle. And Sharok also realized that this was another chance for him — he could become Beria's man. Choosing his words, Sharok said, "It seems to me that the plans for infiltrating Trotsky's circle were unrealistic to begin with. The idea was to get a White Russian into his circle, and generals Turkul, Miller, and Dragomirov were preparing people for this. They would have some chance at this in Turkey and Europe, but no hope at all in Mexico. Trotsky's bodyguards are American and Mexican, and that's where we have to find our man. A Mexican would be best, or at least someone who speaks Spanish."

"All right," said Beria, and there was something in his voice that told Sharok he had hit the mark, that his thinking coincided with the plans these men were making. "The founding Congress of the Fourth International is convening on September third. You should leave for Paris first thing tomorrow and follow that gabfest."

"Yes sir, Comrade Beria!"

He did not use Beria's title, "Deputy People's Commissar." It would have been stupid, considering that the man would be commissar any day now.

"Your superiors." Beria nodded toward Sudoplatov. "You've already met Pavel Anatolyevich."

"Yes, sir."

Beria turned to the other man and introduced him. "Naum Isaakovich Eitingon."

Eitingon offered Sharok his hand and smiled. "Let's get to work."

∾ 15 ∾

AFTER HE RECEIVED THE ORDER, Vadim's position was so strengthened that he was given a one-day pass to the October Hall of the House of Unions to attend the trial of the "anti-Soviet Rightist Trotskyite bloc." This was an honor bestowed upon the most prominent writers, who could be depended on to create the necessary public opinion.

Vadim had no doubt he would live up to their expectations. His reaction would not be a simple newspaper review, like the hundreds being written by his fellow journalists — "Punish severely the filthy band of killers and spies," "Destroy!" "Finish off!" and so on through the other clichés. He would write a vivid study of the psychology of political crime, he would draw a line from Bukharin's speech at the First Congress of Writers in 1934 to today's trial. A speech on poetry . . . the spy and killer had given a speech on *poetry*. Where was the line separating intellectual from criminal? Pletnev, Levin, Kazakov were doctors dedicated to healing and saving, and they became collaborators of Death. Where was the line separating humanist from criminal? He would answer these questions clearly and with dignity. True intelligentsia and humanitarians were those who loyally served the party of Lenin and Stalin. That was how he would begin and the rest would write itself.

Like everyone in the room, Vadim followed the proceedings with bated breath. God! Bukharin and Rykov were former leaders of the Party and the state and Yagoda was the all-powerful head of the NKVD, whose name alone brought fear to the hearts of men. And these People's Commissars, secretaries of the Party's Central Committee, who held the fate of millions in their hands, were now pathetic and crushed, on the defendants' bench, standing up obediently, sitting down obediently, and readily admitting the most horrible crimes. Vadim did not know, and did not want to know, how those confessions were obtained. He could guess. He remembered the barber Sergei Alexeyevich, who had innocently but stupidly repeated a joke about Stalin, with his teeth knocked out and those horrible bruises on his face. But he did not feel the least bit of sympathy for these people. Didn't they create this system, where everyone was forced to be a "Vaclav"? Enough pangs of conscience!

Vadim sat in the back row, but the October Hall was not large and he could see everything. He recognized Bukharin and Rykov right away; everyone had seen their pictures. He also recognized Professor Dmitri Dmitriyevich Pletnev, his father's teacher, who had often been to their house. Vadim's father called him a great talent, even a genius, one of the world's greatest physicians. Last June *Pravda* printed an article called "The Professor Is a Rapist and Sadist." Allegedly, during an examination the professor bit his patient on the breast, and as a result of this trauma, the woman became a permanent invalid. They also ran her letter, which the newspaper called "an amazing human document." The very next day the newspaper campaign against him began. Professors, celebrated doctors, and medical collectives heaped shame on the sixty-five-year-old "rapist and sadist." Vadim did not find his father's name in that list nor did his father, Andrei Andreyevich, speak out at the special meetings of the All-Russian and the Moscow medical societies. Vadim's position was precarious. His father did not want to speak out and his silence could cost Vadim dearly. But he did not dare bring it up for he was afraid of his father's anger and his response. He was afraid his father would accuse him, that he knew about "Vaclav." Could he have left a denunciation on his desk by accident? Could his father have read it? It would be horrible. Perhaps that was why he did not congratulate Vadim on his success and had stopped asking him about his work. But back then, in June of 1937, Vadim had asked his father, "What is this business with Dmitri Dmitriyevich?"

"You read the papers, you must know."

"Of course, I read them. And I read the response from his colleagues. His colleagues condemn him."

"Not all of them! Far from all! Yegorov, Sokolnikov, Gurevich, Kannabikh, Fromgolts, and Myasnikov refused to support that vile business. And your father, incidentally, also refused."

"Everyone has the right to his own opinion," Vadim said placatingly.

There was nothing else he could say. No one knew whether Pletnev had confessed or not. He got two years probation and was arrested again soon afterward, and this case was being heard in the October Hall and Pletnev confessed to much greater crimes than the attempted rape of some hysterical woman.

Vadim listened to Pletnev's questioning with special attention. Say what you will, but there was something special about Soviet power that could crush the greatest authorities and reputations. An awesome, invincible power, and woe to him who stands in its way.

What would his father say now? Pletnev admitted his crimes! And what crimes! Now, Pletnev could expect to be shot. And anyone who defended him was in danger of being shot, too. Now, his father couldn't weasel out of it. He would have to state his opinion. Pletnev was his teacher, his friend. So what! People were denouncing their mothers and fathers, brothers and sisters, sons and daughters. It was nothing at all to denounce work colleagues, teachers, and students.

You were not allowed to take notes in the courtroom. But he would have to write down his thoughts and impressions while they were still vivid in his mind. Vadim did just this as soon as he got home. He worked obliviously.

His father came home soon after, took off his jacket, and put on a housecoat, but left his tie on, as usual. He looked grim and weary. Vadim realized that talk about Pletnev would be unpleasant, but he did not resist. There was no reason to put it off. His father would not dare to disagree, and there was nothing he could say anyway. He would force his father to fire Fenya and to break off all contact with Vika, which his father maintained through that woman Nelli Vladimirova. And he didn't want to deny himself the pleasure of paying back his father for their last conversation about Pletnev. Now his father would not dare to use the words he had used then — farce, vileness, baseness, delirium, provocation. He would have to find other words and expressions.

Gnawing on a chicken leg — Vadim liked cold chicken and Fenya prepared a cold supper when she left for the day — Vadim said, "I was at the trial at the House of Unions. A creepy spectacle, I must tell you."

His father ate in silence.

"Bukharin, Rykov, and Yagoda are lousy, political vipers, and I understand their story. But the doctors — Levin, Kazakov, and most of all, Dmitri Dmitriyevich Pletnev. I couldn't believe my own ears, what he was confessing to."

His father, bent over his plate, continued eating.

"I looked only at him. I thought maybe they were using an actor. But no, it was he, Dmitri Dmitriyevich. I've seen him here many times, right in this room. It was he. His manner of speaking, his way of holding himself."

His father continued eating in silence, without looking at Vadim.

"I don't understand. What made him do it? Murdering Kuibyshev and Maxim Gorky. . . ."

Andrei Andreyevich put down his knife and fork, wiped his mouth with a napkin, leaned back in his chair, and, looking past Vadim, said calmly, "Dmitri Dmitriyevich did not treat Kuibyshev."

"But —"

"I repeat." Andrei Andreyevich raised his voice but still did not look at Vadim. "Dmitri Dmitriyevich did not treat Kuibyshev. Kuibyshev died from heart paralysis. There was an autopsy and the cause of death was a clot in the right coronary artery of the heart. But, no matter what it could have been, Dmitri Dmitriyevich did not treat Kuibyshev."

He took a breath. "As for Gorky, he had lung disease for many years — chronic bronchitis with bronchiectasis, pneumosclerosis, emphysema, and heart and lung insufficiency. He always coughed and smoked constantly, even though his doctors demanded that he quit smoking. He even had bleeding of the lungs. He was better when he lived in Capri or in the Crimea, but every return to Moscow brought on pneumonia. The same thing happened in June 1936. He was treated by Konchalovsky, Lang, and Levin. In their presence, Dmitri Dmitriyevich consulted him several times. The treatment was absolutely correct, but it was impossible to save Gorky. His death certificate was signed by the People's Commissar of Health, all the physicians treating him, and additionally, Professor Speransky and Professor Davydovsky, who did the autopsy. Yet not one of these doctors was called into court as a witness. Not one! There was no need! They blamed everything on Pletnev and miserable Levin. 'A gang of ruthless villains,' they called them!" Andrei Andreyevich struck his fist on the table. "They are not ruthless villains. The people who are judging them are the ruthless villains!"

"Father!" cried Vadim. "Stop! Think! What are you saying? The court was given the results of the medical experts."

"Experts!" Andrei Andreyevich looked Vadim in the face, and there was so much scorn and hatred in his eyes that Vadim looked away. "You call those scoundrels 'experts'? Burmin, who was in charge, is a mediocrity, a toady, and a coward! He spent the last ten years working on the Narzan mineral water of Kisolovdsk and he forgot what little he had ever known. Who did he bring into his commission? Two endocrinologists — how can they be called in as experts in this case?" He gave Vadim another look of hatred and disgust. "This is shameful! And one of them was a friend of Pletnev's, he was welcome in their house, and he betrayed him. Traitors, traitors all around, everywhere there are traitors."

Vadim squirmed. The hatred in his father's eyes, the words — did he know?

Andrei Andreyevich seemed to catch his breath and get a hold of himself. Trying to speak more calmly, he went on. "The only one who had a *professional* right to be called an expert was Vinogradov. He's no great physician, but he's not bad, and he was a student of Pletnev's. And now, the student betrays his teacher. Out of fear."

He was breathing heavily. He looked at Vadim, raised his forefinger in the air, and spoke in a trembling voice. "God will not forgive them. Or the unrighteous judges. Or the false witnesses."

What his father was saying was more than enough to get shot. If he were to say the same thing to his colleagues or friends tomorrow, he would be arrested the next day. And how would that make Vadim look? His father a convicted enemy of the people and his sister in Paris married to an anti-Soviet. No medals and orders; no "Vaclav" — the code name under which he informed on his colleagues — would help him then. Big deal, "Vaclav"! Half the defendants in all these trials were Vaclavs themselves.

"Father, don't get excited! You know you shouldn't get upset," Vadim said. "But just think. Pletnev is our greatest internist. You called him the 'pride of our medicine' yourself. What reason would the government have for destroying him? Especially if, as you say, he isn't guilty of anything?"

"He is guilty!" Andrei Andreyevich shouted, unfastening his collar and shaking his head. "He isn't guilty of what they're accusing him, but of knowing too much.... Yes, yes! When they killed Ordzhonikidze —"

Vadim stood up. "Father, think what you're saying!"

"Sit down! I know what I'm saying. They killed Ordzhonikidze, or he shot himself, but there was a bullet wound. However, the death certificate read 'Heart paralysis.' Dmitri Dmitriyevich refused to sign the certificate. He told me about it himself. He is an unwanted witness, so they're getting rid of him. First they slandered him as a rapist and now they're presenting him as a killer."

"But he confessed to everything."

"They tortured him and he confessed. They all confess in these trials of yours."

Vadim made a move to protest.

"Oh, yes! Don't jump around. I mean your trials. You beat confessions out of people in the cellars of the Lubyanka. Your criminal regime —"

"Father! Father, stop!" Vadim screamed.

Shaking his head and tugging at his tie, Andrei Andreyevich repeated, "Criminal regime.... Criminal regime.... You are all criminals, killers.... And you, too.... You're a criminal.... Your articles are vile and disgusting. You persecute and destroy decent people.... That criminal regime has bought you ... I know...."

Oh God, he was going to bring up Vaclav. No, no, he couldn't let him! Vadim shouted, "And I suppose they haven't bought you?"

The old man stared at him, stunned. "Who? What are you saying?"

"You go to see them, you treat them," shouted Vadim. "They spoil you. People have nothing to eat, but they heap food on you." He pushed away his plate. "Where did this chicken come from? From them! Yes, I serve the regime, but I serve an idea, and you serve them for chicken." He gave the plate another push. "You sit on the people's back and you pour filth on it. Gorky did everything he could for you and your kind. He helped you out and saved you. Who got this apartment for you? Gorky! And how did you pay him back? You people poisoned him."

Andrei Andreyevich, unable to say a word, gasped for air and waved his hands at Vadim.

"I heard it with my own ears," Vadim continued. "Right here in this room, you were laughing. 'They've named theaters, streets, and cities after Gorky, and now we'll have to call the whole regime Gorky. How funny, just because Gorky means bitter!' I heard you with my own ears! I was honored with an order and you didn't even congratulate me, but when you were given the title of Honored Worker in the Sciences, you gave a banquet, you celebrated and enjoyed it. But I'm nothing but a scoundrel and mediocrity? I'm sick of it! I know how you feel about me. For Vika's sake, you put up with that Nelli Vladimirova. But Vika is married to a foreign spy and you apparently approve of that. You're planning to go abroad this year, to meet with Vika, and she'll hand you an espionage assignment from her darling husband, and you're so stupid that you'll gladly do it. And I have to live with the threat that they'll come and take you and me away for being foreign spies. Oh, no! I will not live with that threat! I will not listen to anti-Soviet talk even from my own father. I will not! I'm sick of it! Do you hear me? I asked you a long time ago to trade this apartment for two separate ones, but you refused. Well then, I'll do it myself, I have the right. The law is on my side. And I don't recommend trying to stop me. I certainly don't! Don't force me to tell the truth in court about why we can't live together anymore!"

During Vadim's monologue, Andrei Andreyevich worked at his tie and shook his head, trying to say something. But he could not manage anything more than "you . . . you . . ." and finally fell silent, his eyes shut. His head dangled to one side. Vadim leaped up and tried to lift his father. The old man gasped again and opened one eye. There was no awareness in his gaze. His eye shut. Vadim dragged him over to the couch, put a pillow under his head, took off his shoes, and covered him with a blanket.

Andrei Andreyevich lay with closed eyes, gasping occasionally and then being perfectly still, as if he were not breathing at all.

Vadim needed to call an ambulance.

But this had happened to his father more than once. Andrei Andreyevich had a bad heart. He had always gotten by without the ambulance and he refused to let anyone call for help. After lying down for a bit and taking his drops, valerian or something, he improved. And he would improve this time, too, of course. The paramedics would come, and his father would be feeling fine. It wasn't right to bother people for nothing, to make paramedics rush over with the ambulance.

His father had not opened his eyes. Vadim bent over him and listened. He seemed to be breathing. He picked up his hand and searched for a pulse. He thought he found find it. Thank God, he would make it. Poor father. What was awaiting him? He didn't fit into modern life. He was doomed to be arrested and imprisoned, to suffer pain and shame. Vadim could not live in expectation of the catastrophe that would befall him if his father were arrested. And he could not take it if his father suddenly called him Vaclav. Vadim went to the telephone, listened to the dial tone, and then hung it up. His thoughts were confused.

God, what should he do? How could he live, expecting catastrophe every hour, every day, every night? His father was asking to be arrested. His father refused to understand that there was no room for concepts like decency and conscience these days.

And what if this attack did not go away? What if this wasn't like all the others?

Vadim picked up the phone and dialed 03. Busy.

But why were old people so egotistical? There they are, one foot in the grave and they are not afraid of death, but why drag others into the coffin with you? Take pity your son, father! Your son hasn't even started living yet! Twenty-eight is only a beginning. . . . No, he would not allow himself to be destroyed. Sorry, Father, he would not! Oh, God, what should he do?

Vadim looked at the clock. Eight-thirty. Fenya, who spent the evenings with the Feoktistovs, returned around ten.

Vadim went to the bathroom. The medicine chest on the wall, with a small snake engraved on the glass door, held a vial of valerian drops. He looked at the date. Last year. It should be thrown out anyway. He put the vial in his pocket and returned to the dining room. He went over to the couch and bent over his father.

"Papa!"

His father did not reply. Vadim stared at his face. Even the eyelids did not move. He picked up his hand. It was cold. He let go. It fell lifelessly and touched the floor. Maybe his father was asleep? Well, that was good. A little sleep and he would feel better. Vadim opened the window to let in some air. Of course, everything would be all right. The thoughts he had just had were nonsense. He shouldn't worry about those things. What would be, would be. In the meantime, he would go down to the pharmacy for new medicine. The old was no good, so he would go get some more.

Out on the street Vadim reached into his pocket and opened the top of the vial of valerian. He poured out the contents, through his pocket, onto the dirty, spring snow. The valarian drops were old, no good, but still he did not want to be seen pouring them out. People might misunderstand. On the street he ran into people, careworn and weary, hurrying home from work. There were so many unfamiliar faces on the Arbat now. Everything comes to an end. And everyone leaves. Once upon a time his mother used to walk here, and she had been gone a long time. Vika used to walk here, and thank God, she would not be returning to Moscow. The barber Sergei Alexeyevich used to walk here, and he was gone forever. And Sasha Pankratov rotted away in Siberia, and Yuri Sharok was never around — he must have been transferred to another city, or maybe he had been shot. They treated their own the same way they treated everyone else. Lena Budyagina was in exile, Nina Ivanova had vanished. Everyone was swept away, no one was left. And his father would leave. And he himself would leave when it was his time. Everything was temporary, ephemeral. A year more or less, to history a human life was the blink of an eye. On the corner of Arbat, he slipped the empty vial into a waste receptacle.

At the pharmacy, Vadim waited patiently in line. He knew the cashier and the clerk. "Something for the heart," Vadim said. "My father is complaining about his heart." They gave him some valerian drops. Vadim thanked them and a thought flashed through his mind — it was a good thing that he had come here, it was good that he had been seen. He didn't know why he thought it, but he did. He would go home now. He hoped his father would be better. He would show him the medicine he had bought. I had looked in the bathroom, there was nothing, and I ran to the pharmacy. Here, take your medicine, and most important, don't get upset. You see what happens when you do.

Andrei Andreyevich was still lying in the same position. Vadim called his name, but his father did not answer. Vadim leaned over him, but he did not feel his father's breath. He picked up and dropped his father's hand. It fell lifelessly to the floor once again.

Vadim dialed 03 and asked for an ambulance to be sent immediately to Professor Marasevich's house. What was the matter? A heart attack. Address? He told them the address.

About twenty minutes later, a young doctor, a white coat slung over his topcoat, came into the apartment with two orderlies and a stretcher. The orderlies were wearing white coats on top of their overcoats.

Fenya arrived almost simultaneously. She ran around muttering in agitation. Vadim shouted at her to calm down.

The doctor sat on the couch next to Andrei Andreyevich, felt his pulse, listened to his heart, opened his eyelids. Then he rose. "We don't take corpses."

∽ 16 ∽

THERE WERE IRON BEDSTEADS along the wall, towels draped on their heads, no cloth on the table, four chairs, and a kitchen stool piled with dishes. Clothing hung from nails in the wall. If not for the baby cot, the crowded room would have resembled a college dormitory.

"Masha, our former maid, lives with us," Lena explained. "She's got a job as a cleaning woman at a factory now, and she spends her free day baby-sitting, while I go to various offices."

Varya had never before seen such hopeless poverty. Everyone was poor, but it was a long-standing, accustomed poverty. This had befallen Lena in an instant — she had been thrown out of her apartment, fired from her job, and deprived of any way of making money.

Lena was dressing Vanya and getting ready to go to the store. Varya offered to go instead.

"There's a line," Lena warned.

"Won't they let you go to the head of the line with a baby?"

"Who gets to go to the head of the line nowadays?"

"I'll wait."

"Well, all right, thank you. Here's the money. Get me two bottles of kefir."

"Do you need anything else?"

"Not at all. Nothing else."

Besides the kefir, a liquid yogurt, Varya bought some sour cream, processed cheese, eggs, and marmalade.

"Want to have a feast?" Lena shook her head reproachfully. "Next time, don't do that. It makes me feel uncomfortable."

"We'll see about next time," Varya replied with a smile.

Toddling on slightly bowed legs, Vanya came over to Varya and clutched the hem of her skirt. Cute and fair (like his father, Sharok, thought Varya), he stared at her with his big blue eyes. Lena picked him up and seated him at the table.

"We were searched three times." She poured kefir in a cup, handed her son a piece of bread, and kissed him on the top of the head. "One search at the apartment on Granovsky Street, when they took away my father, another at the dacha, and a third here, when they took Mama. They took everything — money, jewelry, bonds, books, my dresses, Papa's suits. It was all imported, how could they leave it? They sealed two rooms right away. Everything that had been inside was lost immediately — my parents' documents, the record player, even Vladlen's bicycle. I wrote a complaint, asking them to return the most necessary things, but no one replied. After the search they made me sign a paper stating that I had no complaints against the NKVD. They threatened me. 'If you don't sign, we won't leave you anything at all.' They stole right in front of us. They broke locks on our suitcases. They took everything, even the chiffonier. I guess our poor old chiffonier turned out to be anti-Soviet, too."

She kissed her son on the head once more and looked up at Varya. "They fired me as soon as Papa was arrested. They just got rid of my job. A week later they reinstated it and hired someone else."

"What kind of work were you doing?"

"Translating from English. I know French, too. But no one will hire me. 'Call back in a week,' then another week, and one guy simply said, 'Change your name.' And this was when I was trying to get a job as a cleaning woman at night, washing floors and toilets. I saw an ad: 'Mail carriers needed.' That suited me. I could do the rounds before Vladlen left for school, he could keep an eye on Vanya. I went to apply. They said, 'Fill out a form and come at six A.M. tomorrow.' I came back the next day, and they couldn't look me in the eye. 'Sorry, the position is filled.' A few days later, I noticed that the sign was still up. But I keep trying. . . . And I go to all the places — the NKVD, to 24 Kuznetsky Bridge, to the procurator's office, to the military procurator. I looked for Papa in all the prisons, and then for Mama. . . . I didn't find them. They were sentenced 'without the right to correspondence.' That means they're dead. . . . Why don't they just say so! Instead of making people go from prison to prison, from window to window!"

"I know that."

"Yes? Was someone in your family arrested?"

"I brought parcels to Sasha Pankratov."

Lena darkened. "We're all so guilty before Sasha. We didn't help him then."

"What could you have done?"

"I don't know what, but we should have tried. Writing letters, declarations, going to the NKVD, the procurator's office, fighting for our comrade. It was only starting then. And we were silent. And now we're paying for it. Me, and my father, and Sasha's uncle, thousands, millions of people are paying for it."

"It started earlier — with collectivization and getting rid of the kulaks."

"Of course." Lena let the little boy down. He went to play with his blocks on the floor. "I was living abroad then and didn't see any of it happening. But Sasha happened before my very eyes. We didn't know it would affect us. And now, when I see people turning away from me, I think, 'It will reach you, too, and then you'll remember the people you avoided.' You know, all these three, actually, four years, I never went to see Sasha's mother. I didn't want to get involved in other people's sorrow. I was protecting my own peace of mind. And now I'm punished for it. I have these thoughts all the time now, Varya. I'm so ashamed."

"We all have things we're ashamed of," Varya said.

Lena sighed. She looked at her watch, and then at Varya. "Vladlen will be back from school soon. I have to prepare you. He's thirteen and he's completely under the influence of propaganda. He reads the newspaper accounts of the Bukharin-Rykov trial and he believes every word. He curses the defendants and says that they should be kept in cages, like animals, and that people should spit at them. He curses our parents, too. He says, 'They're just like Bukharin and Rykov.' He dreamed of becoming a pilot, but he knows that now he'll never be one, even though he makes model planes and is talented. But they wouldn't send him to a regional competition. He feels like an outcast and he blames his parents for it. He even condemned them at school."

"He's not the first."

"Yes, but I know other children. Our parents fought for their ideas. Who knew that it would all be engulfed in blood. . . . But I just can't get that into Vladlen's head. He doesn't have a drop of pity for his mother or father. Of course, our parents were never close to us. They didn't have time for us. They were busy with Party and government work."

Lena looked over at Vanya, who was playing quietly. "Have you guessed his father?"

"Yuri Sharok."

"A horrible, unworthy connection. My greatest mistake," Lena said calmly, looking into Varya's eyes. "But do you know what attracted me to him, besides everything else? Strangely enough, it was his family."

"Really?" Varya shrugged. "I've never seen more disgusting people."

"Now, I see that. But then, compared to my house, I thought they were a real family, close and friendly. While we were . . . I can't remember a single occasion that all four of us were at the table. We all ate separately. And that's how we grew up. . . . Don't ask Vladlen about our parents and don't bring up politics. Like all teenagers, he is very harsh in his convictions."

Varya nodded. "I'll keep it in mind."

There was noise outside. Lena went to the window and beckoned Varya to follow. "This happens every day in this building."

Four moving vans were unloading — a new family was moving in. A fat NKVD man in uniform with a pistol strapped to his belt, his noisy, screeching wife, and two blond girls around seven or eight years old. The man bullied the movers, nine or ten of them, as they unpacked.

"At our house, almost all the furniture belonged to the state. It all had numbered labels," Lena said. "People were indifferent about possessions. But these people have antique furniture, mirrors and tables, armchairs, even a grand piano!"

"It's all been stolen," Varya said. "If I had a machine gun, I'll shoot them all to hell!"

"Varya, never say things like that. Never, not to anyone, not to your closest friend!"

"Why ever not?" Varya chuckled. "I was talking about the moving men. They're as slow as molasses. Why can't they give better service to an officer of our glorious state!"

"Don't say that even about movers."

"All right, I'll keep quiet."

Vladlen returned from school, coldly greeted Varya, and tossed his worn canvas briefcase onto the bed. Lena gave him lunch — cabbage soup without meat and wheat porridge. He ate and left without thanking her or saying where he was going and when he would be back.

"I have to do something about Vladlen," Lena sighed. "Last week, eighty-five families from our building were exiled from Moscow. You should have seen it! A pogrom! They did everything but cut open the pillows. The courtyard was full of NKVD men, who threw people and suitcases into cars. There are rumors about another sixty families, and I'm probably on the list. What will I do with Vladlen in a new place? I can't feed him even here, and he's a growing boy. He needs nourishment. If his shoes wear out, how can I buy him new ones? There's nothing left to sell. I'm wearing everything I own. It's hard to face, but I think I'll have to give Vladlen to an orphanage. I went to the regional Party committee and they sent me to Danilovsky Val, to the NKVD children's department. It's horrible, like a children's prison."

"But they send them on from there to orphanages where it will be better."

Lena sighed again. "That's what other people told me. Many mothers turned their children over to them before they were exiled. I guess I'll have to give up Vladlen. He wants it himself. Once when there was nothing to eat, and he was making a fuss and driving me crazy, I said, 'I'll give you to an orphanage where they'll feed you.' He replied, 'Wonderful. At least I'll be rid of this damned surname.'"

"If you're exiled, what will happen to Vanya?" Varya asked.

"He'll be with me. I'll get a job. They won't try to starve us to death."

"Who'll take care of him while you work?"

"I don't know.... But I can't abandon my own child! Well, we'll die together. Some families were allowed to choose their city of exile, but I don't even know what to choose. We have some distant relatives in Motovilikha, in Baku, but I don't know them, I don't even have addresses for them. And people are afraid, too. Sometimes I just want to fall asleep and not wake up into this nightmare again."

"If you're given a choice, say Michurinsk. My aunt lives there. She's old, but full of energy and very kind. She lives alone. You could stay with her. If they won't give you Michurinsk, ask for Ufa."

"Why Ufa?"

"Why Ufa?" Varya repeated. "You know, Sasha is free."

"Yes."

"He's served his term, but he's not allowed to live in big cities. He's working as a chauffeur in Ufa. Sofya Alexandrovna writes to him care of the post office. When you get there, drop him a line."

Lena thought about it and shook her head. "That's no good. Sasha has a record and I'm the daughter of an 'enemy of the people,' which will make things even worse for him. I don't have the right to do that to him. If I'm allowed to choose, Michurinsk is better — at least I'll have a place to go straight from the railroad station for the first night. But it's more likely I will not be asked where I want to go, but simply sent away."

"But if they do ask," Varya persisted.

"Then I'll say Michurinsk. But will your aunt take me with a baby?"

"Certainly. I'll write to her."

"Thank you. That will be a big help."

❧ 17 ❧

SASHA AND GLEB usually dined at the restaurant. It was only
a little more expensive than the cafeteria, but they could stay as late as
midnight if they wanted. Sometimes they drank a lot. Gleb was used to
it, and Sasha was getting addicted. Who knew what tomorrow would
bring, let's enjoy today.

One night Gleb said, "Some important lady from Moscow is on tour
here, a friend of Marya Konstantinova's. So she's giving her a party — at
Semyon's expense, of course. Nonna's with them, too."

"And we are pushing our way in?"

"They're by themselves, we're by ourselves, dearie. They're going to
have *suprème de volaille,* we'll have vodka and herring."

Sasha and Gleb had their usual corner table. Semyon Grigoryevich
and his group were in the middle of the room, with waiters and the
female maître d' fluttering around them. They were VIPs.

Sasha could see the whole table from his seat — Semyon
Grigoryevich and Nonna, and the two beautiful, pampered, well-
dressed women, Marya Konstantinova, a brunette, and the important
guest from Moscow, sumptuous and red-haired. There were around
thirty-five guests and they attracted attention. The orchestra played
movie tunes. No Gypsy singer tonight.

"They're only playing official Soviet music tonight, all the
Dunaevsky and Blanter hits, because of that lady," Gleb noted. "They're
ideologically pure, but they're good-looking women!"

Semyon Grigoryevich turned around and looked at Sasha and Gleb.
They caught his eye but pretended not to notice. The ladies turned
around, too.

"Semyon is showing off his team." Gleb winked at Sasha. "Marya is a power here, and she's very choosy about the men she lets near her. I made a pass at her and she sent me packing. So now Semyon Grigoryevich is showing off his goods. That's you. He's singing your praises; 'What an intelligent assistant, with a college education, from Moscow.' He's trying to impress the ladies. The Muscovite, by the way, is a Central Committee instructor on theater. A big shot. She was at school with Marya. That's why Marya is so bold. She has a friend in Moscow who can help her out if there's a problem. It's good having a friend in Moscow, isn't it?"

"Must be nice."

"She's very powerful. If she wanted, she could help me in an instant. In their own, Central Committee, way, of course." Gleb's voice rang with authoritarian steel. 'We've been looking at the works of an artist called Dubinin. Interesting.' You see, dearie, they never give an evaluation. 'Interesting,' that's all. 'There is an opinion.' See? Not a decision, merely an opinion. 'The comrade should be helped' — that means not officially, but in a human way. 'We are sending Gleb Vasilyevich Dubinin to you to be chief artistic director of the theater.' And they would take me, without a murmur."

"You should be an actor."

"There's nothing I can't do."

The next day both ladies, accompanied by Semyon Grigoryevich, showed up at the Palace of Labor. They sat down in comfortable armchairs, with their coats on adjoining chairs, not planning to stay long.

Many of Sasha's former students were in the class helping him. Whenever Sasha clapped his hands and said, "Attention" or "Ready," they all watched him. Today they were learning the first steps of the Boston waltz, the most complicated lesson. You had to spin but with a long first step. The turn was hard for people who had not mastered the waltz.

Sasha saw that Semyon Grigoryevich and his entourage were watching him. He could feel their eyes on his back. When he danced near them, Semyon Grigoryevich beckoned to him. Sasha clapped his hands. "Stop! Now you practice on your own." He turned to his former students. "Help them with the turn."

He went over to Semyon Grigoryevich, who introduced him to the ladies. "Ulyana Zakharovna, Marya Konstantinova, meet Alexander Pavlovich."

"So, this is what you're like," Marya Konstantinovna said. "You got here and immediately became a celebrity."

There was something Buryat in her high cheekbones and dark brown, narrow eyes. She was friendly, but you wouldn't call her face kind.

Sasha pointed to the dancing room. "That's my entire celebrity."

Ulyana Zakharovna gave him a smile.

She was beautiful and stately and wore her red hair braided and wrapped around her head like a crown. Her wide-set gray-green eyes were smiling, gently, but there was a spark of something else. Sasha could not quite place it — curiosity, perhaps?

Semyon Grigoryevich stood and spoke with an actorly familiarity of the master. "Well then, Sasha, why don't you grab a bite with our guests while I work with your students?"

"No, no." Marya Konstantinovna had also risen. "Take me to see the director." She looked at her watch. "We still have twenty minutes. We are going upstairs to the theater," she explained to Sasha. "We dropped by on the way."

The object of this maneuver was obvious — to leave him alone with Ulyana Zakharovna.

"Sit down." Still smiling, she looked up at Sasha, narrowed her big eyes, and, in no hurry to break eye contact, patted the chair next to hers.

"Thanks." Sasha sat down.

She turned to him, and he got a whiff of her expensive perfume. She leaned her elbow on the armrest, almost touching him with her breast. "I was told that you're from Moscow."

"Yes, I am. From the Arbat."

She widened her eyes and again there was a flicker that Sasha did not understand. "We're neighbors. I live on Granovsky Street."

"Not in the Fifth House of Soviets?"

Damn! He let that slip. Now she'll want to know how he knows the house and will ask the names of his friends there. Whom could he name? Executed Budyagin? Judging by the lists of enemies of the people that appeared in the newspapers, all the former tenants were gone. And in their place lived the new elite, like her.

"You guessed it." She leaned even closer toward him. "Do you have friends there?"

"Some of the kids from that building went to school with me. Petya

Voroshilov and the daughters of Mikhailov, Vera and Tamara. It was a long time ago, ten years at least, I've forgotten most of them."

She put her hand on top of his. Her hand was plump and warm. She said with a confidential smile, "Maybe we were at school together, too? Where did you go to college?"

"At a transport institute."

"Transport?" she asked in surprise. "What does transport have to do with dancing?"

"I was a poor engineer. I was always drawn to music and dancing. I'm not the only one."

This conversation was beginning to bore him. Pretending to stretch, Sasha moved his shoulders, freed his hand, and leaned back in the chair.

"Give me your hand." She held it in hers. "I won't let you go so quickly. What if I want to take dancing lessons? Will you teach me?"

"Of course. How about right now?"

"Marya and I are going to the theater now. It will have to be later. You're right, Sasha." She lingered over his name. "You're right. Many performers have an education that is far removed from their current professions. I could do something for you. I know the directors of all the ensembles — Alexandrov, Igor Moiseyev. It's difficult to get in, but the comrades will try to help you. But here comes Marya. We'll continue our discussion. When do you finish your classes?"

"At ten."

"The play lets out at ten-fifteen. Wait for us, and we'll go to Marya's and have a nice talk."

Without waiting for Sasha's reply, she rose. Sasha handed Ulyana her coat and watched her go.

"She really fell for you," Gleb said.

"Seems that way."

"There's a lot of work for a man there."

"She's too much of an executive type for me."

"But very experienced. That's how she got ahead."

"She asked me to wait for her. The hell with it! I'm not in the mood. I won't go."

"Are you crazy, dearie? They worked all this out beforehand. Why do you think they came? She had her eye on you last night. And they've got the food and drink at Marya's house all ready. And if you don't go, Marya Konstantinovna will never forgive you. Don't forget, you're in her debt. And in a month or two when your residency permit expires, and you go back to her for help, she'll say, "Sorry, Alexander Pavlovich, you were too high and mighty for us, and now you can stop counting on me.' And she'll be right."

Sasha hesitated. It was tempting, of course. But something was holding him back. She was from the Central Committee. What would they talk about? What did he need with all this?

"She's so beautiful!" Gleb continued. "Only a fool would refuse. A Venus! An Aphrodite! If she were a local, you'd be chasing her. But because she's from Moscow, a VIP, your morality is raising its ugly head: 'What will people think of me? They'll say I'm a fortune hunter. I'm not one of Catherine the Great's favorites, no Potemkin, no Count Orlov, but a highly moral person . . .' "

"Isn't that reaching a bit?"

"Dearie!" Gleb smiled, showing his white teeth. "You're no Potemkin. What can she do for you — take away the restrictions from your passport? No one can do that, and you wouldn't ever bring it up anyway. So if anything were to happen, it would just be whatever happens when pleasant people are having a party and a woman like that is near you."

~ 18 ~

A SMALL, ONE-STORY HOUSE in a quiet side street not far
from the theater. A balcony, a carved wooden porch, a swept sidewalk.
There was a runner on the floor in the hallway, with a tall coatrack
on one wall and a mirror on the other. Ulyana hung up her fur coat
and sank onto the chair near the mirror. Marya gave her slippers to
wear in place of her boots. Ulyana got up and shrugged uncomfort-
ably. "I wish I could get out of these clothes. Is your dining room
warm?"

"There's heat. I'll give you a robe."

Ulyana looked up at Sasha. "Do you mind if I wear a robe?"

"Of course not!"

They went into the dining room. "Sit down," Marya said. "We'll be
right back. Come on, Ulyana."

The women left.

Sasha looked around. The wall clock had a pendulum, miniatures
were tastefully hung, a lace cloth covered the top of the upright piano,
which supported figurines, and a telephone stood on a round table with
a heavy, curved pedestal. It was mahogany furniture. Sasha was no expert, but he could tell it was old and expensive. There was a Dutch stove
tiled in the Russian manner. A warm and cozy room.

Marya came back in homey clothes — skirt and sweater and slippers.
She folded back half the heavy patterned tablecloth and covered that end
of the table with a white cloth. She set it for three, with plates, stemmed
glasses, and shot glasses.

"Well, Sasha, how do you like it?"

"It's luxurious. Even better than my place."

She shook her head in rebuke. "Sasha. You know I just keep that apartment for people who need a living permit. After all, you don't actually live there."

"Of course."

"If you had come to me as soon as you had arrived, I would have gotten you a place in the center of town. But you were already late when I got your papers and I had to send you there."

"And I'm terribly grateful to you," Sasha said sincerely. "I was too careless about the whole thing, and you rescued me."

She squinted at him, as if to say: You can't fool me, I know why you didn't register, but this isn't the time to discuss it.

Ulyana, in a robe and with her glorious red hair loose, entered the room. The terry cloth robe was long and practically unfastened. He could see her strong white legs and round knees. It was very blatant, and he understood the look in her green-gray eyes. She was a businesslike Central Committee lady and she would not play games. She would get into bed matter-of-factly, and it would be up to him to do his best. She had to pretend to be highly moral at the Central Committee, but here, away from her bosses and subordinates, she could do what she wanted. Marya, naturally, had not told her his background.

"I'm sure you must be starving," Marya said as she set out platters of *zakuski.* "What will you drink? Sasha, you probably want vodka, right? And how about you, Ulyana?"

"I'll have a little, too."

Ulyana moved her armchair closer to the table and sat with her legs crossed. The robe fell away, exposing her legs completely.

"Move closer," Marya said, laughing. "Sasha's gotten a good look at your gorgeous legs. Haven't you, Sasha?"

"What does he care about my legs?" Ulyana said. "He sees legs all day at his classes. All kinds — white legs, black legs, polka-dotted legs."

"I've never seen polka-dotted ones," Sasha replied with a laugh.

"All right, children." Marya poured vodka in their shot glasses. "Let's drink to our meeting."

Ulyana raised her glass. And a serious look appeared in her eyes. "Let's drink to the capital of our homeland — to Moscow. Sasha and I are fellow countrymen, almost neighbors, you know."

This was for insurance. If she slept with him, no one would know. But who could have any objections to her raising a toast to Moscow at a friend's house?

They drank and ate. Sasha had not seen such a rich array of *zakuski* in a long time — caviar red and black, smoked salmon, ham. And vodka that did not reek of fuel oil. A sea of berry-flavored vodkas, too. They liked the good life. They had learned to enjoy it.

Ulyana handed Sasha a plate. "Sasha, give me a little of everything."

Marya nudged the salad bowls of marinated mushrooms, cucumbers, and tomatoes toward him. "Try my pickling."

Ulyana tasted and praised. "This is good. Did your cook Petrovna do this?"

"Yes."

"Homemade is always best. I just don't have the time myself."

She kept her plate on her knees instead of eating at the table. It wasn't very comfortable, but she wanted to sit in a revealing pose.

"I also have a hot dish, *pelmeni,* made here, in Ufa."

Ulyana looked at her watch. "It's after eleven. I'd better call the hotel." She went to the telephone and dialed the hotel. "This is Bolshakova. I'm still at a girlfriend's house and it's too late to call for a car. I'll just spend the night here. Take down the telephone number."

"Why did you leave the number?" Marya asked. "They'll bother you tonight."

Ulyana came back to her chair. "No one's going to call, no one needs me in the middle of the night. Except for Sasha, maybe, if he doesn't find me unattractive. Do you like women like me, Sasha?"

"Like what?"

"Redheads who are brazen and shameless."

He laughed. That was exactly the way he would have described her. "Who doesn't?"

Ulyana resumed the discussion. "I gave the number just in case someone wants to find out where I spent the night. You know, everybody watches us comrades from the center very closely and hopes to put a monkey wrench in our works."

Marya got up. "I'll bring the *pelmeni* now. Just don't misbehave while I'm away."

She was an experienced pimp. . . . Ulyana bent over toward Sasha and looked at him with her big green eyes. But what she said was unexpected. "I slave sixteen hours a day at my job and wait for a lightning bolt to hit me at any moment. Don't I deserve a little relaxation? With a good man? What do you think?"

He didn't know what to say. He merely shrugged to indicate his complete agreement.

Ulyana never took her eyes off him. "You're a good man, aren't you? A decent one?"

He laughed and shrugged again.

"So we're agreed." She leaned closer. "Come on, kiss me."

"Marya's coming back."

"So what. She's a friend."

"And what's this?" Marya's voice interrupted them. "I warned you. Can't you wait just a minute?"

She set down a large bowl of *pelmeni* on the table and served them. "There's sour cream, there's vinegar and pepper, whatever you want on your dumplings. They're authentic *pelmeni*. The filling is half pork and half beef, with a little lamb thrown in."

"*Pelmeni* like this call for a drink," Sasha suggested.

He needed one. Was Ulyana speaking sincerely, or was this merely a self-justification? Did it matter? He wasn't the man she thought he was, either. So they were even. She wanted to have a good time, and he had no objections to that. And they needed a drink.

"Right," Marya said. "Have a big one and give us smaller ones. Come on, Ulyana, vodka is better than a tranquilizer."

Ulyana joined them. She had one dumpling, stared at Sasha all the time, and then put her hand on his.

"Ulyana! Let the man eat!" Marya cried.

"Let him eat. Who's stopping him?"

Marya wiped her lips and got up. "All right, kiddies, you're on your own, but I have to be at the office by nine. So good night." She pointed to the telephone stand. "The keys are over there, Ulyana. I'll get them back from you tomorrow. And remember, Petrovna comes in at nine to clean." She kissed Ulyana and Sasha and patted him on the cheek. "Good boy!"

Sasha was awakened by the light streaming through the chinks in the curtains and the rattle of dishes in the dining room. Ulyana stirred next to him and whispered into the pillow, "Don't get up. It's Marya clearing the table."

He shut his eyes. Eventually the noises stopped and then he heard the front door slam.

"Marya's gone." Ulyana got out of bed. "I'll be right back."

She returned and climbed under the cover, cuddling up to Sasha. "Brr, it's cold." Then she reached for her watch on the night table. "Look, it's almost nine." She cuddled up to Sasha again. "I could stay like this forever. But I have to show up at work. Come on, darling, time to get up." She pulled back the blanket from his side. "Get dressed."

Sasha got up and dressed.

"I'll let you out. Then I'll dress and leave. I need a half hour just to do my hair. If Marya's cleaning woman finds me here, there's no problem. But you understand, we can't both be here. Tell me, when will you be in Moscow? I'm leaving today, you know."

"Really?"

"Yes, darling, tonight. So when will you be in Moscow?"

"I promised Semyon Grigoryevich to go to Saratov."

"Big deal, Semyon Grigoryevich, senior assistant to the junior janitor. Do you have an apartment in Moscow?"

"My mother lives in Moscow."

"So why do you have to drag yourself all over these other cities? I'll get everything set up for you in Moscow."

He sat on the bed. "Are you so all-powerful? Where do you work?"

She gave him a suspicious look. "You don't know?"

"How could I?"

She hesitated and then said, "I work in the Committee, in the arts section. When you go to Moscow, get my number from Marya. I'll tell her to give it to you."

"I'll call you," Sasha said. He knew he would never call. "But I'm too old to be starting a new career. I'll never be a soloist, and I don't want to be a chorus boy. But I do have a request for you. You saw my accompanist, didn't you?"

"The blond?"

"Yes. He's a theater designer. He used to work for Akimov in Leningrad and then at the Youth Theater in Kalinin. He didn't get along with the artistic director and left. If you could help him, it would be great. His name is Gleb Vasilyevich Dubinin."

"Is everything about him in order?"

"In what sense?"

"You don't get it? . . . Do you realize what times we live in?"

Sasha shrugged and gave a short laugh. "He doesn't belong to the Party and he doesn't have a record."

"All right." She looked at her watch and got up to put on her robe. "Tell him that you saw Marya Konstantinovna home last night and told her about him. And she wants him to drop by. I'll help him through Marya. Come on, I'll let you out."

She leaned against the wall in the corridor and watched Sasha put on his coat and cap.

"So, just do as I said. Walk calmly down the street and don't look back."

～ 19 ～

WHY HAD SHE MENTIONED Ufa to Lena? Why had she reminded her about Sasha? Sasha always sent regards when he called his mother. Varya was grateful, but she didn't believe it very much. Sofya Alexandrovna was just being polite, or maybe trying to console her. Sasha had written her off. He couldn't forgive her for her marriage to Kostya.

Sometimes she tried to persuade herself there was another reason. Sasha was wandering around the country, his life was full of danger, and he did not want to subject her to that. But her dreams of a quiet and peaceful life in the provinces were gone now, too. No one could have a quiet life. All she needed was to know Sasha loved her. And for him to know she loved him. To talk on the telephone, write letters, and come visit him for even a day or two, when she was off. And it did not matter that they would never have a house and children. It was a bitter thought, but it was better than nothing. The important thing was to know that they needed each other.

But one night she dreamed about a tiny red-haired baby, who was her son. She was carrying him wrapped in a flannel blanket around the room and cuddling him and kissing him and crying over him. And she kept wondering, why did he have red hair? Sasha had dark hair and so did she, but the baby was a redhead.

When she woke up, she did not want to get out of bed. Maybe she would dream of the baby again. At least they could have a baby in her dreams!

But strangely enough, the dream brought her to her senses. She had still been hoping that whatever misunderstanding there was would clear itself up and that Sasha would write to her. She didn't even go to see her aunt when she had vacation. Her aunt had called, cajoling, and promised they would pick raspberries together and make jam. But Varya was afraid to leave, in case a letter came from Sasha just then to make a date to meet. She would die if she missed it.

But that morning, in the metro on her way to work, standing by the back door so that people would not notice her puffy, tear-stained eyes, she looked into the black tunnel and realized that nothing would be cleared up and that she would never see Sasha again. In the year and a half since his release, Sasha had not written her a single line and had called only once — at Sofya Alexandrovna's insistence, Varya was sure. If he were afraid of joining their lives, he could have written, "I don't know what will happen to me tomorrow. I do not have the right to risk your life and your freedom. Forget me." He was direct and honest, and that was definitely what he would have done. And he hadn't. That meant the problem was Kostya. And he did not want to write about that. He simply dropped her, once and for all, and she had to accept it. He had a terrible break in life, he was persecuted, and he had believed in her. The news about Kostya had stunned and humiliated him. He was a determined man, and he cut her off. There was no room for her in his anxious life. He had simply forgotten all about her. But she would never forget him. How could she forget that day at the Kazan Station, when she saw him marching between two armed guards, his suitcase in his hand and a pack on his back? Or how he had sensed that she was looking at him and turned, and she saw his paper white face and Gypsy black beard. But he saw no one, not even her, and he walked on between the guards toward the train standing on the farthest platform. That day had turned her life upside down. For the first time she felt the horror of this ruthless and unjust world. She would never forget that day. She would never forget Sasha. She would always remember and love him, she would be true to him, she would never abandon Sofya Alexandrovna. Varya called her every day and dropped by on the way home from work sometimes. But now she had someone else to worry about. She spent all her spare time with Lena Budyagina.

Igor Vladimirovich's attempts to find her a job came to nothing. His influential friends, when they heard her name, refused to help, and the few who were willing to send her application to personnel found that it would go no further.

Lena had turned her brother over to the children's distribution center. "If you could have seen our farewell," she told Varya bitterly. "Vladlen didn't even kiss me. He nodded, as if we were strangers. I was told that in a month's time I could learn to which orphanage he was sent. But will I have a month? We got bad news here."

"What?"

"Everyone who had been exiled from our building was arrested in the new place and sent to the camps. Clever. If a wife of an enemy of the people is arrested here, her relatives stay on in the apartment. This way, the whole family is sent to Astrakhan or someplace, leaving the apartment free in Moscow. They'll get to us soon enough. There are only twelve families left. It's a matter of days. I'll be sent to the camps, I guess, and Vanya to an orphanage."

"Would you really give up your son?"

"What else can I do? If I lived on the tenth floor, I'd jump with him from the window. But where can you jump from the first floor?"

"You're talking nonsense."

"I know. But any other conversation is useless."

"Why not go away?"

"Where?"

"I've already told you. To Michurinsk."

"Varya, sweetie, how can your aunt feed Vanya and me? So I'll go looking for a job, and I'll have to fill out the application and tell them who my parents are. And they'll arrest me on the spot. In the sticks. At least here I'll be arrested in the capital. You don't agree?"

"I don't. Why are you all going off to prison and exile so docilely? You don't even save your own children! Millions of people are in the camps, the prisons, in exile, with restrictions in their passports. If they were all to run away, who could ever catch them? You'd need a hundred NKVDs."

Lena sank wearily into a chair. "It's too late, we don't know what to do. If I could only save Vanya, but how?"

"You have to leave him with reliable people and disappear."

"Where are these reliable people? Do you know any?"

"Wouldn't your relatives in Motovilisha or Baku take your child?"

"They wouldn't even if I could find them. They wouldn't."

"All right, then why don't I take him for a while? If you manage to get away and find a good safe place, I'll give him back. And if you don't, I'll bring him up."

"Thank you, Varya, but that's not realistic. You have to work and study. Who'll watch him?"

"Sofya Alexandrovna, Sasha's mother, will help."

"She works too. No, I'd never burden you or her with that."

"Does your Masha have relatives in the countryside?"

"Her relatives were exiled for being kulaks. And she had to run off to the big city when she was just a young girl."

"Take your boy and leave for Michurinsk today. I'll go with you and help you settle in with my aunt."

"I can't take the risk. The camps, exile, that's better than landing in a strange place without work or a piece of bread, with a child and the threat of arrest at any moment."

Varya was upset when she left.

They were all cowards, quietly awaiting their turn. She felt sorry for the boy. He was so blond, tender, and warm, that little blue-eyed boy. He'd be sent to an orphanage for children of enemies of the people. How many toddlers survived that? And even if he did, he wouldn't even know who his parents were, who he was. And if Lena survived, she wouldn't know where her child was.

On her way home, Varya stopped at the post office, where Nina's letter was waiting. Nina wrote to the poste restante, faithfully every week. In her early letters she announced, "Everything is fine. I am teaching history in the upper grades. They need teachers here. Maxim and I are married, and now my name is Kostina." Varya realized that Maxim had made her change her name. Good! Now they'd never find her. But, then again, who was even looking? The ones who had been looking were in prison themselves.

In her later letters, Nina did not write about anything momentous — no news, everything was fine. But today's letter was anxious. "You naturally know about what's happening out here. I hope that everything ends well."

What was she talking about? The letter was dated August 1 and today was the fifteenth. Mail took two weeks. What was going on in early August? Varya did not read the newspapers on principle and she listened to the weather report and nothing else on the radio — she did not wish to hear or read their lies. Of course, some things did reach her.

There were skirmishes with the Japanese in the Far East. But they were always skirmishing with the Japanese samurai.

The next day at work Varya learned what it was. There had been fierce fighting from July 29 until August 11 in the region of Lake Khasan between Soviet and Japanese troops. The Japanese had been repulsed and they signed a peace treaty. So that was what Nina was writing about. Max had been in the war, and Nina was worried about him. Had he survived?

This was the first time that she thought of war as a real possibility. Varya had read about the World War and the Civil War. They had studied the wars in school, but it was all remote and long ago. And now, it seems that Max could have been killed in a war. Naturally, he was a military man and it was his duty to fight, but why was there war? When she was a girl, she was taught at school and she remembered Nina and her friends saying, "Humanity will never forget the World War that took ten million lives. The workers of the world will not allow an attack on the Soviet Union." And now all you hear about is the "threat of war" from Germany and Japan. And now the Japanese had attacked our territory, Lake Khasan in our country. Varya bought a copy of *Pravda* and found the reports from the Far East. In the evening she turned on the radio and listened to the news from beginning to end.

But if something had happened to Max, Nina would have let her know. What if she weren't allowed to tell? Anything was possible in our country. The newspapers report the Japanese casualties, but not ours.

What could she do? Send a telegram? To Nina Sergeyevna Kostina: "Inform about health." Nina would understand whose health interested her. But would that create problems for them? Everything was secret, everything was classified.... They would ask, "Why is your relative worried? Does she know that Comrade Kostin was in battle? How does she know? Did you tell her? Why?" Damned country! Every step, every move could cause danger.

Maybe she should drop by Max's family. They lived around the corner. Just stop by and ask about the war? But she had not been to school with Max. They weren't chums and she had never even been to their apartment. She barely knew his parents. How could she just show up and ask? No, that wouldn't work.

Varya shared her anxiety with Sofya Alexandrovna, who promised to ask Max's mother. Two days later Sofya Alexandrovna called. There was no bad news in the family. That did not relieve Varya. They could hide the truth even from his own mother. All right! She would wait another week and then send a telegram.

She did not have to do that. A few days later Sofya Alexandrovna called her at work. "Varya, look at today's paper. There's something about Max."

"Something bad?"

"On the contrary."

Varya opened the paper. The participants in the battles near Lake Khasan were given medals and decorations. Several thousand men. But the newspaper mentioned only the names of the Heroes of the Soviet Union. And one of them was Maxim Ivanovich Kostin, battalion commander.

Max — a Hero of the Soviet Union! That was the country's highest honor. Now Nina was as safe as houses with him. No one would dare touch her now.

And then Varya thought that Nina and Max could take little Vanya Budyagin. They could adopt him. They had no children and they must have enough money, and there had to be nurseries and kindergartens in a military town. Where did the child come from? Easy, it was her sister Varya's child. She got pregnant by some stranger, the whore, and they couldn't leave the child to be brought up by her, could they? They wanted to bring him up as a real Soviet citizen and a staunch defender of the socialist homeland. She came and dropped off her child, the bitch, and left them with a note, "I agree to the adoption of my son, Ivan, by M. and N. Kostin. V. Ivanova." What could they do but take him? It would be easy to get the paperwork done. It wasn't Moscow, after all. And Max wasn't just anyone. He was a Hero of the Soviet Union!

Would Lena agree? A mother must think about her child first. Would Nina agree? How could she refuse her best friend? The Party couldn't have destroyed everything decent in her! And Max would do whatever Nina said, he was a kind man. She would bring the child herself. Let them try not to take him!

It turned out you needed a pass to go to the Far East. Varya went to the 8th Division of the militia in Mogiltsevsky Alley, where she was told that she had to have an invitation properly filled out. They knew how to do that "there."

Varya immediately sent Maxim a telegram: "CONGRATULATIONS ON THE STATE DECORATION [the hell with them, it would make the telegram go faster]. I'M TAKING VACATION. QUICKLY SEND INVITATION FOR ME AND MY SON VANYA TO GET PASS. VARYA."

20

KLIMENT VOROSHILOV had never lived through a more frightening two months than those of the summer of 1938. For two months Voroshilov was not invited to meetings of the Politburo and Stalin did not respond to his telephone calls. Stalin called in only Shaposhnikov, chief of the General Staff, to report to him. Voroshilov could not sleep at night. He would get up and wander to the kitchen and drink cold water in slow sips to calm down. What would happen, what would happen? Would he be arrested and shot, as had tens of thousands of officers, as had almost the entire command of the Red Army, as had several configurations of the Politburo? Yet he had always agreed to these arrests and executions — executions of people he had not known at all and people he had known to be stalwart officers and talented leaders. Never once had he questioned a single arrest. On the contrary, he had demanded the harshest punishments in order to please Koba, to keep Koba happy. Ever since 1919, in Tsaritsyn, he had devoted his life to Koba and he served him faithfully and truly. He was the first, back in the twenties, to write about Comrade Stalin, the main organizer and commander of the Civil War, glorifying him in every speech and struggling against his enemies. And now they would come for him at night and throw him in prison where they would beat him and torture him and force him to sign things, and he, beloved by the people, hero of the Civil War, would go down in history as a traitor and spy. His wife and children would be tortured and then killed or sent to the camps where they would die felling wood.

A sob burst from his throat. Koba mocked him. "Don't let them in, if they come for you!" How could you not let them in? They'd break down the door and twist your arms. Shoot himself? Then they would announce that he had died of a heart attack and give him a funeral with honors in Red Square. They would leave his family alone. He would remain in the national memory as the person he really was — the first Red officer. And yet, how could he die in good health, strong and young? He was only fifty-five and could pass for forty-five or forty-seven. And he looked like that in his pictures, too. How could he die at the pinnacle of power when the whole country knew him! And now it was all over. Koba, Koba, you don't appreciate loyal men. With whom are you going to replace me — that idiot Budyonny? And for what? All right, he had acted rashly, but it was a trifle, not a crime. And no one but Koba and he knew about that conversation. Koba could forgive it. But he didn't.

The whole problem was that his wife, Ekaterina Davidovna, had gone off to the dacha, and he was home alone when the Kondratyevs called. They were passing through Moscow and he invited them to come by. He had invited Misha Kondratyev in the past, when he was in Moscow, and Ekaterina Davidovna always received him well and warmly. She knew that Misha Kondratyev had saved his life in 1919, when he took in the chest a White Guards' bullet meant for Voroshilov. Last year the Kondratyev daughter applied to Moscow University, and Ekaterina Davidovna had her in their house and helped her get into the university. But she never allowed Natalya in the house because she knew about the business in Tsaritsyn. Although it was nothing much, really. He was attracted to Natalya, but so was everyone else — she was like a flame. But she married Misha Kondratyev, who had been demobbed as an invalid after his heavy wounds. Klim lived in their place, as did other comrades, including Stalin, for instance. . . . They were good people. So Ekaterina Davidovna was wrong to hold anything against Natalya. But you can't change a woman. She was smart and educated, but Ekaterina Davidovna had a temper. They had a peaceful home, and he did not want any conflicts in the house, so he never invited Natalya. Misha was always in town alone. He worked in the banking system and came on business.

But this time he called and said they were both in Moscow. Voroshilov was home alone; Ekaterina Davidovna and the maid were at the dacha. This meant he could invite Natalya, too. Why not see his old comrades-in-arms, Communists, who were not in any opposition grouping, who had no relatives abroad, whose daughter was at Moscow

University and whose son was still a schoolboy? They were reliable people. Comrade Stalin himself knew them. He wanted to see what Natalya looked like twenty years later. And he wanted her to admire him, Marshal of the Soviet Union. It was hot — July — but he put on his full uniform with the decorations and medals because he knew it suited him and that people were used to him in it. Natalya must picture him this way from the official photographs, so this is the way she should see him, in all his glory.

Voroshilov opened the door. Misha had hardly changed at all from his last visit to Moscow, although his hair was gray. And how old was he? Just over forty. But Natalya brought an air of youth with her. She still had a wonderful figure. The Cossack women were like that, a figure eight with a big bosom and wide hips. And her eyes were still fiery black and her voice still had a singsong and enticing quality.

Voroshilov played the host in a restrained way and invited them to the table. They sat down, but they did not touch the vodka, wine, or *zakuski*. They came straight to the point. They had business with him. Their son, Sergei, was mentally ill. No one knew what caused it. They had taken him to specialists in Moscow and to local doctors, and they all agreed that he was incurable. He was a quiet boy, who just muttered under his breath, incomprehensible muttering. After spending a year in a psychiatric hospital, he was an outpatient now. He had been released two months ago and had started a job gluing cardboard boxes at a paper factory. They had a meeting and somebody said that Sergei had shouted "Down with Stalin!" He couldn't have shouted that because he was not interested in politics and he never shouted. He spoke softly and mumbled. And if he had said something wrong, people had to remember that he was mentally ill. Instead he was arrested and condemned to execution by shooting, "For calling for a terrorist act." The boy was only sixteen! So, Kliment Efremovich, please help us save our son!

Voroshilov knew that no one should help in a case like this. If the boy had really said, "Down with Stalin!" (it was terrifying even to think those words), then no one would intercede — not Vyshinsky, not Kalinin. It didn't matter if he were crazy or not, a boy or a man. Only Stalin could help in this case. And that could happen. Stalin knew the Kondratyevs. He had lived at their house. He knew Misha and he had his eye on Natalya. She was in her eighth month of pregnancy and that was the only thing that had saved her. Otherwise Koba would not have let her get away. Voroshilov wouldn't have to tell Stalin the words, "Down with Stalin!" He'd just say that the mentally ill boy had cried out something and they wanted to shoot him.

And so Voroshilov promised to help. Natalya had approached him beseechingly with her black eyes, which betrayed such devotion and suffering. Those eyes had rekindled so many memories — and Voroshilov wanted to look the all-powerful hero. He said, "All right, don't worry. I'll try to help. We'll settle it."

And they left full of hope. Voroshilov thought about it and realized that it had been a mistake. It was dangerous to get involved. He was sorry that Ekaterina Davidovna had not been home. If she had been home, he would not have asked the Kondratyevs to come and he would never have heard their story. It was all an accident. Another random event made things worse for Kliment Efremovich.

Voroshilov was in Stalin's office a few days later. Stalin was in a good mood, reminiscing about Tsaritsyn of all things, and Voroshilov suddenly asked, "Koba, do you remember the Kondratyevs?"

"Who?"

"You lived in their apartment in Tsaritsyn."

"A young couple, very assiduous, husband and wife?"

"That's right. Them."

"How are they?"

"Not bad. He's working at Stroibank and she's a principal of a technical school."

"Give them my regards."

"There's a terrible tragedy in their family."

"What?"

"Their son has been mentally ill since childhood. He spent a year in a mental hospital. He's out now, but he's still crazy."

"How can he be helped?"

"What is there to do? He's incurably ill. But they do need help. You see, he shouted out something at a meeting and he was arrested and condemned to death. The boy is only sixteen. He shouldn't have been let out of the hospital, but they released him."

"What did he yell?"

"Something . . . What can you expect from him? He's crazy."

Stalin raised his heavy eyes and looked at Voroshilov. "What exactly did he shout?"

"Koba, you know a madman can say almost anything."

Stalin kept staring at Voroshilov. "What exactly did he shout?"

"How should I know?" Voroshilov said nervously. "He's crazy."

"If you're trying to help him, you must know."

"It was a big hall." Voroshilov was sweating and cursing himself for ever getting involved. "It was noisy, no one could hear for sure, but two people say that he allegedly shouted . . . 'Down with Stalin!' "

Stalin looked away and after a while said, "We do not need madmen like that."

Later *he* checked — the boy had been shot. And that was right. Otherwise every terrorist would claim to be mad. And why hadn't that madman shouted, "Long live Comrade Stalin!" Why hadn't he imagined himself to be Stalin? They think they're Napoleon or Christ. No madman shouted "Down with Napoleon!" or "Down with Jesus Christ!" What a fool Voroshilov was — asking on behalf of him! Fool! And *he* allowed that fool to be near *him, he* promoted him, and the fool dared to petition *him* on such things! Making *him* think about such things. A Politburo member! Was he trying to show *him* what kind of things were shouted about Comrade Stalin at meetings?

Stalin refused to see Voroshilov for two months. Let him worry about his future, let him stew.

And that was all Voroshilov could do. He was not removed from his position as People's Commissar of Defense. He went to the office every day, had meetings of the collegium, received regional commanders, and gave orders. As a member of the government he participated in meetings of the Council of People's Commissars, and the other commissars, including Molotov and Kaganovich, listened to him as if nothing had changed. They continued sending him the documents that a Politburo member was supposed to receive. But Voroshilov knew the game Stalin played with a doomed man.

Voroshilov did not tell his children, but he did tell Ekaterina Davidovna. However, he told her he had been expecting Kondratyev alone but he brought his wife unexpectedly. Ekaterina Davidovna, a wise woman, paid no attention to this detail. She said that he should not panic. Whatever would be, would be. But she did agree that death was better than suffering and torture. If they came for him at home, they would shoot themselves. They both had pistols. If they came for him at work, he would shoot himself at the office, and she would kill herself at home. They would not involve the children. They were adults and would make their own decisions. She kissed him and told him that if she had to die, she would die peacefully, grateful for the life they had shared. She had been happy. Voroshilov wept on her breast. He loved her. She had never let him down. She did not try to get into the Kremlin high society. She took care of the house and the children and him. She selected books for him to read, accompanied him to the opera — they loved music — and collected records. She supported his interest in painting and took him to exhibits. She never reproached him for anything. There had been the case of the military specialists, and the Tukhachevsky case, and the other military leaders. She did not get involved. She said nothing. She was a good wife, a real wife! She almost never brought up politics, and when she did, she was always right on the button! And this time, she was right, too. What a woman!

On September 30, when Voroshilov came home for lunch as he usually did, Ekaterina Davidovna asked, "Do you know what happened in Munich?"

"There was something on the radio about some pact. Nothing in the papers, though."

"It will be in the papers tomorrow. Try to find out today. I think it is very serious. It may mean war. Now he won't be able to do without you."

Back at the office, Voroshilov learned that on the night of September 29, 1938, Hitler, Mussolini, Chamberlain, and Daladier — the leaders of Germany, Italy, Britain, and France — signed an agreement in Munich. Czechoslovakia had to turn over the Sudeten region and the regions bordering on it where Germans lived to Germany immediately and also satisfy the territorial pretensions of Poland and Hungary. Czechoslovakia lost a fifth of its territory, over a fourth of its population, half of its heavy industry, and powerful defense complexes to the west. Germany's new border was near Prague, the Czech capital.

By the time Voroshilov had finished reading the reports, he had a call from the Kremlin asking him urgently to come to a Politburo meeting.

Ekaterina Davidovna was right.

～ 21 ～

AT SIX O'CLOCK in the evening they met around a long table covered in green cloth in Stalin's spacious office. People's Commissar of Foreign Affairs Litvinov sat a bit apart from the others.

Stalin in a khaki military coat and khaki trousers stuffed into tall boots, strode around the office — not along the windows, as usual, but along the wall that now held not only a map of the U.S.S.R. but also a map of Europe. Assistants had drawn the new borders of Germany and Czechoslovakia and drawn stripes in the regions taken away from Czechoslovakia by Germany, Poland, and Hungary. Each time he passed the map, Stalin stopped and said angrily of Chamberlain and Daladier, "Traitors! Cowards! Cheap salesmen!" But he did not attack Hitler. Hitler took his own. How could he not take it when it practically leaped into his hands? But the Poles were bastards, they had grabbed Silesia. Spiders in a jar! And the Czechs were cowards.

Stalin greeted Voroshilov as usual, as if they had parted only yesterday. Voroshilov's heart was in his throat. It had passed! He was given his life. The worst was over. Stalin was no longer angry.

Later they went down one floor and continued talking over dinner. Zhdanov, an asthmatic, panted as he commented on the latest reports from foreign news agencies, translated into Russian.

"Representatives of Czechoslovakia waited all day in the reception area. They were received at one thirty in the morning. Hitler and Mussolini had already left. Chamberlain told the Czechs about the agreement and handed it to them to read. The Czech representative asked if they were expecting a reply from his government. The answer was rude: no reply necessary, the agreement was final. Czechoslovakia of the 1918 borders no longer existed. And then . . . Listen to this!" Zhdanov looked around to make sure they were listening. "During his conversation with the Czechs, Chamberlain kept yawning."

"Typical British haughtiness," Stalin said. "I saw a newspaper photo of that Chamberlain. He's very, very tall, and skinny, bony, with a tiny, tiny little head. He looks like a prehistoric animal. I forgot how it's called . . ."

"Pterodactyl," Zhdanov prompted.

"Exactly." Stalin turned toward the *zakuski*.

The table was set with cognac and vodka, smoked sturgeon, caviar, mushrooms, bread, greens, and spices, but no sausages, ham, or canned meats. Stalin did not eat them. Khrushchev jabbed a cornichon pickle with his fork and held it up to Andreyev: "Like Chamberlain's head." Everyone laughed. Like the other Politburo members, Voroshilov put a few pieces of food on his plate, but he did not dare fill his wineglass. Stalin narrowed his eyes at him and laughed. "Even marshals can have a glass of wine."

Voroshilov beamed gratefully and poured himself some wine.

Another table held large tureens of soup and a pile of clean bowls. They served themselves. Stalin lifted the lids of all the tureens and spoke to himself as he checked, "Ah, cabbage soup . . . And bullion here. And fish soup . . . Let's have some fish soup."

Then the waiters brought in the main course. Afterward they had tea, pouring boiling water from a large samovar and tea from a pot on a warmer.

Stalin was still wearing the uniform, but he had changed his boots to soft glove leather ones, a light color with red designs. There was another map of Europe in his apartment, also showing the new borders. Just as in his office, Stalin kept going over to the map and cursing the "Munichiners," Chamberlain and Daladier, Britain and France.

They met again in Stalin's office the next evening at six o'clock and then finished up with dinner in his apartment. By this time they had new information. The people of Prague had filled the streets, demanding that the army be kept at the old borders and that a general draft be declared. People wept. However, on October first, the government of Czechoslovakia announced on the radio that it was capitulating. The same day German troops crossed the border and entered Czech territory.

The Politburo members unleashed their fury on Litvinov.

Molotov was particularly angry. He did not like Litvinov because he was the only one who behaved independently in the Politburo. Now he had an opportunity to get rid of him. So, Molotov said, this is what Litvinov's bias toward Britain and France has led to, his blind faith in those imperialist predators! Of course, Comrade Litvinov had lived in England for many years and considers himself a man of British culture. He speaks English better than Russian and his wife is an Englishwoman, but is that any reason for such a shortsighted policy? These are bourgeois reasons, not Party reasons. And, Molotov added significantly, at best these are bourgeois reasons.

Kaganovich, his cold blue eyes regarding Litvinov with hatred, accused him of overlooking the interests of the Soviet Union in his desire for cheap popularity with the Western bourgeoisie. Why hadn't he foreseen Munich? Why hadn't he warned the Party leadership? Ruthless conclusions had to be drawn regarding Litvinov and his apparat.

The cautious Mikoyan lowered the heat of passion by a few degrees. He spoke of the trade situation between the U.S.S.R. and the West and said that the German side was stalling on signing a mutual trade and credit agreement.

Voroshilov, still reeling from his months of fear, joined the general chorus. Casting meek looks at Stalin, he read out data on Soviet and Czech armed forces. Against 43 German divisions, the U.S.S.R. and Czechoslovakia could immediately launch 133 divisions. That was almost three times as many and Hitler would certainly be defeated. But instead of instilling confidence among the Czechs in the formidable Soviet support, Litvinov was flirting with Britain and France while they made a pact with Germany behind his back.

Litvinov remained calm. Yes, Britain and France were trying to appease Hitler through betrayal. Their hopes were unfounded. Hitler had far-reaching plans. And with new German aggression they would understand that Hitler had to be stopped before they became his victims. Therefore, they could not lose an ally like the U.S.S.R. The situation was difficult but not impossible. They must not lose their heads. The Munich Pact had powerful enemies in the West. When Chamberlain returned to London, he announced, "I have secured peace in our time." And Winston Churchill replied, "We have suffered a total and crushing defeat. And we must not think that it will end here. This is only the beginning." And he was not the only one to think this way. This was the prevalent opinion in Europe.

"You think that Hitler will attack the U.S.S.R.?" Molotov interrupted.

"Britain and France seem like easier enemies than the U.S.S.R. If Hitler starts a European war, he will attack them first."

"You are lowering our vigilance," Kaganovich said roughly. "In whose interests?"

"I have no other interests besides the interests of my country and my Party," Litvinov replied.

"Empty words!" Kaganovich barked and turned his back.

Stalin spoke at the end of the last session. But the Politburo did not hear what they had expected. "Britain and France," said Stalin, "are pushing Hitler into aggression against the Soviet Union. Japan has joined the anti-Soviet alliance and the U.S.S.R. is in very dangerous political isolation."

He stood up and paced the room, along the windows, as usual, looking out on the lights of the Kremlin and Moscow as he spoke. "What should be undertaken in these conditions? Comrade Litvinov assures us that Hitler will attack the Western states. This variant is not impossible, but the Western states must understand this first." Stalin stopped in front of Litvinov and pointed at him. "If you, Comrade Litvinov, are certain that the Hitlerite aggression will begin with France and Britain, then you must persuade the leaders of France and Britain of that. That is the main task of our diplomacy today."

Litvinov and the staff of the Foreign Ministry worked diligently in compliance with Stalin's directive.

However, Comrade Stalin understood the main task of Soviet diplomacy to be something else.

The Munich Pact revealed the weakness of Britain and France and their fear of Hitler. And that would push Hitler to attack the "eternal enemy," France, and the hated England. Litvinov was right about that. But Hitler would attack them only if he had a friendly or at least neutral Soviet Union behind him. Litvinov did not understand that and he would not further closeness between the U.S.S.R. and Germany. Others were doing that for him. Let Litvinov run negotiations with France and England, soothing their vigilance.

Naturally, Hitler would be pleased by the removal of the Jew Litvinov. *He* would do it when *his* relations with Hitler were at the right point. But *he* would not destroy him. It was not clear how things would turn out and Litvinov might still be useful. He had a good reputation in Britain and the United States, so let him go on persuading them. The real policy, *his* policy, would be carried out by others. Kandelaki, the trade representative in Germany, was negotiating secretly. And he reported not to Litvinov, but to *him* directly. And now Molotov had to be brought in on the secret negotiations.

22

LENA CALLED. "Varya, if you can, come over quickly. As quickly as you can."

"I'll be right there."

Varya hung up and went to see Igor Vladimirovich.

"I have to leave," she said.

Igor Vladimirovich looked at her in disbelief. There were due at the Moscow City Council in an hour. Varya was preparing the materials for his report and she was to go with him, as usual.

"I have an urgent matter at home," Varya said. "I'll give the blueprints to Lyova and explain everything to him. He'll go with you. All right?"

"All right, let's have Lyova then," said Igor Vladimirovich.

It turned out that Lena and everyone else in her communal apartment had been given orders to leave Moscow within three days. They asked her where she wanted to go and Lena said Michurinsk, as Varya had recommended.

"Not Michurinsk." Then she said Ufa. She simply couldn't think of any other city. They wrote down Ufa and gave her a ticket.

"I have a child."

"How old?"

"Eighteen months."

"No separate ticket needed."

And the day after tomorrow she was supposed to go to Ufa and report to the local NKVD. Her maid Masha was let go and transferred to Metrostroi, the subway building department, where she would have a dormitory bed. Lena wanted to notarize a power of attorney for Masha, giving her permission to find out which orphanage her brother,

Vladlen, was eventually sent to. But she was not sure that could be done.

"Do you want me to go to the distribution center and find out about Vladlen?"

"Varya, they won't tell a stranger. That's the rule. Masha can at least show them her passport and show that she had lived with us both at the old place on Granovsky Street and here. That might help."

"All right, let her do it," Varya said. "But let's sit down for a bit. I want to talk to you."

They sat down. "I'm glad you're going to Ufa. When you find Sasha, he'll be able to help you."

"No. I won't look for Sasha. I don't want to get him in trouble. You know they must have a reason for letting you choose the city. They're not humanitarians, you know. I think they want to find out where our relatives are so that they can start a new round of arrests and exiles."

"Up to you. But you can't take Vanya with you. If they arrest you there, he'll perish. And if they don't, both of you will."

Lena looked up at her. "What are you proposing?"

"Tell me, haven't you ever wondered whom Nina married and where she was living?"

"It wasn't hard to guess, Varya. She married Max and went off to live with him."

"Right. At the battle of Lake Khasan, Max was made a Hero of the Soviet Union."

"Really?" Lena grew animated. "I'm so happy for him. He was a good man. Simple and modest. Sasha really liked him. Thank God, he's survived."

"I propose," Varya said, "that you leave Vanya with me. And I'll take him out to Nina and Max. They will adopt him. He will be safe with them. We'll save the child. You'll know that he's alive and you'll know where he is. And if your circumstances change for the better, you can work it out with them. If necessary, I'll go get him and bring him to you."

Lena lowered her head. She thought for a long time, and then asked, "Will they take him?"

"Don't doubt it for a minute. I'll take care of everything. I've already wired them to send me and the child an invitation so that we can get travel documents. I'm due for a vacation at work. I'll take care of Vanya until the paperwork is done. Sofya Alexandrovna will help me. Just pack his things now."

Lena still sat with her head down. Her mother and father had been shot, her brother was in a NKVD orphanage, and now she had to give up her son, forever, probably. And she had to face the end her parents faced. Let her son survive at least.

God, where did this courageous and selfless girl come from to help her? How did she survive this vicious, bloody world?

"I'll give you Nina's address," Varya said. "But don't write it down and don't write to them. Memorize it. They're in the army. If you cause them trouble, your son will suffer for it. You'll have to correspond through me. Write to me at poste restante. That's reliable and safe."

"All right."

Lena smiled sadly. Then she looked at Varya. "You are so good! Do you know that?"

23

ON JANUARY 13, 1939, the correspondents accredited in Berlin reported on the opening of the new building of the imperial Reichstag. They described its size, many times greater than the former Reichstag, reported on the huge marble columns and the marble slabs that paved the inner courtyard, on the massive five-meter-high doors, and on the gallery that led to the main hall, which on Hitler's orders was twice as big as the gallery in the palace of Versailles. The colossal office was decorated with a bronze sculpture, as large as a man, of a sword half out of its sheath. That sword, Hitler allegedly said, would instill fear in diplomats. The new Reichstag was opened with a large reception for the diplomatic corps.

But the main item in the newspapers was the fact that during the reception Hitler made a point of speaking with Soviet ambassador Merekalov for a long time. After Hitler, Ribbentrop and General Keitel approached Merekalov. The Soviet ambassador found himself the center of attention.

Merekalov was cautious in his report back to Moscow: "Hitler said hello, asked about life in Berlin, about my trip to Moscow, said he knew about my meeting in Moscow with the German ambassador Schulenburg, and wished me success." Merekalov's caution did not surprise Stalin. Merekalov was not aware of the secret contacts, and he also was not very good at German, while Hitler had spoken without an interpreter. But the significance of the fact was clear. Hitler was sending Stalin a signal — he knew about the secret negotiations, he approved, and was ready to improve the relations between the U.S.S.R. and Germany.

Confirmation of this was the cessation of attacks in the German press on the leaders of the Soviet Union.

But an even more important confirmation came in the report laid on Stalin's desk from the anti-fascist group of Schultz and Boisen within the German Aviation Ministry. On the morning of March 8, Hitler gave a speech to the higher generals and admirals and ordered them to occupy the rest of Czechoslovakia no later than March 15; and by autumn, when the roads would be washed out, to occupy Poland; and in 1940–41, to wipe the "eternal enemy" France from the face of the earth and establish sovereignty over England, capturing its wealth and possessions all over the world.

Stalin could congratulate himself. His prognosis was correct. Hitler was aiming at France. Now it was up to him. Stalin's response came in his speech at the Eighteenth Party Congress, which he gave two days later, on March 10, 1939.

In preparing for the Eighteenth Congress, Stalin paid greatest attention to the composition of the Central Committee, which was to be reelected. He took the list of the Central Committee members from the Seventeenth Congress, crossed out those who had been executed, which was the majority, put a heavy X next to those who were doomed to be shot, and drew circles around some names, like nooses, and lowered them from the list to the list of candidates. Then he put nooses around some names on the list of candidates and pulled them up to the list of members. Then, based on his own calculations, he added new names.

And he dictated an addition to his speech at the Eighteenth Party Congress. Noting that Britain and France had not repulsed Germany, Stalin said, "The main reason . . . is the desire not to interfere in Germany's involvement in a war with the Soviet Union, to let all the participants become entangled in the swamps of war, to let them weaken and exhaust each other, and then, when they are weak enough, to appear on the scene with their fresh forces and dictate terms to the weakened participants of the war. Cheap and easy! . . . However, it is necessary to note that this dangerous political game could end up as a serious failure for them."

They understood Stalin's reply in Berlin.

On March 15, German troops entered Prague. Czekhia was annexed into the German empire as the "Protectorate of Bohemia and Moravia." After that, German troops took the Lithuanian port Klaipeda (Memel).

On March 23, Madrid fell, and Republican Spain was defeated. The open military conflict between the U.S.S.R. and Germany on Spanish soil had ended.

Thus, the road to an alliance with Hitler was cleared. But an alliance with fascist Germany? The political repercussions of such a step had to be minimized.

The people? The people were not a political power. They became a political power only in the hands of a political leader. Resistance to this sharp turnaround could come only if there were a political opposition in the country. There was none. It had been destroyed, eradicated forever. *He* led the people, and the people were used to *his* unexpected turns and maneuvers. The Party was in *his* hands — a lever of incredible strength and obedience, ready to turn instantly in whatever direction necessary. The people were merely subjects of the state.

The West? The reaction in the West would be ambiguous. The bourgeoisie would be hysterical and so would the social democrats. The Communists? The Communist Party was in *his* hands. They lived on Soviet gold. The opponents of *his* course would be found among the Western intelligentsia. Of course, they would need a leader. And there was such a leader. Trotsky. He had a name, the glory of being a hero of the October Revolution, and he personified socialism, which the Western intelligentsia wanted so badly. And most important, Trotsky has been predicting an alliance between Stalin and Hitler over and over, and in the eyes of Western workers and intellectuals, who were not sophisticated in the ways of major politics, he would appear to be right. In his latest works, Trotsky wrote:

> The fall of Czechoslovakia is the fall of Stalin's policies. . . . Now Soviet diplomacy will try to have a rapprochement with Hitler — at the cost of new retreats and capitulations. . . . The rapprochement of Stalin and Hitler is very likely. . . . Having destroyed the Party and beheaded the army, Stalin is openly declaring his candidacy as Hitler's chief agent.

What a bastard! He understood the necessity for political maneuvers, yet he poured such filth on *him*. It would not be hard to predict how Trotsky would howl with glee when *his* pact with Hitler took place and that miserable Fourth International turned into a major force. You could not deny Trotsky his political sense. He knew his future chances very well.

The destruction of Trotsky was turning from revenge to the liquidation of a dangerous foe. Now instead of Slutsky and Speigelglass, Sudoplatov and Eitingon were handling this at the NKVD. Beria assured *him* that they were preparing the operation thoroughly. Too slowly! *He* had to talk with those men.

Eitingon was away. Beria arrived with Sudoplatov. Stalin knew him. Two years ago he had come to see him about Ukrainian affairs. He was nervous then. Now Sudoplatov seemed more confident.

He made a gesture inviting them to sit down. They sat on either side of the long table. Stalin paced the room and spoke softly.

"You, of course, know how much evil Trotsky has caused our people. His cohorts suffered a deserved punishment. But their leader? Alive and well." Stalin stopped talking and walked from corner to corner. Sudoplatov looked over at Beria and Beria shook his head almost imperceptibly. The pause did not mean that Comrade Stalin had finished speaking. He would continue. "Trotsky has been abroad for ten years. Can it be that no one could disarm him in ten years? Of course they could. They did not want to. Sabotage! The guilty will pay dearly for this. But we cannot wait any longer. In the present international situation we cannot put up with this any longer. War is coming. Trotsky has become a helpmeet of fascism. Trotskyites are infiltrating the leftist movement, disorganizing it, and thereby weakening the assistance the progressive forces could give to the Soviet Union. We must strike a blow against the Fourth International. How? By removing its head."

Stalin stopped in front of Sudoplatov, looked at him with his heavy eyes, and said harshly, "Trotsky must be liquidated within the year. I hope you will be able to manage this. Go to Mexico. All the necessary conditions will be created for you and you will get all the help you need."

Sudoplatov rose to reply.

"Sit!" Stalin ordered.

Sudoplatov sank back down in his chair, but even seated he spoke as if he were at attention. "Comrade Stalin! We will do everything to fulfill your command. However, I should not go to Mexico. I do not speak Spanish and I will attract unnecessary attention."

"What about Eitingon?"

"That was what we had planned, Comrade Stalin. Comrade Eitingon will head the operation locally."

"What kind of a man is he?"

"He is forty. An experienced intelligence officer, reliable, quick-witted, tough. Party member since 1919. Graduate of the military academy, worked with Comrade Dzerzhinsky. Acquitted himself very well in Spain. Fluent in English, German, French, and Spanish."

"What is the plan of operation?"

"There are several versions planned. The final decision will be made in place. What they all have in common is that it will be carried out by a Communist who has been trained in the Soviet Union and who fought in Spain."

"Well then," Stalin said, "go ahead! Spare no expense. Bear in mind" — and he regarded Sudoplatov once more — "the liquidation of Trotsky is an assignment from the Central Committee of our Party." He extended his hand. "I wish you success. Good-bye!"

Stalin and Beria were left alone.

"What do you have?" Stalin asked. Beria put down a sheet of paper in front of him. It was a denunciation by someone from the Foreign Ministry stating that in a private conversation Litvinov spoke negatively about the foreign policy actions of the leaders of the Party and the government.

Knowing Litvinov, Stalin could believe that Litvinov would dare do that. And in general, it was time to move on to broader negotiations with the Germans. Litvinov was not suitable for that.

Of course, *he* had not forgotten how Litvinov had saved *him* in London from the drunken dockers. Of course, *he* valued the fact that in the intervening thirty years Litvinov had never told anyone about it. But there is a limit to gratitude. The head of state cannot have personal friends. *He* has the great work *he* is doing. And people are divided into those who help *him* do it and those who get in the way. Too bad that Comrade Litvinov did not understand that. That lack of understanding cost many people their lives. However, Litvinov's life must be saved. Litvinov might still come in handy.

In the corner of the denunciation, Stalin wrote, "Into the file." He returned the paper to Beria and said, "Do not touch Litvinov yet. But I must know his every word. Wherever he may have said it."

On May 3, Litvinov was removed from the post of Commissar of Foreign Affairs and replaced by Molotov, who remained Chairman of the Council of People's Commissars. Malenkov and Beria were present that night during the process of removing Litvinov and installing Molotov.

Beria's presence was not accidental. By the summer of 1939 they had arrested five of Litvinov's deputies, 48 ambassadors, 140 staff members of the Foreign Ministry, and the majority of workers in Soviet embassies abroad. Some embassies were completely destroyed. New people were called in to handle Stalin's new foreign policy.

～ 24 ～

THEY HAD TWO HOURS before classes started, and Sasha and Gleb went to the post office to pick up their mail. Gleb's aunt wrote rarely, but Sasha had a letter from his mother, a calm letter. Sasha had sent her money several times, and she always scolded him for it, worried that he was depriving himself. But she was gradually accepting the thought that Sasha tried to instill in her. Everything was fine and he was staying in Ufa because he had a fine apartment and was making better money.

Sasha stood by the window and read his mother's letter. Gleb was chatting up the girls on the other side of the counter. He knew them all because they had taken dancing lessons last year. It had been a good group and lots of fun. Just then a tall woman in a black coat and dark gray beret approached the pickup window and showed her passport. Sasha thought there was something familiar in the face he had glimpsed and he kept staring at her. She stood looking down while the post office girl flipped through the letters in the box while holding her passport open in her other hand. She closed the passport and returned it. No mail.

The woman straightened and turned. My God, it was Lena Budyagina!

"Lena!"

Still beautiful with a matte, elongated face and slightly curved lips, she had what Nina Ivanova used to call a "Levantine profile." But the eyes were weary and there was something new, something grim about them.

She looked up at him. That familiar look reminded him of their class, their school, their gang. He could smell the Arbat.

"Hello, Sasha. I'm happy to see you."

She spoke calmly. There was no surprise at meeting so unexpectedly. Yet they had not seen each other in five years. Could she have known he was in Ufa?

Gleb joined them. He smiled at Lena, his white teeth flashing. Lena smiled at last. A polite smile, not shy, as it used to be. Sasha introduced them. Lena was a schoolmate, a friend of his childhood and youth. Gleb was his best friend.

They walked down the street together. Sasha asked her about Moscow, about their friends, and how long she had been in Ufa. She answered briefly. She came to Ufa six months ago. Friends? Max was in the army, Nina was married and moved away. Vadim seemed to be in Moscow. She was reserved, she did not use surnames, and she did not mention Sharok even though he was the father of her baby. She did not say where Nina had gone even though she was in the Far East with Max, which Sasha knew from his mother. And Max was a Hero of the Soviet Union. That was in the papers, yet Lena did not specify about which Max she was talking, nor did she mention her parents or how she had ended up in Ufa.

They reached the bus stop. "Which one do you need?" Sasha asked.

She looked at the sign. There were three routes. After a pause, she replied, "It doesn't matter."

It had to matter. They went in different directions.

"Why don't you give me your address, I'll drop by," Sasha offered.

"No, I live quite far. I could visit you, or we could meet somewhere. It's spring and it's warm now."

"All right. Write down my address."

"I'll remember it."

He gave her his address and they agreed on a day and time. Lena got in the next bus.

"Pretty," Gleb said thoughtfully. "Careful."

"She was the prettiest girl in school," Sasha said. "Careful? Who isn't careful nowadays? She knows I was arrested five years ago and exiled, and now she suddenly sees me in Ufa. She doesn't know what my situation is now."

He trusted Gleb with everything. But with his own things, not someone else's. Maybe Lena was living under a different surname. She might have gotten married. He wouldn't tell Gleb anything about her yet.

"Dearie, she was being so careful because of me. And she's right. How does she know who I am? We could have run off from Siberia together for all she knows. She got away from us on the first bus that came along. I'm not criticizing her. On the contrary, I'm impressed that at least someone from your school grew up more clever than you."

"Fine then," Sasha said. "Let's take a look at the newspaper."

"What's to see? It's all about the Congress."

But he stopped with Sasha at the billboard that displayed the day's newspapers.

The papers had been full for days with reports on the Eighteenth Party Congress. All the same, all the same. . . . Reports, speeches, greetings, words in honor of Comrade Stalin, and stormy applause.

But here was the speech by the writer Mikhail Sholokhov. Sasha read it and brought it to Gleb's attention. "Take a look at this."

Gleb started reading. " 'Soviet literature, having purged itself of its enemies, has become healthier and stronger. . . . We are rid of spies, fascist intelligence agents, and enemies of every stripe, but all those vile creatures were not really people. . . . They were parasites sucking on the living, full-blooded body of Soviet literature. . . . Now cleansed, our writers' milieu has profited from it.' I can't go on," said Gleb. "It makes me sick. Let's go!"

"Read it. The country must know its heroes."

" 'The way it is, and will be, comrades, is that in joy and in sorrow we always mentally turn to him, the creator of our life. For all the profound human modesty of Comrade Stalin, he will have to tolerate our outpourings of love and loyalty to him [applause], because not only we, who live and work under his direction, but all the working people in our land, tie their hopes for a radiant future for mankind to his name. [Applause].' Listen, why should I read this? Let's go!" Gleb repeated.

"All right, all right. But what do you think?"

"He's a flunky!"

"But he wrote *The Quiet Don,* a great novel."

"In the twenties there was doubt about his authorship. They even had a special commission to investigate."

"I heard something about that."

"Akimov told me. The real author was some White officer. But no one would acknowledge that. Don't be silly, dearie! Here they had a man of the people to take credit. If *The Quiet Don* is a work of genius, the author cannot be a flunky. As your beloved Pushkin said, dearie, genius and evil are incompatible."

"Not every genius can overcome fear. And Sholokhov is no genius."

"Trampling executed comrades is what you call fear?"

"Yes, it is fear."

"No, dearie, it's just our Russian flunky spirit at work. A flunky bows down to his master and will gladly beat another flunky to death at his master's wish. We're all flunkies, from top to bottom. The entire 'great Soviet people' that you intellectuals talk about with such reverence."

"The intellectuals are bad, the people are bad. And who are you, then?"

"Me, dearie, I'm a flunky like the rest. I'll tell you about something I saw with my own eyes. Would you like to hear it?"

25

SASHA LAUGHED. "Go on. You always have a suitable story."

"Just listen to this. It was around 1929 or 1930, when I was in love with a very nice girl, a village schoolteacher. I used to come visit her. She told people I was her brother since we have the same patronymic — both our fathers were Vassily. We spent the night frolicking in bed, of course, we were good at that, and in the daytime I went out into the woods and fields with my sketchbook and easel. A country idyll. The locals treated me with benign condescension, you know the way a man of the land treats a city man with an easel — a rich man's folly sort of thing. Well, one morning we were sleeping — it had been a busy night — when there was a lot of noise outside. What was it? She got up and went to the window. She shifted the curtain and said, 'They're dekulakizing the Golodukhins.' Actually, dearie, they were all Golodukhins there. The village used to be called Golodukhino. It was changed later to a more modern name, 'Threat to Imperialism.'"

"Come off it!"

"I swear. This impoverished little communal farm, but they called it Threat to Imperialism. Really scary."

"It's a joke!"

"But that's not the point of my story. The point is that everybody had the same surname in the village — Golodukhin. They were all relatives, near or far, but relatives. And now they were arresting some Golodukhins for being kulaks, rich and exploiting peasants. Naturally I pulled on my pants and made for the door. This was something to see. But Klavka said, 'Don't go, there's militia and all kinds of officials. You're not a local. They'll pick on you and ask for your papers. And the villagers will say he comes to stay with our teacher, Klavdia Vassilyevna, and I don't want that. Watch from here, you can see everything from this spot.'

"I stood where she told me and I saw two wagons near a house, and the militiamen dragging women, children, and old people out. The homeowners weren't resisting. They knew that resisting would be added to the other charges. The women were throwing their things, their pathetic belongings, into the wagon. There was a very old granny who couldn't walk. The militia had hauled her out of her bed and carried her to the wagon and tossed her in. There was an infant and the other kids were small, too. Crying, wailing, shouting, I tell you, it was a horrible, revolting picture. People were being torn out of their home, their nest robbed, and sent to Siberia, to their deaths in fact."

Gleb stopped and walked on in silence. Then he went on. "But the main thing, dearie, is this. There were men and women watching, standing in silence, even the children were quiet. And they were all Golodukhins, just like the miserable family being deported. They were relatives, in-laws, godparents. They had lived all their lives together. And this wickedness was happening before their eyes, and it was being done by some scrawny official in a jacket and skinny militiamen. And from the way those strong healthy and grim peasants and the strong women were watching, and from the readiness on their faces, I thought they would attack those weaklings, beat them up, throw them in the wagon, lash the horses, and send them packing out of the village. I was waiting for that. But no. . . . The militiamen had the whole family out of the house and in the wagon. The women were wailing and the children were howling, and then the militiamen flicked the whip at the horses and off they all went. . . . And then, dearie, the whole crowd went into action. Not to catch up with them, not to save their kin — no, they rushed into the house to grab up what was left, what those poor wretches couldn't take with them. And then our kind, pitying women walked out all happy and pleased, with their children, carrying pots or plates or a hearth grate they pulled out of the stove with the wires still dangling. They were in a hurry to loot before the chairman of the village Soviet sealed the shamed and robbed house. I was nineteen or twenty then. And at that moment I realized that our people were flunkies, from the peasant to that flunky writer Sholokhov, from a simple peasant woman to a Politburo member who will admit to being a spy or saboteur if ordered to do so. And everything that those Dostoyevskys and other philosophers write about our special soul, our special mission, our special significance — it's all bull! Tutchev's line 'Russia cannot be understood by the mind . . . ,' that's all poetic malarkey, poetic fantasy."

"Did the whole village take part in that?" Sasha asked.

"Not the whole village, of course, but what does that matter?"

"A lot. A gang of looters is not the people. Every country has its bandits."

"Then why didn't the 'good people' come to defend their neighbor?"

"Did you? Did you defend him?"

"Dearie, I'm a flunky like the rest."

"Then don't expect more from others! Especially from the peasants, who were put down all throughout history, who were robbed, exploited by the landowners, overseers, their fellow flunkies, Cossacks with knouts, soldiers with rifles, agitators and commissars with Mausers, and the ones who gave orders for dekulakizing and the ones who carried out the orders. But we don't blame them, that's too dangerous, and we want to live and dance and drink and eat."

"Speaking of eating," Gleb said as they passed the restaurant. "Let's drop in."

"We just had lunch. Why don't you just admit it? You want a drink."

Gleb laughed. "All right, dearie, let's have a drink before classes start."

Sasha looked at his watch. "Not enough time. Let's get it over with and then go out for a drink."

"Fine, if we must," Gleb said. "Until this evening then. But there's something I want to say to you. You scolded me, but what about you?"

"I'm just like you. But no matter how bad I am, I'm not going to blame exhausted, cowed, and deceived people for my behavior. I don't despise them. I despise myself."

Gleb walked on in silence for a while and then he said, "I'm not talking that way about our people because I'm a German or some other foreigner. No, dearie, I'm a pure Russian. We're allowed to be proud of that now. Patriotism is in fashion. All those movies like *Alexander Nevsky, Minin and Pozharsky,* and *Peter the Great,* why do you think they're being made? To inculcate patriotism, and Russian patriotism at that, dearie. I'll tell you something else, and only you. I'm from the nobility, an ancient line. My ancestors took Kazan and Astrakhan with

Ivan the Terrible, and crossed the Alps with Suvorov to fight Napoleon. We have mayors and Decembrists, landowners and People's Will radicals among us, all kinds, but no Germans. Our line did get weaker. We married with merchants and turned into intelligentsia instead of aristocrats. We started getting university degrees, and there were professors and artists among us, so no one has guessed about my nobility, thank God. But I don't consider my aristocracy to be anything important, dearie. There was a document from the sixteenth or seventeenth century, a relative showed it to me, and our ancestor the boyar signed it to the tsar this way, 'Your faithful flunky Ivashka, son of . . .' et cetera. Can you imagine a French or German nobleman signing that way! . . . That's typically Russian. They were all flunkies then, even the boyars, and that's why we're like this now."

"Don't tell fairy tales about the French and Germans. They've got a lot on their consciences, too. Think how free the Germans were after the war, what democrats! And they saddled themselves with Hitler, through free elections at that. They rushed from the Kaiser to freedom, and as soon as they had a whiff of freedom, they hurried back under the knout. So don't set up others as a model. And don't tar all our people with the same brush."

They reached the Palace of Labor. Gleb took the doorknob in his hand but did not open the door. Unexpectedly, he said, "That school friend of yours, Lena, she's interesting."

"You usually say 'Madonna *colossale*' in these cases," Sasha chuckled.

"No," Gleb replied thoughtfully. "This is something more significant."

26

MOLOTOV WAS A SLOW THINKER, *he* mused. He could be too late, but there could be no lateness. Hitler intended to occupy Poland before the autumn mud on the roads, which meant he had to regularize his relations with the Soviet Union. Now not *he,* Stalin, but Hitler would be looking for ways to agreement and making concessions. *He* would not force Hitler to humiliate himself. A man does not forget humiliation, and at the very first opportunity, he takes his revenge. But *he* would show Hitler that *he* understands his moves. This would be a negotiation between the leaders of two of the most powerful nations, between people whose interests coincide.

The U.S.S.R. and Germany against Britain and France. *He* had predicted this ten years ago and now it had come to pass. Hitler would destroy Poland in a month or two. But if France and England were to get into a war with Hitler, that would be for a long time. The Great War lasted four years, and this one would be longer. They would exhaust themselves in the struggle, and in the meantime the U.S.S.R. would become the most awesome military power in Europe, and *he* would dictate *his* will to an exhausted Europe.

On *his* orders the counselor of the Soviet embassy in Berlin, Astakhov, visited the German Ministry of Foreign Affairs and had a conversation that boiled down to the fact that in questions of foreign policy, Germany and the Soviet Union had no contradictions.

A week later the German ambassador, Schulenburg, told Molotov, "It is time to improve relations between Germany and the U.S.S.R. In the resolution of the Polish question, Russian interests will be taken into consideration. Britain cannot and does not want to help the U.S.S.R.

Rather, Britain will force the U.S.S.R. to pull its chestnuts from the fire." That was a good statement. But in Berlin, Astakhov was told, "If the U.S.S.R. wants to get on the side of Germany's enemies, the German government is prepared to become an enemy."

That had a threatening sound. That *he* would not allow. Hitler was nervous. There were only three months remaining before the attack on Poland, but he had to keep his nerves in check. Hitler was an hysteric. After Hindenburg swore him in as chancellor of Germany, he wept. Such a sensitive kraut. And he wrote in *Mein Kampf* that when he learned of the November 1918 revolution in Germany, he also wept. Touched by his return to his homeland, he wept when he arrived in Vienna after Austria was annexed to Germany. Crocodile tears, of course. He did not drink or smoke and was a vegetarian. And he calmly sent thousands of people to die. An unbalanced personality. But he would have to weigh his words with *him*.

Stalin ordered Molotov to break off political negotiations with Germany and to demand that the U.S.S.R. and Germany first sign a trade agreement. Molotov was a master of such tactics. Dragging things out, backpedaling — that was his element, his nature. In June and July all German attempts to continue political negotiations came up against Molotov's cool restraint and demands for the signing of a trade agreement. And it was only on July 22 that the Soviet press could publish the announcement, "Negotiations on trade and credits between the German and Soviet sides have been resumed."

And finally, five days after that, Astakhov sent a report on his talk with the leading German diplomat, Snure, which took place on July 25 in Berlin, in a private room at the fashionable restaurant Evest. They must have had a good meal. Diplomats like sophisticated food. They're gourmands, and they eat and drink at government expense.

Snure stated, in the name of the Führer, "The German policy is directed against Britain. That is the decisive factor. From our side there can be no talk at all of a threat to the Soviet Union. Despite all the differences in worldview, there is a common point in the ideologies of Germany, Italy, and the Soviet Union — resistance to capitalist democracy. What can England offer Russia? Not a single goal that suits Russia. What can we offer? An understanding of mutual interests that will be beneficial to both sides."

His tactic was the right one. Hitler's main worry was that Stalin would come to terms with England. But what was Hitler offering concretely?

Stalin dictated a telegram to Astakhov. "If the Germans are sincerely changing the guard and truly want to improve relations with the U.S.S.R., they must tell us how they concretely visualize this improvement. Things depend entirely on the Germans here."

Molotov would sign the telegram. But this was not the telegram of a diplomat. It was Stalin's text. Hitler would understand.

Hitler understood, and Hitler was in a rush. This was the reply: "From the Baltic Sea to the Black Sea, there will be no problem. There is enough space on the Baltic for both states. The question with Poland will be regularized by the Germans within a week. If the Russians wish it, Germany will sign an agreement with them on the fate of Poland."

On August 7 an intelligence report was placed on Stalin's desk. "Starting August 20, must consider the beginning of military action against Poland."

The next day Voroshilov appeared with an urgent report. "In Mongolia, in the region of the Khalkhin-Gol River, the Japanese have concentrated troops under General Kamatsubara for a general attack."

The threat of war on two fronts, which Stalin had feared most of all, was becoming a reality.

"You will report on Khalkhin-Gol as events develop," he said. "How are the negotiations with the British and French military representatives?"

"The negotiations begin tomorrow. The main difficulty is that Poland refuses to allow our troops to pass through its territory. We can't beg Poland on our knees to accept our help, after all."

"England and France," Stalin said, "are counting on Hitler's wanting to attack the U.S.S.R. once he occupies Poland because he will be tempted by the proximity. They do not think about the fact that Hitler could attack them, instead of us. Well, let's try to convince them one more time. Let's see what your negotiations with their military representatives will yield. I doubt that they will become wiser."

He spoke with a strong Georgian accent and chopped at the desk with his hand.

"Start negotiating, stand firm, and we'll see," Stalin concluded.

27

THE INVITATION CAME QUICKLY. Varya received the pass from the militia without any delay. Max's title as Hero of the Soviet Union had its effect.

There was a small complication along the way in Khabarovsk. A young lieutenant, checking passes, asked, "Why isn't the child on your passport?"

"He is in his father's."

"There is no mention of your marriage here."

"We aren't married."

"Where is the child's birth certificate?"

"Do you expect me to carry the child's birth certificate around when I'm visiting family? Comrade lieutenant! All my documents were checked inside and out when I was getting the pass. Don't you trust Moscow?"

"The rules are the same for all citizens. Don't violate them next time!" He glared at Varya as he stamped the pass.

Even though Max was now famous throughout the country as a Hero of the Soviet Union and had received a promotion, there was no sense of joy or peace in their house. Nina had a gray streak in her hair, and it was early for that.

"Papa went gray early, too. It must be hereditary."

"Don't worry, it looks good on you," Varya said.

Max and Nina were restrained in conversation, but Varya could tell that the situation in the Far East, despite their recent victory, was the same as in Moscow. The newspapers were full of the same vicious hysteria. Almost the entire officer corps had been arrested in 1937, and this year, they arrested their replacements.

Nina did not want to discuss this, and Varya kept quiet — there was no point in antagonizing her. She needed to get Vanya settled. However, Nina was the first to talk about it. The previous evening Max had stayed late at a Party meeting, came home after Varya had gone to sleep, and left in the morning before she had gotten up. At breakfast, Nina complained, "These Party meetings are killing Maxim. They are recruiting soldiers to be informants and forcing them to denounce their commanders. You criticize a soldier and he runs to the special officer with a pack of lies, and those lies get you a court martial."

She left the table and did not bring it up again. Varya felt sorry for her. But who didn't live in fear now?

Max and Nina listened to Lena Budyagina's story in silence. But once they were alone, Nina said to Varya, "When we got your telegram, I assumed that the baby was yours and Sasha's, and that one or both of you were in trouble and you needed help. Max and I did not rule out the possibility that Sasha had been arrested again. They could come for you, too. We even thought we might have to get you married out here. We did not hesitate for a minute. You are my sister and you know how much Sasha means to Max. By the way, how is Sasha?"

"He's traveling from town to town, working as a driver wherever he can," Varya replied briefly. Nina obviously thought that things were fine between them and Varya did not want to disabuse her, even though it hurt every time Nina brought up their life together.

"Poor Sasha," Nina said with a sigh, "he had a tough time. On the other hand, maybe he was lucky. If he were arrested now, and he certainly would have been arrested now because he's too independent and principled, he would be shot."

"It looks that way."

"In any case, we assumed you and Sasha wanted to leave the child with us. And I repeat, we had no hesitation about it at all. But the son of Lena and Sharok, the grandson of Budyagin . . ."

"I don't think Sharok is part of the picture," Varya noted.

"I just mentioned it," Nina said. "The real problem is that he is Budyagin's grandson. If they find out, Max will be charged with aiding an enemy of the people and who knows what else, and they'll find out about me, and it will be a catastrophe."

"You're afraid?"

"Yes, I am. It's all so unexpected. I have to get used to the idea. I have to think about it. Is there any guarantee that the truth will never reach here about him?"

"It's impossible! Lena would not admit his whereabouts under torture. She realizes that if something happens to you, it's the end for Vanya, too. Her story is that she left him at a railroad station. People are doing that all the time, now."

"Does Sofya Alexandrovna know?"

"I told her that he was the son of a friend whose husband was arrested and who was afraid she would be next. She fled Moscow and asked me to take her child to her family in the Far East."

That was what she had said to Sofya Alexandrovna, even though Varya could tell that Sofya Alexandrovna did not believe it. She had already told the older woman all about Lena Budyagina and even consulted with her on what to do about Vanya. Nevertheless, Sofya Alexandrovna pretended to accept the story. A reliable person.

"All right," Nina said a little uncertainly. "Now the second question. The boy has no documents."

"Your neighbors know that your sister came to visit with her son. Everyone has seen me — I take Vanya for a walk every day. People here know every time someone sneezes."

"Well, all the men around here have been eyeing you."

"One fine day I'll vanish. You and Max — "

"Varya, call him Maxim. Max is what he was called in school. It doesn't sound Russian. And here, the slightest foreign sound is regarded with suspicion."

"Fine. You and Maxim are in shock. Some sister, abandoning her child like that. You can blame it all on me — feckless, irresponsible, a floozy."

"That's too strong!" Nina grimaced.

"Don't worry, your regimental ladies will rub their hands with glee over the story, and add details, too. The sassy flirt wiggled her hips all over the place and made eyes at all our men. You could tell what she was like. Poor Nina Sergeyevna, stuck with the kid."

"You have some imagination," Nina said with a smile. But the smile was forced.

"Not imagination. This is reality. They'll gossip away about me and forget about the child. Register him as Kostin because you don't even know the name of the father and you believe that your sweet sister doesn't, either."

"Enough of that!"

"I'm just giving you ammunition. As for the stuff about bringing up a Soviet man, a future defender of the homeland, I think you'll find the right words."

"Drop the sarcasm, you've outgrown that age. And I've grown up, too, by the way."

"But if you still think that Vanya will make things difficult for Max, I mean, Maxim, I'll take him back."

"And what will you do with him?"

"I'll bring him up as a single mother."

"Don't try to scare me. Let's wait. We'll think about it. Maxim makes the decisions."

The next morning Nina was up at dawn waiting for Varya to wake up. She went straight to the point. "I don't like your story. 'Abandoned the child . . . Ran off . . . We don't know where to look for her.' It's not serious."

So, she had discussed it last night with Maxim. Varya thought that Maxim was still under Nina's heel, but the situation had changed. Nina seemed to be in charge, but she always looked over her shoulder at Maxim. He was taciturn and expressed his opinion tactfully, but Nina accepted his opinion instantly.

"Maybe, we could put it another way. You wanted to find work here, but couldn't, and announced that you were going to work in the North, seeking your fortune there. And we insisted that you leave the boy with us. Vanya's not even two. How can you let the poor baby live in barracks and in the cold? Once you get settled and married to a decent man, you'll take the boy. What do you think?"

"I love it," Varya said with a laugh. "I'll go north or south! Perfect! That does sound more convincing." She couldn't resist needling Nina a little. "Tell Maxim I like the idea."

After Maxim first heard Varya's story about the boy, he asked no more questions and did not bring up Lena again. He came home late. As a new regimental commander, he had a lot of work, and he was a demanding officer. In his free time he chatted with Varya about inconsequential things and played with Vanya. He liked the boy, and the boy always met him joyfully.

And then, in late August, he said that he had made arrangements for Vanya to start nursery school on September 1.

"Once he serves a year there, we'll promote him. At age three, he'll be in kindergarten," Maxim chuckled.

The next day Varya left for Moscow.

Sheltering the grandson of an enemy of the people — Maxim realized the risk involved. But he could not send the boy away. Lena was his wife's best friend, and he had known Lena since childhood. He had been at their house on Granovsky more than once. He loved the place and he loved Ivan Grigoryevich Budyagin. He did not believe that he was an enemy of the people any more than he believed that his faithful comrades in combat were enemies of the people. And he trusted Varya. She did everything right and it was unlikely anyone would learn about it. And even if they did, he couldn't be to blame. They just stuck him with the kid.

Maxim did not like to lie, but when forced, he did it with a sly peasant simplicity that was terribly convincing. He went for advice to the regimental commissar and the secretary of the Party organization. He spread his hands in amazement and said, "Let's give this some thought, boys. The girl has a fatherless son. She came here planning to get married. She would have found a husband easily because she's beautiful and educated. We have a deficit of eligible girls here. They'd take her even with the boy. But I know my sister-in-law. If she stayed here, there'd be turmoil. All the women would break up with their husbands. And over whom? A relative of the regiment commander! I had to refuse her. I told her to go find herself a man somewhere else. And she said, 'Oh, so, you don't want to help me bring up my child? Then I'll go north!' Then my wife got upset. Go wherever you want, but don't drag the poor boy into the polar nights. He's skin and bones as it is. We won't let you. We'll take care of him here. And the sister said fine. And left. And who knows when she'll be back, if ever. Well, I figure, if this is the way it is, then we'll bring up the son of the regiment commander without her. And that will preserve the necessary moral climate in the regiment. That's the decision I'm thinking about. Your opinion, comrades?"

The comrades agreed with him. A high moral climate in the regiment was the most important priority because the moral climate was an inseparable part of the political climate.

28

AFTER VOROSHILOV LEFT, Stalin called Molotov. "Tell Berlin that we are interested in negotiations. But the Germans are rushing us. They must be given to understand that we are not in a hurry. We have no reason to hurry. Find a strategy — gradually, step-by-step — that will force them to show their cards. If their proposals suit us, then we will hurry, too."

Three days later, on August 15, Molotov came in with Ribbentrop's reply. The text made it clear that Hitler had dictated it and that it was intended for *him*.

Stalin, thinking over every word, began reading the message out loud slowly. Molotov listened attentively even though he had already read it himself.

"The road to the future is open for both countries. Germany has no aggressive intentions with regard to the U.S.S.R. German-Soviet relations have come to a turning point in their history. The decisions taken now will have decisive significance for generations of German and Soviet people — "

Stalin stopped reading and looked at Molotov. "That Austrian enjoys flowery speech."

"An orator!" Molotov replied, knowing that Stalin always imbued the word with sarcasm.

Stalin resumed his slow reading. "The interests of Germany and U.S.S.R. are not in conflict anywhere. Between the Baltic Sea and the Black Sea there are no questions that could not be settled to the complete satisfaction of both states (the Baltic Sea, Southeastern Europe, and so on). The German and Soviet economies can supplement each other. . . . The imperial minister of foreign affairs is prepared to come to Moscow for a brief visit in order to express the views of the Führer to Mister Stalin."

Stalin lowered the paper to his desk and leaned back in his chair. "The proposals are clear. In addition to the Polish territories, Hitler is willing to talk about the Baltic states, Finland, and Bessarabia. . . . However, our people could never understand or approve of a union with an *aggressor*. We could conclude an agreement on nonaggression. Our people would understand and approve such an agreement. The agreement would mean that the U.S.S.R. would not fight and that the Soviet people are guaranteed peace and tranquility. Does that mean that we refuse our interests in Poland, the Baltics, Bessarabia, and other regions of Europe? No, it does not. But that must be determined by a separate, *secret, protocol*."

He paused and then continued. "Of course, someday our descendants will learn of this secret protocol and ask why Stalin and Molotov concluded a secret protocol. After all, the Bolsheviks were always against secret treaties. Yes, the question could be raised. And there is an answer. Treaties concluded by the Tsarist government against the interests of the people is one thing, and secret treaties concluded by the worker and peasant government in the interests of the people is another. They are different things. And future generations will understand us. How are the trade negotiations moving?"

"Successfully. I think they'll conclude this month."

"The question has to be put this way — first the trade agreement, then the agreement on nonaggression. Then the Germans will accept all our terms. For the Germans, a nonaggression pact means that the U.S.S.R. will not interfere when Germany attacks Poland."

"England and France have given Poland their guarantees," Molotov noted.

"They're afraid of Hitler. Well, and even if they do decide to wage war with Germany, all the better. They'll all be sucked up in that war, exhausting themselves, and it will end like the last war — with revolution. And finally, it is time to stop the Japanese provocations. That should be up to Germany since it is an ally of Japan. Thus," he said, raising his finger, "you will respond to Ribbentrop this way. Is Germany prepared to sign an agreement on nonaggression with the U.S.S.R.? As for the secret protocol, all mention must be oral, only. Let's see what they propose."

The next day, August 16, Molotov passed along these questions to Schulenburg, the German ambassador.

And on August 17, Schulenburg read Molotov Ribbentrop's reply. "Germany is prepared to sign a pact on nonaggression with the U.S.S.R. and to use its influence to improve Japanese-Soviet relations. Ribbentrop is prepared to fly to Moscow tomorrow, August 18, with the Führer's authorization to sign the corresponding agreement."

Molotov hesitated. Neither he nor Stalin could receive Ribbentrop the next day — the documents were not prepared. Therefore, Molotov had told him that at the present it was impossible to determine even approximately the date of his arrival.

Stalin was not pleased with this response. "Hitler may take this response as an unwillingness to receive his minister. 'I can't tell you even approximately.' Why can't you? You can. As soon as they sign the trade agreement, we will receive Ribbentrop. Find the German ambassador immediately and give him that reply. And hand him a draft of the nonaggression pact. They'll sign any pact now. They're running out of time."

Molotov roused his staff and told them to find Schulenburg and invite him back to the Kremlin. Schulenburg arrived. Molotov handed him the draft of the nonaggression pact and announced that Ribbentrop could come to Moscow immediately after signing the trade agreement.

On August 20, the trade agreement was signed. And on August 21 at 3 P.M., Stalin was handed a personal letter from Hitler.

To Mister Stalin. Moscow.

1. I sincerely welcome the signing of a new German-Soviet trade agreement as the first step to the restructuring of German-Soviet relations.

2. The conclusion of a nonaggression pact with the Soviet Union means for me the determination of Germany's long-term policy. Therefore Germany is renewing the political line that was beneficial for both states during the past centuries.

3. I accept the nonaggression pact that Mr. Molotov sent to me and I consider it necessary to clarify questions related to it.

4. The supplemental protocol desired by the Soviet government may be developed in the shortest time possible, if a responsible government figure from Germany can come to Moscow personally for negotiations.

5. Poland's behavior is such that the crisis may occur any day.

6. I suggest yet again that you receive my minister of foreign affairs on

Tuesday, August 22, and at the latest, Wednesday, August 23. The imperial minister of foreign affairs has the authority to compose and sign both the pact on nonaggression and the protocol. I will be happy to receive your speedy reply.

Adolf Hitler

They could drag it out no longer. Hitler had taken over the negotiations and there could be unexpected consequences from any action.

That same day, at 7:30 P.M., Stalin sent a reply to Hitler.

To Chancellor of the German State Mister Hitler.

Thank you for your letter.

I hope that the German-Soviet pact on nonaggression will become the decisive turning point in the improvement of political relations between our countries.

The people of our countries need peaceful relations with each other. The agreement of the German government to sign the nonaggression pact creates the foundation for the liquidation of political tensions and for the establishment of peace and cooperation between our countries.

The Soviet government has authorized me to inform you that it agrees to the visit of Mr. Ribbentrop to Moscow on August 23.

J. Stalin

That same evening, during a meeting of the military representatives of the U.S.S.R., Britain and France, Voroshilov's adjutant handed him a note: "Klim, Koba said that you should shut down the show." The note was not signed, and the handwriting was indecipherable. It looked liked Molotov's.

The negotiations were stopped because they had reached a dead end.

All day and night of August 22 was spent in preparations for Ribbentrop's arrival. They prepared the documents, the building, the guards, and the reception at the airport. They could not find German flags — red with a black swastika in a white circle. They finally found some at Mosfilm studios where they were used in anti-fascist films.

Stalin did not go to his dacha. He spent the night in town, approving documents and planning his conversation. He read the information sheet on Ribbentrop — he needed to know with whom he would be dealing. In his youth, Ribbentrop had been a commercial traveler selling wines and had joined the Nazis, became ambassador to England, and was now minister of foreign affairs. Göring's note caught Stalin's attention. After all, he was the second most important man in the German government after Hitler — "Lazy and incompetent, vain as a peacock, haughty and without a sense of humor. When I criticized Ribbentrop's candidacy, saying that he would not be able to handle British affairs, the Führer told me that Ribbentrop knew this lord and that minister. To which I replied, 'The whole problem is that they also know Ribbentrop.' "

Hitler naturally encouraged such needling. A ruler could not tolerate a united entourage, which might conspire behind his back. So Göring's words had to be taken with a grain of salt. Hitler would not keep a lazy incompetent politician as minister of foreign affairs. Journalists, on the contrary, described him as a hardworking and determined man, rough and arrogant. The success of German foreign policy confirmed that. As for haughtiness, in a diplomat that was a tactical measure, especially when the policy was aggressive. But in the coming negotiations Ribbentrop would be sucking up to them. There was only a week until September 1. Ribbentrop and Hitler were in *his* hands. And if Ribbentrop did behave arrogantly, *he* would soon put him in his place.

Now, on the eve of Ribbentrop's arrival, *he* had to decide things for himself. *His* decision would determine the fate of the Soviet Union, of Europe, and of the whole world. The main question was: Did *he* trust Hitler? Would German divisions march through Poland only to then attack the Soviet Union?

In politics you trust no one. In politics you trust only yourself. They say that Hitler has a special intuition. Nonsense! Intuition is always the result of cold calculation. Calculation shows that after Poland, Hitler will attack France. They say that Hitler is unpredictable. What they consider unpredictability is the ability of great politicians to change course sharply when their genius foresees the need. The fact that *he* signs the pact with Hitler will also be seen as unpredictability. In fact, it is a calculated step that corresponds with the long-term interests of the Soviet Union.

Of course, Hitler as a person is difficult to understand. A man with bangs hanging down onto his forehead, with a Chaplinesque mustache and a beaky nose pitted with blackheads and a strange habit of clasping his hands somewhere below his belly, does not resemble a great political figure. And yet, he indubitably was a great political figure. They say that

Hitler suffered from megalomania, constantly showing off his genius and his higher purpose. "Providence entrusts the genius with leading a great nation. . . . In order to save the nation, a dictator with an iron fist is needed." Of course, that kind of egotism is unfamiliar to the Soviet people. The Soviet people value modesty in a leader above all. Apparently, the Germans have another concept of leader. Germans like pushiness. However, only a man who believes in his genius is capable of instilling that faith in others. But as for actually talking about it . . . he never spoke of his genius. Others did that for him. Megalomania is a mania without the greatness. But you had to admit that in six years Hitler lifted Germany out of the ruins, conquered chaos, established order, achieved industrial acceleration, liquidated unemployment, created and armed a powerful army, navy, and air force, broke the chains of Versailles, annexed Austria and Czechoslovakia without losing a single German, increased the country's population by ten million, took an enormous and strategically important territory, and turned an unarmed and bankrupt Germany into a powerful state that made England and France, those rotting, fading countries, tremble as they suffered defeat after defeat.

On whom should *he* bet? On Hitler, who had time on his side, or the Western democracies, whose time was passing? Whom would *he* defend? The arrogant Polish elite that had enslaved four and half million Ukrainians and a million and half Belorussians? Poland, which only last year attacked a dismembered Czechoslovakia like a vulture and stole Silesia? It was not *his* fault that Poland was ruled by pompous fools. Why hadn't they returned Danzig to the Germans? Danzig was a German city, after all. Why did they refuse to allow Soviet troops to cross their territory? Were they so strong that they could quarrel with Germany and Russia at the same time? The Poles were always implacable and now they did not wish to be realistic. Let them pay for that. Now it was too late for Poland to think about its mistakes. Tomorrow Ribbentrop would be in Moscow, and *he* would sign an agreement with Hitler. *He* had been thinking about this pact for a long time, and *he* was certain that Hitler would want such an alliance. Now *his* confidence was paying off, as it had to. Allying yourself with the Western democracies was dooming yourself to defeat. *He* understood it and so did Hitler.

All these years *he* had thought about Hitler a lot and found much in common with him in both character and fate. Like *him,* Hitler had written poetry in his youth, had sung in a children's choir, had been sickly, alienated, and lonely as a child, loved history, and refused to learn foreign languages. Like *him,* Hitler had an unbending will, was persistent and decisive in reaching his goals, felt the slightest danger and reacted quickly, knew how to pick top people and how to get rid of unreliable ones permanently. Like *him,* Hitler was capable of maneuvering.

How could they — the two greatest figures of modern times, men of similar fates, brought to the top of power only through their own efforts and who turned their countries into the most powerful in the world, uniting their people by the noble concept of statehood — how could they destroy their people, countries, and themselves in a mutual war of destruction to the joy of the international bourgeoisie, to the rejoicing of the plutocrats, whom they both hated? Could it be that there was not enough space on this planet, exploited by the British and French imperialists, for *him* and Hitler, their people, their countries? The world was large and there was enough territory for Russia and for Germany. When they took over the world, they would find a way to coexist. And if their descendants could not maintain their inheritance, too bad for the descendants.

Hitler had written about "territories in the East" back in 1924. Russia then was weak and looked like easy prey. Hitler kept that thesis in order to the fool the West, to keep the West from interfering as Germany rearmed. Now there was a different distribution of power in the world, and he was no longer maneuvering. He was headed for his primary goal.

A few days ago, President Roosevelt had sent a telegram to Molotov. "If the Soviet government forms a union with Hitler, it is as clear as day that as soon as Hitler conquers France, he will move his troops against Russia." What did Roosevelt understand? He understood only the interests of American bankers. Undoubtedly, American bankers did not want to see a strong, united Europe against them. They preferred to deal with another Europe — a Soviet Union in ruins, a Germany in ruins, a rotting France, a fading England, a Europe that will obey the American bankers. Roosevelt would not see such a Europe.

He had made a decision. A final one. Now Hitler had come to the same final decision.

~ 29 ~

THE SPANISH COMMUNIST Jacques Mornard was coming
to Paris and he should be put in touch with Zborovsky. Zborovsky
would introduce Mornard to the American Trotskyite Sylvia
Ageloff, who would participate in the coming Trotskyite congress. That
was the assignment from Eitingon. Sharok passed it along to Zborovsky
and asked him for information about the lady.

"The young lady," Zborovsky corrected. "Translator, fluent in
French, Italian, Spanish, and English naturally. She also knows Russian;
her mother is Russian. Her sister, Ruth, works in Mexico, in Coyoacán,
as part of Trotsky's personal staff. Whenever Sylvia visits Ruth, she is
also put to work in the secretariat. Both Lev Davydovich himself and
Natalya Ivanovna Sedova, his wife, like her and trust her implicitly."

Zborovsky clearly liked her himself. He had even liked Lev Sedov,
which had not kept him from killing him. However, he still represented
Trotsky's interests in Paris, publishing the *Opposition Bulletin*. This was
why, Zborovsky said, Trotsky would not let him come to Mexico — he
was needed in Europe. But it was also possible, according to Zborovsky,
that Trotsky and his wife found it painful be near a man who would be
a daily reminder of their late son. Sharok did not argue, but he was convinced that Trotsky or someone close to him distrusted Zborovsky. That
was why they kept him far away. Therefore, infiltrating Coyoacán,
as sketched out by Sudoplatov and Eitingon and which Sharok had
brought up himself in such a timely way, was the only correct move.

Sharok had no trouble recognizing Mornard, a tall and handsome
Spaniard with spectacles, mustache, beard, and sideburns. He had seen
him in February 1937 at the NKVD intelligence training center near
Moscow. Back then he had neither beard nor mustache, and his name

was something like Ramón or Lopez. A young man of twenty-three or -four who spoke French and was polite and tactful, he spent a few days there before he was transferred to another school, probably the one where they trained "Yasha's kids." They worked intensively on Spanish affairs then, infiltrating various political movements, particularly the Trotskyite POUM, and sending in agents and running small jobs on liquidating political enemies. The young Spaniard was a new recruit. Sharok remembered him because the Spaniard had tagged along on a ski trip with him. The Spaniard had never skied, but now he wanted to try. Three of them went: Sharok, Arvid, who was a Swede or a Norwegian, and the Spaniard. Arvid raced off ahead of them into the woods, but the Spaniard trailed after Sharok stubbornly, even though he kept losing his skis and falling down. And he wasn't dressed warmly enough. He didn't even have a hat, and a snowstorm came up. It was February. Sharok took pity on the fellow and said, "Why don't you go back. You'll catch cold." The Spaniard gave him a hurt, even an angry look, and went back. The unexpected anger and aggression in that seemingly mild and pleasant man stayed with Sharok. The Spaniard left the very next day, without having said good-bye to anyone.

So he wasn't Jacques Mornard. He had a Belgian passport, which was naturally picked up in Spain, from someone in the International Brigade. As soon as a volunteer came to Spain, his passport was taken away. They went in big bundles to Moscow. Passports of people killed in the war were handed out to intelligence agents, after careful study of the deceased's biography, family, and friends. Passports of the living were also used, once they were supplied with new names by master forgers.

Sharok did not know whether Mornard had the passport of a dead Belgian or a forged one, but according to the passport Mornard was thirty-three. That means they had added around seven years to his age. That was why he had grown the facial hair, to look older. Sylvia Ageloff, whom he was supposed to seduce, was twenty-eight.

Sharok also had a beard and mustache. Would the Spaniard recognize him? It was hard to say. He gave no indication. And did not utter a word of Russian. A self-controlled man. He was his usual polite and tactful self, but now with an added unhurried gait and marked dignity, even an aristocratic air, that was part of the character he was playing.

Sharok brought Mornard and Zborovsky together. Mornard told them the biography Eitingon had developed for him: Mornard's father was the Belgian consul in Teheran, and Mornard had broken with his illustrious family out of ideological considerations. He saw the social injustice prevalent in the world, but he was indifferent to politics and did not want to take it up. He planned to work in Paris as a photo correspondent in the Belgian press agency. Besides which, Eitingon instructed him to use Sylvia to gain the trust of the Rosmers, Trotsky's closest friends. The Congress was to take place in their villa in the town of Recigny, outside Paris.

Sharok was impressed by Eitingon's plan: he had selected the best profession for Mornard — a journalist not interested in politics. As Sharok realized from his few conversations with Mornard, the man was poorly educated and could not have passed as someone interested in politics. The Rosmers would have smelled a rat instantly.

A few days later Zborovsky called to say that the meeting would take place in a café on rue Nicolo at one o'clock tomorrow. He and Mornard would show up about ten minutes early.

Sharok arrived a little later, walked past Zborovsky and Mornard, and sat down where he could see them.

Two women entered the café. Zborovsky rose to meet them. Sharok had no difficulty in guessing which one was Sylvia from the description: a blonde of medium height, with a good figure, but not a beauty by any means. She was dull and not attractive. He did not envy Mornard. And who would believe that such a good-looking man would fall in love with her? But there was no way out of it now, that was his assignment.

Zborovsky led the women to his table and Mornard stood up. They all shook hands and sat down. From his vantage point, Sharok could observe them easily. They were talking animatedly, though quietly, and voices rose only occasionally. Sharok heard only random words. Was Sylvia falling for Mornard? She was a bluestocking, involved in politics. Women like that either turned into old maids or married ugly fellow activists. But Mornard was a political ignoramus. What would they have in common? Only a physical attraction. Would she be afraid of getting involved with someone that handsome? Every woman knows her limitations, what nature has given her to work with. Sylvia's only hope was her figure. That was a strong point. If a woman has a good body, men assume she's good in bed. When he first saw Kalya at a trolley bus stop, he noticed her full hips. When a woman has hips like that, you can take her from many positions, which is what he did, many times. But it was unlikely that they would continue in the same way. He could still see Abakumov pawing her. And even though Sharok had sworn to Kalya never to bring it up, he kept remembering it. He did not call her before he left for Paris. She'd get over it. And then he'd see. Who knew when he'd be back in Moscow — in a month, a year, two years?

In the meantime, the conversation at Zborovsky's table was getting livelier. Mornard was telling a story and Sylvia was laughing. Sharok paid and headed for the door, thinking that Mornard did have a chance.

Mornard knew how to use his opportunity. According to Zborovsky, he was seeing Sylvia every day, going out to the theater and restaurants. Mornard drove Sylvia in his car to see the Rosmers in Recigny and then picked her up. Sylvia introduced them. Everything was proceeding well.

The founding Congress of the Fourth International took place at the Rosmer villa. Zborovsky gave Sharok the manifesto and other documents from the Congress. He also gave him a copy of Trotsky's article that had been published in the newspapers. "It took the Kremlin clique ten years to stifle the Bolshevist party and turn the first workers' state into a grim caricature. . . . Just ten years. . . . But in the course of the next decade the program of the Fourth International will become the guiding star for millions, and they will know how to storm the earth and the sky!" Sharok sent it all on to Moscow.

At last Sharok had the following information: Mornard and Sylvia had moved into a two-room flat in the middle of Paris, near Notre Dame. They ate at the Pan Am American bar in the Place de l'Opéra. Eitingon's assignment had been carried out. Now Sharok had to give Mornard money. Lots of money.

∾ 30 ∾

ON THE SET DAY AND HOUR Lena rang the doorbell. It was hard to figure out how long it would take with the Ufa buses, which ran however they wanted, but she had — punctuality had always been her strong suit.

"Have any trouble finding it?" Sasha asked, helping her with her coat.

"Your directions were so precise, I couldn't have gotten lost."

Sasha made tea, set out sandwiches with sausage and cheese, chocolates, and a bottle of red wine, which he had gotten the night before. Lena refused the wine. "My head spins from a single drop."

She was more relaxed than at the post office.

"But I'll drink to our meeting." Sasha poured half a glass and drank. "So, Lena, first I'll tell you about my life and then you can tell me about yours. After my exile, I was given a passport restriction, which meant I could not live in big cities. So I'm wandering around the small ones. My record creates problems for me in ordinary jobs, so I'm doing something extraordinary: I'm teaching ballroom dancing. Gleb, whom you met with me, is my accompanist and a loyal, tested comrade. You don't have to worry about him. I speak regularly on the telephone with my mother. She is alone. My father is working in another city and he has a new family. My uncle Mark was shot. That's my life. What do I know about yours? Ivan Grigoryevich and Ashkhen Stepanovna were arrested in 1937. You have a son, whose father, so I heard, is Yuri Sharok, but you seem to have broken off with him. About our friends: Max is in the Far East, a Hero of the Soviet Union. Nina Ivanova is his wife. Vadim Marasevich is a successful critic and as far as I can tell, a real bastard. That's all that I know about myself, you, and our friends. Now you can tell me whatever you feel is necessary."

She looked up at him. "Do you think that I don't trust you?"

"Lena, distrust is the mood of the times. And I'm not asking you to be frank. But maybe you need my help. I'm ready."

"Sasha, I always believed you and I believe you now," she said seriously. "You know the basics. Here's what I can add: I'm sure Father was shot, because they wouldn't accept a single parcel for him from me. They say that is the first sign that the prisoner has been executed. Mother must have been shot, too. My brother Vladlen, you remember him, is in the NKVD children's distribution center. My son, Vanya, is being brought up by good people. I was ordered to leave Moscow and asked to pick a city. I chose Ufa, and every month I check in with the NKVD on Egor Sazonov Street. I work at Neftegaz refinery and live in the dormitories."

"What do you do there?"

"Construction and repair of the railway tracks. It's hard work, but the pay is good."

"You haul ties?"

"Sometimes. It suits me: I am able to send money to Masha, Vladlen's former nanny, and she'll keep an eye on the boy."

Sasha coughed, shook his head, poured himself more wine, and caught Lena's look. "Are you worried I've turned into an alcoholic? Don't worry, I haven't. So, that's the kind of work you do, hauling ties and track. Do they give you gloves at least?"

"Yes. It's all temporary, of course. All the members of families of enemies of the people, exiled from Moscow, have been arrested. I'm on the list. There's a camp nearby, so they can simply move me from one barracks to another, behind barbed wire this time. As for our friends, you're right, Nina went off to be with Max. It's a secret, but if you already know, I can tell you about it. Vadim? His sister, Vika, married a Frenchman and is living in Paris. Now he has relatives abroad, so Vadim is trying extra hard to please the regime."

"Why aren't you eating?" Sasha insisted. "Have some tea before it gets cold."

She took a sandwich and sipped from her glass of tea.

"Tell me, if it's not a secret, what your last name is."

"Budyagina."

"Have you tried looking for other work?"

"Like what?"

"You know languages."

"Sasha, sweetheart, who would give me a job with languages? Who would let me teach school?"

He got an idea. "Listen, you play the piano very well, don't you?"

"I play. I'm not so sure I'm very good at it."

"Are you free today?"

"Why?"

"Come with me to the Palace of Labor, I teach dancing there. You'll see how I work."

"Today?" She looked at her watch. "All right. I have trouble picturing you as a dance teacher."

"And I can't picture you working on the railroad."

"I know." She went on, "I sometimes think that it is retribution."

"Retribution? For what?"

"For the sins of our fathers."

"What do you mean?"

"Everything. The Red Terror, the Cheka, the GPU. For everything that went on. They ran the country, they were responsible for the fate of the people."

Sasha poured some more wine into his glass and then looked at Lena and laughed. " 'Daddy, don't drink!' Remember where that's from?"

She frowned. "It's very familiar. But I can't remember . . ."

" 'Anna on the Neck.' Chekhov."

She burst out laughing. "Of course. 'Anna.' Right. 'Daddy, don't drink!' "

"You can't lump them all together, Lena. There was White Terror as well as Red, both sides performed evil deeds. Revolution is cataclysm, avalanche, and the guilty ones are the people who could not prevent it."

Sasha finished the wine and spoke again. "In nineteen twenty-one the Civil War ended and they saw that communism could not be built by violent means. And things moved back again. NEP, the New Economic Policy, was intended for gradual and painless transformations. But NEP was discarded and now see what we have and who we have.

That is the fault of our fathers. They did not prevent it; they had power and they turned it over without a murmur to criminal hands. They are guilty. And so am I. . . ."

"Of what?"

"Do you remember Sonya Shvarts in our class?"

"Of course, I saw her after graduation. She went to university, now she's a physicist, like her academician father."

"I ran into her once on the Arbat, too. We talked about our class and the kids and teachers, and she said with a laugh, 'You know, Sasha, I used to be afraid of you at school.'

" 'Afraid of me? Why?'

" 'I don't know why. But I was really afraid.'

"And I thought to myself, Why could she have been afraid of me? Was I scary, did I bully people?"

"Not at all. We all loved you!"

"Not her. And I figured it out. I was a Komsomol member and I personified the system based on fear. I instilled that fear in her and that is my guilt. So your father is guilty and so is your mother and so am I. But not you! And there are thousands, tens of thousands of people like you — wives, children, parents — why should they pay? You call it retribution. I call it caprice."

"But if our fathers," Lena said musingly, "gave up power so readily, that means that their ideals weren't so powerful, their ideas were not so right in the first place. After all, the Revolution was predicated on those ideas."

"Someone said that revolutions are begun by idealists and ended by the scoundrels who destroy the idealists. You and I see that and our goal is to survive. Maybe better times and changes await us."

"Do you really believe that? Or are you just trying to cheer me up?"

"I believe it. That's why I'm telling you that we must survive, if only for the sake of our loved ones: you have a son, I have a mother. By the way, have you seen her recently?"

She lowered her head. "Sasha, I'm very ashamed. I haven't seen her once. And I'm paying for that now, too."

Sasha laughed. "I asked you about my mother not to find out if you've been visiting her, but for another reason. It's just that at the post office, I got the feeling that you were not surprised to see me here, and I wondered if my mother had told you that I was in Ufa."

"I did know that you were here. But not from your mother. Varya, Nina's sister, told me."

"Varya . . . You've been seeing her, you're friends?"

"I saw a lot of her lately. You must remember her as a little girl, right?"

"As a schoolgirl," Sasha replied curtly.

"She's no schoolgirl now. At times I felt that she was older and wiser than me. Not to mention stronger. She pulled me out of trouble, literally hauled me out of it. After my parents were arrested, I was fired, and I couldn't get a job washing floors. And I had my brother and son to take care of . . ."

She got up and walked to the window. She did not want Sasha to see how upset she was. "All my friends vanished with the wind And suddenly I ran into Varya. By accident. On the street. If I believed in God, I would have to pray for her every day! Which, incidentally, I do: I don't know prayers, so I use my own words. I'm not talking about the fact that she fed us for months on her tiny salary: she's an ordinary draftsman, she needs every ruble she makes. She saved Vanya."

Lena turned to Sasha and looked at him, testing him. "She took my son to her relatives."

"To Nina?"

"Yes. No one knows about this, Sasha."

"And no one ever will. Don't worry."

"It wasn't easy taking him to the Far East. Vanya's birth certificate says: mother — Elena Ivanovna Budyagina. But the pass for the train says Varvara Sergeyevna Ivanova. Can you imagine the great risk she took? They could take away the child. They could accuse her of kidnapping him. But she's a saint and that's why she got away with it. I swear, she's a saint! So young, so beautiful, and she spends her life worrying and taking care of others!"

"Wait, wait a minute!" Sasha was stunned. "I don't understand. What pass are you talking about?"

"You can't go to the Far East without a pass. Max had to send one to Varya for her and her son. While they were waiting for it, Vanya lived with her and your mother. Sofya Alexandrovna took care of him, too. She would do anything for Varya. Varya helped her a lot, too, Sasha. She carried parcels for you to the prison, she stood in those horrible lines. Do you know about that?"

"Of course."

"Nina and Max probably thought that Vanya was Varya's son."

"I heard that she had been married to some billiard player?"

"Yes. A stupid story. She was seventeen years old. And is my affair with Sharok anything to be proud of? And I was older. We all make mistakes. That's how we get smarter."

She suddenly smiled and looked up at Sasha. "By the way, Sasha. You're somewhat at fault for her marriage, you know. Obliquely."

"How's that?'

"You were sent off to exile from the Kazan Station, accompanied by two guards and a commander."

"Right."

"You had a beard and carried a suitcase."

"Yes."

"Well, at that time the graduates of the military school, including Max, were leaving for the Far East from a different platform. Nina and Varya were seeing him off. Varya saw you, she saw your pale face and your big black beard. She told me that it was the most powerful impression of her life. She thought that you were walking docilely be-tween the guards, docilely carrying your suitcase, docilely going off to exile. She was seventeen then, Sahsa. Don't be offended. She thought that you had allowed them to humiliate you. That you should have resisted, they should have had to tie you up and carry you. So that people would not walk past, indifferent to your suffering, so that the newly graduated commanders wouldn't be so happy, not even noticing that a man was being led off by guards. That was how she felt. And she decided that she would not live that way, she would not turn into an obedient slave. And she found a man who did not work anywhere, who invented things, who made big money, and who was independent of the government. And she married him, in order to be independent. However, she quickly learned that it was all a bluff, that he was a gam-bler and maybe even a hustler. So she threw him out. In rather dramatic circumstances."

"Apparently he wanted to kill her?"

"Oh, you've heard about that? I guess I'm wasting your time with this story."

"No, no. I've only heard about that final episode. She threw him out, and he threatened to kill her. My mother told me that at the station during a very brief meeting. The rest I'm hearing for the first time. It's all very interesting. Please go on."

"Varya learned from that: independence is not given by anyone. You become independent on your own if you can do good in spite of everything. And that is how she works now. And I'll tell you this. If not for Varya, I would never have lived through everything that befell me. It was Varya who told me, 'When they give you a choice of cities for exile, tell them Ufa. Sasha is there. Find him, send him a postcard, and he will respond instantly.'"

My God! Then Varya had not forgotten him. . . . "Why didn't you send me that postcard?"

"Your situation is complicated enough as it is. Sasha, I didn't want to be a burden."

31

PLEVITSKAYA PUT ON AN ACT and did not admit to anything. Nonetheless, the facts and the very disappearance of Skoblin
pointed to her guilt. The entire press covered the case. The newspapers,
of which Sharok read every single one, accused the French government
of giving safe haven to Bolsheviks, and accused the police of helping
Miller's kidnappers cover their tracks. But neither the investigation nor
the court case led to any Soviets resident in the country; no one was
named. Plevitskaya was sentenced to twenty years of hard labor, which
essentially meant lifetime imprisonment. The émigré community was
jubilant. Burtsev declared, "May she rot in prison."

But the ROVS was for all intents and purposes destroyed. As before, Tretyakov carefully recorded conversations at the headquarters,
but they held no interest. The headquarters stood empty for weeks at a
time and there were no funds to pay even the security guard's wages.

During Plevitskaya's trial Sharok decided that now was an oppor-
tune time to make contact with Vika Marasevich. Vika had been at
Plevitskaya's in Ozoir-la-Ferrière, a town whose name the Russian-
language newspapers spelled every which way. Vika was intimidated,
and if someone were to intimidate her even more, she would give in. For
the time being there was no practical use to which she could be put, but
there might come a time when she would be needed. However, by that
time she might have regained her composure, and she might announce
that they were blackmailing her. He knew Vika's character. She had
gotten away from them in Moscow, and in Paris she was all the more
capable of doing so. But now she was demoralized and despondent, the
Plevitskaya case was continuing — there was nowhere she could run.

Sharok assigned the Vika operation to a staff member whose nick-

name was "Sukhov." He would get in touch with her himself when
matters required. "Sukhov" phoned Vika in Sharok's presence and said
that he had brought her a letter from her brother and that it would be
best for them to meet in a museum, perhaps at the Louvre. The only day
when he could meet her would be tomorrow, preferably during the first
half of the day, but Vika could name the time. He could send her the
letter by mail, but Vadim had warned that the letter contained nothing
of substance, and that the main news was what he would convey to her
in person.

After a certain silence, Vika asked, "Excuse me, what is your name?"

"Pyotr Alexandrovich."

"Tell me, Pyotr Alexandrovich, has something happened there?"

"Sukhov," carefully instructed by Sharok, answered, "Victoria
Andreyevna, you are putting me in a difficult position. Excuse me for
the Moscow turn of phrase, but this is not an appropriate subject for
a telephone conversation. Among other matters which I must discuss
with you are those relating to the inheritance. By the way, I wish to
express my deepest condolences on the passing of your esteemed father."

Sharok had learned of Professor Marasevich's death from the newspapers. The "inheritance" was a lure that should make Vika bite.

However, Vika said nothing. Sharok gave "Sukhov" a sign and the
latter said, "If you don't wish to meet with me, then I have no reason to
insist. To the contrary, that will be easier for me. Let Vadim search for
other ways. Then let me say good-bye."

"No, no." Vika interrupted him. "Wait. I'm thinking about when it
would be convenient for us to meet. In the Louvre at twelve o'clock at
the ticket window, is that all right with you?"

"Fine."

"How will I recognize you?"

"I have been to Starokonyushny, at Vadim's, and I remember you
very well. Maybe you will remember me too. I will be by myself as, I
hope, will you."

The next day at twelve Sharok and "Sukhov" pulled up to the
Louvre. Vika was walking up and down by the ticket window. Sharok
pointed her out to "Sukhov." For several minutes they studied the people near the museum to make sure that Vika had not brought anyone. That is, "Sukhov" studied them while Sharok gazed at Vika

and recalled the princely Marasevich apartment on Starokonyushny and the illustrious people, smiled upon by fame and good fortune, who had been guests there. Vika had looked great in Moscow and still did; she was definitely the kind of woman who stood out in a crowd.

Once he made sure that she had no one tailing her, "Sukhov" approached Vika. They greeted each other and went into the museum. Sharok followed them, went up the wide staircase, and entered one of the galleries. Vika and "Sukhov" sat on a bench. Sharok walked the length of the gallery, pretending to study the pictures.

Vika had learned about her father's death from Nellie Vladimirova, and Charles had brought her the issue of *Izvestiya* containing the obituary. There had been no word from Vadim. And his life did not interest Vika. Issues relating to the inheritance? Mother's jewels had always belonged to her, and she had them now. Vadim wanted to divide up what their father had left? That was out of the question. He was a miser and a skinflint. And she had no desire to see any Soviets, anyway. But she agreed to the meeting nonetheless. Who knows! Maybe they had found something serious in her father's papers? After all, their forebears had been related to the Cossack chiefs. Possibly there were rich relatives in Europe, maybe even property that she had a claim to. Maybe her father had medical discoveries or patents registered in the West which the Soviets did not know about? Maybe Vadim himself wanted to take to his heels and come here as a correspondent and stay. After all, it was terrible, what was going on in the Soviet Union. She had absolutely no use for Vadim here, but if there were patents or property, then there was no way of getting them without him — he was also an heir. In any case, she would not allow him to become a burden to her. What she needed was to find out everything.

She did not remember Pyotr Alexandrovich at all. He was a thin young man, even skinny. Modestly dressed. Smiling. He drew an envelope out of his jacket pocket, took a paper out of it, and showed it to Vika without letting it out of his hands.

"Are you familiar with this document, Victoria Andreyevna?"

She took a look at it and grew cold. It was a promise to collaborate, given by her at one time in Lubyanka. Oh, the accursed past, the accursed country! Pyotr Alexandrovich folded the paper, put it in the envelope, and repeated his question:

"So, Victoria Andreyevna, do you remember it?"

What would they do to her? This was not Moscow! She would call the police and hand this Soviet spy over to them! How dare he try to blackmail her with this forged paper. Above all, the paper proved *him* guilty.

"No," answered Vika. "I am not familiar with this paper. Shall we stroll over to the police station and clarify things there?"

"We don't need the police, Victoria Andreyevna." Pyotr Alexandrovich smiled. "Reporters will come running, the document will be published in the newspapers, it will be hard for you refute the results of handwriting analysis, and hard to explain your links with Mrs. Plevitskaya and your visits to Ozoir-la-Ferrière. All of this will be of great interest to the public. Mrs. Plevitskaya will be exposed and the tie to you, an NVKD agent, will add new charges against her and will expose you as well. You need to think things over carefully before going to the police."

This scoundrel's words, pronounced with a friendly smile, were no empty threat: they could ruin her life and Charles's too. They carried out their work abroad with the same impunity that they did in Moscow at the Lubyanka! They had kidnapped General Miller in broad daylight, and before that General Kutepov, and they had killed the defector Ignatii Raiss. Just think: Skoblin was a general, and Plevitskaya was a famous singer, and even they were their victims!

"I don't intend to burden you," Pyotr Alexandrovich added. "We may ask you to render us some minor services, which will in no way violate the laws of France. We have never once disturbed you because the necessity has not arisen. Now the necessity has arisen in connection with the Plevitskaya case. You were at her home, and we would like to know what you talked about."

"Nothing special! Nadezhda Vasilyevna told about her life, sometimes she sang, reminisced about Russia, she is a person of deep religious faith and she showed me their church. I am stunned, shocked, by everything that has happened!"

"That's excellent! Write all that down. Bring it here next Thursday at the same time. But I warn you, Victoria Andreyevna, don't even think of doing anything stupid. Just one disloyal step on your part, and your photographs and your promise to collaborate will appear in all the newspapers right away, along with the dates of your meetings with Plevitskaya. I hope that you will see reason."

After this meeting, Sharok ordered "Sukhov" to "reel her in slowly, whatever you bring in will be fine. Keep her on a long leash. Meetings should take place only in public places: museums, galleries, exhibits."

Eitingon soon arrived. He approved of the operation with Vika, but advised caution. She was from wealthy stock and had no need of money and she had no ideological motivations. So there was only fear, and in this instance it was an unreliable motive. Vika did not interest him now, so Sharok switched his focus to the Spaniards, sending them off to Mexico and putting together there a powerful diversionary group. He did things on a big scale and didn't pinch pennies.

Eitingon conducted himself as confidently in Paris as he had in Moscow. He didn't even hide his mistress, which made Sharok envy him; Eitingon felt in control, whereas Sharok was timid and lived like a monk. He was afraid of having dealings with prostitutes — you could catch some nasty bug and then end up shelling out all your money for treatment, or get into some entanglement with a pimp and then you might as well kiss your career good-bye. He needed to find a steady woman, and he would have liked that woman to be Vika, rather than anyone else, but where Vika was concerned Eitingon turned out to be right.

As had been arranged, a week later "Sukhov" accompanied by Sharok pulled up to the Louvre. They went into the gallery. Vika was waiting on a bench. But "Sukhov" did not approach her. He looked at pictures with Sharok and they went into the next gallery, without letting Vika out of sight. "Sukhov" had changed his appearance by putting on a mustache and a beard. There were not many people around. "Sukhov" and Sharok noticed two characters who did not leave the gallery for an entire hour. It was not hard to guess what sort of people they were. Then the two characters left, and Vika left after them.

Eitingon suggested that maybe Vika had confessed everything to her husband, that he had gotten in touch with Sûreté and with the counter-intelligence service and proposed that through Vika they might discover some Soviet agents. Then they would forgive her her youthful transgressions in Moscow.

"Don't touch her yet," Eitingon said. "We don't need her. There will come a time when you may consider using her."

Spending a lot of time with Eitingon and Mornard and meeting with people from Spain and dispatching them to Mexico, Sharok got an idea of who the major players were in the present operation. In Moscow Sudoplatov was directing it, and here Eitingon was in charge. That woman, Eustasia Maria Karidd del Rio, was not only Eitingon's mistress, but also his aide. The daughter of a rich Cuban, she was married to a Spanish aristocrat named Mercader who lived in Barcelona and she had five children by him. She was a woman of passionate enthusiasms and she had left her husband, lived with her children in Paris, returned to Barcelona, joined the Communist Party, and been recruited by Eitingon. The children were strongly influenced by her. One of them, Ramón Mercader, was now called Jacques Mornard. Like his mother, he had been recruited by Eitingon, had gone to Moscow, and there, at intelligence training school, Sharok had seen him. He had stayed in Moscow for a bit more than a year, come to Paris already under the name Mornard, become involved with Sylvia Ageloff, met the Rosmers, and had done all this with one sole purpose — to get to Trotsky in Coyoacán.

An official communication came: Yezhov had been relieved of his duties as People's Commissar for Internal Affairs. So that was over. Yezhov was as good as dead now. It made no difference whether they put him in prison and shot him in a week, in a month, or in two months. Beria had been appointed to replace him. How would the new broom sweep things out? Of course, Sharok wanted to discuss all this with Eitingon, but he couldn't make up his mind to do so; it was better not to show his concern. Eitingon let slip during a conversation that Kobulov, who was the person closest to Beria, was championing Abakumov. That meant that Sharok had influence in high places. Time would tell. There would be a shakeup, but their department was not likely to suffer, the "boss's" main task was Mexico, and whoever was working on that would not be touched. They would be touched if they did not carry out the task. Maybe things were going slowly, but everything was going well. Sylvia returned to America. Mercader remained in Paris for the time being, mentioning commercial affairs as the reason. In actual fact, Eitingon had decided to exchange his passport for a more reliable one. This turned out to be the passport of Tony Babich, a Canadian citizen of Yugoslavian extraction who had died in Spain. The "T" was remade into an "F," the "o" into an "a," between the "F" and "a" an "r" was inserted, and the "y" at the end of the first name was changed to a "k." The name became "Frank." The same thing was done with the last name, and "Babich" became "Jackson"; the Canadian citizen Frank Jackson, born in Yugoslavia on July 13, 1905, naturalized in Canada in 1929. The passport was forged in Moscow by highly experienced masters. All of this was ready in August. Ramón Mercader, a.k.a. Frank Jackson, a.k.a. Jacques Mornard, finally got the opportunity to go to America, where Sylvia was waiting for him.

～ 32 ～

THE LARGE GERMAN DELEGATION, accompanied by security and servants, flew out of Berlin on two four-engine Condor airplanes. Ribbentrop flew on one of them, the Führer's personal plane. They landed in Moscow at noon on August 23. The delegation was taken to the building that had formerly housed the Austrian embassy, and had now been transferred to Germany. After a quick lunch, Ribbentrop hurried to the Kremlin. Negotiations with Molotov were set for 15.30. In the evening there would be a meeting with Stalin. However, entering Molotov's office, Ribbentrop saw Stalin there.

That was Stalin's move; he had decided to catch Hitler's minister off balance right away. But he behaved simply, was welcoming and well-wishing. He was not a diplomat, he was in charge here, he was the arbiter. He could resolve an argument with a phrase or a single word. He sat in an armchair, attentively listening to Molotov, Ribbentrop, and Pavlov, one of the interpreters. The Soviet draft of the pact was brief: the U.S.S.R. and Germany would refrain from using violence or aggression toward each other, and from attack. If one party became the object of military action by a third power, the other party would not support that power. The parties would resolve their differences using exclusively peaceful means. The agreement was concluded for a period of five years and would go into effect after ratification.

Ribbentrop proposed an amendment: that the treaty be concluded for a period of ten rather than five years and that it go into effect immediately after signing. They were in a rush, and so they wanted to get it approved. Well, they could work together on that, the Soviet people would support it: if the treaty went into effect immediately, that meant that peace would immediately go into effect.

They moved on to the secret protocol. Ribbentrop drew from his pocket a sheet of paper folded in quarters and gave it to the interpreter Hilger. Hilger read it point by point. Ribbentrop looked at Stalin without taking his eyes off him. But it was impossible to read anything on Stalin's face. He listened with his eyes half-closed as Hilger read in Russian the protocol about the demarcation of each side's sphere of influence in Eastern Europe . . . Hitler was opening the way for Stalin in the Baltic States and was giving away half of Poland, and they would decide the question of its actual existence later on. *He* needed to think some more about what was more favorable for *him:* to have a shared border with Germany, or to preserve between them some fragment of Poland.

"That is all, Mr. Stalin." Hilger put the paper on the table.

Stalin began speaking slowly, pausing to give Pavlov the opportunity to interpret.

"I think that the protocol, for the most part, is acceptable. It would be useful to mention the Soviet Union's interests in Bessarabia. Everyone knows that Bessarabia was always a part of Russia and was occupied by Romania in 1919."

Listening to the interpretation, Ribbentrop said, "I understand, Mr. Stalin. I will immediately inquire about Mr. Hitler's consent to this. I hope that the answer will be speedy and in the affirmative."

The answer came in two hours.

"Yes, agree. Hitler."

They moved the signing of the documents to midnight.

Stalin ordered that Chief of Staff Shaposhnikov be invited to the signing ceremony. The presence of the former Tsarist army colonel would make an impression on the German generals who had formerly been officers of the Kaiser. Let them know that *he* had destroyed only certain traitors, and that the majority of officers supported *him.*

Molotov and Ribbentrop signed the treaty and the protocol. According to accepted practice, they exchanged folders and handshakes. Ribbentrop asked to be put through to Hitler by telephone. A direct line had been set up the previous evening. Excited and pleased with himself, Ribbentrop joyfully reported to the Führer that all documents had been signed and that the mission had met with complete success. Speaking with Hitler, Ribbentrop by mistake lowered himself into Molotov's chair.

"He's gone completely mad with joy," thought Stalin.

They went into another room where a table had been laid with wines and hors d'oeuvres. Here reporters and photographers awaited them. Everyone drank and nibbled standing up.

Stalin seated himself in an armchair by the wall and invited Ribbentrop to sit down next to him. The German interpreter Hilger stood near Ribbentrop, and the Russian interpreter Pavlov stood near Stalin.

"I wonder what is Mr. Ribbentrop's view of Soviet-Japanese relations?" asked Stalin.

Ribbentrop listened to the interpretation and in a sign of sincerity, put his hand to his heart.

"Mr. Stalin, I can assure you that German-Japanese friendship is not directed against the Soviet Union under any circumstances. Moreover, we, Mr. Stalin, are in a position to make a contribution to the settling of differences between the Soviet Union and Japan. I am prepared to act energetically in that area."

Several hours before *he* had been handed a dispatch from the Far East. The Soviet troop offensive in the Halhin-Gola region was going successfully, and the main Japanese forces were completely surrounded. Ribbentrop, of course, did not know that.

"The Soviet Union is not afraid of war and is ready for it," said Stalin. "If Japan wants peace, all the better. Of course, Germany's help could be useful. But we are not asking for help from anyone. We are relying only on our own strength."

"Of course, of course, Mr. Stalin, you are absolutely right. There will be no new German initiative. I will simply continue the talks with them which I have been conducting already for several months."

He understood! Göring had no grounds for saying that he was incompetent.

A person with a camera appeared next to them.

"Mr. Stalin," Ribbentrop pronounced with great solemnity, "allow me to present to you Mr. Hofman, Mr. Hitler's personal photographer and friend."

Stalin shook Hofman's hand, smiled, and gestured to the table.

"When Mr. Ribbentrop and I go over to the table, we will drink to your health."

The agitated photographer answered, "Your Excellency, it is a great honor for me to convey to you warm greetings and heartfelt good wishes from my friend Adolf Hitler. He would be glad to meet personally the great leader of the Russian people."

"May I request of you," answered Stalin, "that you convey to Mr. Hitler that that is my wish as well."

Then Hofman took a step back, set up his equipment, photographed Stalin with Ribbentrop, thanked them, and went over to the table.

"And what do you think of Turkey?" asked Stalin. "Turkey has a common border with the Soviet Union, it controls the straits, the Bosphorus and the Dardanelles. This is the Soviet Black Sea Fleet's route out to the Mediterranean and, consequently, to the ocean. The straits have been an acute problem in Russian politics for a long time."

"Oh, Mr. Stalin!" Ribbentrop exclaimed. "I am doing everything possible to achieve friendly relations with Turkey. But it's very hard to come to agreements with the Turks, Mr. Stalin."

"Yes," said Stalin. "The Turks are always wavering."

"That we understand, Mr. Stalin." Ribbentrop picked up on this thought. "England has spent five million pounds sterling on anti-German propaganda in Turkey."

Stalin snorted.

"The English plutocrats are certain that everything can be bought and sold. Their military representatives came here and talked on and on for ten days. We never did understand what it was they really wanted. If we could have been bought, they probably would have known what to say. But, as you understand, we cannot be bought."

"Mr. Stalin," Ribbentrop nodded his head, "forgive me, but I can tell you that England is weak, I assure you, Mr. Stalin. I was ambassador to England and I know that England is weak and wants other countries to support its arrogant claims to world supremacy."

He's sidling away from the question about the straits and switching the topic to England. Never mind. Hitler can't get away from a resolution of that problem; the U.S.S.R. must dominate the Black Sea. Time would pass, and *he* would demand the straits, too, as well as many other things that Hitler did not now want to give up.

"I agree with you." Stalin paused to give Ribbentrop a chance to evaluate this acknowledgment for what it was worth. "England dominates in the world thanks only to the stupidity of other countries. Just a few hundred Englishmen run India. Is that ridiculous, or what? But they will wage war persistently, playing deftly on the contradictions between different countries. On top of that, France, England's ally, has an army that must be taken into account. . . . Let's ask Molotov here."

He signalled for Molotov to come over.

Molotov put his plate on the table and walked over.

"Mr. Ribbentrop and I are discussing France's military might," said Stalin. "What do you think?"

"I think that France has an army that deserves attention."

"You see!" Stalin said to Ribbentrop.

"Perhaps you, Mr. Stalin, and you, Mr. Molotov, have more reliable data," Ribbentrop replied, "but remember, gentlemen, that the 'Western rampart' is five times stronger than the 'Maginot Line.' "

Stalin laughed to himself. As did Molotov. They knew perfectly well that the German 'Western Rampart' was merely an incomplete fortification that ran from Luxembourg to the Swiss border, and that as a unified line of defense it existed only on paper. And Ribbentrop knew that, of course. Nonetheless, in order to add persuasiveness to his words, he stated haughtily, "If France tries to fight with Germany, it will definitely lose. Germany has allies. . . ."

"From the anti-Comintern pact?" Molotov asked ironically.

Ribbentrop rose, then sat down, and said, agitated, "Mr. Stalin, Mr. Molotov, gentlemen. I want to bring complete clarity into this question. I want to state with complete firmness and definitiveness: the anti-Comintern pact is in no way directed against the Soviet Union, it is directed exclusively against the Western democracies."

"The only people frightened by the anti-Comintern pact were small-time English shopkeepers," said Stalin. "That pact could not frighten anyone else."

Let Hitler understand: he needed to choose the names of his alliances more carefully. *He* was not afraid of any anti-Comintern pact.

Ribbentrop did not understand, or he pretended not to understand, Stalin's derision. "Precisely, Mr. Stalin, precisely. I too doubt that that pact could frighten the Soviet people, Mr. Stalin. I guessed that by reading the Soviet press. The Germans understand all that well. You know, Mr. Stalin, there is a joke that has been popular among witty Berliners for several months now: 'Stalin is planning to accede to the anti-Comintern pact.' "

Stalin grimaced. The little German lacked a sense of humor. Göring was right about that.

"Berliners like a good joke, I see," said Stalin. "And how do the German people feel about the settlement of relations between Germany and the Soviet Union?"

"It is welcomed, Mr. Stalin, at all levels of German society. Even the simplest, least sophisticated people understand that England's intrigues are the only obstacle."

"Simple people always want peace," said Stalin.

"Yes," corroborated Ribbentrop. "The German people want peace, but, on the other hand, their indignation about Poland is so great that everyone is ready to fight. The German people are not going to endure Polish provocations anymore."

Stalin had not planned to discuss war between Germany and Poland. Without listening to the full interpretation, he rose, and with a movement of his hand invited Ribbentrop over to the table.

The waiter poured out champagne. Stalin raised his glass. Everyone grew silent.

"I know," said Stalin, "how much the German people love their leader, and so I want to drink to his health."

Everyone drank to Hitler. At that moment the German photographer clicked his camera. Stalin called him over, nodded at an empty wineglass, and the photographer hurriedly poured some champagne and clinked glasses with Stalin.

"Tell him," Stalin turned to the interpreter Pavlov, "that that photograph should not be published. Such a photograph might be misunderstood by Soviets and Germans. Soviets and Germans might think that we are having a drunken revelry, rather than providing peace for the people."

"Excuse me, Mr. Stalin, excuse me." The photographer was embarrassed. "You are absolutely right, I will open up my camera and give you the film right now."

Stalin stopped the photographer with a movement of his hand.

"No need! I believe him. Tell him that his word is enough for me."

Stalin was wrong in believing the photographer, who deceived him, as did Hitler. Some time later, the photograph showing Stalin drinking to Hitler's health appeared in the German press, and then in the world press.

Molotov raised his glass in honor of Comrade Stalin.

"It was Comrade Stalin in his speech in March of this year, a speech which was correctly understood in Germany, who completely changed the political relations between our countries."

Molotov was referring to Stalin's speech at the Eighteenth Party Congress.

Then Molotov proposed toasts to Ribbentrop, to the German Ambassador Shulenburg, and to the German people.

Ribbentrop's toast to Mr. Stalin, Mr. Molotov, and the Soviet government took the form of a long and florid speech.

Day was already dawning outside; the morning of August 24 had arrived. The reception ended.

Seeing Ribbentrop to the door, Stalin stopped and through the interpreter Pavlov spoke slowly, weightily, and, it seemed to him, in heartfelt tones: "Convey to Mr. Hitler that the Soviet government takes the new pact very seriously. I give you my word of honor that the Soviet Union will never betray its partner."

"Mr. Stalin," answered Ribbentrop, "you may rest assured that those will be the first words which I shall convey to Mr. Hitler."

On August 31 at a special session of the Supreme Soviet of the U.S.S.R., the Non-Aggression Pact between the U.S.S.R. and Germany was ratified.

On September 1 at dawn, the German army crossed the Polish border and moved toward Warsaw from the north, the south, and the west. The Second World War had begun, the bloodiest war in the history of humanity.

33

HOWEVER, at first this was a strange war. England and France did not fire a single shot, but stood by calmly observing as Germany's tank armadas routed the Polish army in a matter of two weeks and, passing through the whole country, occupied Brest.

Was the West leaving *him* to go one-on-one with Hitler? Had a new Munich Conspiracy been concluded behind *his* back? Were they sacrificing Poland in order to direct Hitler's strike toward the Soviet Union? Had *he* miscalculated? Had Hitler deceived *him*?

On September 17, Soviet troops entered Poland, and, encountering no opposition, they came all the way to the line agreed upon with Ribbentrop. So Hitler had not deceived *him*. Everything took place precisely, efficiently, and properly. While Brest and the other cities were being handed over to the Soviet troops, the Germans and Soviets organized joint military parades which took place in an atmosphere of warmth and friendliness. A neighbor like this was someone one could live with.

On September 27, Ribbentrop once again arrived in Moscow. This time he was met by Molotov himself, an honor guard was formed, and the airport was decorated with flags bearing the swastika — this time they had made enough of them.

The negotiations began in Stalin's office at ten o'clock in the evening and continued until dawn. They concluded a Treaty on Friendship and the Border. They divided up Poland. The U.S.S.R. received all of the Baltic states. They drew a new "final" border on the map. Stalin signed it with a dark blue pencil, and Ribbentrop, with a red one. Poland as a state ceased to exist. At the session of the Supreme Soviet, Molotov stated: "It turned out that brief strikes by the German Army and then by the Red Army were sufficient that no trace of this deformed offspring of the Treaty of Versailles remained."

The next day, Stalin held a ceremonial dinner in honor of Ribbentrop. In the evening they saw the ballet *Swan Lake* at the Bolshoi Theater. Later Ribbentrop would write to Stalin: "At times it seemed to me that I was mingling with old Party comrades."

After Ribbentrop's departure, the Soviet Union positioned troops, navy bases, and airfields in Estonia, Lithuania, and Latvia. On October 12, negotiations with Finland began as well. Stalin had no doubt about their outcome; surely, insignificant little Finland could not be planning to go to war with the great and mighty Soviet Union!

In the face of successes of such worldwide historical significance, what was the gleeful crowing and cackling of Trotsky! But he did not subside, continuing to shoot out sprays of venomous slaver:

"Now we have learned that the Kremlin has long sought a military agreement with Hitler. Stalin fears Hitler. And it is no surprise that he fears him. Fascism strides from one victory to the next. The German-Soviet pact is Stalin's capitulation to fascist imperialism, done for the sake of self-preservation of the Soviet oligarchy. . . . Hitler is conducting military actions while Stalin carries out the role of quartermaster. . . . Terrible military threats lie in wait for the Soviet Union. . . . In two years Germany will attack the Soviet Union. The only guarantee is Ribbentrop's signature on a scrap of paper."

Stalin tossed the Trotsky article aside. The swine! He was finished as a politician, he had no supporters left, he hadn't even fathered children who would support him when no one else did, and yet he didn't quit! He holed up in his cave and issued prophecies: in two years Hitler would attack the Soviet Union! Where did such exact forecasts come from? Why was he going to attack in 1941, specifically? In 1941 the world would be completely different, and Trotsky would be forgotten, along with his idiotic forecasts. The man's days on earth were numbered. Sudoplatov and Eitingon wouldn't dare not to carry out *his* order!

And that old jackass Litvinov was busy pontificating too. He kept quiet in public, but at home he held forth to his wife, although he knew that his apartment was bugged. That was why he had not named *him* even once, reserving his criticisms for Molotov only. But *he* understood who Litvinov was really talking about.

The retyped notes were put on the desk before Stalin.

"Hitler has occupied a position right on the western borders of the U.S.S.R. The Soviet Union is now faced with a western front. . . . (Coughs.) The agreement draws the U.S.S.R. into an amoral collaboration with Hitlerite Germany. Molotov hopes that he will be able to establish stable relations with Germany. This is a dangerous illusion! (Sneezes . . . Does he have a cold or what, the blockhead?!) Germany has been Russia's enemy since earliest times. The pact and the agreement have cleared the way for a second world war."

Litvinov should be shot. What made him any different from Trotsky? But now was not the time to lay a finger on him. The alliance with Hitler was getting stronger, and sooner or later measures would have to be taken in regard to the Jews. By no means would the Soviet Union give up its internationalist essence, *he* would not give away such a trump card. Then at the final, decisive moment *he* would play that trump card against Hitler's nationalist swaggerings. This was a matter for the distant future. However, it was not out of the question that en route to this future some ideological concessions might be necessary; *he* might have to take the Jews down a few notches, to toss a bone to Hitler. This bone would consist of Litvinov, along with other Jewish loudmouths. If necessary, Litvinov would go on trial. And his loose talk to his wife would be thrown up at him then.

Returning Beria's dispatch, Stalin said, "Add the following words to Litvinov: 'Molotov's diplomacy reflects his own stupidity and narrow-mindedness,' and then show the dispatch to Molotov."

Let these denunciations make Comrade Molotov jump a little; he was far too calm and imperturbable. He needed to be shaken up.

Beria gave the paper to Molotov. However there was no reaction on his part. He continued to report to Stalin about routine matters in the same calm and imperturbable manner. Among the matters he reported on was a communication from the Soviet embassy in Berlin. Telman's wife, Rosa, had been there. She asked Moscow to try and wrest her husband, Ernst Telman, leader of the Germany Communist Party and true friend of the Soviet Union, from the fascist torture chambers. In passing she mentioned that she had nothing to live on, and that she was starving, but that she requested help not for herself, but for Telman, the head of the German proletariat, and she was convinced that Germany would not dare turn down such a request from the Soviet Union.

Telman's wife was at liberty? She was strolling around Berlin and stopping in at the embassy? She had been sent. And it was clear why. First of all, Hitler wanted to show that unlike *him* he did not repress his enemies' families; he was saying that he was so strong that he had nothing to fear from a few wives and children. Second, Hitler was testing *his* loyalty. *He* had shown his loyalty by giving Hitler several hundred German antifascists. But if in exchange *he* asked him to free Telman, then that was not loyalty, but rather a business transaction.

"What did they tell her at the embassy?" Stalin asked.

" 'We cannot help you in any way.' Then she started crying and said, 'Has all of Telman's work on behalf of communism been for nothing? Then at least give me some advice: Can I appeal to Göring?' They answered, 'That is your personal affair.' "

"Well," said Stalin. "They gave the right answer."

He did not wish to get into negotiations with Hitler on this matter. The Communist movement in Germany was well developed, and what happened to Telman would have no impact on that. And *he* could care less whether or not Hitler repressed the families of his enemies. As far back as 1937 *he* had personally dictated and signed a Politburo decision that stated: "Henceforth it is established that all wives of those exposed as traitors to the homeland or rightwing Trotskyite spies are subject to imprisonment in camps for a period of not less than five to eight years." And at the same time he had expressed his credo: "We will destroy every enemy, even if he was an Old Bolshevik, we will destroy his whole family and all his kin. We will ruthlessly destroy everyone who threatens the unity of the socialist state by his actions or by his thoughts, yes, even by his thoughts."

And now the task at hand was to reestablish Russia's past borders. Finland and Bessarabia were all that still had to be restored. Molotov reported that the Finns were being stubborn. The Finns were being stubborn? The Balts had not let out a peep, and here the Finns were, being stubborn. How many Finns were there? Three or four million. . . . And they didn't want to give in to the Soviet Union? They had forgotten that it was the Soviet authorities who had given them independence. They had given it to them, and they would take it away. Stalin ordered Molotov to summon a senior official of the Finnish government to Moscow.

The experienced diplomat Paasikivi arrived. Our ambassador reported from Helsinki that all of Finland had sung the national anthem as they gave him his send-off. How sentimental they were, it turned out! And he had thought that the Finns were a phlegmatic people.

Stalin went to Molotov's office. As he appeared, Paasikivi rose. He was a tall, bony Finn. With a nod, Stalin indicated that he might sit down and through the interpreter requested him to explain what the difficulty was. After all, the U.S.S.R. was offering such good conditions: the Finns would move their border back from Leningrad, in exchange for which they would receive much more territory in Karelia. What was wrong with that?

The interpreter translated Paasikivi's answer.

"You see, Mr. Stalin," Paasikivi said, "according to our constitution, only the representative assembly can decide territorial questions. And an affirmative decision requires no less than a two-thirds vote. I fear — "

"You don't need to fear anything," Stalin interrupted him roughly. "You will get more than a two-thirds vote, and on top of that you will figure in our votes too."

The threat was unambiguous. But it had no effect on the Finns.

"Well, then," Stalin said at a meeting of the military council, "the artillery will go into action. At the first salvo the Finns will put their hands up."

Both Voroshilov and Timoshenko agreed with him completely.

On November 30, the Soviet Union went to war against Finland.

However, the Finns did not put their hands up. Not for nothing had they sung their national anthem on Paasikivi's departure day. The war with little Finland lasted not nine days according to plan, but one hundred and four days. The U.S.S.R.'s losses in the war included seventy-six thousand killed and one hundred and seventy-six thousand wounded and frost-bitten. And without achieving a complete victory, the U.S.S.R. ended the war on March 13. As the whole world watched, the Soviet Union displayed its military weakness.

34

VARYA SENT A TELEGRAM general delivery from the Irkutsk Station to Lena in Ufa. "VACATION OVER GOING HOME." She did not sign the telegram — Lena would be able to guess, and in the space for the return address Varya wrote: "SIDOROVA — IN TRANSIT." Arriving in Moscow, she found letters from Lena at the post office, brief and businesslike: found work and space in a dormitory, how are things with you? Not a word about Vanya, as they had agreed. Varya telegraphed right away: "GOT LETTERS, ALL HEALTHY, MOOD CHEERFUL, DETAILS BY LETTER." In the letter she wrote that she had had a wonderful vacation, that she was rested and had put on weight and gotten a suntan, and that her relatives had received her warmly. Lena would understand that all this had to do with Vanya. She felt that the contents of the letter were effectively veiled.

Igor Vladimirovich had learned that she was going to the Far East and had obtained a ticket for her in a compartment, which had caused her some distress — she would have been willing to go by coach.

"Allow me to make you a small gift," said Igor Vladimirovich. "I wanted you to have at least *some* comforts on your trip."

"Is that the thing now — to give women train tickets as presents?"

He laughed. "Flowers are customary. But when I gave you flowers you returned them."

On that jocular note they had parted. And he met her joyously upon her return and didn't ask any questions, saying only: "I made arrangements about a job for your acquaintance. But I understand she no longer needs it."

"What makes you think that?"

"She didn't call."

"She's been sent away from Moscow," Varya answered briefly, desiring to cut the conversation short. Of course, Igor Vladimirovich was able to guess at a great deal. When he was getting the ticket, Varya had given him her pass: with a child, it said. He was smart enough to figure out a thing or two. But to draw him into the details would mean making him an accomplice. There was no need for that.

But she did not succeed in cutting short the conversation. Choosing his words, Igor Vladimirovich spoke slowly and in imposing tones:

"Varya, I want to say, just as your friend: be careful."

"What have I done?"

"Sometimes you express your thoughts far too openly, at the wrong time. This could be construed in ways harmful to you."

"I don't understand what you're talking about."

He continued to choose his words with the same painstaking care.

"I have the feeling that your name has started to attract an unhealthy interest and that certain people are starting to take note of your behavior. Or, to put it in technical terms, as the level of danger increases, the degree of caution must also be increased."

"Still," Varya insisted, "the interest in me hasn't just come out of nowhere, has it? Do your fears have something to do with Lena Budyagina?"

"I don't know. But for a while now I've felt that there is a certain coldness toward you on the part of the Party Committee. I doubt I'm mistaken."

"Maybe I should go somewhere else?"

"Under no circumstances. You would be even more unprotected. Things will be calmer and safer for you, Varya, with me. And," his voice shook, "by my side. But I urge you to be careful, Varenka, I implore you."

What was behind his warning? It was not a casual warning. Nor did he make it in order to dispose her favorably toward him. Igor Vladimirovich did not hide the fact that he was in love with her, but he was not one to intimidate her with imaginary dangers. There was something to it. Were the women at the studio wagging their tongues? No, that was not it.

A Short Course in the History of the All-Union Communist Party of the Bolsheviks came out and people began to study it in all the offices, organizations, and educational institutions, as it was obligatory for all employees. Sessions were once a week for two hours after work. Everyone bought the text, and was required to read a chapter each week, which was discussed at the sessions. The facilitator would ask questions aimed at finding out whether each employee had read the chapter assigned the previous week and whether he or she had understood it the way it was supposed to be understood.

Varya bought the *Short Course,* as did everyone else. They were brought to the workshop and cost a ruble and change. On the metro home she leafed through it, and the crap she found printed there almost made her throw up — at the beginning Lenin was mentioned in every other line, and then Stalin was mentioned in every line. Of course she did not appear at the first session, announcing that they were doing the *Short Course* at the college. This was her usual ploy.

However, this time her ploy did not work. They required her to bring in official notification from the college stating that they were indeed studying the *Short Course* there. And at the college they announced that everyone should do the *Short Course* at their workplace and on those evenings the students were excused from their classes. Study of the *Short Course* by the country's citizens was considered a matter of exceptional significance to the state.

As Lyova put it, "Varya's gotten herself into a bind." Rina had nothing to say.

On that same day Varya was summoned in to see Iraida Tikhonovna, chair of the local committee, a fat, bustling woman with a mellifluous voice. She was an engineer in the sewage and water supply section. As an engineer she was lacking in gifts and so she devoted herself to trade union work. But she was not a malicious woman, and given the opportunity she could even be helpful. She was the one who had said some time back, in defense of Varya, "She's going to school; the young comrade is developing her professional skills." Iraida Tikhonovna maneuvered to get spaces at the spas and sanatoria for employees and placed their children in Pioneer summer camps, including the famous Artek on the shores of the Black Sea. She was basically a person who was useful to everyone, to the employees and the administration, as well as to the Party bureau, of which she was a regular member. In her post Iraida Tikhonovna did not do much, but her signature was affixed to designs and blueprints, she received prizes, and she was making her way up the career ladder.

The room that served as the office for the local committee had been furnished by her efforts and everything there was as befitted such a place. The table was covered with green baize, in the corner was a red banner presented for outstanding service, and on the walls there were portraits of Lenin and Stalin, a list of the obligations of socialist competition required from the collective, portraits of shock-workers, and honorary certificates. In short, everything was as it should be in a reputable organization. To make things cozier, Iraida Tikhonovna had brought potted geraniums in from home — the red flowers stood on the windowsill and next to them was a watering can with some water in it that had been left to stand out before being given to the plants.

"Varya," said Iraida Tikhonovna, "you know how I feel about you. All of us here value you as a growing young professional. But, Varya, you deceived us: you said that you were doing the *Short Course* at the college, and that turned out not to be true. You really let all of us down, Varya."

"Who did I let down?"

"There is one hundred percent attendance in all organizations. And on our staff we have only forty people, so every absent person brings the numbers way down."

"And because of those numbers I'm supposed to miss classes?"

"The night schools allow students to miss their classes on those days."

"I am not a Party member, and I am not required to study the history of the Party."

Iraida Tikhonovna went rigid: what nerve! Not required to study the history of the Party!

"Comrade Ivanova!" Iraida's voice became official. "You read the administration's order, it was announced to all the employees and is hanging on the wall."

"I don't remember — there are lots of things hanging on the wall."

"I will remind you then: 'All employees are required to attend study sessions on *A Short Course in the History of the All-Union Communist Party of the Bolsheviks*. You violated the order."

"That's possible," Varya answered tranquilly. "I guess I'll receive a reprimand then."

"And your statement that non-Party members don't have to study the history of our Party places Communists in opposition to non-Party members."

"Yes?" said Varya with surprise.

"Yes, yes! In our country Communists and non-Party members are one bloc and you are trying to split them apart."

"I am capable of splitting such a powerful bloc?"

"Ivanova! Don't play games with me! I defended you, and now I'm sorry I did. You have other things working against you too, Ivanova, a lot of things. You've been deceiving us for a long time now, using the college as your cover. You didn't participate in a single May Day or November demonstration, you slipped away from all the assemblies and rallies. You're the only one in the studio who signed up to lend your salary for three weeks, when the other employees signed up for a month, or, like me, for two months."

"You are richer than I am," said Varya. "I am an ordinary technician, and you are a senior engineer, and your husband has a similar position, he's a senior engineer somewhere too."

Iraida Tikhonovna's cheeks flushed and her eyes narrowed.

"Yes, my husband is an engineer," she hissed, "and your husband has been convicted of fraud and misappropriation of socialist property."

"That's not true. I don't have a husband and have never had one. And who I sleep with is nobody's business. I am not interested in who you sleep with or even if anyone sleeps with you."

Iraida Tikhonovna looked Varya in the face, silently and with hatred, then, breathing deeply, she said, "Ivanova, this conversation today will cost you dearly and things will come back to haunt you — your husband who was convicted, and your sister, who was removed from the Party, and the exiled Trotskyite whom you correspond with. We know all about you. We will drag out of you everything there is to know. We are stronger than you are, remember that."

"I will remember your threats. In all likelihood you will have to answer for them."

Varya stood up and left the office. Varya herself did not know why she had promised to remember Iraida's threats, and why she threatened her with having to answer for them. She had wanted to have the last word, and not walk out of that vile office humiliated.

But where had they gathered all that information? Apparently they had been gathering information for a long time. Igor Vladimirovich's hint was not a casual one. Thank God they apparently knew nothing about Lena Budyagina.

Before the affair became a political one, she needed to leave — they would forget about her. Architectural engineers were in demand every-where. Igor Vladimirovich would give her a good recommendation. It was a pity, of course; she had worked here for four years, she was used to it, had considered them all her friends more or less, but there was nothing else to do.

Igor Vladimirovich read her statement. It was short. "I request to be dismissed by my own wishes." He read it over, put it on the table, and asked:

"Can this wait until tomorrow?"

"What will change tomorrow?"

"Are you free this evening?"

"I have to be at the college."

"Cancel it. I want to talk with you. It's very important. Let's go the National Café. Do you remember? That's where we met."

35

So HERE THEY WERE, sitting in the National Café at a little table by a window looking out on the Mokhovaya. In front of them were the red-brick building of the Historical Museum and the slope leading to Red Square and to the left was the Hotel Moskva, on the site where their design studio had once been. Then the hotel had been built and the studio had been moved to Ordynka Street. On the right was the Alexander Park, where she had wandered with Igor Vladimirovich the day they met four years ago. But they hadn't sat here then, that time they had gone to the restaurant on the second floor. Vika had been with Erik the Swede, the beautiful Noemi had been accompanied by a Japanese man, and Nina Sheremetyeva had been with an Italian. Vika was in Paris now, Noemi was married to a well-known writer, and Nina Sheremetyeva was married too, to someone who was practically a king or a prince. Varya knew that from Lyova and Rina. All that had been a long time ago, it felt like a hundred years had passed, and she had no nostalgia for that life — to the contrary, she felt revulsion: it had been like a feast in the midst of a plague. The only good memory was the meeting with Igor Vladimirovich. He had liked her, and then his feelings had changed to a love that was steadfast and patient, although it was not shared. If she had returned his love then, her life would have turned out differently, and she wouldn't have had the sordid experience with Kostya. True, then there wouldn't have been Sasha, but Sasha was gone forever anyway. Now, sitting here, she remembered how she and Igor Vladimirovich had danced in the little area in front of the orchestra and when he had asked her what kind of music she liked, she had answered: "Loud music." And everyone laughed, and then later, in Alexander Park, they ran away from the guard and she ripped her stocking and Igor Vladimirovich had sympathized with her plight. All this was gone, as if it had never happened. Gone was the joyful amazement at life, the anticipation of happiness in a world which had seemed so inviting and lovely. Now she knew that the world was unjust, cruel, and merciless.

Igor Vladimirovich ordered himself some wine, and coffee and cake for her. She did not want to eat much because she'd had lunch at work. Varya saw Igor Vladimirovich's agitation; he was worried about the situation with the *Short Course.* He was no fighter. But then, who was a fighter now? He was a decent man, and that was a lot in today's conditions, in fact, it was a great rarity now.

The waiter brought everything and left them alone. Igor Vladimirovich leaned toward Varya slightly because he did not want their conversation to be heard at the neighboring tables.

"Varenka, we are about to have an important conversation, the most important conversation of my life."

He drank down some wine from the glass and inhaled deeply on his cigarette, looked at the ashtray, and put out the match.

"And Varya, I ask you to take seriously what I have to say, and trust it completely. I want you to consider me a reliable friend."

"I have always considered you a reliable friend," answered Varya, thoroughly touched by his agitation. "And I am also your true friend."

"Good. So, you have applied to leave your job, and you hope that that will put a stop to this nasty uproar. Varya, you should realize that you won't achieve anything this way. They will find you everywhere, they have been observing you for a long time. They keep tabs on all of us. There is a personal file on every employee that contains information on family, acquaintances, work history, as well as recommendations and any incriminating or compromising material. We are surrounded. With the *Short Course* you have given them a pretext to stir things up. I talked to Iraida Tikhonovna and she is furious. Apparently you offended her personally."

Varya shrugged.

"It was a typical catfight. She insulted me, and I answered back. What of it?"

"I understand. But she gives everything a political coloring. 'Non-Party members are not required to study the history of the Party, let the Communists do that.' (That's what you supposedly said to her.)

Your sister was removed from the Party and you hid that; you are corresponding with an exiled Trotskyite and are going to continue the correspondence."

"I didn't say that."

"She can think up whatever she likes. She is kind only for the sake of appearances: it gives her a better chance of keeping on the committee and she 'has more authority in the collective,' as they say, but essentially she is the same type of nasty creature as all the rest of them. And you must confess, Varya, you have permitted yourself to do many things that no one in our society is allowed to do. And it will be very easy for Iraida Tikhonovna to cook up a case against you. You are powerless against them. You could drop everything and go to your sister, but the summons and the permit will take time to get ready, and I'm not sure that you'll make it in time. But even if you do, what will you do there? Work? You'll have to fill out an application, they'll ask where you worked last, you'll tell them MosDesign, and they'll find out everything, it will all come out. What else could you do? Marry some lieutenant, change your last name, and become a housewife so you don't have to fill out any applications."

Varya nodded. Nina had gotten a job at a school without references from her previous job in Moscow. The Far East was out for another reason: little Vanya was there, and there was that made-up story about how she had been recruited to work in the North, so she could not show up there.

Igor Vladimirovich interpreted this gesture in his own way.

"Yes. I think so too: Is that the kind of life for you? And who will your unknown future husband be?"

He grew silent, stroking the stem of his wineglass with his slender fingers and thinking.

"Once you said that you loved someone else and that you were waiting for him. I have no reason not to believe you. But where is that person? At that time you said, 'He will return in a year.' Three years have gone by already. If he exists, is he capable of helping you out, taking you in and giving you safety? If yes, then I will give the order to take care of the paperwork and you should go to him right away. But, Varya, if he does not exist, if you said all that just so you could refuse me politely, then there is only one thing you can do." He paused briefly, and looking Varya in the eye, added in a firm voice, "Marry me."

Varya was silent. When Igor Vladimirovich said, "We are about to have an important conversation, the most important in my life," she had realized that he was going to propose to her.

Why couldn't she get out the word *yes?* She was very fond of Igor Vladimirovich, she trusted him, she respected him, but something stopped her, something kept her from responding. Sasha? Everything with Sasha was over, that was clear. But Sasha, Sasha whose place in her destiny had remained unfilled, was still a part of her life, and sweet, good Igor Vladimirovich was somehow outside of her. She did not love him. And so she could not say "yes."

Igor Vladimirovich's voice brought her out of her pensive state.

"I understand, Varya, that it's hard for you to decide right away. But I want to add something for you to think about. The practical side. If you accept my proposal, we can sign the marriage papers tomorrow."

"Is it possible to sign the papers immediately?"

"They will register us. And tomorrow you will leave your job. In a month or two, when everything has calmed down, I'll get you a position — if you want it, of course — in another studio where I'm transferring after the New Year. I'm starting a big new project. Or, and this would be preferable, you can matriculate as a full-time student and then you'll be free in the evenings. After all, in addition to work there are theaters, concerts, the conservatory, exhibits, all of which you have no time for now. But that's for you to decide yourself. That's how the events in the studio look to me. You will be my wife and you won't work there anymore. And if anyone starts an attack on you, it will be an attack against me as well."

"But it's not your sister who was removed from the Party, it was mine."

He burst out laughing.

"To a certain degree it will become a fact in my biography too. But they won't make a move against me; they're smart enough to know that I have contacts in high places. So that won't be an issue. But there is something else, Varya."

He drank down the remainder of the wine, lit another cigarette, watched again as the match burned down, and tossed it into the ashtray.

"More than anything, Varya, I was afraid that you would think that I have decided to take advantage of your situation. That's not the case. You have always kept me at a distance, I am used to that, and I probably would have been willing to continue putting up with it. But I cannot allow you to be destroyed, Varya. Not only because I value you highly as a person, but because I love you. You are brave and you are willing to risk danger for the sake of others. But everything is much more serious than you think, believe me. My proposal resolves all the problems — with me you will be safe. And now here is the most important thing I want to say. I am not proposing a marriage of convenience, which would be humiliating for me and insulting for you. I offer you my love and devotion in the hope that you will love me. And you can accept my proposal only if you desire to answer my love with your love. You yourself would never strike a deal, you are too noble for that, but I want to be completely clear about this question. If you accept my proposal, then you will be my wife, I will be your husband, God willing, we will have children, and we will love them, and finally, we will have a shared life. There are things, Varya, which stand above time and you and I are creating something of that order. It will not free us from human problems and sorrows, but it will mean that we can give people some minuscule joy and consolation from our work, our art. You are very gifted, Varya, and you have a great future ahead of you. I know that you think now that the help you give the persecuted and the needy is higher than any art you might produce. And I agree with you. But in the position you are capable of achieving, you will be able to offer help and charity in much larger measure."

He leaned back in his chair and looked at her with a sad smile.

"Whew . . . I've never given such long speeches. I've worn you out. Now it's your chance to speak, Varya."

She also smiled in response.

"Today at work you asked me, 'Can it wait until tomorrow?' Now I want to ask you that same question."

He sighed.

"Well okay, until tomorrow then, I guess, until tomorrow."

They went out onto Gorky Street.

"You don't need to see me home," said Varya. "It's only three subway stops."

"All right," Igor Vladimirovich assented. "So we'll talk tomorrow. But remember, Varya, that whatever you decide, whatever turn your fate takes, I am ready to follow wherever you may go."

～ 36 ～

VARYA WALKED HOME. She didn't feel like fighting the crowds in the metro.

Her situation was serious. They would call meetings, demand that the collective be purged of the "hostile element," and then the authorities would take up her case. It was a well-known scenario.

Marrying Igor Vladimirovich was her only chance to be saved. Did she have the right to use that chance? Sasha was not the problem, as far as Sasha was concerned she did not exist and it was long past time for her to reconcile herself to that. But she had convinced herself many times that she did not love Igor Vladimirovich. He was not repellent to her, he was even pleasant, but for some reason from the first day of their acquaintance he had not struck her as a possible husband. Maybe because then she had been just a girl and he had seemed old to her. But actually he was no older than Kostya. Kostya did not seem old to her and Igor did. Kostya then had had an aura of independence from the regime and Igor Vladimirovich was dependent on it. By her standards of that time, Kostya did not accept the existing order, while Igor Vladimirovich did. The comparison was stupid. Kostya was a pool-player, a wheeler-dealer, a cardsharp, he operated by the laws of the criminal world, and this was no better than the lawlessness of the state. She had to envision whether or not they would be able to live together. Would she be proud of him or ashamed? As a talented man, a distinguished person, she would be proud of him. But who and what did talented people serve today? Everyone was in service to that same mustachioed countenance. And Igor Vladimirovich had his patronage as well. What was there for her to be proud of? Exhibits, receptions, newspaper articles filled with praise, congratulations? So

many scoundrels and nonentities had been favored with similar attentions!

Would she be ashamed of him? In all these years there had been only
one occasion when he had made her wince — that was the time when
he gave her a performance review at a trade union meeting in minc-
ing, bureaucratic tones and then after the meeting, at the Kanatik, he
had yelled at Kostya's whore Claudia Lukyanovna in an unexpectedly
shrill voice, saying, "So, it's been a long time since you spent the night at
the police station? Well, I can arrange it for you right away!" Someone
else would have sent her fleeing from their table, and all he could say
was something about calling the police. At the time she had thought,
"Coward!"

But she was wrong to think that, unfair. He was not used to trade
union meetings and had decided to speak to them in their own language; he wasn't used to ugly scenes with prostitutes. And so many
years had gone by since then, it was not kind of her to remember
those things, he could remind her of much worse things: Kostya, for
example.

She would not be ashamed of him. Yes, he served, but after all,
so did she. He was the main creative force behind the reconstruc-
tion of Moscow, which would put the stamp of the great Stalin epoch
on the city for future ages. She was a rank-and-file technician, but
she served too, like everyone else. A person had to live, to eat and
drink, and no matter what anyone said, to build cities as well. And
Igor Vladimirovich had achieved his position not through obsequi-
ousness or dirty tricks, but thanks to his talent. And in his soul he
sympathized with people who were persecuted and dispossessed; he
had interceded on behalf of Lena Budyagina and helped get Vanya
away.

She remembered how once they had been walking along the
Volkhonka past the square where the Palace of Councils was being constructed. She asked him why he hadn't participated in the competition
for the design of the palace; everyone had been surprised and confused
that he hadn't.

He laughed.

"Do you know who was most afraid that the Palace of Councils
would be built? You'll never guess."

She named several names, but did not guess. It turned out it was — Hitler! If Moscow were to erect that towering monstrosity, then they would outdo Berlin, which the Führer didn't want.

"So, you didn't want to upset Hitler?"

"It looks that way, doesn't it?"

"But seriously, what was the reason?"

"Seriously? They're building the palace on the site of the Church of Christ the Savior, which was destroyed. You can think what you like about religion and churches. But it was built in honor of the victory over Napoleon, using public funds raised kopeck by kopeck from all over Russia. I could not participate in its destruction."

Yes, life with Igor Vladimirovich would be righteous, insofar as it could be righteous in this country.

But still . . . what would Sasha think when he heard that she had gotten married for a second time? The first time to a successful cardsharp, and the second time to an architect at the height of his career? He would think badly of her. He was being buffeted from place to place around the country, persecuted, oppressed, homeless, without a roof over his head, and she would be living in a lovely apartment, visiting the conservatory, attending premieres. Things were over with Sasha, but she did not want him to see her as a cheap husband-hunter, looking to marry money.

Why hadn't Sasha wanted to meet with her then? She would have come to Kalinin, they would have sat at the train station and talked, maybe he would have understood everything, and then everything would have turned out differently. But now Sasha linked her name in his mind with disappointment, yet one more betrayal. And it was impossible to change anything.

Nothing had worked out or would work out with Sasha and it was time to forget her illusions. Circumstances were forcing her to get married. She would not find a better husband than Igor Vladimirovich, someone who was so intelligent, decent, loving, concerned. And there was no need to put it off, he was in a hurry, tomorrow or the day after tomorrow she would move in with him on Gorky Street. And after that . . . well, after that, there were many things which made her uncomfortable. How would she start addressing him with the more intimate "thou"? She was used to using the more formal "you" when she spoke to him, and she was used to referring to him by first name and patronymic. How would she kiss him, and how would she get into bed with him? She would have to break down her internal resistance. Well, that would all come later. What was important now was to clear up everything with Sasha. Of course, Sasha would find out that she had married again. But Sofya Alexandrovna could tell him that this person had waited for her for four years, as she had waited for Sasha for years. And had given up waiting. And had decided that she had the right to determine her own fate.

She would give Igor Vladimirovich her consent, but first she would tell him everything. About Kostya and about Sasha. But that was past, and in the future she would live with Igor Vladimirovich and she hoped she would be a good, devoted, and, of course, faithful wife.

In the courtyard Varya looked at Sofya Alexandrovna's windows. There was a light in the windows. So she wasn't asleep. Varya went up to her room.

She knew the corridor, the apartment was familiar. There were new tenants in Mikhail Yurevich's room, and Sasha's room, which she and Kostya had rented at one time, was inhabited by a woman she didn't know. In response to Varya's question about who she was, Sofya Alexandrovna answered evasively, "An acquaintance of my husband's." Apparently, it was someone from Pavel Nikolaevich's new family, but Varya did not ask any more questions.

Much had changed. But still, as she went in to see Sofya Alexandrovna, Varya thought sorrowfully about how much still linked her with this room — they had put together packages for Sasha here, read his letters, she had addressed parcels to him and sealed them. Now this house would cease to be her second home; of course, she would not stop seeing Sofya Alexandrovna, but it was unlikely that she would manage to call on her as often as she had before. And the only memento of this apartment would be the books that were presents from Mikhail Yurevich.

Varya's account worried Sofya Alexandrovna.

"This could end badly. Go visit your aunt in Michurinsk for the time being, and the situation will be clearer there."

And then Varya said that Igor Vladimirovich had proposed to her.

"Well, that's wonderful," Sofya Alexandrovna brightened. "You did praise him, after all."

"Yes, he's a decent person. He hasn't even joined the Party, although they are demanding that he do so. The director of a studio, and not a Party member. There are very few cases like that."

"For me the most important thing is that he is ready to protect you. Of course, heads aren't rolling the way they were before, but his reasoning sounds very logical, with him you will be safe. Marry him, Varenka. Save yourself. It will make your life easier."

Varya was silent. Sofya Alexandrovna took her by the hand and looked into her eyes.

"What's bothering you? Tell me! Sasha?"

By remaining silent, Varya confirmed the other woman's question.

"Varya, darling . . . Of course, I made a mistake when I told Sasha about Kostya. It would have been better if you had told him yourself. But Varyusha, that wouldn't have changed anything. Sasha lived in Kalinin for half a year, now he's in Ufa. He said that he went there on business, but I found out that Kalinin has been proclaimed a closed city and so he had to leave. Tomorrow Ufa could be made a closed city, and that would mean more wanderings, and perhaps exile or the camps. And there's no light at the end of the tunnel. Sasha is a marked man, he's doomed, he's the kind they're after. Does he have the right to wreck your life the way his own life has been wrecked? If he knew about your current situation, he would say without a moment's thought, 'Get married right away, especially if he's a decent person.' I feel bitter saying this, I know that you would have been a wonderful wife to Sasha, but if everything is ruined for Sasha, at least you can have a decent life."

Varya was silent and then said, "Perhaps you are right about Sasha. Probably he really should be free. But I would not have been a burden to him in any case, I don't think. And Igor Vladimirovich truly is a fine person. But I am not sure that I love him."

"Varyusha, darling, you think that the best marriages are love matches? You are mistaken. . . . Love, even the strongest love, is no guarantee of a happy family life. I was very much in love with my husband, Sasha's father. My family was against the marriage: they said he was stubborn, narrow-minded, and intolerant, and I thought that he was that way out of independence and a sense of his own merit. I was blinded by love, Varyusha; he was very handsome. And I ruined my life. He turned out to be an egoist, and heartlessly vain. So there's a love match for you! Join your life only with someone who has a heart, with a genuine human being. Igor Vladimirovich has waited for you for four years, that means he loves you. Marry him, don't change your mind!"

"Do you want me to do what you say?"

"Yes, because I wish you happiness!"

The next morning Varya went into Igor Vladimirovich's office.

He rose and looked at her questioningly.

"Igor Vladimirovich," said Varya, "let's go out again somewhere today, there are some things I want to tell you."

"Of course, that's fine, but tell me Varya, just one word: yes or no?"

Varya smiled at him.

"Yes."

37

G LEB MET THEM in the foyer of the Palace of Labor. He smiled.

"I knew that Sasha would bring you here."

"Did you?" Lena responded with a smile.

"To show off his art to you."

"He calls himself a friend," Sasha uttered sadly, "and presents me as a heartless careerist. I've brought you a pianist!"

"That's perfectly wonderful!" Gleb exclaimed. He sat Lena next to him. He looked at her and sounded the first chords.

Never had Sasha worked so joyously as he did today, never had Gleb's familiar melodies had such an effect on him.

"... *Ach, those black eyes have captivated me, they are impossible to forget, they burn before my eyes ...*"

Lena's story had shaken him. What an amazing coincidence! They had taken him to the station then in the Black Maria. First the Red Army soldiers jumped out of the vehicle, and he lingered, gazing at the people, the free people, the sky with its low clouds, the wet asphalt, all this made an impression on him after his time in prison. . . . The commander yelled, "Come on, come on, the train isn't going to wait for you, get out!" And scowling, the little man in the long wool military overcoat rushed ahead, anxiously pushing his way through the crowd. Feeling someone's eyes on him, Sasha looked around, but he did not see a single familiar face and, flanked by two Red Army officers, he went on toward the railcar. And that was Varya looking at him and crying. Fate itself had brought them together before a separation, but they hadn't even had the opportunity to look at each other. It hadn't worked out. And after that he had ruined everything himself. How could he have spoken to her so cruelly on the telephone! He recalled her crestfallen voice as she said, "Then you have nothing else to say to me, Sasha?" He would call her. Just to hear her voice, no matter what she said. Let her know that he valued her, was proud of her, and blamed himself for that conversation. . . .

Gleb played on and on.

". . . *Black eyes, passionate eyes, lovely, burning eyes, how I love you, how I fear you, I first laid eyes on you in an unkind hour . . .*"

Moving around the room, Sasha saw Lena, and she also looked at him from time to time and at the group and smiled at Gleb's jokes, and when Sasha announced a break and came over to them, it seemed to him that her face grew calmer.

"So, how are things?" asked Sasha. "Is it boring?"

"I am very impressed!"

"Could you accompany me, like Gleb does?"

"Accompany? I doubt it. I can play only when I have music to read from."

"What do you need music for?" Gleb smiled. "Do you remember any tangos?"

"Of course I remember. 'Droplets of Champagne,' 'Weary Sun . . .' "

Gleb played a couple of chords.

"Is this it?"

"Yes."

He stood up. "Sit down, play."

Lena sat down at the grand piano and played the tango. She raised her eyes from the keyboard.

"I haven't sat down at a piano in a hundred years. How was it, all right?"

"Fine, wonderful!" exclaimed Gleb.

"And you say you have only one profession, foreign languages," said Sasha. "It turns out you have a second one."

"I never thought of it as a profession."

"Well it's time you did. I bet it's better than hauling railroad ties."

Gleb raised his eyebrows in surprise, and Lena frowned.

"Don't frown," Sasha said to her. "It won't hurt for Gleb to know what kind of work you do. He and I will try to get you a job as an accompanist. What do you think, Gleb, will we be able to?"

"We'll try."

"And we'll rent you a good apartment, and we'll keep watch over you; you're too pretty for the natives."

"Not only for the natives," added Gleb.

Lena stood up.

"It's time for me to leave. I have a long way to go, and I have to be at work tomorrow."

"When is Stasik supposed to come?" Sasha asked Gleb.

"Around eight."

"Excellent. Hang in there, Lenochka."

Sasha turned toward the auditorium and clapped his hands together.

"Let's continue. Please rise and stand in pairs."

"... *Farewell, farewell, farewell, my dear, I will never in my life love anyone again, and all I have is memories of you and I send you a farewell tango ...*"

Sasha turned his attention to the group again, thinking about Varya as before, turning over again and again in his mind all that Lena had recounted about her. "So young, so beautiful," she had said, "and completely consumed with other people's problems and concerns." And she had written to him in exile, "How I would love to know what you are doing now. . . ." And she had wanted to buoy him up with her love and had taken Lena's son to the Far East. . . . He and Gleb had concluded that the people were lackeys, stooges . . . no, not all of them were lackeys! Sasha mechanically squeezed his partner's hand, and his partner looked at him in surprise.

"Did I do something wrong?"

"Excuse me," he apologized. "You're fine, you're doing everything right. My mind was elsewhere. . . ."

Gleb started a new melody: "*The trip is over, my heart is weary and wants to rest awhile ...*"

He could arrange any melody to fit the rhythm of the dance, even Gypsy songs, which he knew Sasha loved. Lena was sitting near him and he was saying something to her, obviously explaining to her how to accompany. Stasik appeared and also seated himself near the piano. People from the next group started arriving.

Finally Sasha let his students go and looked at Gleb.

"Will you take Lena home?"

"No need, I can get home myself."

"He'll drive you home in the car and stop wherever you say and let you off."

"You have a car?"

"All the cars in this city belong to us," laughed Gleb.

"Don't be a stranger. You know where to find Gleb and me. In the mornings we're at home, and in the evenings we're here. We'll try to get you into our brigade."

"I need to think it over."

"Think it over, but not too hard."

When Gleb got back, the second group was already finishing up.

"Well, pal, I want to report to you, that she lives behind the oil processing plant, it's dark, there are some little houses, and barracks farther on. She wouldn't let me drive any farther. And she wouldn't let me see her to her door. Of course, I insisted, saying I wouldn't let her go by herself. I went with her partway. The barracks are in a straight line, like in the camps. There is a streetlight by each one, but the barracks themselves were dark inside — they probably go to bed early, or maybe they have to put their lights out at a specific time, who knows. So as soon as we got to the barracks, she said good-bye and rushed off but I noticed that she went into the second barracks on the right."

Sasha told Gleb Lena's story over dinner. Gleb listened attentively, although these days there was nothing unusual in Lena's fate; they were surrounded by people with similar tales.

"I decided that she was a teacher: she enunciates her words very clearly."

"She lived abroad for a long time, that's what that's from, and after that she worked as a translator at some technical publishing house."

"Her father could have gotten her a better job."

"No, her father is of the old school! And she wouldn't have gone for it herself. I used to think that way too, you know: the country needs engineers and all that."

Gleb snickered.

"What idealistic babes we were. . . ."

"That's for sure," Sasha said with a laugh. "We wanted to serve the socialist fatherland, but it turned out we weren't needed."

"A woman like that," said Gleb, "she knows three languages, and they've forced her to haul railroad ties, lay rails, and hammer spikes. There's a poem for you about a lovely lady."

"Okay, enough, let's have another round."

"Well, how about that," said Gleb, amazed, "*you* want another round? What happened?"

"I've got problems."

They drank and ate.

"You see, the thing is, I was in love, back when I was in Moscow," said Sasha. "I mean, I don't know, would you call it love? A young girl, seventeen years old, she liked me, she was a nice girl, pretty, smart, with personality. Then I was put away, she went from prison to prison, brought packages, looked out for my mother, wrote to me in exile. I wrote back, dreamed of seeing her. Her name is Varya. And then when I returned, I found out that she was getting married. It's true, she got divorced quickly. I felt like I'd been punched, and of course I called everything off, put an end to it. And now Lena told me how things really were, and now everything looks completely different. It's a long story, but basically I was wrong; I rejected her harshly and unfairly, she waited for me and I tossed her aside."

"Did you love her?"

"I did."

"And now?"

"Now too."

"And what about her?"

Sasha shrugged his shoulders.

"I don't know, we haven't seen each other in five years."

"That's a tough one. . . ." Gleb paused. "Of course, a young girl isn't going to sit by the hearth waiting for you for so many years. But on the other hand, it was first love! That's a hard thing to forget."

"I'll call her," said Sasha.

"That's the spirit," said Gleb. "Have her come here. We'll get her the best hotel room there is to be had. And figure out what's going on."

"How can she come here? She's working and she's in school."

"The May holidays are right around the corner, and then she can take a few vacation days, and there's your honeymoon. Let's drink to that, pal!"

It was a good thought! And Lena was in Ufa. He would tell Varya, "Come see us for the holidays! We'll all get together."

"Now about Lena," said Sasha. "We need to set her up in our division; she'll wither away working on the railroad."

"Yes, by all means," Gleb agreed. "I'll talk Lena and Stasik into it, we'll make room for her. I'm afraid that Mashka won't go for it, since she was exiled."

"Kanevsky is playing in the local symphony orchestra and he used to work with us and he's an exile too. And the last name? It's possible Mashka won't recognize that last name — she's not too bright when it comes to politics."

"Let's assume that. And Semyon? He'll say again that they don't need pianists."

"If Semyon doesn't want her, then I'm dropping everything and leaving tomorrow."

"Really?"

"Really. Without a second thought."

"I'm not having second thoughts, pal, I'm just thinking things through, figuring how it will all work out. Resigning would be the right move. And I'll chime in too and say, 'If Sasha's leaving, then so am I.' "

Usually Sasha called Moscow on Sundays. But it was three days until Sunday. It would be unthinkable to wait that long. The next day he called Varya.

Taking his request, the operator asked: "Who will pick up, or who should I ask for?"

"Varvara Sergeyevna Ivanova."

"Wait."

Then she said: "Not home."

The next day was the same story. She was probably at the college.

On Sunday he called his mother first. She was waiting for his call, as always. How's your health, how do you feel. . . . At the end of the conversation he asked:

"How's Varya getting along?"

And he felt suddenly that his mother was stalling.

"Varya," his mother repeated. "Varya has gotten married, Sashenka."

"Married?"

"Yes. To a good, decent person. They have known each other for many years, but everything was decided in just one day. That's just how things worked out. Do you understand me? It's the times we're living in, Sashenka, you don't need me to tell you that."

"When did it happen?"

"Two weeks ago."

"Well," said Sasha. "Give her my congratulations. My deepest, sincerest, and most heartfelt congratulations."

∽ Part II ∽

And the marble of lieutenants — a plywood monument.

— B. Slutsky

PART II

✑ 1 ✑

GLEB HAD NEWS. Marya Konstantinovna instructed him to bring over documents confirming that he was a theater set designer.

"Moscow requested them, they're looking for a theater for you."

"Your Ulyana is effective," Gleb told Sasha.

Sasha winced. The reminder about Ulyana cut him to the quick. "His" Ulyana, indeed!

"We'll see what kind of hole in the wall they offer me. In the meantime, we have to find work for Lena."

Semyon Grigoryevich didn't even want to hear about a new accompanist — the groups were ending, there was only a month, a month and a half of work left. But when Sasha and Gleb threatened to leave, he gave in. Very well, he would listen to their friend, then decide.

But Lena didn't show up.

"Let's go over and see her," Gleb suggested. "I saw which barrack she went into."

"She doesn't want us to go and see her," Sasha replied. "Let's wait."

Lena showed up at the Palace of Labor about two weeks later.

"We worked without any days off."

Coatless — the weather was warm — she wore a simple gray blouse over an equally simple dress; she was tall, strong, and tanned.

Sasha was working with a group, and when he saw Lena, he gave her a friendly wave.

Gleb was overjoyed and broke into a smile; he seated Lena beside him again, showed her how to accompany again, even made her play a little instead of playing himself. Things seemed all right, it was working out.

During the break Sasha came up to them, he put his arms around Lena's shoulders.

"We've arranged everything. Gleb will train you a little, then you'll show the boss your stuff. The main thing is to know when to pause, when to repeat, all this will come with time.

Unexpectedly Lena said no: "Thanks, but this doesn't suit me."

"Why?!" Sasha was amazed. "Were you promoted to a better job?"

"I still have the same job as before. But it suits me. It's dependable. Workers are always in demand. Especially to haul railroad ties. With you, there's no stability. You're here today, you're gone tomorrow. What will I be left with?"

"We'll set you up with the Concert Tour Bureau. Men and women singers come here on tour, they need accompanists at concerts."

She shook her head in disagreement.

"I'm inconspicuous at the factory, but here I'll be in the public eye. If I'm an accompanist at concerts, that means my name will appear in posters. 'Ye. Budyagina at the piano' — isn't that the way it's written?"

"We're talking about working with us now, we'll see about the future later."

"Sashenka, there's only one thing that *I* can see: I won't be staying *here* very long. Do you understand?"

"Lena," Gleb interrupted, "I understand you, too. But, you know, the situation is changing. There aren't any 'Yezhov gloves' anymore, they say that Yezhov himself has been imprisoned. And some people are already being freed, rehabilitated."

"Possibly, possibly," Lena replied sarcastically, "but if they free me, too, why should I flit from one job to another? I'll wait — maybe they'll send me back to Moscow and send my parents back."

Her irony was understandable. What rehabilitation? A faint rumor had gone around that they had supposedly freed several generals and were supposedly beginning to imprison fewer people. Well, since half the country was already in prison, if they decided to imprison the second half — who would remain, whom would Stalin lead? Lena's reasoning was sound. Of course, the fact that she was inconspicuous at the factory was a relative matter; whoever was supposed to know about her, did. But she had the *semblance* of inconspicuousness nonetheless, and this reassured her.

"Decide what you think is best," said Sasha. "Frankly, I thought it would make you happy — if it doesn't, it doesn't — but come around to see us anyway. Don't disappear for a long time."

Gleb looked at Lena with yearning.

Had he fallen in love?

Lena began coming to see them on her days off. She would sit beside Gleb, sometimes she would replace him at the piano, just for the pleasure of playing.

Gleb would perk up when she appeared, even become affectionate. Sasha had never seen him like this — even-tempered, cheerful, looking over at Lena, beaming with happiness.

Then they would walk her home, sometimes the two of them, more often only Gleb; Stasik would replace him at the piano; no one could replace Sasha.

Once, right on her day off, the group was canceled — there was an urgent meeting called in the establishment.

"Maybe we could spend a little time in a restaurant?" Gleb suggested.

Lena shrugged her shoulders.

"I'd rather go to the movies. I bought a *Pravda* on my way over. Eisenstein extols Romm's latest film, *Lenin in 1918.*"

They bought tickets for the 6:00 P.M. showing. Sasha could barely sit through it to the end. The glorification of Stalin — well, all right, everybody was doing it now. But the scene in which Bukharin assists in the attempt to assassinate Lenin was repulsive, nothing could be more despicable. Sasha had seen Bukharin once, at the Pioneer gathering in Khamovniki, where Bukharin gave a speech when he was elected an honorary member; he walked with them along Bolshaya Tsarintsynskaya Street, down the middle of the street, a small, stocky, broad-shouldered man with a beard and merry blue eyes, who laughed and joked and walked with them to Zubovskaya Square and then got into a car that was waiting for him there. There weren't any bodyguards, he was simple, cheerful, charming. "The Party's favorite" was what Lenin called him. And now he had been executed as a traitor, spy, and murderer. And director Mikhail Romm was in a hurry to trample his mutilated body.

They walked out of the theater silently. Got on a bus. Lena refused to hail a cab: "I don't want to stir up any unnecessary talk."

On the bus Sasha asked her for the copy of *Pravda:* "Let me have a look at what Eisenstein has to say."

"The movie gets to the core," Eisenstein wrote, "it grasps the very heart of what makes Bolshevism great — humaneness. . . . The theme of the Revolution's humaneness, the great humaneness of those who are bringing it about is reflected in all the nuances of the characters' personalities and their actions. . . ."

And Eisenstein was doing it, too! As a young boy, Sasha had seen his *Battleship Potemkin* in the Khudozhestvennyi Theater on Arbat Square. The cashiers, ticket-takers, cloak-room attendants, all were dressed in sailors' uniforms; it looked just grand, it set the mood. The world had acknowledged *Battleship Potemkin* as the best film and Eisenstein as the greatest director. Now the "greatest" was loyally serving the tyrant and executioner. Here was an example for his argument with Gleb about genius and villainy.

Gleb also read the paper and gave Sasha a meaningful glance.

"Well then, one more sycophant."

This meant Gleb also remembered their conversation.

Lena's visits made Sasha happy. Memories of childhood and youth would be stirred up: they were sad, pleasant, made his heart ache. Looking at her, he often thought: That's what Ivan Grigoryevich's blood line means! He had passed will and courage down to his daughter. She knows that they're going to take her away any day now, but says not a word about it. Only once did she mention in passing: "It's possible that they'll transfer me from one barrack to another, but the next time will be behind barbed wire."

His situation had been far easier than Lena's present one, just because of the unexpectedness of his arrest. He couldn't imagine how he would have gone to the institute, met with his friends, ate and drank, thinking about the same thing all the time: "This is your last step as a free man." It was torture for Lena! And torture for her son! Maybe she had already said good-bye to him without the hope of ever seeing him again. Her only solace was that he and Gleb were close by, so it wasn't so completely lonely after all, and in Moscow she didn't feel so alone, with Varya next door there.

Sasha had steadfastly endured the news about Varya's new marriage. At least it seemed that way to him.

"Well, what about your Varya?" Gleb asked. "Should I expect her in Ufa or not?"

"Varya got married. She knew this man for many years, but everything was decided in a single day. Maybe it's better that way."

What, strictly speaking, would have changed if he had had time to talk with her? Well, they would have seen each another. No matter what he would have said to her, no matter what she would have replied, he had to disappear from her life anyway. And now it turned out that it was she who had disappeared from his life. And she'd done the right thing: at best, he was doomed to wander, at worst, the camp lay ahead of him. So she wouldn't have been able to wait for him in any case. Maybe her new husband helps people just like she does, that was what had brought them together. Only he was sorry that he hadn't apologized. Should he call now? It would be awkward — he hadn't called, he hadn't written, and now he finds out that she's gotten married and reappears to congratulate her and ask her to pardon him for the past? Maybe someday he'd see her, and he'd apologize then.

Depressing, of course, but what can you do? And what lay ahead? Where should he go after Ufa? Drag along after Semyon Grigoryevich to Saratov? If Gleb were to come along, that would be different; after all, he was a loyal friend. Go to Ryazan? How could the brother of the late Mikhail Yurevich help him? What kind of work should he look for in Ryazan? Everything was in a fog. And his dissatisfaction with himself gnawed at him. In exile he had worked on French, he had written essays about the history of the French Revolution; here the French textbook and the essays were thrown into his suitcase, and he hadn't looked at them once, he hadn't read a single book. He was dancing and drinking. That's what his life had come to.

2

IT TOOK HITLER two weeks to annihilate the Polish army, one of the strongest in Europe; he conquered a nation whose population was nearly ten times that of Finland. *He* had waged war for more than three months and had failed to defeat a people whose population was one-fortieth of that of the Soviet population. *He* had put *his* trust in the military, *he* had underestimated the strength of Finnish resistance. Well then, every politician has failures, every military leader suffers defeats from time to time as well.

But the people have to continue believing in the invincibility of their army as they had before, they have to know that we'll only fight on foreign soil — we had fought only on Finnish land — they needed to be convinced that they were winning and would win with little bloodshed. That's why our losses should not be reported. The U.S.S.R. is a large country, and if a few people are unaccounted for in its innumerable cities, villages, and rural settlements, no one would find out how many people we actually lost. There was only one thing that the people needed to know: *he* had moved the border with Finland from a distance of 32 kilometers to 150 kilometers, thereby ensuring the security of Leningrad.

And the people also needed to know that there is a war going on in Europe. It was through *his* efforts that peace is being maintained in the Soviet Union. The world is fragile and unsafe. It can become strong and safe if the U.S.S.R. becomes the mightiest power in the world, one that no one would dare attack. To this end, the nation's economy has to be converted into a military one; the production of airplanes, tanks, and the newest weapons has to be increased. This would require much strength, much sacrifice, but the people would have to agree to this, if they wanted peace and order. The most brutal work discipline has to be introduced: unauthorized absence from the workplace, truancy, lateness, turning out poor production — all had to be punished in the most ruthless manner. The training of the command staff of all ranks has to be increased many-fold; new academies, schools, and courses had to be created — the military profession has to become the most prestigious in the nation. Strict order has to be established in the army; a combined military and political command that includes the ranks of generals and admirals has to be introduced. Voroshilov has to be removed from the position of People's Commissar of Defense and replaced by Timoshenko. Military reconnaissance has to be declared responsible for the failures in Finland. Proskurov, the head of the Red Army's Directorate of Military Intelligence, has to be executed.

What about the international repercussions? They were bad, unfavorable. But that was temporary. The Soviet Union would show its true strength. Hitler would go to war against the Soviet Union only when he has destroyed England and France; he can't wage war on two fronts. As for France and England — they were not Poland, they could not be conquered in two weeks. The Soviet Union had a reserve of three to four years. In this time *he* would create the most powerful military industry in the world, the most powerful army in the world. Let no one labor under any delusion about our failures in Finland, let no one console himself with talk about the "colossus with feet of clay."

England and France had been assisting the Finns, sending arms, forming an expeditionary corps; volunteers from all over Europe had come to Finland. Under these conditions, the continuation of military operations would have inevitably led to a war between the U.S.S.R. and England and France. This was what Hitler wanted, he wanted to draw the U.S.S.R. into the war on his side. But the Soviet Union wasn't ready for such a war. *He* would come forward when he had fortified his position and they were weakened. That is why *he* stopped military operations and signed a peace treaty with the Finns.

Yes, yes, that was exactly why *he* had signed it, to show Hitler that *he* was just as smart as Hitler was, and Hitler realized that he had failed to draw the U.S.S.R. into the war, that he would have to fight alone. And that was what he was doing. In April the Germans occupied Denmark and made a landing in Norway. At the beginning of May, Holland and Belgium capitulated. The road to France was open.

England had barely managed to evacuate its expeditionary corps from Dunkirk.

Chamberlain's government fell, and Churchill came into power. Of course, Churchill was a sworn enemy of the Soviet regime. But Churchill had condemned the Munich Pact and would not conclude a new treaty with Hitler. England would continue the war. While Germany had a Western front, the U.S.S.R. was secure against a German attack.

On May 24, Beria informed Stalin about a telegram that had just been received from New York: "Operation completed. Results to be clarified later."

And so they finally had gotten to Trotsky. But why would "the results . . . be clarified later?" Had the scoundrel been killed or not?

Stalin had to wait for the answer to this question for several days. Beria finally arrived. Judging by his face, the way he hid his eyes behind the lenses of his pince-nez, the way his voice quavered, Stalin understood that the operation had failed.

Without shifting his heavy glance from Beria, Stalin snapped: "Report!"

Beria reported.

"The operation was carried out under the direction of the famous artist Siqueiros. At three in the morning a group of twenty-two people, armed with submachine guns and a machine gun, drove up to Trotsky's house and instantly disarmed the guards outside. Our man, standing guard at the gate, opened it up for them. Siqueiros's people disarmed the inside guards and opened a barrage of fire at the windows and doors of Trotsky's bedroom. The machine gun was aimed directly and fired long charges, more than two hundred bullets at the bedroom alone. Finishing the operation, the group tossed a bomb and escaped. However . . ."

At this point Beria's voice broke off.

" 'However' what?" Stalin asked menacingly.

"Trotsky and his wife hid behind the bed, the bed was their cover. Only their grandson in the neighboring room was slightly wounded, and it was nothing, a small scratch.

"Was the bedroom large?" Stalin asked, without turning his head.

"It was small. . . ."

"And you want me to believe that two hundred bullets fired into a small bedroom did not hit the people who were in that room?"

"Comrade Stalin —"

"I know that I am Comrade Stalin! I'm asking you: How could this happen? Two hundred bullets and not a single one struck the target?"

"The distance between the window and the bed was half a meter. Trotsky's wife pushed him into that space and lay down on top of him. They fired at the bed, at the entire room through the window, but they were hiding in a place that was out of the line of fire."

"And the bomb?"

"The bomb did not explode."

Stalin slammed his fist on the table. The expression on his face was terrifying.

"Who is deceiving whom?"

Beria remained silent.

Stalin slammed his fist on the table again.

"I'm asking, who's deceiving whom: Siqueiros — Eitingon? Eitingon — Beria? Or is Beria trying to deceive Comrade Stalin?"

Beria remained silent.

"Why are you silent?" Stalin yelled.

"Comrade Stalin," Beria said, "our man has infiltrated Trotsky's circle. Your order will be carried out."

"When?"

"In the near future."

"Now then," Stalin uttered sternly, "I'm giving you three months; everything has to be completed in August. Pass this on to Sudoplatov and Eitingon. At the same time, remind them about what happened to Speigelglass."

On June 6, the new English ambassador in Moscow, Stafford Cripps, passed on a personal message from Churchill to Stalin. Churchill warned that Hitler's ambition was to conquer all the European countries including the U.S.S.R., and he proposed that they work together.

Having read the message, Stalin answered: "I am well acquainted with several of Germany's leading figures and didn't notice that they had any aspirations of devouring the European states."

This conversation, as well as the text of Churchill's message, was passed on to Hitler the very same day — Stalin demonstrated his loyalty to him.

Within a week, on June 14, the Germans occupied Paris.

This news stunned Stalin. France, the most powerful state in Europe, had been brought down in a month. Was Hitler unconquerable? Would Hitler really deceive *him?*

In the speech that he gave at the Reichstag in honor of his conquest of France, Hitler stated: "At this hour, I suppose, my conscience urges me once again to appeal to England's reason and common sense, because I am not a defeated enemy who is pleading for mercy, I am a conqueror. . . . You must not wait until Churchill flees to Canada, you must begin peaceful negotiations with Germany now."

Stalin waited for England's response with no less anxiety than Hitler. After the lightning-flash defeat of France, a peace with England would make Hitler the master of Europe, which would upset all Stalin's calculations. The members of the Politburo who remained to have dinner with Stalin in the evening sat around subdued; there were no anecdotes told, no jokes. Stalin was gloomy. He would get up from the table, then sit down again, lowering his eyes to his plate. Molotov later complained to his wife: "The tension is so unbearable, my nerves just can't take it."

A few days later, the Minister of Foreign Affairs of England, Eden, rejected Hitler's peace proposal. On August 13, the Germans bombed English cities, and the aerial war over England began. The English, of course, would never forgive Hitler for this. Stalin breathed a sigh of relief. *He* was not left to confront Hitler one on one. Their pact was still in effect. Time was in *his* favor.

Then on the evening of August 21, Beria appeared with an urgent report: Trotsky had died that day in a hospital in Mexico City. The blow to his head had been delivered with an ice pick by the Spaniard Ramón Mercader, the same NKVD agent-infiltrator in Coyoacán about whom Beria had reported to Stalin the previous time. The operation was supervised in Mexico by Eitingon and in Moscow by Sudoplatov.

They had finally finished off the scoundrel! This man had poisoned *his* life, worried *him* needlessly for thirty-five years. *He* saw him for the first time in 1905 at the London Congress: young, handsome, surrounded by male and female admirers, he delivered spectacular speeches and didn't even notice *him*. And in Vienna in 1913, Trotsky also gave showy speeches; he was also the center of attention and he didn't notice *him* either. And in 1917 he played the role of leader and guide of the Revolution, and during the Civil War he considered himself the main organizer of the victory — he didn't care one whit for *him,* he behaved arrogantly and impertinently. And for the past fifteen years he had slung mud at *him,* shamed *him* at very turn; they say he even wrote a book about *him,* just hadn't managed to get it published. It was obvious what the book was about: Trotsky was a genius, while Stalin was a mediocrity. No! Comrade Stalin ruled over the destinies of the world, while Mr. Trotsky was stretched out in the morgue with a smashed skull. Serves him right!

Beria also handed *him* Trotsky's will, written in February before Siqueiros's attack. He had anticipated his own death, the scoundrel, he understood that he could not escape revenge. But he couldn't die like other people. He maintained his pose right up to the edge of the grave. Well then, let's just have a look at what he'd scribbled here.

Stalin opened the folder that Beria had handed to him.

WILL

The end, apparently, is near. These lines will be published after my death.

There is no need for me to refute the stupid and vile slander of Stalin and his network of agents: there is not a single stain on my revolutionary honor. I have never entered, either directly or indirectly, into any secret agreements or negotiations with the enemies of the working class. Thousands of Stalin's opponents have perished as victims of such false accusations. New generations of revolutionaries will restore their political honor and give the Kremlin executioners their just deserts.

I fervently thank my friends who remained loyal to me in the most difficult hours of my life. I am not naming anyone individually, because I cannot name everyone.

I consider that I have the right to make an exception for my friend, Natalya Ivanovna Sedova. Fate granted me the good fortune to be her husband along with the good fortune to be a fighter for the cause of socialism. In the course of almost forty years of our life together she has remained an inexhaustible source of love, generosity, and tenderness. She has endured great suffering, especially in the last period of our life. But I find comfort in the fact that she has also known days of happiness.

For forty-three years of my adult life I was a revolutionary, I fought under the banner of Marxism for forty-two of them. If I had to start over,

I would naturally try to avoid making certain mistakes, but the general direction of my life would remain unchanged. I will die a proletarian revolutionary, a Marxist, a dialectical materialist, and, consequently, an atheist. My faith in the Communist future of humanity is no less fervent, and even stronger, than in the days of my youth.

Natasha has just walked over to the window and opened it wider so that air can flow more freely into my room. I see a bright green patch of grass under a wall, a clear blue sky above it, and sunlight everywhere. Life is marvelous. May future generations cleanse it of evil, oppression, and violence, and may they enjoy it to the fullest.

February 27, 1940
Coyoacán

L. Trotsky

～ 3 ～

THE FIRST INTELLIGENCE reports about the attack that Germany was preparing on the Soviet Union began to arrive in June 1940. Stalin attached no importance to them. The talk by some Germans was idle chatter, the training of several thousand parachutists who knew Russian was the fabrication of an idiot, the transfer of German units onto Polish territory was normal military life in an occupied nation, the concentration of German troops on the Soviet border was disinformation; Churchill was being duped, his attention was being distracted from the preparations to invade England.

A more serious warning came in October from an agent in the German General Staff: Germany would start a war with the U.S.S.R. in the spring of next year; the goal was to split off the Ukraine. His report should not be believed either — Hitler won't be able to end the war with England by the spring of next year, he wouldn't be crossing La Manche in the winter.

And the stubborn idiot Litvinov also kept going on and on about the inevitability of the German attack, about Molotov's erroneous policy, meaning Stalin's policy of course, not Molotov's.

"The devastation of France means that Soviet policy is totally bankrupt. Hitler has no second front now; England is not a second front. Now the Reich can rely on the entire continent of Europe for resources. Bribing Hitler with gifts is the policy of an ostrich hiding its head in the sand."

He doesn't understand a thing, the old blockhead! Hitler will not attack the Soviet Union. Of course, given his impulsive nature, it depends on whether or not he is given a good reason to do so. Hitler has to be convinced of *his* loyalty. *He* will transfer Litvinov from Central Committee member to Candidate-member of the Communist Party. Hitler will see that *he* is ridding himself of Jews. And *he* will remove Zhemchuzhina from the Central Committee altogether, let Hitler marvel at the fact that *he's* even sacrificed the wife of Molotov, a government leader.

On October 5, the plan for the nation's defense was discussed in the Politburo: Timoshenko, Shaposhnikov, Zhukov, and one of the heads of the General Staff and the developer of the plan, Vassilevsky, who presented the plan.

Everyone was seated at a long table. As usual, Stalin paced around the office; sometimes he would walk up to the map that Vassilevsky traced with a pointer, then walk away from it, listening to Vassilevsky, trying to form a final opinion about him. This was already the third time *he* had listened to him, and with each time *his* impression grew more favorable.

Vasilevsky was from a priest's family; his father still had a parish in a remote village. Beria gave him a positive recommendation. A rare instance. Beria would unfailingly add something negative while giving the most positive review, so as to cover himself. But in this case he added nothing negative. Vassilevsky had attained the rank of staff captain during the Great War, has been serving in the Red Army from May of 1919, graduated from the Academy of the General Staff, served in the General Staff from 1937. A knowledgeable, mild, considerate person. Zhukov, of course, was a warrior, but a martinet who aroused irritation, whereas it was impossible to get irritated by Vassilevsky; once, *he* said to him: "Comrade Vassilevsky, you probably wouldn't even hurt a fly. . . . Be more tough." And he has a good, mild voice, and a pleasant face, light brown hair, blue eyes; he'd pass for a rural schoolteacher if he were dressed in a *kosovorotka,* the peasant side-buttoned shirt. Stalin listened to him without interrupting; only at the point when Vassilevsky spoke about reinforced regions, did he ask: "What, are you planning a retreat?"

"No, Comrade Stalin, by no means! We're planning only an advance, but that doesn't rule out creating a defensive line at the border."

Stalin stopped, turned to Vasilevsky.

"Right, it doesn't rule it out. At the new border! Now the Soviet Union has a new border! That's the one to reinforce. Whereas you've also been planning to reinforce the old border. But the old border doesn't exist any longer and never will. Forget about it."

"But it's well armed and equipped, Comrade Stalin," Vassilevsky timidly objected.

"Wonderful. That gives you ready equipment. Dismantle it and move it to the new border. And give the underground buildings to the collective farms, let them use them to store grain. By leaving the old defense structures intact, you're saying to the troops: 'Don't be afraid, you have somewhere to retreat, you still have a powerful defense line at your back.' This means cultivating retreatist attitudes in the army, everything's teaching them to retreat instead of advance. Continue!"

Vassilevsky continued. The plan was thorough. Vassilevsky presented it clearly. When he finished, a silence fell in the office. The military said nothing, they had already said everything with their plan; the members of the Politburo were also silent, they didn't know what Comrade Stalin thought about it.

Continuing to pace around the office, Stalin began speaking: "I don't quite understand the objective of the General Staff. . . ."

As usual, he spoke slowly, clearly, quietly, forcing everyone to listen tensely to every word.

"What is the General Staff's objective? It is to have our main forces concentrated on the Western front. What is this objective based on? It is based on the assumption that, in case of war, the Germans will, of course, attempt to deliver their main strike along the shortest route: Brest-Moscow. Can one agree with this objective? I don't think it's possible to agree with this objective. I don't think that the Germans will move along this shortest route. All the intelligence reports says that the Germans want to capture the Ukraine. Can these intelligence reports be believed unconditionally? Of course not. There is a lot of disinformation, lies, and nonsense. Nonetheless, it's no accident that the Ukraine is mentioned. Why not? If you think it's possible that Hitler will become involved in a war with the Soviet Union, it will be a long war; the U.S.S.R. is not Poland and it isn't France, and such a war is impossible without grain, without fuel, without raw materials. This means that Ukrainian grain, Donbass coal, Krivoi Rog iron ore, Nikopol manganese are of particular, exceptional importance to the Germans. It follows that Hitler will prepare his main strike not by moving east, but southeast. Moreover, Hitler has already established himself in the Balkans and it will be easy for him to strike from there. A plan based on this objective has to be developed."

He fell silent, then asked: "Do you have objections, comrades?"

Timoshenko and Shaposhnikov and Zhukov and Vassilevsky knew full well that, according to the plans of the German General Staff, the main forces of the Germans were aimed at Smolensk and Moscow. Moreover, as Hitler conquered the nations of Europe, in order to end the warfare more quickly, he would first break through rapidly to their capital cities. This was his well-developed, tested, and proven tactic.

But not a single one of them had the courage to raise an objection against Comrade Stalin.

"Well then," Stalin concluded, "there are no objections. I request the General Staff to rethink and report its plan in ten days."

On October 14 the plan was again presented in the Politburo. In this revised plan, in which the main strike was anticipated in the southwest, they envisioned the highest concentration of Soviet troops there as well. Vasilevsky reported clearly, thoroughly, and convincingly, just as he had the previous time.

Stalin was satisfied and after the meeting invited everyone to go down one floor to have some lunch in his apartment.

The lunch was simple. Let the military see how modestly Comrade Stalin lives, let them follow his example. The first course was a thick Ukrainian borshch; the second, well-prepared buckwheat groats and a lot of boiled meat; the third course was cooked fruit compote and fresh fruit. Stalin drank Khvanchkara, a light Georgian wine. But the officers did not follow his example in this; they applied themselves to the cognac.

Stalin raised a glass to toast Comrade Vassilevsky's health, and after taking a few sips from his wineglass, asked an unexpected question:

"Comrade Vassilevsky, why didn't you become a priest after you graduated the seminary?"

The embarrassed Vassilevsky mumbled something about the fact that he and his three brothers chose a different path in life.

"So then," Stalin said with a smile, "that wasn't what you wanted, that's understandable. Whereas Mikoyan and I wanted to become priests, but for some reason we were rejected." He turned to Mikoyan. "What do you say, Anastas, did they reject you?"

"They did, Comrade Stalin," Mikoyan confirmed.

"You see" — Stalin made a helpless gesture with his hands — "we still don't understand why they rejected us."

Everyone smiled, happy with the leader's joke and his good mood.

Stalin was silent for a little while, then raised his eyes up at Vasilevsky.

"Tell me, please, Comrade Vassilevsky, why don't you and your brothers help your father out financially? As far as I know, one of your brothers is a doctor, another an agronomist, and the third a pilot. You are financially secure people. I think that if all of you would have helped your parents, then the old man probably would have been able to abandon his church a long, long time ago. After all, he needs it only to survive somehow."

Now no one smiled, unsure what the leader was driving at and how it would all turn out for Vassilevsky.

"You see, the point is, Comrade Stalin," Vassilevsky explained, trying to hold back his nervousness, "I broke off all contact with my parents back in 1923."

"You broke off contact with your parents?" Feigning sincere surprise, Stalin repeated the question, "Why, if it's not a secret?"

"Otherwise, I couldn't have become a member of our Party, I couldn't have served in the Red Army, especially within the system of the General Staff."

"Do our Party and our army really have such kinds of rules?" Stalin again asked with surprise.

Everyone knew very well that the Party and army had exactly these kinds of rules, but no one confirmed this for Comrade Stalin. What's more, Comrade Stalin himself was well aware of this.

But Vassilevsky understood that he had to prove that what he had said was true, or else he would look like a liar in Stalin's eyes. So he said: "Comrade Stalin, with your permission, I'll tell you about this incident. . . ."

"Go ahead."

"Two weeks ago, unexpectedly I received a letter from my father, the first one in many years. I have been indicating in all applications since 1926 that my father is a priest and that I don't keep in contact, either in person or by letter, with him. And now suddenly there was this letter. I immediately informed the secretary of my Party organization about the letter. And he demanded that I not answer this letter and that I continue the former policy in my relations with my parents."

With a look of surprise, Stalin surveyed the members of the Politburo who were sitting at the table. Finally they understood what was expected of them, and echoed his expressions of the same surprise, puzzlement, and even indignation.

"Your secretary is a fool," said Stalin, "he has no right to work in the General Staff; the General Staff needs intelligent people, not block-heads. The Red Army must be united and monolithic, not stratified by social origins. Lenin's father was a member of the gentry and, as you know, Vladimir Ilich did not renounce his parents. I want you, Com-rade Vassilevsky, I want you and your brothers to immediately estab-lish contact with your parents and give them regular financial support. And pass this on to the secretary of your Party organization, if he's still a secretary and still working in the General Staff by then, of course."

～ 4 ～

MARYA KONSTANTINOVNA passed on a letter to Gleb from Moscow: the Committee on Arts Affairs was offering him a choice of cities where he could work as an artist in a Young People's Theater. Kalinin was one. There was a new artistic director there; at one time Gleb had left the theater because of the old one. Gleb chose Kalinin.

But he dragged out his departure, and it was obvious that it was because of Lena. He would wait impatiently for her to appear at the Palace, take her home, return sullen, preoccupied; he would undress and go to bed. He had fallen in love. He stopped seeing women. Sasha also stopped, because he was tired of it. And they stopped drinking heavily.

Gleb called Kalinin to inquire about arrangements, he called Leningrad to pressure them for the necessary documents. He went to local theaters to see plays and look at stage decor.

One day he came to the Palace looking agitated.

"They arrested Misha Kanevsky. And a few others. They're cleaning up Ufa."

"Let's go over to see Lena after class," said Sasha.

"At night we'll scare everyone in the barracks. We have to go now, while it's still light."

"Work with the group, take our places," Sasha asked Stasik, "play for them, let them practice."

They caught a ride over to the factory settlement.

Three women sat on a mound of earth that served as a bench near the barracks; one, old and gray, was leaning on a walking stick, the others were younger.

"Dear ladies" — Gleb broke into a smile — "I have a request, please ask Budyagina, Elena Ivanovna, to come here. We're afraid to go in ourselves."

"What are you afraid of?" the old woman asked. She had lively, restless eyes.

"Your barrack is all women, the girls will capture us and won't let us go."

"That's possible." The old woman burst out laughing. "You're that good-looking, are you? Where are you from?"

"From the same village, we dried our felt boots on the same stove."

"A joker." The woman shook her head. "What's your name, what should I tell Lena?"

"Your two village boys are here, they've brought gifts for you, dear."

Lena came out in the same simple dress that she wore when she came to the Palace of Labor, looked at them with surprise, and for some reason behind her.

"Go to the children's play area," the old woman hinted, "there's a bench there."

Something was shining in the grass near the sandbox, Lena bent over and picked up a rusty shovel with paint peeling off its wooden handle.

"Someone lost it."

"One of the pianists we know, an exile from Leningrad, was arrested," said Sasha, "and someone else was taken away. They're picking up exiles from here. Maybe they'll get you, too."

She listened silently, wiping the shovel with a handkerchief. She finally lifted her eyes.

"Things are calm here at the factory."

"It's a matter of time."

"No doubt, but I think they won't bother anyone until the construction of the factory is finished, especially ordinary workers, there aren't enough workers to go around."

"When will the construction be finished?"

"By the end of the month."

"Do you intend to wait around to be arrested?"

"What can I do?"

"Leave."

"Where to?"

Gleb got up from the bench.

"Lena, let's not waste time. Let's go to Kalinin. Right away. I have a house there, a job, my *own* people. We'll register our marriage, you'll take my last name, your son will live with us, he'll become my son."

She stopped twirling the shovel, put her handkerchief in her pocket, looked askance at Gleb.

"Dear Gleb, thank you. I know that I'd be happy with you. But they'll find me anyway, and then you'll suffer along with me. And I don't want you to suffer."

"No one will ever find us," Gleb objected. "I'll protect you."

"When my case began," Sasha said, "our neighbor advised me to leave. I didn't listen to him. And I should have. Now you're making the same mistake."

She shook her head.

"You were free and unrestricted then to go wherever you wanted. But I'll be making an escape when I leave Ufa, they'll announce a nation-wide search, they'll find me and try me as more than just a 'member of the family.' It's a pity, Gleb, that we didn't meet earlier; I would have accepted your proposal without a moment's hesitation." She looked at him with affection. "Gleb, you're offering me your hand and heart, aren't you?"

"Yes, but I'm also offering you freedom."

"With me, you'll lose it yourself. And it's frightening to live with the thought that any minute you and those dear to you can be arrested." She put her hand on Gleb's shoulder. "And you, Gleb, are dear to me. . . . I'll tell you honestly: for people like me there isn't much difference between all this" — she pointed to the barracks, the gloomy factory building — "and a camp. I think it's even more tranquil in a camp."

It was a quiet summer evening, still light, but there were lights inside the barracks and Venus, the evening star, had already appeared. Smoke from the factory smokestacks was rising above the roofs. A peaceful landscape, dammit!

"That means you'd feel more at peace in a camp?"

She looked carefully at Sasha, heard an unkind edge to his voice.

"Yes, that's what I think."

"And whom will you feel more at peace about? Your son, maybe? They'll pass kisses on from him to you, and chocolates from you to him?"

"You're speaking cruelly to me, Sasha."

"I'm speaking the way you deserve to be spoken to. Hasn't your parents' experience taught you anything? They let themselves be swallowed up, they offered up their heads. You're afraid of a search! What court tried you? None! What sentence were you given? None! You were *illegally* ordered to go away to some other city. And all of you submitted without complaint, you left to wait around here for the camps. But you've got a clean passport. In three days you and Gleb will register your marriage and you'll be issued a new passport with a different name. And no one will find you. But you're afraid, you're being cowardly! We're used to living like slaves, and we'll die like slaves. And it serves us right!"

She lowered her head and said nothing, silent for a long time. Then she said to Gleb: "Gleb, you're facing the barracks. How many women are there are on the bench?"

"Four."

"And when you arrived, there were three?"

"Yes."

"Is the fourth one wearing a green blouse?"

"Yes."

"She's one of the ones who keeps track of us. That's why I didn't let you accompany me up to the barracks. And if I leave now with you and spend the night, and especially if I don't come out to work in the morning, they'll start searching for me right away. Can we leave now? Is there a train?"

"The Leningrad train is a day train, at noon."

"You see! I'll only be able to leave on my day off."

"When is that?" Sasha asked.

"The day after tomorrow."

"It's risky to wait," Gleb said. "We don't necessarily have to go by train; we can go by boat and then transfer somewhere."

"Dear Gleb, they have their people at the train station and at the pier, even at the bus station. A few people tried to leave from here, but they were caught. It's important that they only notice your absence later, that's why you have to *escape* on your day off." She laughed. "What a word — 'escape'. . ."

"I like it," Gleb tried to joke.

Sasha got up.

"The day after tomorrow in the morning we'll be waiting for you at our house. Try to come earlier, some other possibilities may turn up."

"I'll come precisely at nine. Without any of my things, you under-stand." She smiled — at last it was her former shy smile. "Gleb, you'll have to get me a whole new wardrobe."

The next day Gleb submitted his resignation. Semyon Grigoryevich frowned, but there was no escaping it: a person has to leave for his new job. Gleb told him that he would leave in about three days, but got tickets for the Leningrad train for the next day; he had friends at the city ticket office, who arranged everything.

At home in the evening, while he was packing, Gleb said to Sasha: "They'll notice her absence too late, she'll already be in Kalinin; by the time they wake up, she'll already be Dubinina Elena Ivanovna. Sound good?"

"Yes, it does."

"A nationwide search? That means police, residence permits, per-sonnel departments. They won't poke around in registry offices. Espe-cially since they'll void her old passport and give it to me. I know the girls there, and I'll burn it. We'll pick up her son, and before you know it, we'll have our own. What do you think?"

"It's simple enough to do."

Gleb finally closed his suitcase, put his bayan on top of it, sat down at the table.

"Well, then, one for the road?"

"With Lena around, you'll have to cut back on the booze."

"Don't worry. Everything will be within reasonable limits. After all, dearie, I'm nearly thirty now. What was it that your Pushkin said about marriage?"

" 'At twenty be a playful dandy, but at thirty marriage brings income handy.' "

"Let's drink to that!"

They had a drink. Gleb capped the bottle, put it in the cupboard.

"That's it! I'm leaving the rest for you."

He sat down at the table again. "I don't want to be long-winded . . ."

"I know how taciturn you are." Sasha burst out laughing.

"Exactly. But I'll tell you one thing. When I saw her at the post office, I knew right away — this was my destiny. And the point isn't that she's a beauty, knows languages, the point is something entirely different."

He fell silent for awhile and then continued: "Well, she's the same breed as you — refined. But in her this quality arouses tenderness and reverence in me, pardon such high-flown words. You are a man and have to be a bulldog with a lethal grip in this world. But she's a woman, she can't be a bulldog. Now your Ulyana . . ."

"You can have her."

"It doesn't matter whose she is. Ulyana is a bulldog. But Lena's a woman, and I want to protect her, defend her. When I found out that she was hauling railroad ties, I wanted to go over there and beat up all those directors and foremen — why don't you haul them yourselves, you bastards. I can't forgive myself for not taking her away two weeks ago, as soon as I got the letter from Moscow. I got scared, dearie. What a woman! How to approach her? How to say it? How to make the offer? But when I found out about Kanevsky, I decided right away — I have to rescue her, save her, no matter what. Whether she loves me or not has no meaning, the main thing is get her out of here. . . . And now, did you hear? 'You are dear to me.' Ah! 'I would be happy with you.' How's that, dearest! Has anyone ever said words like that to you? No one has ever said them to me!"

"Lena is wonderful," said Sasha. "I've known her for many years. I'm happy for you and I'm happy for her. But now let's go to sleep. We're used to dozing until midday, and we've got to get up early tomorrow. . . ."

They were ready at nine o'clock, but Lena was late. Gleb kept walking up to the window and looking to see if she was coming; he was dashing around the room.

"Something held her up," Sasha calmed him, "she'll be here."

It was getting close to ten, then eleven. . . . The train was leaving in an hour.

"Maybe she went to the train station?" Gleb suggested.

"She wouldn't do a fool thing like that; more likely they canceled her day off."

At twelve o'clock they went over to Lena's.

The same old woman was sitting on the same mound of earth, leaning on her stick. When she saw Sasha and Gleb, she said quietly: "Go on, go on, guys, Lena's not here."

"When did they take her away?"

"Yesterday, go on, go on."

They didn't budge.

The old woman beckoned Gleb with her finger.

"Son, what nationality is she?"

"She's Russian."

"And what about her religion? Is she Orthodox or something else?"

"Orthodox."

"May God bless her . . . ," the old woman whispered.

~ 5 ~

IN THE LOBBY of the NKVD building on Egor Sazonov Street, they filled out an application: Budyagina, Elena Ivanova, born in 1911, address — Neftegaz settlement, requested by — Dubinin, Gleb Vasilievich, relationship —

"Write fiancé," Sasha advised.

"No, I'll write cousin, that's more reliable."

"Don't suggest that you are related to the Budyagins, understand? Write fiancé!"

"Anyone can call himself a fiancé, they'll send me to hell! But a relative? Just let them try not to give me the information!"

"Just don't go looking for a fight. Don't get carried away!"

"I know that, dearie! Butt out, you'll spoil the whole thing."

He walked up to the little window, knocked on it, and handed in the application.

"Wait."

They waited for a long time, even though there weren't very many people in the lobby. They would take turns going outside the building to smoke. Sasha bought a *Pravda* in the newspaper kiosk on the corner and looked through it: Hitler's victories in Europe, inviolable friendship with Germany, Trotsky's murder, committed by "one of his closest intimates and followers. . . . He was killed by his own supporters, his life was ended by terrorists whom he himself had taught to murder on the sly, treachery and evil deeds."

Of course they had killed him themselves! They considered everyone idiots!

Gleb paced back and forth around the reception room, impatiently glancing at the little window.

"Dubinin!"

Gleb walked up to it. Sasha stood next to him.

"Passport!"

Sasha grabbed him by the arm — don't hand it in!

"Why do you need my passport?"

The bureaucratic voice from behind the little window replied: "Information is issued upon the presentation of an identification document."

Gleb took out his passport, pushed Sasha aside, and handed it over.

The little window slammed shut.

They walked off to the side.

"Why did you hand over your passport? You could have said, 'I don't have it with me.' Now they'll jump at the opportunity — they found a relative of Budyagin's in Ufa. Let's get out of here before it's too late! You'll get a new passport in Kalinin."

He pulled Gleb toward the exit, but Gleb pushed him away again.

"No frigging way! I won't leave until I find out where Lena is."

It was impossible to dissuade him. Gleb, always so careful, was now going for broke. The door next to the little window opened, and a fat squat NKVD man wearing glasses appeared. He raised a piece of paper to his eyes.

"Dubinin!"

"I'm Dubinin."

The NKVD man looked him over carefully, opened the door wider, and holding it open, said: "Let's go!"

"Why?"

"They'll tell you why there — let's go!"

Gleb's face, distorted with anger, moved closer toward him. Gleb's face . . .

"Why there, and not here?"

The NKVD man moved back half a step and lifted the paper to his glasses once again.

"You're requesting information about . . . Budyagina, Elena Ivanovna?"

"Yes I am."

"Well, that's where they'll give it to you."

Sasha walked over to them.

"Gleb, we're late for work."

The NKVD man stared at him.

"And who are you?"

"A comrade. We were on our way to work, he asked me to drop by here with him. So we did."

"Now go on. Your comrade will catch up to you. Let's go, Citizen Dubinin."

"Gleb!" Sasha grabbed him by the sleeve.

The NKVD rudely shouldered him aside, walked in after Gleb, and slammed the door.

Loathing, despair, and the feeling of his own powerlessness choked Sasha. Should he scream, protest? A dozen square-faced hulks would jump out, tie him up and beat him, drag him into a cell, and there was only one road out of there. A band of criminals had seized power in the country; how to fight them? Embrace certain death? His death would not give anyone anything, no one would even know his fate.

Sasha walked out on the street, stopped a car, gave the driver Semyon Grigoryevich's address. He was an old friend of Gleb's; besides, Semyon gave lessons at the NKVD club, he must have some sort of connections, maybe he could pull the right strings and rescue Gleb.

Semyon Grigorievich listened to Sasha's story and promised to look into it. But at the end of the day, he reported that he hadn't been able to find anything out, and looking past Sasha, added in his beautiful actor's voice: "I'll finish up your two groups myself, Sashenka, and Nonna can pay you for the hours you worked."

So. He was getting rid of him. And he won't rescue Gleb.

"Well then," Sasha agreed, "I can be fired. But that isn't all, Semyon Grigoryevich."

Semyon Grigoryevich looked at him expectantly.

"Firing me isn't all," Sasha repeated; "you have to give me a certificate: worked here from such-and-such a date until such-and-such a date, make a note in my passport that I was fired, oh yes, apropos my . . ." He took some documents from his jacket pocket, found his union card, and looked at it. "Exactly, my union dues haven't been paid for the past three months. What an irresponsible debtor I am."

"Sasha. . . . But don't you understand? You'll have to stay around here longer."

Sasha shrugged his shoulders.

"I'm not in a hurry. Maybe I'll find another job."

Semyon Grigoryevich's eyebrows inched up.

"I thought you were more sensible. They arrested your closest friend. And the woman, whom you recommended to me, was also arrested."

"My, my, my," Sasha burst out laughing, "turns out you've created quite a little nest for yourself, Semyon Grigoryevich."

He took pleasure in his frightened look. He wants Sasha to disappear immediately. Well, he won't! He won't bolt, he won't run way! He'll leave when *he feels like it.* They'll put him into prison? Let them. But he's not going to run like mad. Yes, he's powerless, he can't do a thing for Lena and Gleb, but he won't just desert them like that.

"Now look here . . ." Defensive overtones appeared in Semyon Grigoryevich's voice. "I never even saw this woman, and as soon as I heard her name, I immediately refused to hire her."

"You think this is to your credit? Fine, we won't moralize anymore. It's clear: you want me to leave. Did you get instructions from Marya Konstantinovna?"

"Yes, Marya Konstantinovna also thinks it best for you to leave."

"She didn't advise you to leave?"

"We still have to finish two groups."

"I'll bet. . . . 'Two groups.' You won't be finishing them, Semyon Grigoryevich. You'll disappear far from harm's way. You'll return the money for the unfinished classes, to avoid any claims, so that they don't start a search for you. And you'll fill out all your applications just as you're supposed to. That's exactly what I'm asking for. My documents also have to be in order. Let Marya Konstantinovna know about this."

Marya Konstantinovna shot a hostile glance at Sasha, stamped his passport, pasted the stamps in his union card herself, and issued him certification of his employment with the Bashkir Republic Concert Tour Bureau. The certificate was on official stationery, but signed: "Course director, S.G. Zinoviev." And she picked up the telephone receiver, letting Sasha know: that's it, go now, don't just sit around here! Her gesture was contemptuous and rude.

"Thank you." Sasha took the document, unhurriedly put his passport and union card in his pocket. "I'll probably be in Moscow. Any instructions on what to say to Ulyana Zhakharovna?"

"Ulyana Zhakharovna?" She looked at him impertinently. "Are you acquainted with her?"

What a broad!

"You forgot?" Sasha feigned surprise on his face. "And I also forgot a little bit. With whom did I drink vodka and snack on mushrooms in that cozy little room, with whom did I lie on that little bed under the little mirror? Maybe you remember?"

She sat at the table without lifting her head, but her cheekbones stood out sharply.

"Nothing to say?" Sasha nodded at the telephone. "Why aren't you calling the police? Why aren't you screaming for help? There's someone misbehaving in my office! . . . Are you afraid? Afraid that I'll talk about the mushrooms and the little bed? Don't be afraid, I won't. I don't want to dirty my hands with you!"

Gleb did not return the next day or the next week. No one came for his things. The bastards, the scum! Sasha had never experienced such loathing, such a desire for revenge. If he could only survive until revenge would be his.

He settled his bill with his landlady, got Gleb's suitcase, got Lyonya the bayan player's word that, if Gleb did not return in a few months, he would send Gleb's suitcase to his aunt. Gleb left the house in a short-sleeved shirt and bare sandals. He wouldn't survive in transit to the camps without warm clothing. And his aunt might be able to send some to him.

At the post office, the girls packed Gleb's bayan into a plywood crate, sewed sackcloth around it, and wrote on it: "Careful, glass." Sasha included a letter to the aunt in the package with an explanation of what had happened, where he had left Gleb's things, and advice about whom she should contact.

He called his mother. He spoke in his usual calm, cheerful way. He didn't mention a word about the fact that he was leaving Ufa. At the end of the conversation, as if in passing, but sufficiently clearly, he said: "Lena was here, the one I went to school with."

"Yes, yes, I know."

"She got sick, for a long time. . . . Tell her relatives, the ones you know. Did you understand me?"

"Yes, I understood, I'll let them know."

Of course, Mother had Varya in mind. She'd let her know.

∾ 6 ∾

NINA WAS HAPPY with Maxim's transfer to Moscow. It would be more difficult financially, but then it would more peaceful. People were also being imprisoned in Moscow, but Maxim wasn't as conspicuous in Moscow. But here everything was congested, a small fenced-off military town, closely built two- and four-story houses, the same faces, the guarded looks. Maxim was a Hero of the Soviet Union, but it was precisely the fact that he was a Hero, who already commanded a regiment, who had outdistanced many in the service, that aroused envy, a feeling that was alien to both Nina and Maxim: they always acknowledged superiority of mind and talent. Now the new standards of conduct were duplicity, lies, and denunciation. The wives of commanders did not know during the day whether their husbands would return from work, and when they were already at home, they didn't know whether someone would come for them at night. Like everyone else, Nina was afraid to talk about the arrests, but how could you not say at least a few encouraging words to your neighbor whose husband had been taken away at night? What do you do — turn away when you see her on the stairway?

They arrested Flerovsky, the commander of the Air Force; Viktorov, the commander of the Pacific Ocean fleet and his entire staff; they executed Fedko, the commander of the Primorsky group of forces; then Levandovsky, his replacement; then the legendary Pokus, who had led the assault of Spassk during the Civil War. . . . Maxim, smiling glumly, reminded Nina of a line from a well-known song, a favorite of their youth: " 'And there will remain, as in a fairy tale, like beckoning lights, the stormy nights of Spassk, the days of Volochaievsk . . .' " They had been proud of the country then, they had glorified their heroes, and now, all they could think about was who was going to be executed with a bullet to the back of the head?

There was talk in hushed tones about Marshal Blukher. They summoned him to Moscow, criticized him in the Politburo. However, Stalin was peaceable with him, he asked his advice about the construction of a new strategic railway line, Voroshilov offered him and his family a rest period at his Sochi dacha. That's where they seized him, brought him to Moscow; four interrogators tortured him, they knocked out one eye. . . . "If you refuse to talk, we'll knock out the other one." They brought him to Beria, and Beria shot him. His wife got eight years in the camps, the children were doled out to orphanages, the youngest, an eight-month-old infant, disappeared without a trace.

Nina did not know if this was true, but that's what people were saying. She asked Maxim and he answered: "Don't listen to that talk!"

"Well, what's going to change if I don't listen to it?" Nina exploded. And she left the room.

Then she changed her mind; she regretted it. Maxim's nerves were on edge, he himself was under the observation of the political section and the Party bureau and the NKVD; he was responsible for every person that he supervised and for every word they said. That's why he had reacted the way he did to her question: it was difficult for him to talk about this. She should keep silent in response, she had to endure it, they were living out their last months in the small town. In September his studies would begin; Maxim had already received his orders.

She opened the door, and as if nothing at all had happened, called Maxim: "Come say 'Good night' to Vanya. He's waiting."

For Nina, the Soviet regime and the Party remained the sacred notions they had been before, but no matter how bitter it was, she had to admit it: that Party, that regime no longer existed. Of course, there would be trouble if they were to dig up her past Party membership in Moscow, but it was not likely that any of the people who handled her case were still in the regional committee. And supposedly there were different people in the NKVD as well, no one in the house on the Arbat knew anything, and besides, they were planning to live in the Military Academy dormitory, not on the Arbat.

Varya lived at her husband's place, but kept a room on the Arbat; she had not officially signed off the apartment registry and hadn't signed Nina off either, and she gave her the keys right away. Nina began to go over there often, sometimes staying overnight, and then she moved over to the Arbat altogether. The room at the dormitory was tiny. Vanya interfered with Maxim's studying, and it was more convenient on the Arbat — Maxim's mother lived in a neighboring building off the same courtyard, so when Nina had to go out on business or to see Maxim, she would leave Vanya with his grandmother.

No one at the house noticed her return, just as at one time no one had noticed her departure. Maxim was the one who made an impression. Everyone, of course, remembered him — this little boy, the elevator operator's son, had once run around here and now look at him, a Hero of the Soviet Union. Delegates from the school where he and Nina had studied came to see him and announced that the school was proud of him, that his photograph hung in the Lenin corner; they asked him to give a speech to the pupils, talk about his feats, about the heroic deeds of the valiant Red Army, about the crushing defeat of the Japanese samurai.

One day Nina saw Yuri Sharok's mother in the courtyard, but the older woman did not recognize her or pretended not to. And she did not know that her son's son, her grandson, was walking with Nina. And thank God — Nina had no desire to get into a conversation with her.

Nina telephoned Sofya Alexandrovna, Sasha's mother, and asked her if she could drop by. More than anything else she was afraid of an unexpected encounter in the courtyard, of being unable to say anything in public, of the conversation being constrained, of remaining, in Sofya Alexandrovna's eyes, someone who had deserted Sasha. Nina wanted to tell Sofya Alexandrovna that she had not been disloyal to Sasha, had not betrayed him, that on the contrary, she had written a letter in Sasha's defense, she had collected signatures, and that a charge had then been brought against her for it and that was why she had been forced to leave Moscow. The reason for her distance had been something else. Sofya Alexandrovna had allowed Varya and the man who was her husband at the time to live with her, and seeing Varya *with that person* was more than she could bear. She probably should have overcome her antipathy and not abandoned Sofya Alexandrovna, she should have continued coming to see her and not paid attention to Varya and her husband. What could she do? She hadn't been able to control herself.

Nina had prepared this logical and convincing explanation.

But when she walked into the familiar room, holding Vanya by the

hand, and saw tiny, gray Sofya Alexandrovna, who had grown thin-
ner and older, when she saw Sasha's large portrait on the chest of
drawers, she started crying. And these tears reconciled them without
explanation.

What was she crying about? She cried about their youth, about their
unfulfilled hopes and unrealized dreams, so honest and beautiful, now
lost, executed, and crucified, she cried about Sasha, Lena, pushed out
of the life that they had believed in and to which they had been so
selflessly devoted, she cried about Ivan Grigoryevich, about Alevtina
Fyodorovna, her older comrades, all destroyed in the name of the Revolution to which they devoted their lives. In their stead, dull, ruthless
careerists and self-seekers had appeared. We'll have to submit to these
people; we'll have to live with our heads bowed.

She sat on the edge of the sofa, sobbing, wiping her eyes with a
handkerchief. Vanya hugged her knees, fussed with her sleeve, "Mama,
what is it, Mama, why are you crying?" Nina never allowed herself
such weakness, but now, here, at Sofya Alexandrovna's, she couldn't
hold back — Sasha's mother, the only dear soul who had received her
in this house; and she was a mother to Varya, too, and Nina had dis-
tanced herself from her then, and no explanations could justify it, at
that time fear was already creeping into her, dominating her, distorting
her soul.

Looking at Nina, Sofya Alexandrovna also shed a few tears. She had
no hard feelings about the past. Children who had been deceived, a lost
generation, an unfortunate country. And the good-looking blond boy
who was hugging Nina's knees, he's only four, and he'd already been
deceived, he doesn't know where his mother is, who his father is, and
he'll probably never know. Thank God, he had Nina, he had Maxim,
he hadn't rotted in an NKVD orphan reception center.

Sofya Alexandrovna extended her hand and stroked Vanya's head.

"Mama hasn't been in Moscow for a long time, she got homesick, she
came back and saw all of us and began to cry from happiness. Do you
understand me, Vanyusha?"

The boy didn't answer and looked inquisitively at Nina.

"Isn't what I'm saying true, Nina?"

Wiping her eyes and swallowing her tears, Nina uttered: "Yes, it is."

"See?" Sofya Alexandrovna stroked Vanya's head again. "How is it,
do you like it in Moscow?"

The boy looked at Nina again, shifted his gaze to Sofya Alexandrovna, and said seriously: "I like it."

A few days after Nina and Maxim's arrival, Varya invited them over.

She lived with Igor on Gorky Street in a new house looking out on Soviet Square — the Obelisk of Freedom was in the middle of the square, and on the other side of the street there was a new house with a store and a restaurant, and the Mossoviet was on the right side. It was a large apartment, a spacious one, but Nina noticed that Varya had brought nothing from the Arbat — neither her favorite lamp, nor her books or photographs. Perhaps she didn't want to strip the room bare.

Varya came to meet them at the train station, picked Vanya up in her arms, covered him with kisses, pressed him close.

"Put him down," Nina cautioned, "his shoes will dirty your elegant suit."

"He won't, he's too smart."

And Vanya clung to her, you couldn't pry him loose.

"Look, he remembered me, he recognized me!"

"You think so?" Nina was doubtful. "So much time has passed. He just likes you. I noticed this a long time ago: Children love those who are beautiful."

Varya talked them into going over to the Arbat, having dinner, relaxing, spending the night, and Maxim would find out about the room in the dormitory in the morning.

"Why should the whole tribe of us trudge to the Academy?"

She stayed with them until evening, bathing Vanya and putting him to bed. As she watched Varya kiss him and whisper something affectionate in his ear, Nina thought: She regrets that she didn't keep the boy herself, or she's grieving that she doesn't have her own child. Her eyes were sad.

She asked Varya if Sasha knew about her marriage; she simply asked, without attaching any special importance to it.

Varya was silent for a while, then uttered a strange sentence:

"Maybe he does, maybe he doesn't, I don't know."

And she broke off the conversation.

And now, as her guest, seeing this spacious, well-lit apartment that Varya had not seemed to make her own, for some reason she immediately remembered that strange sentence, and everything sort of connected together.

On the way back, Nina said to Maxim: "I think that Varya only really loved Sasha."

They liked Igor Vladimirovich: he was nice, well-bred, friendly, he wanted to make friends with his wife's relatives. They had a chuckle over the fact that he had cultivated "nepotism": after graduating the institute, Varya worked as an engineer-builder in the planning organization headed by Igor Vladimirovich.

"Sit down to dinner," Varya instructed, "otherwise the meat will be overdone. As for the drinks, let Maxim give the orders."

Maxim read the names of the wines — Mukuzani, Tsinandali, — and let his gaze settle on the bottle of vodka.

"I'd prefer this."

"Let's drink vodka," agreed Varya. "Igor, pour!"

Igor Vladimirovich went around the table with the bottle and filled the vodka glasses. Varya lifted hers:

"Nina, Maxim, to you! To your return, to a good life in Moscow, to Maxim becoming a general!"

Maxim smiled good-naturedly.

"It takes a long time to become a general."

"What about Budyonny," Varya objected, "Chapayev, Shchors, Kotovsky, who else did I see that film about? Simple noncommissioned officers, but they commanded armies, and also bragged: 'We never graduated from no academies'!"

"Varenka," Igor Vladimirovich gently interrupted her, "you made a toast, let's drink. To you, Nina, to you, Maxim!"

Nina detected a quarrelsome note in Varya's voice and decided to change the subject. Why talk about the army? She praised the beans.

"Did you cook them?"

Varya nodded toward the window. "No, I ordered them from the restaurant. It's a Georgian restaurant, The Aragvi, they use special spices, I don't even know which ones."

However Maxim continued the conversation on his own:

"That was a different time, Varya, the technology was different and it was a different war — a civil war. The old standards can't be applied to modern war."

He was silent for a while, then lifted his gaze to Varya. "If we approach the army with outdated ideas, then we'll lose the coming war."

Igor Vladimirovich moved his chair away from the table slightly, put his hand on Varya's shoulder, looked at Maxim with interest. It took courage to speak about the possibility of defeat in these times.

"You're right, Max," Varya said guiltily, "I was fooling around. Nonetheless, I still want you to become a general, and Nina, a general's wife. It's nice to have a sister who's a general's wife."

"Good," Maxim agreed, "I'll do my best."

"Do you think that there will be a war?" Igor Vladimirovich asked.

Maxim replied tersely: "There has been a world war going on for two years."

Maxim's remarks about the army expressed the anxiety that was overpowering him. After the best military leaders were executed, the leadership of the People's Commissariat of Defense was seized by soldiers from the First Cavalry Army headed by Voroshilov, men who were uneducated and not very bright, whose lives were informed by their experiences in the Civil War. The newly appointed Marshal Kulik declared that the Red Army soldier did not need the submachine gun — a bourgeois invention — but an old-fashioned .30-caliber rifle with a bayonet; he said that a bullet is a fool, but the bayonet is a fine fellow! The same Kulik rejected the need for mortars, asserting that the artillery should be horse-drawn because nothing mechanized would withstand our roads. And this was the leader of the Main Artillery Sector. The other military leaders were a good match for him. What would become of the army under their leadership?

With his thoroughness and prudent management, Maxim was a good regimental commander. He loved order, he knew how to create it with a firm hand, not an iron fist. He was born in Moscow, graduated from one of the best schools in the capital, grew up in a circle of children of the Arbat intelligentsia, and was superior to his comrades in the service in his development and education; he read a lot, he subscribed to many magazines, and ordered books from Moscow.

Naturally, he didn't believe in trials, open or closed — everything was transparent. He didn't believe that commanders who had fought in Spain, in Khasan, in Khalkhin-Gol were enemies of the people. But defending them meant sharing their fate, meant ceasing to serve his country and do his work. He didn't defend anyone, but he managed to avoid condemning them. He got away with it for a time, but people started looking askance at him. He had to leave, and the courses at the Academy turned out to be a very timely excuse. He didn't want to part with his own regiment, but he had no alternative.

However, Maxim did not attain peace of mind in Moscow either. He met many of his friends, some of whom he had served with in the Far East, some with whom he had gone to military school. They were the same generation, the Komsomol youth of the 1920s, and all of them in general shared the same thoughts. Time had made them cautious, but nonetheless by means of allegory and hints, sometimes as if telling a joke, they talked about many things. Representatives of the armed forces who came to the Academy gave speeches that went beyond the limits of the newspaper reports. And there were still some professors of the old left, who were permitted a certain geriatric political naïveté by the authorities. For example, a military history instructor quoted the opinion of a certain military commander: "It's not the enemy's heightened battle-readiness that provokes the aggressor; on the contrary, it is the enemy's lack of preparedness for war." To people who understood, it was obvious: this was about us, about our fear of preparing for defense, in order not to anger Hitler. After all, everyone knew where, on which borders, 140 German divisions were concentrated. In November 1940, Field Marshal Brauchich inspected these troops with the top generals and checked their battle-readiness.

Another professor, analyzing the operations of German troops in Europe, said that the Germans had to transfer a minimum of thirty divisions in order to invade England, and this would require a certain number of ships, barges, tugs, launches, not to mention an escort and support fleet.

"Does Germany have that many ships?"

And it was obvious by the way he shrugged his shoulders that the invasion of the British Isles by Germany was problematic and that the Soviet leadership's certainty that Hitler would invade England first was groundless.

The same professor, emphasizing the critical role that the large German tank formations played in their victorious operations, did not hold back:

"While we've eliminated our mechanized corps . . ."

Then suddenly remembering, he added:

"Apparently a different strategy has been chosen."

But those who understood tactics knew that, because of its obtuseness, the military leadership refused to restore the mechanized corps. And that the infantry divisions had only half their staff. And this was on the eve of a war.

This was the way Maxim and his comrades lived. Everything was grasped by inference, through half-sentences, hints, guesses; given the backdrop of soporific official reports, you had to extrapolate meaning on your own.

The instructors were good, the professors of the Academy, but they were constrained by a program based on a single strategy — advance only! The tactics of forced retreat, encounter battles, combat in a situation of encirclement were forbidden topics of discussion. "The advance strategy" led to the depots being moved up to the border itself ("We're going to advance"), and in case of a sudden and successful attack by the Germans, they would immediately wind up in the hands of the enemy.

Why weren't the nation and the army preparing for the inevitable war? No one dared ask this question, and no one would have dared to answer it.

Instead of an answer the students were compelled to study Voroshilov's book, *The Defense of the U.S.S.R.,* thoroughly. In this book they could learn that "Comrade Stalin, the first marshal of the Socialist Revolution, the great marshal of victory on the fronts of the Civil War, the marshal of Communism, knows better than anyone what has to be done today."

7

AFTER THE "MOLOTOV-RIBBENTROP" PACT was concluded, after the Red Army entered Poland, arrests of Russian émigrés in France who were suspected of contact with the Soviet Union began, along with the noisy anti-Soviet campaign, which reached its climax when the U.S.S.R. invaded Finland.

Before his departure for America, Eitingon said to Sharok: "Military laws and courts are in effect here now. Go into hiding. Zborovsky will probably leave Paris, he's afraid of the Germans."

Eitingon unexpectedly said this sentence in German — he was testing his knowledge of the language. "Take care! Speigelglass was executed, but they're checking on how his assignments are being carried out."

They continued the remainder of the conversation in German.

"Do you think they'll get here?" Sharok asked.

Eitingon shrugged his shoulders. "I consider it likely that the Germans will end up in Paris sooner than the French will see Berlin. If the Germans get here, do you think they'll hand over the White Guard to us?"

What a devil, dammit! He's making small talk, because he wants to speak German.

"I don't know what agreements were made," Sharok replied.

"They won't hand over the White Guard to us, but they might give us the Russian Trotskyites. As a Jew, Zborovsky doesn't suit the Germans, as a Trotskyite he doesn't suit the Russians. He'll leave. That leaves only Tretyakov. Make your contacts with him more cautious: change your apartment and your telephone, stop meeting in person, use secret drops. Distance yourself from everything else. The situation will become clearer in a year or two, when our enemy will become apparent. Did you understand what I said?"

"Of course."

"I'm asking because your German isn't very good. You should practice more."

"I'll do my best. But I have a question for you as well: Do you rule out a German attack on the Soviet Union?"

"The Second World War has just begun, the disposition of forces is still unknown."

"And your prognosis?" Sharok insisted. Left in a complex situation, he wanted some sort of reference point or guideline.

After some reflection, Eitingon replied: "An agent has to keep several scenarios in mind, otherwise he won't be prepared for unexpected turns in politics."

That could mean that he doesn't rule out a conflict between the U.S.S.R. and Germany. Comrade Stalin maintains that the pact guarantees our people a long-term peace, but Eitingon doesn't believe in the certainty of this peace. And Trotsky also thinks that this peace is insecure, and Eitingon is leaving to murder Trotsky.

Eitingon gave Sharok a significant look.

"You have to look ahead; the main thing is to disappear into the shadows, live like an average man. A paycheck, an apartment, a decent wine with dinner, a small circle of Russian émigré friends — these are your interests. It goes without saying that as a patriot, you are concerned about the future of France."

Thank God, he's being ordered to go into hiding. To be sure, now is a very convenient time to slip away. It would be a real windfall for the French, English, and Americans to pick up an agent like him. He could tell them a great deal, he could turn Eitingon's entire network over to them. They'd hide him. But for how long? They didn't stand on ceremony with traitors: if you betrayed the others, you'll betray us. They'd squeeze everything they needed out of you and dump you. And no one knew how the war would turn out. What if Hitler did not wage war against the Soviet Union? What if he attacked France and England together with Stalin? Where would he go then?

No, it wasn't time. According to Eitingon, the situation would become clear in a year or two. God willing, he would live through it peacefully.

Sharok checked the secret drop in the Vincennes woods — everything was in order, the place was safe. He arranged for a meeting with Tretyakov on the outskirts of town, got in the last car of the metro and left it last, so that he could see all the passengers, then he transferred to a different line and repeated the entire procedure. Convinced that he wasn't being followed, he sat down at a table next to Tretyakov in a café.

Tretyakov had been anxious of late. Although arrests had affected only the pro-Soviet part of the emigration, the suspicion of the authorities and the average Frenchman included all Russians. Tretyakov complained that an entirely respectable-looking gentleman had called him a "lousy foreigner" (*sal étranger*). In a shop, in public. And no one defended him. All the French were infected with Russophobia now. And how could it be otherwise. Kirill Vladimirovich gave his daughter in marriage to the son of the former German Crown Prince, "the former" were marrying "the former," thinking that a minus plus a minus would add up to a plus, how do you like that?

Sharok did not grasp the logic in this digression and changed the subject. His suggestion that they stop meeting in person and switch to contact through the secret drop made the old man happy — fewer meetings, less risk. Yes . . . but what about the money? Sharok reassured him, paid him a three-month advance, promised to pay him promptly in the future.

"And take inflation into consideration," Tretyakov begged.

"Of course," replied Sharok.

In the spring of 1940 Nadezhda Vasilyevna Plevitskaya died in prison. An Orthodox priest heard her confession and administered last rites before she died. This put Sharok on guard. Laws about the sanctity of confession did not exist as far the police were concerned; they must certainly have installed a listening device in the cell. Sharok calculated the possible dangers. He had not met with Plevitskaya. Skoblin did not know his name or his address, and he had already changed his apartment and telephone number twice. But did Plevitskaya know about Tretyakov? Anything was possible. For the last two days Skoblin had been hiding at his place, now Tretyakov was dangerous, they could be following him. Sharok reported his thoughts to the resident, who instructed him to break off his contact with Tretyakov without explanation. "If we need him, we'll find him."

Only it wasn't clear what was happening in Mexico. Were they really doomed to fail again?

Of course, Trotsky had to be finished off. And Eitingon would accomplish the deed. That wasn't bad either — one Jew would kill another. But if Eitingon succeeded, then he, Sudoplatov, and Beria would all receive awards. While he, Sharok, wouldn't get a thing! An insignificant pawn. They wouldn't even remember that it was he, here in Paris, who had transferred people to Mexico and introduced Mercader to Sylvia. Of course, the point wasn't the awards, but that his career had suffered a setback. Yezhov had planned to promote him over Speigelglass in the future, and maybe over Slutsky, that's why he had transferred him to the Foreign Department. That's what he was counting on. That was past history — gone. Yezhov and Speigelglass had been executed, Slutsky had been poisoned, while Sharok was stuck in his former position without any hope for promotion. It made him resentful. Others got awards and he didn't get a bloody thing!

But if they didn't succeed in finishing off Trotsky, Eitingon's head would roll, and so would Sudoplatov's, possibly even Beria's. Abakumov, his present patron, could also come crashing down along with them; new bosses, new people would appear — you go and figure how to approach them! So it was better if these two, Eitingon and Sudoplatov, remained; that would be more peaceful. This was why Sharok favored a successful outcome to the operation, he read the newspapers carefully, but found no reports from Mexico.

All the rest didn't worry Sharok. The French were dismissing the possibility of war, writing nonsense: theatrical premieres, about the races and exhibits. True enough, there were a lot of military men in the streets, a blackout was in effect in the evenings, the famous *chansonier* Maurice Chevalier sang new patriotic songs, and sometimes German airplanes would appear, but they didn't drop bombs. The customers that came to see Sharok's boss argued that the Germans would not cross the Maginot Line. It was beyond their capabilities!

However, the Germans invaded Norway and Denmark, then Belgium and Holland, and, skirting around the Maginot Line from the northwest, they rushed into France. On the morning of May 16 the news broke — the French Army had been routed, and the road to Paris was open.

A panic ensued. From the east and the north of the country, crowds of

refugees surged through Paris pushing wheelbarrows, handcarts, children's carriages overloaded with belongings. Old cars, their tops loaded
down with suitcases, bundles, mattresses, with beds and sofas, bicycles
with sacks on their frames, carts, carriages, wagons, hearses, hitched up
to horses, donkeys, oxen moved on through. The sky was covered with
a black fog. Some said that oil tanks were burning, others claimed that
Rouen was burning, and still others swore that it was a smokescreen.

Sharok came into his office; his boss, an Alsatian, was tidying up the
foyer with his youngest son. Their maid Marie usually did this.

It turned out that Marie had resigned that morning and was leaving
with her parents.

"I can report an equally sad piece of news to you." Sharok grinned.

The café where they often dined had closed down. There was a lock
on the door, the windows were boarded up; Jews had run it, they had
cleared out of Paris.

"It's all right, everything will turn out all right," Sharok's boss
reassured him.

His voice was cheerful.

The words "everything will turn out all right" were to be understood
to mean that the Germans would enter Paris.

Sharok did not fear the arrival of the Germans. To some degree, this
made his situation easier — they were allies. Should he fail, they would
return him to Moscow; he was working against the Russian White
Guard, not against Germany. And Sharok approved of the pact with
Hitler. It was the right move. We feel more kinship to Nazi Germany
than to the English and French plutocrats.

On June 13 there were reports that the Germans were moving to en-
circle Paris, cutting it off from the rest of France. Clouds of smoke
leapt over the Ministry of Foreign Affairs — the archives were being
burned. Highly placed officials were hurriedly escaping in long black
cars. Several young people threw themselves across the road at the turn
of the Quai d'Orsay, a crowd encouraging them by yelling: "The scoundrels, they're running away, they've abandoned us!" "Traitors!" "Turncoats!" The police intervened, clearing the traffic. Paris was declared an
open city, and the troops were ordered not to engage in combat.

Sharok trudged home. The heat was ghastly. To have a sip of cold
beer somewhere, but the cafés and stores were closed.

On June 14, German airplanes flew low over the city, black crosses visible on their wings.

The instructions of the military governor of Paris were broadcast over the radio: Residents were not to leave their houses for forty-eight hours, during which time the Germans would complete their occupation of the city. From their windows, those who lived in the center watched the German troops parade in review. The Fascist generals reviewed the parade from the Arc de Triomphe.

For the past few days Sharok had seen the German troops passing through the city: the motorcyclists wearing leather and steel helmets, their faces immobile, looking like statues, the infantrymen in open cars, the soldiers with their shoulders held back, their chins tucked in, submachine guns on their chests. Sharok was surprised at how many soldiers wore glasses — we reject the nearsighted for combat service. And finally, the tanks, their caterpillar tracks rumbling terrifyingly along the Champs Élysées, crawling along the streets, filling the city with smoke and clanging. Yes, this was real power!

However, the fear that the Parisians had felt soon disappeared. The Germans behaved properly. Even after a few drinks, the soldiers didn't pick fights, but noisily sang their songs and roared with laughter as they used sign language to negotiate prices with prostitutes.

Many of those who had fled Paris came back and reopened their houses, cafés, shops. To be sure, the enormous flags with swastikas flying from Town Hall, the Arc de Triomphe, and the Tomb of the Unknown Soldier offended the national pride of the French. And the Parisians walked by the Opéra stone-faced: musicians in gray-green uniforms sat playing their German marches on the steps of the building, as if they owned it. But Sharok went to hear them play for several days in a row. Splendid marches, they created a mood. All in all, Germany was a mighty power, and Hitler knew what he wanted, while the French didn't — they jabbered on in the newspapers, in the Chamber of Deputies, and look where their talk got them. Eitingon had predicted long ago that the Germans would occupy Paris; would he really turn out to be right about another thing, that Hitler would attack the Soviet Union? That would be bad! Fighting a war against Germany would be difficult, especially with France defeated and the English hiding out on their islands. And a war with Hitler would mean a return to the endless Communist talkathon, to "internationalism," to "the Socialist fatherland," none of which promised anything good for Russia.

In the meantime, Sharok bought a cheap German-French dictionary and applied himself to his German. Dictionaries lay piled up on counters, just like the German-language guidebooks to Paris. But they weren't especially popular; soldiers were more eager to buy postcards of the Eiffel Tower and obscene photos.

The Germans left the Russian émigrés alone. Sharok had assumed that Stalin, in returning many German Communists to Germany, would demand at least the most active White Guard soldiers in exchange. It was not clear whether Moscow had asked for them, but she didn't get a single Russian. And the German occupation proved to be financially advantageous for everyone: the Germans gave many people work as chauffeurs, janitors, managers of dining halls, and those who knew German served as interpreters.

Sharok thought that he, too, could find work with the Germans, because he knew the language fairly well. But he didn't receive any instructions to work for the Germans.

At the end of August, reports about Trotsky's murder appeared in the newspapers. Now Sharok kept careful track of the newspapers and finally put together a relatively complete picture of the operation that had been carried out.

The first assassination attempt was made back on May 24 by a large group, headed by the Mexican artist Siqueiros. It proved to be unsuccessful. The Parisian newspapers had not reported it at the time or had reported it only in passing, and Sharok had missed it — the event was insignificant against the background of the nation's invasion by the Germans.

It was Ramón Mercader who succeeded, the same one who lived in Paris under Sharok's tutelage as Jacques Mornard, and then followed Sylvia Ageloff to America as Frank Jackson. Of all the possible plans, the one that Sharok had prepared was successful. And Sharok thought again with bitterness that no one would remember this, that others would get the laurels.

From America, Ramón and Sylvia had headed to Mexico, where Ramón supposedly ran a business, and Sylvia worked on Trotsky's secretarial staff. As Sylvia's fiancé, Mercader sometimes frequented Trotsky's home, made friends with his grandson Seva; guards had gotten used to him and let him in freely. Mercader performed various services for the family and its guests, drove them to shops, and once they all took a trip to the seacoast, a distance of 400 kilometers. A likable, obliging young man, a businessman of unconstrained means, Mercader had no personal contact with Trotsky himself, did not seek to become close to him, and kept a respectful distance, a person uninvolved in politics.

Mercader's unexpected request that Trotsky read one of his articles surprised him, but Trotsky considered it awkward to refuse the fiancé of the favorite of the house, Sylvia. Their first meeting alone took place on the August 17 when Mercader brought his article to Trotsky's office. It lasted several minutes. Trotsky made some notes on the manuscript and gave Mercader permission to return in several days with the corrected text.

On August 20, Mercader came again. Although it was a hot day, he was wearing a hat and carried a raincoat on his arm.

"Why are you so warmly dressed?" Natalya Ivanovna, Trotsky's wife, said with surprise. "It's sunny."

"Not for long, it may start raining," Mercader replied.

Had she suggested that Mercader hang his raincoat on the coatrack, everything would have unraveled then and there. Mercader would not have handed over his raincoat — there was an ice pick and a dagger in the pocket — she would have suspected something was amiss and called the guards. And that would been the end of it! The guards couldn't be blamed that they didn't know about the ice pick and the dagger: Trotsky had forbidden them to search people who frequented his house regularly, instilling in them that distrust demeans people.

Reading these lines, Sharok smiled. These were the kinds of notions the "leader and founder of the Red Army" lived by. That's why he had lost both his destiny and his life.

The guards also didn't notice that Mercader had parked his car outside the fence so he could make a quicker getaway. And there was a second car waiting for him around the corner, they also missed that; Ramón's mother, Caridad, and Naum Isaakievich Eitingon were sitting in that car.

The second and last meeting also lasted several minutes. Trotsky sat down at his desk and began reading the article. Mercader put his raincoat on the edge of the desk and, when Trotsky leaned over to make a note on the manuscript, pulled the ice pick out of his raincoat pocket and brought it down on Trotsky's head. Sharok imagined the power of this blow: not only was Mercader physically strong, he was certainly well trained. The assumption was that such a crippling blow would cut down Trotsky instantly and that Mercader would have enough time to flee the house and drive away.

However this assumption proved to be incorrect. Trotsky screamed, jumped up, and threw himself on Mercader, who pushed him away. Trotsky fell, but was able to get up on his feet and run stumbling out of the room. The guards immediately seized Mercader and started beating him brutally with their gun butts.

Mercader wailed pitifully: "They've got my mother. . . . I had to . . ."

"Don't kill him," Trotsky gasped, "he must be forced to talk."

Trotsky also remained conscious in the hospital. He even joked before his operation: "Tomorrow the barber is supposed to visit me, now I'll have to postpone the appointment."

However, Mercader's blow proved to be fatal. Trotsky died twenty-six hours later.

The long-awaited operation was finally done. The only thing that surprised Sharok was how crudely they covered up their tracks. The Soviet version, that the murderer was "one of the people in Trotsky's most intimate circle," was meant for domestic consumption. But they found a letter in Mercader's pocket that mentioned that Trotsky had instructed him to go to Moscow to kill Stalin. Mercader didn't want to carry out this mission and was forced to kill Trotsky himself. Capital punishment does not exist in Mexico — the highest form of punishment is twenty years' imprisonment, which was the sentence that Mercader would have received no matter what the scenario had been, so they could have come up with something more intelligent. However, Eitingon was indifferent. He had carried out Stalin's assignment and, in doing so, had avoided the fate of his predecessor, Speigelglass — he saved his own life.

Sharok found out much later that Eitingon and Caridad spent eight months in hiding in Cuba and California and returned to Moscow via China in May 1941. Those who took part in the operation were generously awarded the highest medals, and Mercader was awarded the title of Hero of the Soviet Union by a secret resolution of the Central Executive Committee of the U.S.S.R.

8

THE KAZANSKY TRAIN STATION again, the tower clock with the zodiac signs, Kalanchevsky Square again, the automobiles, the trams, the passengers with their bags and suitcases, the stands and kiosks, the crowd, the bustle and crush. Only the Assyrian was missing: the bootblack and his stall were gone.

Sasha did not experience the fear and humiliation that he had felt here three years ago when he returned from exile. If they ask for his documents, here they are, he's in transit through Moscow, in transit, understand? Here's my ticket. Are you literate? Read it!

It was just a shame that he wouldn't be able to visit his mother. If he went to see her, they would notice, then they would start dragging her back and forth, the sons of bitches, they were capable of doing anything. Calling her would just upset her. He was in Kalinin, then in Ufa, now Ryazan, why, what for? He would call her from Ryazan: I found a better job and am closer to you.

But he would go to the Institute. They were obliged to issue him a certificate of graduation from the Institute. Here it is, his student record book, he had passed all the subjects, and all his grades were filled in: he was an A student, but he hadn't defended his degree. Those who did not defend their degrees were issued certificates of graduation from the theoretical course. Some Moscovites did not defend their degree deliberately, so that they would not be forced out into the provinces after graduation; they stayed in Moscow and got jobs there: even without degrees, they were specialists who had completed an engineering education.

Sasha didn't know why he needed this certificate. He wouldn't be going to work in any official institution, there were applications there, personnel departments. He'd have to drive again! He didn't need a certificate for that. The best thing was to do hackwork at dances. But Gleb was gone, Semyon was gone. And Ryazan was not Ufa — Moscow was not far away, so people had probably learned to dance the fox-trot. He had to find something else. In Ufa he had come across guys like himself, rolling stones who made do working on various projects; people were chosen at random, the bosses were far away, and the "organs of State Security" were far away. What was wrong with surveying for highway construction, for example? He had studied in the Automotive Roads Department, where they had courses like "Highways," "Bridges," and they had geodesics and topography. Maybe he should go around with a theodolite. Then he would need a certificate. The main thing was that it was established procedure! And if it was the procedure, then they had to give it to him!

He stared into people's faces on the street, in the tram. It was an ordinary Moscow crowd: tired, preoccupied, sullen people, guarded and unfriendly. And for some reason, unexpectedly alien. Or rather, he himself was the alien here; he had been excommunicated from Moscow.

And familiar Bakhmetievskaya Street and the Institute where he had studied for four years were alien. He hadn't been here for seven years, but felt no excitement, nothing moved in his heart. He remembered only how he was expelled, trampled, tortured, mocked. The walls, doors, stairways, hallways were repulsive, and the same disgusting smell of cabbage gone sour wafted from the dining hall. He had come in vain — to see these ugly faces again, to plead, convince, demean himself. No, he would not demean himself! He would demand what was established procedure.

Sasha didn't find his department; it had been turned into a separate institute and transferred to the Leningrad Highway.

The administrator didn't even look at Sasha's student record book.

"Go to the archive, let them find your personal file."

The archive was still in a half-basement, in a crowded and badly lit building. The keeper of the archives, a shriveled-up, bilious old man wearing a worn-out suit and black oversleeves, sat behind a desk that was crammed between bookcases. There were bags under his eyes, and his eyes were as dim as the lightbulb hanging from the ceiling.

Sasha stated his case. He had entered the Institute in 1930, had finished up the theoretical course at the beginning of 1934, here was his student record book, he had passed all the subjects, did not complete his practical work, did not defend his degree, and now was requesting that he be issued a certificate. The administration requested information from the archive.

The old man listened to Sasha with his head hanging.

"Why didn't you defend your degree project?"

He lisped, either because he didn't have enough teeth or because his dentures were loose.

"I left Moscow due to family circumstances."

"Why didn't you return for six years to get your certificate?"

"I didn't need it. And I didn't return to Moscow at all."

"Give me your record book."

The old man leafed through the record book, then got up with difficulty, leaning both arms on the desk, and walked over to some distant bookcases, pulled out a narrow drawer, picked through cards for a long time, finally found the right one, came back, sat down, read it, looked at Sasha, read it over again, extended it to Sasha.

Yes, it was his card. His surname, given name, patronymic, the year and place of his birth were all correct, the year he entered the Institute was also correct. The reason for his expulsion: "Sentenced for anti-Soviet, counterrevolutionary activity."

Now the old man wasn't looking at the desk but at Sasha, and something alive, interested yet restrained, had appeared in his gaze, or so it seemed to Sasha, something even slightly mocking that said: So that's what your "family circumstances" turned to out to be.

"Well, so what?" Sasha asked in a challenging way.

"That is . . ." The keeper of archives did not understand.

"Certificates are issued to all who didn't defend their degrees, irrespective of the reasons they failed to do so."

The old man looked away from him and said nothing for a long time again.

"I don't issue them, the administration does. I have to deliver the registration form to them."

"Give it to me, that's why I'm here."

"It isn't issued to you personally; they'll send for it from the administration." He chewed his lips and added, "I have difficulty nowadays walking up to the third floor from here."

And then as he looked at the desk again without lifting his head, he said: "The reason for your expulsion is indicated here."

"Does this deprive me of the right to receive a certificate!?"

"The director . . . ," the old man began and fell silent, then repeated: "The director will be thinking about *his own* right, not *your* right. He'll probably have a consultation before he issues you such a document."

The hint was obvious. The director would pass it on to the Special Section and they would call the NKVD. They'd say that so-and-so has come, he's strutting around here, demanding things. And the old man was asking him plainly: Did Sasha understand what this could lead to? Could it be that in this basement, within these disgusting bureaucratic walls, he had nonetheless met a human being?"

"Do you live in Moscow?" the archivist asked.

"I have a strike against me, I'm not given permission for residence in large cities."

"I remember your case," the old man said, "it was when Glinskaya was still here, and Krivoruchko was here, your dean at the time, I think, was Yanson or this . . . Lozgachov." He turned to Sasha, and something alive, restrainedly interested and mocking appeared on his face again. "Everyone turned out to be enemies of the people, you understand, what a case, they turned out to be enemies of the people. And you say — I have the right."

He fixed his stare on the desk again.

"When do you have to leave?"

"Today."

"Do you have a passport?"

"Yes."

"Show it to me."

He leafed through the passport, then returned it to Sasha. He put Sasha's registration form and his student record book into a folder and, bracing himself against the desk, stood up again.

"Let's go."

They walked up to the third floor to administration. The old man walked slowly, held on to the bannister, stood on each landing for a long time. Sasha wanted to support him under the elbow, but the old man moved away from him.

They finally got there.

"Wait here."

The archivist walked into the room with the sign "Personnel" on it.

There wasn't a single bench. Sasha walked up and down the familiar corridor, at the end of which was a bust of Lenin on a plaster pedestal, framed by red banners. There were slogans on the walls, the official notice board, the Institute newspaper, various announcements. . . .

He had come here for the first time ten years ago, when he had handed in his documents to the reception committee. Ten years! Now he was twenty-nine; he had been nineteen then. Dull Stalinist sayings were drummed into their heads, the main textbook was Stalin's book, *Questions of Leninism;* they learned it by heart — you could get thrown out of the Komsomol for a mistake. New, different times had come: "the iron boys" of the Revolution were replaced by the neat "Regional Committee boys" — obedient bureaucrats, soulless administrators.

The archivist had communicated curious things to him. That Glinskaya, Yanson, and Krivoruchko had to be imprisoned was obvious. But Lozgachov, the careerist and opportunist, he also got the 58th Article! Sasha pitied Yanson most of all; his students loved him. A kind, decent human being, the son of a Latvian peasant, he worked as a farmhand, fought for the Revolution and in the Civil War, then received a higher education, one of those millions of people that the Revolution raised up from the lower classes and introduced to culture. When someone was failing, Yanson would summon him to his office to have a "heart-to-heart talk."

"The nation is taking care of you, giving you a free education," and he would inject his favorite, "giving you the opportunity to make your way in the world, but you don't appreciate it."

He was a pure man.

The archivist walked from the personnel office to the director's. Sasha looked at the clock. The old man had spent exactly an hour in the personnel office; he wondered how long he would be in the director's office.

The archivist spent an hour and a half in the director's office — they sure racked their brains for a long time, maybe they were "having a consultation" with the appropriate people. The secretary would dart out, certain people walked in and out, although it could be that they were coming to see the director regarding other business and not his case, while the archivist sat in the reception area and waited.

He appeared, looked at Sasha, said nothing, then headed to the personnel office again. They're correcting or clarifying something, Sasha thought, seeing the old man return to the director's office again.

Sasha waited patiently. If it turns out well — that's good. If it doesn't — the hell with them! He had lived without a certificate, and he could continue to do so.

Finally the old man came out and handed Sasha's record book to him.

"So, this is yours."

He handed him a form.

"And this is yours."

The certificate was genuine, typeset in the printing office. Sasha's surname, given name, patronymic, the dates of his entrance and graduation, his subjects and grades were all there, according to established procedure, written in black India ink. But at the very end, after the sentence "Did not defend degree project," it said: "Due to his arrest."

"This was all that I could do for you."

Undoubtedly, the director had ordered the addition about the arrest. He didn't give a damn! He would fold the form where the addition about the arrest was, it would wear off with time.

Sasha looked at the old man with gratitude.

"Thank you so much. As we say good-bye, tell me, what is your name?"

"What for? Good luck, all the best to you."

He turned and began descending the stairs.

Sasha walked out of the Institute. From here to the train station, from there to Ryazan. What was in store for him in Ryazan? He'd been lucky at the Institute; would he perhaps also be lucky in Ryazan?

9

AND SO, Stalin was pleased with his marshals and generals: they were dependable and obedient, they didn't poke their noses into politics, from his conversations with Vasilevsky, they understood that he knew the whole truth, warts and all, about each of them.

Germany's actions were not entirely clear. It had stationed its troops in Romania and in Finland, it had signed the Tripartite Pact with Japan and Italy. Japan became Germany's military ally, if war broke out in the West, a second front would be formed in the U.S.S.R. in the East.

In reply to Molotov's question, Ribbentrop proposed that the Soviet Union join the "Tripartite Pact," turning it into a "Quadripartite Pact." However, this would draw the Soviet Union into a military conflict with England and the U.S.A., for which the U.S.S.R. was not prepared. The decision was made to initiate long, drawn-out diplomatic negotiations in order to gain time.

Molotov arrived in Berlin on November 12 and met with Hitler twice. Hitler assured him in long speeches that England would be defeated in the near future, that what lay ahead for Germany and the Soviet Union, along with Japan and Italy, was the prospect of dividing up the British legacy. Hitler deflected Molotov's attempts to bring up the issues of the German troops in Finland and Romania, the Black Sea Straits, the situation in the Balkans; he didn't listen, continuing as before to hold forth on the global partition of the world.

The talks with Hitler amounted to nothing. Seeing Molotov off, Ribbentrop said: "The main issue is whether the Soviet Union is ready to collaborate with us in annihilating the British Empire. Everything else is absolutely insignificant."

These words required a response. Again the decision was made to delay an answer and, in the meantime, to settle relations with Japan independently. Japan was preparing for an assault on Indonesia, Malaysia, Singapore, Burma, and naturally needed to make itself secure in relation to the U.S.S.R.

On April 13, 1941, the U.S.S.R. and Japan concluded a neutrality pact in Moscow. Stalin was exultant. *He* had shown Hitler again that *he* had guessed his intention. Hitler had made certain moves in order to test *his* reaction. This was a chess game in which the pieces were peoples and nations. And every move *he* made in response surely earned Hitler's admiration: *he* was a worthy rival, a worthy ally.

As Matsuoka, the Japanese minister of foreign affairs who had signed the treaty, was leaving Moscow, his train was delayed at the Yaroslavsky Station. Stalin himself had come to see Matsuoka off. This was the first and only time in the history of the Soviet state that Stalin had met and seen off foreign representatives. On the platform Stalin placed his hand on Schulenberg's shoulder and, turning to Matsuoka, solemnly stated: "We have to remain friends and do everything possible to ensure this." And shaking the hand of the German military attaché, Krebs, he said sincerely: "We remain friends."

After these ceremonies, the train started off and Matsuoka, sitting in his salon car, could serenely reflect on the current situation about which Stalin, in spite of his powerful intelligence network, apparently knew and suspected nothing. Before the signing of the treaty, he had met with Hitler in Berlin, who declared to him: "In a few months the U.S.S.R. will be finished as a great power." That was when Matsuoka informed Ribbentrop about the possible conclusion of a pact with the U.S.S.R.; Ribbentrop did not express any objections. That meant that Hitler did not need an ally against the U.S.S.R.; he expected to cope with it himself.

Matsuoka also recalled his visit to the Chief of the Red Army Staff, General Zhukov. The request for this meeting was unexpected, but Matsuoka considered it essential. Was it possible that Stalin and Molotov were not informed about the imminent German attack?

Dyed-in-the-wool politicians could put on a show for him. Zhukov would be easier to size up. What could the Chief of the General Staff be thinking about on the eve of a war? Naturally, only about the war. As Matsuoka later reported in Tokyo, in front of him stood a soldier who awkwardly, by order from on high, tried to be courteous, who admitted that he had never been abroad, but had read a lot about Germany,

Italy, and England, and primitively reasoned that it was easier to get to know a country on a personal visit than from books. But Matsuoka simply couldn't figure out whether Zhukov was informed about Germany's imminent attack.

Stalin was satisfied with the Japanese pact: The Soviet Union did not have a second front, Germany did — England. And until Hitler had dealt with England, he would not attack the U.S.S.R. That is, if he weren't given a reason to, if their trust and sympathy were strengthened. That was why *he himself,* as the official head of the state, had to create policy. In early May Stalin became Head of State, the Chairman of the Council of People's Commissars. Molotov remained the People's Commissar of Foreign Affairs.

As before, Stalin refused to trust a single report about the attack on the Soviet Union being prepared by Germany — this was all petty moves of pawns on a chessboard. Even the dull-witted Molotov, even he had said at a Politburo session: "You can't depend on intelligence agents. Agents can push you into dangerous positions that you can't sort it out. There are countless provocateurs both here and there."

He was right. Half of our foreign agents have been recruited by the other side and they report what their masters want them to. It's no accident that many refuse to return and defect to the enemy side.

However, it wasn't just the agents — our troop commanders are also reporting on the concentration of German units on the new border of the U.S.S.R., about the uninterrupted movement of echelons of tanks, artillery, cars, and weapons toward the new border, on border violations, on the continual flights of German intelligence airplanes deep into Soviet territory.

Many commanders are expressing their bewilderment: Why are they forbidden to repulse these provocations? Even Zhukov dared to ask *him* this same question.

Having reprimanded Zhukov for this, Stalin, as the head of state, nevertheless wrote in a personal message to Hitler that the concentration of German troops on the Soviet border surprised *him,* that it created the impression that Germany was preparing to wage war against the Soviet Union. In response to which Hitler also immediately wrote in a personal letter as he underlined, *confidentially,* to Stalin, that Mr. Stalin's information was correct, that large military formations really were concentrated in Poland, but that they are not directed against the Soviet Union;

that he, Hitler, would adhere strictly to the concluded pact, which he guaranteed on his honor as head of state. The reason was that the territory of Germany was being heavily bombed by the English, being well observed by the English from the air — that was why he was forced to move his troops to the East. He, Hitler, hoped that this information would go no farther than Stalin.

The response was sincere, friendly, convincing, and, most important, corresponded to *his* conviction that intelligence agents cannot be trusted.

Nonetheless, German Ambassador Schulenburg invited Soviet Ambassador Dekanozov, who had returned to Moscow from Berlin, to lunch; in the presence of Embassy Counselor Hilger he said: "Perhaps this has never happened before in the history of diplomacy, but I plan to pass State Secret Number One on to you. Inform Mr. Molotov, and he will, I hope, inform Mr. Stalin, that Hitler has made the decision to declare war on the U.S.S.R. on the twenty-second of June. Why am I doing this? I was raised in the spirit of Bismarck, and he was always opposed to waging war against Russia."

Stalin was informed about this. At the Politburo session Stalin said: "Let's consider that disinformation has already reached the ambassadorial level."

The members of the Politburo agreed that disinformation had already reached the ambassadorial level.

Now the intelligence reports and the dispatches from the border unit commanders merely irritated Stalin.

Richard Sorge, the Soviet agent in Japan nicknamed "Ramzai," passed on to Moscow a photocopy of Ribbentrop's telegram to the German ambassador, in which it stated that Germany was planning to attack the U.S.S.R. on June 22.

Churchill warned Stalin about this through his ambassador.

Gerhardt Kegel, a staff member of the German embassy in Moscow, reported on June 11 that an order to destroy secret embassy documents and prepare for evacuation within a week had been received.

On June 12, Rado, the Soviet agent in Switzerland, warned: "The attack will take place at dawn on Sunday, June 22."

However, on June 14, the Soviet people were officially informed in the newspapers and on the radio: "Germany is undeviatingly complying with the conditions of the Soviet-German Non-Aggression Pact just as the Soviet Union is, in view of which, in the opinion of Soviet circles, the rumors about Germany's intention to break off the pact and perpetrate an attack on the U.S.S.R. are devoid of any basis."

On June 15, a new telegram was received from Sorge in Japan: "The attack will take place on a wide front at dawn on June 22."

That same day, Timoshenko and Zhukov reported to Stalin and handed him a packet of the latest messages about Hitler's imminent attack.

Stalin leafed through them cursorily, carelessly tossed them on his desk, and pointed to another folder: "All this rubbish has already been reported to me. What's more, today one of our assholes, who has done well for himself acquiring factories and whorehouses, even deigned to report the date of the German attack — the twenty-second of June. Would you have me believe him? Go back to your work. And strictly forbid your subordinates to panic. Now the commander of the western military district, Pavlov, has already sent me his third telegram: 'Request permission to occupy defense structures along State borders.' Doesn't it seem to you that General Pavlov wants to provoke a war?"

Zhukov brought himself to answer: "Comrade Stalin, we have no grounds to suspect General Pavlov. He's proven his reliability. He's careful and prudent."

"You can serve the enemy well under the pretext of being careful" — Stalin interrupted him. "If Pavlov allows himself any unauthorized action, you will pay for it with your head. 'Prudent!' Pavlov is prudent and the government and Central Committee are not?"

Timoshenko and Zhukov were silent.

"And so," Stalin said sternly, "absolutely forbid Pavlov to even send such telegrams. Explain to him if he doesn't understand that advancing the troops can only provoke the Germans."

On June 16, a report came in from the secret intelligence network in Germany: "There was a meeting in Dresden of 2500 individuals who were assigned to head various departments in occupied Soviet territory." And the names of the future burgomasters of Moscow, St. Petersburg, Kiev, Minsk, and Tbilisi were listed.

Stalin issued an order to send for Merkulov, the People's Commissar of State Security, and Fitin, the Chief of the Intelligence Directorate. They appeared in the Kremlin within a few minutes. Stalin did not invite them to sit down, and they stood in the doorway.

Pacing up and down his office, without addressing Fitin by name,

Stalin said: "Chief of the Intelligence Directorate, report to me on who the sources sending in these messages are, their reliability, and what their opportunities are for acquiring such secret information."

Fitin talked in detail about each agent.

After listening to him, Stalin walked around the office for a long time, then said: "So then, Chief of Intelligence. There are no Germans except for Wilhelm Piek who can be trusted. Is that clear?"

He walked over to the desk, leaned over it, reread a report, wrote something on it, and handed it over to Fitin.

"Go, check everything over again and report it all to me."

Merkulov and Fitin read Stalin's note as they walked out of his office.

"You can send your source on the staff of the German Air Force to hell. He is not a source, he's a disinformation agent."

Meruklov and Fitin had neither the opportunity to recheck anything nor the chance to send anyone to hell.

On June 21, a German soldier, Alfred Liskow, crossed the border and stated that the German Army would begin its attack the next day at 4:00 A.M. The artillery had assumed its firing positions, and the tanks and infantry their starting positions for the offensive.

Stalin was informed of the report. He ordered Timoshenko, Zhukov, and Vatutin to report to him immediately. They did. Members of the Politburo were already sitting at the table in the office.

"Didn't the German generals drop this defector behind our lines in order to provoke a conflict?" asked Stalin.

"No," Timoshenko confidently replied, "we think that the defector is telling the truth."

"What are we going to do?" asked Stalin.

Zhukov read the draft of a directive on getting all the troops at the border into complete battle readiness and the decisive beating back of any attack.

Stalin interrupted him: "It's premature to issue this directive. Let's try to settle everything in a peaceful manner. To avoid causing any complications, our troops should not give in to any kind of provocations."

The military left to draft a new directive. It was almost morning before the Politburo members returned to their homes. Stalin left for his dacha.

A knock on the door awakened Stalin.

"Comrade Stalin, Army General Zhukov requests that you come to the telephone about an urgent matter."

Stalin picked up the receiver.

"Hello."

"Comrade Stalin," reported Zhukov, "German airplanes have just bombed Minsk, Kiev, Vilnius, Brest, Sevastopol, and other cities."

Stalin said nothing.

"Did you understand me, Comrade Stalin?"

Stalin did not answer.

"Comrade Stalin, did you understand me?" Zhukov asked again. "Do you hear me, Comrade Stalin? Hello, hello! Comrade Stalin, answer please, do you hear me?"

In a toneless, hoarse voice Stalin finally uttered: "Come to the Kremlin with Timoshenko. Tell Poskrebyshev to have all the members of the Politburo show up there."

At 4:00 A.M. on June 22, 1941, Germany attacked the Soviet Union, which was not prepared for war and lost twenty-seven million of its sons and daughters.

~ 10 ~

PALE AND SLEEP-DEPRIVED, Stalin walked into his Kremlin office. The Politburo members were already waiting for him. They look calm, but they're pretending. They say, While Comrade Stalin is with us, everything will turn out all right in the end. Let them pretend, what else do they know how to do?

Such a clear, far-seeing policy, developed over the years, the only one that was acceptable to *him* and to Hitler, had collapsed. Who destroyed it? Hitler himself? That was impossible. Had there been a government coup in Berlin? Had German generals bought by English plutocrats unleashed the war? Did that swindler Churchill deflect the attack from himself? Clarity was necessary.

"The German embassy must be called," Stalin said.

Molotov went over to the telephone stand, talked with someone, and, without hanging up, turned to Stalin:

"The German ambassador requests that you receive him concerning a pressing communication."

Molotov looked at him inquiringly. He, of course, thinks that Comrade Stalin should receive Shulenburg. No, Stalin will not speak to him, does not intend to explain himself to him about *such* a subject, does not wish to listen to *such* a report from the German.

"You receive him," said Stalin.

Molotov hung up and went to his office.

General Vatutin arrived and reported: after artillery preparation the Germans assumed the offensive along the entire forward edge of the western and northwestern fronts. But *he* would not be fooled by this maneuver. If this was really a war, then the Germans were distracting our attention from the south, where they were preparing their main strike.

Molotov returned.

"Well, what?" asked Stalin.

"Germany has declared war on us."

Stalin stood up, walked to a far corner of the office, stopped at the window. That means it wasn't the generals or the conspirators or the British agents. That watery-eyed sniveling scum Hitler had deceived him. He was bedazzled by his victories in Europe. But the Soviet Union is not Europe, the Soviet Union is one-sixth of the planet; let the little Germans in their little military coats and caps take a little stroll through Russia. *He* didn't want war. But *he* was forced into it and *he* would fight.

Zhukov stood up.

"The General Staff proposes that we immediately come down on the enemy with all the forces we have in our border districts and stop it from advancing farther."

Stalin remained silent.

Timoshenko knew Stalin better, and so he stated it more accurately: "Not stop, but destroy."

Stalin nodded. "Issue the directive."

The officers walked out.

"The people have to be informed about the war," Stalin said and looked at Molotov. "Prepare the speech!"

A painful silence ensued. Everyone had been sure that Stalin himself would make the speech.

"Comrade Stalin," Vosnesensky ventured, "at such a crucial historical moment, the people, first and foremost, have to hear you."

"What's the difference, whom they hear it from? From the Chairman of the Council of People's Commissars or from his deputy? The people know Molotov."

"Only Comrade Stalin can rouse the people to defend the nation," said Kaganovich.

"The people won't understand why Stalin himself is not making the speech," added Mikoyan.

"The people will understand that the war has begun, and that's the important thing," replied Stalin.

"Nonetheless, it would be better if Comrade Stalin himself made the speech," Kalinin said likewise, shaking his little beard. "Of course, the people know Comrade Molotov, but the people must hear the voice of their leader, the leader of the Party and the state."

They want to push *him* forward, and they themselves would stand behind his back. They didn't realize that he had nothing to say *now*. *He* shouldn't have to *report* but rather explain why, after the assurances that there would be no war, it began nonetheless, and *he* had to think through the explanation. In a few days when the enemy is thrown back, when the Red Army delivers powerful attacks and drives it back, *he* would speak then.

Stalin frowned. "Comrade Molotov has made speeches to the people many times; he has spoken about German affairs a lot. His speech will be logical and understandable to the people. Write your speech, Vyacheslav!

Molotov finally read the text of his speech aloud. Stalin listened to it attentively. Molotov's speech would be *his* appeal to humanity and to history: let them know how honestly *he* behaved and how treacherously Hitler had acted.

And therefore he added sentences at various points in the speech:

"The German troops attacked our nation without asserting any *claims* whatsoever."

"In spite of the fact that the Soviet government *conscientiously* complied with all the conditions of the treaty."

"The German government could not lay a single *claim* to the U.S.S.R."

"Our troops and air force did not tolerate violations of our borders in any single place."

And although the address ended with an appeal "to close our ranks even more tightly around our great leader Comrade Stalin" and the words "Ours is a just cause. The enemy will be destroyed. Victory will be ours," it was an accusation of Hitler's treachery, just as Stalin wanted it to be.

None of the Politburo members dared to object to Stalin's additions.

In the meantime, alarming reports were coming in from the borders. The enemy was advancing to the west and northwest, but Stalin was still as convinced as he had been before that this was a maneuver meant to distract, that Hitler would deliver his main attack in the south, and so gave Zhukov the order:

"Fly out to Ternopol immediately, to the headquarters of the Southwestern front."

"And who's going to command the General Staff at such a difficult time?"

"Leave Vatutin in your place," said Stalin and added with irritation: "Don't waste time, we'll get along here somehow."

Zhukov flew to Kiev and was in Ternopol by evening. Vatutin called him right away and read him Stalin's directive: The troops are to assume the counteroffensive to crush the enemy and move into its territory. Zhukov's signature as Chief of the General Staff had to appear on the directive.

"What counteroffensive?" Zhukov cried out. "We have to sort out the situation, wait until morning."

"I agree with you," replied Vatutin, "but the decision has been made."

A counterattack was out of the question. Soviet troops were not prepared even for defense. Chaos reigned at the fronts. In accordance with Stalin's order, weapons had been removed from the old border, but had not been installed at the new one. After all, Comrade Stalin had said that Hitler would attack next year and would attempt to deliver his main strike in the south. Well, Hitler attacked this year and delivered his main strike in the west, where he had a five- to sixfold advantage. And a few days before the war, Stalin had forbidden Pavlov, the commander of the Western front, to occupy even the defense structures along the border. A nonsensical, preposterous directive, but Zhukov did not dare to take exception.

"All right, sign my name."

Vatutin came to Stalin's office again, and reported that columns of German tanks were not far from Minsk.

"What have you gotten wrong? The enemy advanced two hundred kilometers in five days?"

"Yes, Comrade Stalin, they broke through the Western front."

Stalin slammed his fist on the desk.

"So this is how the General Staff leads its troops! You find out about the situation on the front when the enemy has reached Minsk! Tomorrow you'll tell me that it's already on the outskirts of Moscow!" Stalin tossed the map aside. "Take your worthless documents and in two hours bring me the exact disposition of our troops and the German ones on all the fronts."

The Germans would take Minsk! This was impossible to believe!

Maybe a few German tanks had broken through to Minsk, and there was panic in the General Staff.

Stalin called Zhukov in Ternopol.

"Comrade Zhukov! A difficult situation has developed on the Western front. The enemy has reached Minsk. It's not clear what's happening with Pavlov. Come to Moscow."

That night Timoshenko, Zhukov, and Vatutin stood at attention in front of Stalin, their faces pinched and their eyes red from lack of sleep.

Stalin threw the map of the Western front on the desk.

"Put your heads together and tell me what can be done."

Minsk fell on the next day, June 28. The Germans had completely devastated dozens of Soviet divisions, taken 750,000 Red Army soldiers prisoner, captured equipment and military supply depots. On the very first day of the war they had destroyed 1,200 airplanes, 800 of them on the ground.

It was a catastrophe. In three days' time they would be in Smolensk, and in three days after that in Moscow. . . .

Stalin sat in his office alone. The telephones were silent. Where had everyone disappeared to? They had hung around here at the table, eaten, drunk, argued, and suddenly they had evaporated, vanished. Were they thinking about how to save their skins? They were conspiring about how to foist the defeat on *him;* they wanted to make *him* the scapegoat! Scum! Bastards! And where were they? Molotov swore that the Germans would not attack, he elaborated on his meetings with Hitler, Göring, and Ribbentrop. . . . And he calls himself the People's Commissar of Foreign Affairs! And the marshals and generals! Why didn't they insist, prove that they were right? They had been deceiving *him,* pulling the wool over *his* eyes, leading *him* astray, they hadn't taken the necessary measure for defense. Yes, *he* demanded caution, but caution did not mean inactivity. Now they'll show up, begin making their claims, they'll arrest *him,* drag *him* through the Moscow streets, and give *him* to the brutal mob, which would tear *him* to pieces. How to get out of this trap quickly, quickly?

Stalin pressed the buzzer. He waited. No one appeared. Could Poskrebyshev have run away?

Stalin walked over to the door, and listened. All was quiet. Poskrebyshev had run away! He looked into the reception room. It was empty. Yes, exactly, he had run away, that bastard! He tiptoed over to the next door, eavesdropped — there wasn't a sound in the corridor. He grasped the door handle but before he could turn it, the door suddenly opened. Stalin jumped back. Poskrebyshev stood in front of him with papers in his hands, looking at Comrade Stalin with surprise.

"The car! To the dacha!" Stalin said hoarsely.

11

THE CAR sped through nighttime Moscow. Stalin looked at the backs of his driver and bodyguard from the backseat, clutching a gun in the pocket of his service jacket. He pulled back the corner of the curtain just a bit, but nothing was visible through the window. Moscow had been darkened. Figures, probably those of traffic controllers, flitted at crossroads.

The gates opened, the car drove up to the house, and a guard opened the door. There wasn't a single light on at the dacha, in the guardroom, in the yard. It was dark, gloomy. Stalin quickly went to his room and turned on the light; there were blue blinds across the window, but the room had been ventilated, there was air to breathe. Nonetheless he opened a hinged pane slightly, wanting more air.

Valechka came in to find out about dinner: what should she serve? She saw the slightly opened window and began to fret: "Mosquitoes will fly in toward the light, Josef Vissarionovich, they won't let you sleep, they'll bite. It's just plain awful how many mosquitoes there are this year."

He impatiently twitched his shoulder — she was babbling on and on.

"I'll eat dinner later, tell Vlasik to come here."

And he sank into a chair, closing his eyes.

Was it possible that everything was lost? Great people ended their lives at the peak of success, at the height of glory, that was why they were immortal. Napoleon suffered defeat after his conquest of Europe yet remained the greatest military leader in human memory. Robespierre, a petty lawyer, a Jacobin, an unsuccessful terrorist, had died by guillotine. Was it possible that such an ignominious end also lay ahead of *him? His* "comrades-in-arms" would foist the failure of the war on *him,* would slander *him,* shame *him,* arouse the wrath of the people, provoke the mob to violence.

He could hear a rustling behind his back.

He looked back fearfully. Vlasik stood in the doorway.

"Why are you, you . . . motherfuck, creeping as quietly as a mouse?"

"Did you call for me, Comrade Stalin?" Vlasik mumbled confusedly.

"Don't allow anyone in, and don't call me to the phone!" Stalin ordered.

"Yes, sir!"

"Go!"

Stalin closed his eyes again; it seemed to him that he was dozing off and waking up. How, why had this happened? *He* had created a stable state, one that would last for centuries; everything that could threaten *his* existence and future had been destroyed, burned to the core, reduced to ashes, even the capacity for dissidence had been annihilated. New generations, who did not know and had no desire to know anything other than their childhood inculcation, had grown up; generations for whom the Soviet state was the best, most just, and most ideal one, while all other states were unjust and hostile, who wanted no other way of life but the Soviet one. Was it possible that five million German soldiers could conquer two hundred million of *these* people? Could a mighty empire, founded on enthusiasm and absolute submission, on fear of its leader and on selfless love for him, really collapse? And yet Hitler was penetrating the nation like a knife into butter, he reached Minsk in six days, he's advancing farther, soldiers are surrendering, commanders are doing nothing.

Stalin suddenly heard the sound of boots in the corridor. . . . Are they coming?! The conspirators are coming! They would arrest him or strangle *him,* like they strangled Emperor Paul I.

Stalin jumped up from his chair.

The door opened. Vlasik stood in the doorway, his hand shot up to his cap in a salute.

"Permission to report?"

Stalin looked at him fearfully. Who's there behind his back? There was no one behind his back.

"Why are you stomping around like an elephant?"

"Permission to report, Comrade Stalin. Army General Comrade Zhukov is on the telephone."

"But I told you not to connect me with anyone!"

"Yes, sir, Comrade Stalin!"

Vlasik did an about-face and left.

Zhukov called. . . . What does he want, Zhukov? He wants to report that the Germans have taken Smolensk, that the Germans are on the outskirts of Moscow? The Chief of the General Staff was a mediocrity! *He* and *his* guards will fight to the end, saving their last cartridge for themselves. That was better than being torn apart by the mob. Or, worse than that, winding up in Beria's hands, in his basements at Lubyanka. The "comrades-in-arms" could conspire with Hitler to give away the Ukraine, Belorussia, the Baltic region, the Caucasus with its Baku oil, just to save their skins, and they would blame him for the defeat, the bone-breakers would torture him in the Lubyanka basements, beating out of him the evidence that he had betrayed the Soviet Union. Beria would defect to the enemy in an instant, the old provocateur!

He imagined himself naked, mutilated, on the stone floor. Just the thought of the torture and anguish made him gag. They wouldn't care that *he* was an old man, that *he* was over sixty. Who was it who had complained that they were beating *an old man*. . . . Many had complained, written, but these words stuck in his memory . . . "They beat me, *an old man* . . . ," wrote Meyerhold the director, the People's Artist, who had been executed last year.

Stalin stood up, went over to the cabinet, pulled out a drawer, took out the folder in which he kept the letters which he was not giving the archive; he sometimes even reread them. This was some fifteen to twenty letters of the million letters written to him by those condemned to death.

They included Bukharin's "plea for forgiveness," which he had written several hours before his execution: "There is not a single word of protest in my soul. I should have been executed a dozen times for my crimes. I am on my knees. Allow the new Bukharin to live. This gesture of proletarian magnanimity will be justified."

Yezhov: "My fate is obvious, of course, my life will not be spared. . . . I ask one thing — execute me calmly, without torture. . . . Tell Stalin that I will die with his name on my lips . . ."

There were letters here of other executed members of the Politburo. He was saving them for history — let it be known that the executed were guilty, *this* was what they wrote before they died, and people do not lie when they are about die.

Meyerhold's letter was not addressed to him, but to Molotov. Beria reported that such a letter had been passed on to Molotov, and so he asked Molotov: "Did Meyerhold write to you?"

"He did."

"What did he write?"

In response, Molotov gave him the letter. It wound up in this folder. He took it with other official papers to the dacha, and it just must have been left here. Or was it that he remembered the words, "They beat me, an old man . . ."?

Stalin took Meyerhold's letter out of the folder and reread it:

> They beat me here, a sick old man of sixty-eight, they laid me face down on the floor, they beat me with rubber whips on my soles, my back, my legs. . . . And when these parts of my legs were flooded with profuse internal bleeding, then they beat these red-blue-yellow bruises again with this whip and it was so painful that it seemed like they were pouring boiling water on these painful sensitive places on my legs. . . . They beat me on the face with this rubber, striking with a full swing. . . . I screamed and cried from the pain. . . . Lying face down on the floor, I discovered the ability to cringe, writhe, and whine like a dog, who was being beaten by his master with a whip. . . .

Stalin gagged again. No, *he* wouldn't allow this to happen to *him,* he would not let it come to that. Let the Germans kill *him* right here. Although, why would the Germans kill *him?* What reason would the Germans have for killing *him?* Which of the leaders of the conquered nations had they harmed? No one. Neither kings nor presidents nor prime ministers. Marshal Pétain in France was the head of state. So what? At least he had saved part of France. Later, if things take a different turn, the Germans will leave, and Pétain will turn out to be the nation's savior.

The most important thing was to save one's life, to survive. They won't let *him,* the traitors, the turncoats! They'll save their own mean little lives.

Stalin rang. Steps sounded in the corridor. The dolt was finally walking normally. Vlasik appeared in the doorway, then stopped in his tracks.

"The Germans are dropping paratroopers in our territory," Stalin morosely pronounced.

Vlasik's eyes bugged out and he listened tensely.

"The paratroopers are dressed in our uniforms, they're impersonating NKVD agents, and they speak Russian well."

He fell silent for a while, then looked at Vlasik, who continued staring bug-eyed.

Stalin said again: "They may send a diversionary group here to destroy the head of the Party and the state. The number of guards has to be increased."

"Yes, sir, Comrade Stalin, I'll send for more troops right now."

"No! Don't call anywhere, don't send for anyone! You have enough guards. You have to increase vigilance. So no one can penetrate this place. Understood?"

"Understood, Comrade Stalin, I'll see to it."

"Go!"

He sat down in his armchair again, dozed off again, and rustling woke him up again. But this was familiar rustling — Valechka had brought him supper. He chewed on something, he didn't feel like eating.

Valechka looked at the nearly untouched food, shook her head reproachfully, and took everything away. Before leaving she wanted to close the window, because she knew: Josef Vissarionovich did not like to sleep with it open. But Stalin ordered her not to close it.

He dozed in the armchair again; he should lie down, but he was afraid to get undressed. His boots were the only thing he took off.

That was how he spent the entire night, dozing and waking up in the chair. His thoughts would surface again, become confused, and be forgotten. There was only one clear thought: 200 million, 200 million, 200 million. Was it possible to overcome *this*? If every single person, to the last individual, rose up, who could break through this? Men, women, children, millions, millions, millions of them. A sea of people, ready to die at *his* command — who could conquer them?

In the morning the uproar of birds woke him up. He used to sleep with a closed window and never heard it. He got up, walked toward the veranda, drew the blinds open. The sun was coming up beyond the trees; he had forgotten what the dawn was, but now he remembered.

Everything was quiet. Suddenly he felt like sleeping. He drew the blinds shut, lay down on the sofa, covered himself with his tunic, and instantly fell asleep.

He woke up, looked at the clock. It was 12:30 in the afternoon. The same oppressive silence in the house, outside the window. Valechka brought in breakfast. He ate almost nothing again, ordered her to take it away, sat down in his armchair. And again, fears overpowered him. He didn't know what was happening in the country, he hadn't turned the radio on — what for, he wouldn't hear anything comforting and he wouldn't hear the whole truth either. He didn't want to listen to anything. And he couldn't think about anything, since every thought caused him pain and suffering. Only one thing gnawed at his brain — 200 million, 200 million! Hitler would not be able to force his way through such a gigantic mass. But *he* had been betrayed, betrayed, betrayed. . . .

Evening fell. It was dark in the corners of the dining room, and he dozed off again.

He suddenly heard noise in the corridor and regained consciousness. They were coming!

He wanted to jump up, get his gun. But he did not have the strength to get up. He closed his eyes. And when he opened them, he saw Molotov, Voroshilov, Malenkov, Beria, Mikoyan, and Vosnesensky. . . . It seemed as if they filled up the entire room, that they surrounded him from all sides.

"Why . . . Why did you come?" Stalin exhaled.

"Koba," Molotov said, "something has to be done. The nation has to be brought to its feet, a powerful center — the State Committee of Defense — must be created, it must be granted full powers of authority, the functions of the government, Supreme Soviet, and Central Committee of the Party must be transferred to it. You, Koba, must become head of the State Committee of Defense. Your name will inspire faith and strength in the people, will ensure the leadership of military operations."

Stalin listened silently. He was returning to full consciousness. These people could do nothing without *him,* they were afraid of seizing power, they weren't even capable of serious betrayal. They continue to submit to *him* and only *him,* and the people obeyed only *him.* They were looking at *him,* waiting for *him* to speak. But Stalin was only able to squeeze out a single word:

"Fine."

Now *he* was looking at them. Yes, they obeyed *him,* and the people obeyed *him*. Two hundred million people obedient to *him*. The entire road from Minsk to Moscow will be paved with the bodies of these millions, German tanks will not force their way through these mountains of corpses, the Germans will suffocate in this stench, suffocate in the flames and smoke of the charred ruins of fires. Paris was declared an open city, but in Russia Hitler will not find open cities, everything will be burned, destroyed, and annihilated — cities, towns, villages, the harvest in the fields, the plants and factories, the Germans will not get Ukrainian grain and Donetsk coal, only blood, blood, blood. Hitler will choke on this blood. This will be the blood of millions, dozens of millions of people. Never mind, history will forgive Comrade Stalin for this. But if *he* were to lose the war, surrender Russia to Hitler's power, history would never forgive *him* for that.

Beria interrupted the silence. "I think that the staff of the State Committee of Defense has to be small. Stalin as its head, Molotov, Voroshilov, Malenkov, Beria, its members."

"Fine," Stalin said again and added hesitantly: "Maybe Mikoyan and Voznesensky should be included?" moving his gaze across them.

"Who's going to work in the Soviet of People's Commissars, in the Gosplan? Let Comrades Mikoyan and Voznesensky take care of government affairs."

Voznesensky said firmly: "I think that the SCD must consist of seven people. I think that the individuals that Comrade Stalin named should make up the staff of the SCD."

What was behind their differences? What was it they couldn't share? The crafty Mikoyan said with annoyance: "I think we're wasting time. I consider this argument inappropriate. Let there be five people in the SCD. Both I and Voznesensky have enough responsibilities as it is."

They were not united, they were still divided as before. This was good.

Stalin pulled on his boots, got up, took a walk around the room, walking slowly, waddling somewhat — his legs had fallen asleep. He walked over to the veranda, stood there, looking at the summer garden in bloom. Without turning around, he said:

"Well then, that would be wise, and then we'll see. Prepare a decree about the creation of the State Committee of Defense. What's tomorrow's date? July first. Then publish it tomorrow."

He continued looking at the garden, his garden, at the flowers that he tended, at the woods, visible beyond the fence. Many gardens would be trampled now, many woods would be burned. Scorched earth, burned cities and villages, blood and mountains of corpses — this is what Hitler would get. Now *he* knew what *he* had to tell the people.

"After the establishment of the SCD, the people will expect a speech from its chairman," he heard Molotov's voice behind his back.

"I will speak on the radio on July third," Stalin replied.

Nonetheless, Stalin was nervous, his throat tightened, he drank water, and the clinking of the glass against the pitcher of water could be heard in all the nation's indoor and outdoor loudspeakers. For the first time in his life he said the words ". . . Brothers and sisters, . . . I am addressing you, my friends. . . ."

Of course, he wasn't telling the truth, speaking as if the reason for the failures was the surprise attack, as if the best enemy divisions were crushed. But that wasn't the main thing. The main thing was the declaration of a war of annihilation, a war of extermination.

"Our nation has entered into mortal combat. . . . We must mercilessly fight with all those who disorganize the rear, deserters, panic-mongers, rumor-mongers, we must destroy spies, diversionaries, enemy paratroopers. . . . Do not leave the enemy a single kilogram of grain. . . . a single liter of fuel. . . . Drive off all the cattle. . . . It goes without saying that everything that cannot be hauled away must be destroyed. . . . Form partisan detachments, diversionary groups to blow up bridges and roads, to damage telephone and telegraph wires, set fire to forests, warehouses, carts. . . . Create unbearable conditions for the enemy, pursue and destroy them at every step. . . . Onward to our victory. . . ."

If *he* was fated to perish, *he* would not perish alone. All the people would die *with him*. Every last one of them.

∾ 12 ∾

WHEN THE WAR BROKE OUT, Sasha was in Pronsk, a small town in the south of Ryazan Oblast. He was working as a driver for a geological survey expedition planning the construction of a new highway. Starting in the morning on Sunday, the townspeople spilled out into the central square around the loudspeaker. Not everyone had a radio, and those who did hoped to find out something more here on the square in public than they would hear sitting at home. They listened to Molotov's speech in silence and dispersed in silence. That same day, they bought up all the salt, matches, and soap in the shops.

The next day, the recruits — boys and young men in civilian clothes, local and from neighboring villages — marched along the main street with bundles or backpacks; mothers, fiancees, wives walked alongside the column, searching out their kin, calling to them, talking to them.

Sasha drove along the road in his one and a half tonner "GAZ-AA," picking up the survey workers with their materials and tools. There was moaning and wailing in the villages — they were seeing the boys off to war. The local authorities tried to give the mobilization "a civilized appearance" with demonstrations and speeches, but the villages saw them off in the old way, in the Russian way — with lamenting, songs, dances, vodka, plentiful snacks. All in all, "this our very last little day. . . ."

Sasha was returning with his next party of surveyors to Pronsk, helping pack up the expedition equipment.

The radio blared all day in the room. People responded with distrust to the reports from the front. "Fierce battle in the Brest sector" meant that Brest was in the hands of the enemy. "The enemy succeeded in constraining our units" meant that our troops were retreating, encircled, or destroyed. "Five thousand German soldiers and officers were taken prisoner in a twenty-four-hour period" — where could such a thing have happened, if there were already battles in the Minsk region? It wasn't Soviet troops that were capturing the Germans, but the Germans capturing Soviet troops.

The blackout was introduced in Ryazan, blue paper blinds were hung on windows, window glass was pasted over, slit trenches were being dug in courtyards, recruits were marching along the streets in columns. Mothers, wives, sisters walked alongside them just as in Pronsk; volunteers were busy with drill training in the military commissariat office, local police stations, and schools. Sasha called his mother, warned her that he was going to be drafted for service in the army. His mother spoke calmly; she understood that for Sasha the war would be the start of a new life, that *specialness* that had accompanied him would be left behind.

Sasha dropped in to see Yevgeny Yurevich, the only person in Ryazan with whom he remained friends. Sasha enjoyed him, he reminded him of his brother, Mikhail Yurevich, Sasha's neighbor on the Arbat, similarly mild and cultured, and he looked like him: a pince-nez, thin light brown hair, the same quiet laugh, kind smile. He loved music, used to sit at his large radio in the evenings; now he had to turn it in and make do with the public loudspeaker, like everybody else.

"Well, Sasha," Yevgeny Yurevich said, "are we going to war? I tried to sign up for the People's Volunteer Corps, but they wouldn't take me." He pointed to his pince-nez. "We're digging slit trenches at work and at home. What do you think, will these trenches help during bombings?"

"Probably."

"I am amazed and comforted by the solidarity of the people. There are so many who have suffered unjustly, yet they've forgotten the offenses against them in the face of danger. The newspapers are saying that the Germans are dropping spies and diversionaries into our rear area. This is undoubtedly true, but there will be no treason in Russia. There have never been any traitors among Russians, not during a single war."

"And what if Hitler disbands the collective farms, frees the peasants?"

"If Hitler destroys the collective farms, he won't get any grain. Time will be lost while they divide the land, while they get settled. But Hitler needs grain now."

"He can promise them land."

"Dear Sasha, if Lenin had promised land, had promised peace in 1917, he wouldn't have stayed in power a week. He did it all in a single day, with *one* decree and won because of it. No one believes in promises. No, Sasha, the Russians will not tolerate invaders. I think that they'll trust the people more. Sasha, I hope new and better times will be upon us after the war."

Sasha listened. This was the general frame of mind now: patriotic, militaristic, uncompromising toward the enemy. For him, too, everything retreated before the most important thing — the nation had to be defended.

"I'm waiting for my registration notice from the recruitment office," Sasha said. "Can I leave a few things here? They won't take up too much room — just a suitcase and a bundle of books."

"Why are you even asking? Of course! You'll return and pick them up. Only make sure that you come back a victor!"

"I'll do my best." Sasha smiled.

In a week Sasha received written instructions to appear in the enlistment office with his passport and record of service.

A tired, harassed lieutenant took Sasha's passport, put it into a drawer, looked through Sasha's record of service, searched for his registration card.

"Your civilian profession is driver?"

"Driver."

"Do you have a driver's license?"

Sasha handed him his license.

The lieutenant looked at it, didn't even take it, filled out a registration application, and gave it to Sasha. "Show this at work, get a dismissal notice and everything else you're supposed to, and then tomorrow. . . . Do you know the Selmash plant?"

"Yes, I do."

"Be there by 8:00 A.M."

A motor battalion was being formed at the Selmash plant. The chief of staff looked at Sasha's driver's license and nodded respectfully. "Eleven years of professional experience. And your education?"

The certificate of graduation from the Institute with the note — did not defend his degree due to arrest — was in Sasha's pocket. Sasha replied: "Incomplete higher education."

"Where did you study?"

"At the Institute of Transportation."

"Come with me to the battalion commander."

The battalion commander, Captain Yuldashev, a short, thin Tatar, squinted as he looked Sasha over.

"Why didn't you graduate the Institute?"

"Family circumstances."

"What year did you quit?"

"Fourth year."

"We're receiving vehicles, we need specialists, skilled people. Put yourself temporarily at the disposal of the assistant of the technical equipment unit, Military Technician First Class Korobkov."

Sasha took a steambath, put his clothing through the disinfecting chamber, and picked up some overalls — uniforms had not yet been received at the clothing store — meal chits were also issued here at the plant dining hall. The dormitory was a large, empty shop or warehouse filled with bare-board cots without mattresses, pillows, or bed linen.

"Take any one," said the orderly, "whoever gets a vehicle sleeps in the cabin, but these are all available. Whatever personal effects you have, put them in the storeroom, they'll be more secure there."

Cars were coming into the yard.

When Korobkov, a thick-lipped, awkward fellow wearing boots and overalls over a service shirt with copper buttons and cubed insignia on the collar tabs, found out that Sasha had studied in the Moscow Transportation Institute, he broke into a smile. "Why, you and I are schoolmates!"

That's all he needed here, a schoolmate. But he didn't remember this Korobkov. Besides, what difference did it make. His former life had ended and a new one had begun.

"They turned our department into the MADI, the Moscow Road Transport Institute and transferred it to Leningradsky Prospect," Korobkov continued. "I hustle around here alone. The battalion commander is a former cavalry man, so I'm responsible for all the equipment. The mechanic is the only one who helps; he's experienced."

He called over an elderly man in a worn-out jacket who was near the cars: "Vassily Akimovich!"

Wiping his hands on cleaning rags, he came over to them.

"Get acquainted — this is Red Army soldier Pankratov; he'll be receiving cars."

"Receive me!"

Vassily Akimovich glossed over Sasha with an indifferent look and returned to the cars.

"Let's not waste any time." Walking past a line of cars and trucks waiting to be admitted, Korobkov walked over to two one and a half tonners gleaming with fresh paint. "Start with these. . . ."

Near the cars stood a beefy fellow wearing a service shirt without collar tabs, tied with a commander's belt, and stylish shiny leather boots — executives wore this kind of uniform these days; however, he had a canvas bag on his side, its belt slung across his shoulder like a sword. Sasha determined from this bag that he was a member of supply services.

"Well, City Trade Department," Korobkov said and nodded to him, "did you find the paint?"

"Everything was carried out as ordered, Comrade Military Technician First Class," reported the supply man with bravado.

"I looked at these cars the day before yesterday," Korobkov explained, "they're decent cars, but they looked so hideous, I ordered them to be painted; they begged off, said there wasn't any paint. But they got some. Didn't you, City Trade Department?"

"If the motherland demands it, the country has to produce it," the supply man replied with a grin.

"Very well, Pankratov, get to work," Korobkov said. "I'm leaving."

Sasha ordered the driver to turn on the motor and raise the hood.

"Listen, boss, the technical assistant has already inspected these cars," the supply officer began, "he found them to be in good running order."

"Now I'll take a look."

Sasha listened to the motor at different rpms, then waved to the driver to turn it off.

"I can't accept this car, the motor knocks," said Sasha, lowering the hood.

Sasha also rejected the second car — there was too much play in the steering wheel, the front end was loose, needed tightening.

"And where will you get new kingbolts?" the driver objected.

"That's your problem."

"You're being too picky, boss," the supply man said sullenly and went off to headquarters, evidently to complain to Korobkov.

Sasha did not pass a single car that day — they had defects, bald tires, weak batteries, needed paint.

An unpleasant pastime! Some people who were turning in cars were rude, others fawned, still others gave him pleading looks. Sasha felt sorry for the latter, for he knew that they didn't have the means to do repairs and that they could be prosecuted for not turning in their cars, but he had no right to accept cars for the front that were beyond repair.

Korobkov was stunned.

"Not a single car in good condition? Maybe you're too demanding? After all, I looked at those cars myself."

"If you like," said Sasha, "we can look at them together."

But Korobkov didn't want to look at them with Sasha and said anxiously: "The situation is serious, the schedule is tight. If we're too picky now, we'll have to accept anything old thing that comes in, just to be able to leave on time. No one is going to give us new cars. Here's what I think: if a car has passed a technical check in the auto inspection department and is in running order now, it must be accepted."

"I'm not signing any statements like that," replied Sasha.

Korobkov frowned. "Well then, go and take a walk for now."

Sasha didn't have to take a walk. In the morning there was reveille, breakfast, then training: drill, regulations, rifle, grenade, order of march during marching and in combat, conduct during bombings, artillery shellings, extinguishing cars on fire, field camouflage, sending signals, administering first aid and using a first aid kit, the rules of transporting shells, weapons, gasoline, oil and lubricants, and personnel. The classes were taught by junior military technicians Kornyushin and Ovsyannikov, young fellows who had just graduated the Automotive School and arrived a few days earlier to command platoons in the battalion. In the time free from training, Sasha hung around the shop, which also served as the garage. The drivers cursed — the cars were unfit, wherever did they get them, there was nothing to repair them with, they argued with the commanders: "You get in and drive it yourself!" They treated Sasha well, because they knew that he refused to accept the cars, and they approved of that: well done! And they also came to him for advice — Sasha knew about cars.

There were also political classes. Political instructor Shcherbakov conducted them; he was from the reserves, a local Ryazan worker from the Society for the Assistance to Defense, Aviation and Chemical Construction of the U.S.S.R. They read *Pravda, Krasnaya zvezda* (Red Star). Shcherbakov would order the Red Army soldiers to retell in their own words what they had read. The city drivers would recite lackadaisically, but the rural ones couldn't do it. Shcherbakov would become irritated, give the newspaper to a soldier — "Learn it by tomorrow!"

Naturally, Sasha answered without hesitation. This put Shcherbakov on his guard: obviously Sasha was too educated. He looked askance at him.

About two days later, Sasha was summoned from the barracks to report to the battalion commander. In Yuldashev's office were Korobkov, the mechanic Vasily Akimovich, military technicians Kornyushin and Ovsyannikov, and Senior Lieutenant Berezovsky, the recently returned commander of the First Company, who seemed to Sasha to be a career military man, probably about forty, his black hair streaked with some gray, trim, sullen, and demanding.

"Red Army soldier Pankratov reporting at your command."

Yuldashev pointed to a chair. Sasha sat down.

Shcherbakov, the political instructor, walked in after him, nodded dryly to everyone, and sat down next to Yuldashev.

"Let's have a technical discussion on the admission of technical equipment. Please, Comrade Korobkov."

Korobkov reported. The schedule required the admission of twenty cars a day; they were lagging behind schedule but would catch up.

"Any questions?" announced Yuldashev.

"Permission to speak, Comrade Captain?" said Shcherbakov. "I have a question for Red Army soldier Pankratov. Red Army soldier Pankratov!"

Sasha looked at him inquiringly.

"Red Army soldier Pankratov!" Shcherbakov repeated. "You must stand up when a superior in rank addresses you."

Sasha stood up.

"Red Army soldier Pankratov! You were ordered to accept cars. You have refused them. Weren't they in working order?"

"They were in working order, but —"

"So, they were in working order," Shcherbakov interrupted him. "Why didn't you accept them?"

"A person with one leg, a prosthesis, or on crutches is also in 'working order.' But they're not admitted into the army."

Senior Lieutenant Berezovsky grinned, and fixed his gaze on Sasha.

"Don't show off your wit, please!" Shcherbakov angrily pronounced. "Don't forget, you're in the army, and drop all of these little intellectual tricks of yours. What kind of an example are you setting for the drivers? They're refusing cars, demanding new ones."

Sasha knew that the drivers were demanding cars in good working order, not new ones, but he replied in the following way:

"I am an army private who is a driver and it is not my responsibility to accept equipment."

"You have been ordered to accept it, and you are obliged to do so."

Sasha said nothing. What could he say to this idiot?

"Sit down, Pankratov," Yuldashev said. "Can the defects in the cars that you rejected be eliminated?"

"Not in the battalion — there aren't any tools. But there are motor transport depots, repair shops, an auto exchange, where you can get everything, do everything."

Yuldashev addressed mechanic Vasily Akimovich: "Your opinion, Comrade Sinelshchukov?"

"If the administration wants to get rid of the defects, they'll manage. They need help, of course, from the Party City Committee."

Senior Lieutenant Berezovsky said, "I quickly inspected the cars in my company. The cars are in poor condition, the batteries are weak, the tires are bald."

Korobkov began to protest: "You have to take the circumstances into consideration, Comrade Senior Lieutenant. The bulk of the cars were turned over to the army in June and July. We're getting the leftovers."

"There is only one circumstance to consider," Berezovsky cut him off. "Cars in good working order are needed at the front, you have to fight there."

The Chief of Staff walked in and placed a piece of paper in front of Yuldashev, who read it and said:

"We've received a telegram which reads: 'Urgent that someone come to Moscow to receive a technical assistance vehicle.' Who shall we send?"

"I can make the trip," Korobkov instantly replied.

"The battalion cannot be left without technical supervision." Yuldashev's gaze stopped on Ovsyannikov. "You'll take a driver, Comrade Ovsyannikov, and go. Are there drivers in your platoon?"

"Only one so far." He pointed to Sasha. "Red Army soldier Pankratov."

"Then Red Army soldier Pankratov will go with you." He returned the telegram to the Chief of Staff. "Issue them documents."

Sasha stood up. "Permission to speak, Comrade Captain. I haven't been issued a uniform yet."

"Give instructions to have it issued," Yuldashev ordered.

"Used," the Chief of Staff either said or asked.

"Issue it from the emergency stores."

That meant that they had new uniforms, but probably not very many, which was why they were being tight-fisted with them.

ꙮ 13 ꙮ

WHAT A SURPRISE, what luck! Of course, he was precisely the one that Yuldashev wanted to send. The shrewd Tatar. A clever man. And he also showed that Shcherbakov a thing or two.

Sasha got his things and books at Yevgeny Yurevich's, put aside two changes of underwear, some wool socks, a sweater, a scarf, a towel, razor, shaving brush, soap, toothbrush, small bottle of cologne, his mother's photograph, a two-volume set of Chekhov, and he also put aside *War and Peace* — he would find room in the car, so he wouldn't have to carry it around. He packed the rest in his suitcase and a carryall. In the evening he called his mother to let her know about his official duty trip.

Early in the morning he and military technician Ovsyannikov were already on the train. There weren't many passengers in the car, and very few remained when they approached Moscow — entrance to Moscow was permitted only with a pass or summons from central offices.

Ovsyannikov turned out to be a nice fellow, friendly and talkative. Although Sasha was his subordinate, he addressed him using the formal "you" in deference to his age as well as his "intelligentsia" status. Smiling, he said: "You really blasted that political instructor with the remark about the invalid on crutches, I almost crawled under my seat from fear."

"What were you afraid of?"

"The political staff! With them, if you get one word wrong, they never let you forget it."

He was from the Oblast of Kostroma, had worked on a collective farm, then at a Machinery and Tractor Station driving a tractor. He talked as he looked out the window. "Since I was a tractor driver, they sent me to driving classes in the army, I've been driving a car all my active service, and then, since I had completed seven years of education, they sent me to a military automotive school, and now I'm a junior military technician."

Young, red-cheeked, he was very proud of the cube insignia on his collar tab, spiritedly saluted senior officers, was happy when privates saluted him, but if they didn't he didn't stop them; he was a fine fellow, not conceited. He carried Sasha's suitcase: "You have your hands full with the carryall."

He reminded Sasha of someone. Sasha strained his memory and remembered. . . . The young lieutenant that had brought Max that last New Year's Eve. The little lieutenant had diligently turned the handle of the gramophone, he was shy in their company, couldn't bring himself to talk to Varya. Sasha was amused by his embarrassment and he tried to draw Varya into a conversation with the lieutenant, and she then turned to Sasha, and he saw her Malayan eyes and delicate face up close for the first time. Then he danced with Varya, held her small palm in his hand, she smiled without trying to hide her delight at dancing with him. How old was she then? She was sixteen then, and he was twenty-two. Now she was twenty-four and he was already thirty, his fourth decade was approaching, that was how quickly everything had passed by, rushed by, gone by, vanished.

That lieutenant's name had been Serafim, that's what his name was. . . .

Ovsyannikov had never been in Moscow, and it stunned him. The train station, the square, the people, the trams and cars. He didn't stray far from Sasha, afraid he would get lost. He became timid in front of the military patrol and was nervous as he watched them check his and Sasha's documents.

As for Sasha, what immediately struck him was that the crowds had thinned out, that there were hardly any kiosks. There were hordes of women wearing boots and service shirts, many military trucks filled with Red Army soldiers, silvery balloon barrages on the ground that would lift into the air in the evening, and anti-aircraft weapons on the square.

The motor depot where they were supposed to pick up the mobile workshop wasn't far, in the Krasnoselskaya quarter. They got there on a half-empty tram, found the depot through one of the alleyways;

obviously there had been warehouses here before. It was an enormous yard with railroad tracks, workshops along the perimeter of the yard, with cars under the open-sided sheds, the entrance to headquarters was off the street. There were servicemen, drivers, military technicians in the corridors; they probably also had come for vehicles. In the office a woman clerk checked their documents against some sort of list and returned them to Ovsyannikov.

Go to the Chief of the Depot, to the left, the last door at the end of the corridor.

Ovsyannikov went to the chief, Sasha sat down on his suitcase, regretting that he hadn't called his mother from the train station; the devil only knew how long they would be kept waiting here.

Ovsyannikov came out. "Comrade Pankratov! Come with me. They're requesting your presence!"

Sasha followed Ovsyannikov into the office.

A military engineer, third class, sat at the desk. He lifted his head, looked at Sasha . . . Runochkin! Well, I'll be damned. Runochkin, they had been in the same course together, small, slightly cross-eyed, and lopsided Runochkin!

Runochkin stood up, without taking his eyes off Sasha.

"Sasha, is it you?"

"Seems like it's me. . . ."

Runochkin came out from behind his desk, and they embraced.

Ovsyannikov smiled with embarrassment; he felt shy about being there.

Hiding his excitement, Runochkin said in a somewhat rough way: "Why are you standing — sit down!"

Sasha had few pleasant memories from those accursed days. But he remembered Runochkin with affection — he was a true comrade, the only one who had not betrayed him at the Institute but had shielded him, defended him. Runochkin had changed. Maybe it was the military uniform. He used to be a bit bent, but now he had bearing, he was a short, well-built commander, who behaved confidently, even authoritatively, and didn't look askance, but straight ahead. Only one thing tormented Sasha — he had forgotten his first name. At the Institute they usually called each other by their last names, rarely by their first names. So he forgot it. How should he address him? By rank? Runochkin was addressing him by his name, not as "Red Army soldier Pankratov."

"Tell your command, comrade military technician," Runochkin said, "to thank the Lord God that they sent Pankratov with you. We studied in the same Institute, in the same group, understand? The kind of equipment I'll put together for them no other motor battalion has. Understood?"

"Yes, sir, I understand, Comrade Military Engineer Third Class. Thank you."

"Don't use superfluous words. . . . Simply say military engineer."

"Yes, sir, Comrade Military Engineer."

"You'll get the car tomorrow. Be here at ten zero zero. Comrade Pankratov will stay . . ."

"At my mother's," Sasha prompted him.

"Right, and you, Military Technician, we'll give you a place to sleep in the dormitory; there's a movie theater next door, the Transportation Theater nearby, you won't have occasion to get bored."

He pressed a buzzer. The same woman clerk apeared. Runochkin gave her the documents. "Check off their travel orders, take their ration certificates, Red Army soldier Pankratov gets dry rations, isn't that so, Sasha?"

"Of course."

"It would be better if the military technician comes to our dining mess. What do you say, Military Technician? Do you want to nibble herring in the dormitory or eat hot food?"

"Hot food is preferable."

"Register the military technician in the dining mess and assign him to the dormitory, to room number six."

"Dmitri Platonovich, the commandant requires a personal note from you for room number six."

Thank God! His name was Dima, exactly. Dima, Dimka.

Runochkin wrote something on a piece of paper and gave it to the clerk.

"Military Technician, please go, everything will be arranged for you, and, Larissa, bring Pankratov's documents here. On your way!"

Ovsyannikov stood up.

"Yes, sir, Comrade Military Engineer."

"One minute!" Sasha wrote his mother's telephone number on a piece of paper and gave it to Ovsyannikov. "This is my mother's telephone number, just in case."

"Now that's good. I'll wait for you in the corridor, Comrade Pankratov."

"Why wait for him?" Runochkin asked.

"I'm looking after his things, so they don't get taken away. . . ."

"What things?"

"I have a suitcase and books with me, my property. I want to leave them at my mother's," Sasha explained, "they're in the corridor."

Runochkin opened the door to the corridor, ordered the first Red Army soldier walking by to bring the things into the office.

"Permission to leave, Comrade Military Engineer?"

"Granted!"

Ovsyannikov thrust his hand up to his military cap, did a precise about-face, and left.

"He's more like your orderly than your commander," said Runochkin.

"He's just a nice guy. Dima, would you let me make a phone call?"

"Of course!" Runochkin moved the phone toward Sasha.

Sasha called his mother, told her that he was already in Moscow, that he would be free soon and would come home.

"I swear, Sasha, I still can't believe it. Your military technician put your movement orders in front of me and I saw — Pankratov, A.P. I didn't pay any attention to it, there are hundreds of people passing through, and then something nudged me. . . . Pankratov, A. Maybe it's Aleksandr? What if it is?! Let's see your Pankratov, I say. . . . And here you are! I didn't expect such a meeting, honestly, I thought Sasha had disappeared, perished like the others had. You know, I stopped in to see your mother, and she said you were in the Butyrka prison, and then after the Institute I lost track of you — I was sent off to the provinces."

"She told me that you had stopped by when she came to see me in prison. You were the only one who did. Thank you."

Runochkin waved it off, looked away.

"All right, Sasha, don't mention it. . . . Tell me about yourself."

"Myself? What can I say? I spent three years in exile in Siberia, on the Angara river. Then I was forbidden to live in large cities. The war saved me. Now I'm a soldier, like everybody else."

"But why a private?"

"I was arrested before the Institute could issue me a certificate."

Runochkin shook his head.

"What did they do, the bastards! Almost half the Institute was swept out."

"I know a thing or two about this. . . ."

"Now Hitler has wound up in Smolensk," Runochkin angrily said and dismissed it with a wave of his hand. "Let's not talk about this now! Thank God, at least you're alive! But a private! Here's what, I'll transfer you here."

"How?"

"Very simple. We'll send a summons through the Main Administration to the battalion: detach so-and-so immediately at our disposal for outside duty."

"And what will I do?"

"Whatever you want — brigade leader, chief of a shop, we're going to be equipping a repair train." He pointed to the window. "You see, there's even a railroad branch line here. We'll assign you a rank, you'll live in Moscow for now, and then later we'll see how the war goes."

"Thank you, Dima, but that's not for me. Assign me a rank? You'll have to fill out an application, indicate my convictions."

"Sasha, what are you talking about? Nowadays only fools are filling out their applications honestly. Who's going to check? All the checkers are hiding in their corners."

"And I have too many friends in Moscow. I don't want to walk around being very careful. I did it for four years. I'm sick of it! Enough! With the war, the front, there are no questions!"

"Is having a martinet as a superior better? Who is your battalion commander?"

"Captain Yuldashev."

"I haven't heard his name. And your technical assistant?"

"Korobkov, military technician first class."

"Korobkov? Venka?"

"I don't know his first name."

"I do. He's a first-class military coward. He gets by on his connections; he shuffled papers in the People's Commissariat after the Institute, and he's never even seen a real car. But now he's been quickly recertified, and they gave him the rank of military technician."

"Is this possible in the army?"

"It's whom you know, not what you know, that counts. Everywhere."

"Now I understand why he accepted all kinds of junk in the battalion. And where do you know him from?"

"Do you remember Borka Nesterov?"

"Of course."

"What was the epigram that you wrote about him? 'A pork chop and a helping of rice — that's that best memorial for the grave of Boris.' Is that how it went? That was an expensive little pork chop for you."

"Very expensive." Sasha laughed.

"Borka Nesterov is working in the Main Administration. He was the one who told me about Korobkov. So you never know who you're going to run into in the army. With me you'll have peace of mind here, I'll keep you out of harm's way. Think about it. If you don't make up your mind yourself, I'll do it for you: I'll send the report in today!"

"Dima," Sasha said seriously, "I don't want you to do this. Promise me."

"That's a pity, Sasha. . . . You want to fight? Do you have hopes of restoring your good name at the front, redeeming your guilt? Don't count on it! Up there," he pointed to the ceiling, "nothing has changed. On the contrary!"

"I wasn't guilty then and won't be," said Sasha. "I don't need their forgiveness. And I don't intend to forgive them. But I want freedom at long last. There, at the front, behind the wheel, I'm going to know what I'm living for, and if I'll have to die, then I'll know why I'm dying. My decision is final."

"Very well! If it's final, then it's final. Now let's go have lunch — you just got off the train, didn't you? — and we'll have a bit to drink."

"Dima, I haven't seen my mother for many years."

"I'm sorry, but we have to spend a little time together. Let's call each other, get together, maybe we'll call Borka Nesterov."

"Let me tell you frankly, Dima. Besides you, I'm not particularly eager to see anyone from the Institute. I met you — it's a lucky day for me. As you may know, I haven't had too many of them in the last seven years."

"I realize, Sasha, I do." Runochkin's voice wavered.

"Tell me, is the metro working normally?"

"What metro? I have a whole yardful of cars. We'll zip over there in a flash."

14

THE NARROW deep well of the courtyard, surrounded by eight-story buildings. The courtyard of his childhood. There were barrels of water and boxes of sand near the building entrances, but everything else was the same as before. The same fire escapes on the walls that he climbed to get up to the roof to put up an antenna for his crystal receiver. Nowadays no one knows about these homemade radios; back then, the first Soviet radio station, "Komintern," had just begun broadcasting.

The back doors of the movie theater Arbat Ars, through which the public exited after showings, were next to the gates. In the summer these doors were always open — it was stuffy in the theater, the projector's ray spiraled above the rows of moviegoers, you could hear its whirring and the sounds of the broken-down piano... Max Linder, Douglas Fairbanks, Mary Pickford, the touching, unlucky Charlie Chaplin. That was a long time ago, but he could remember it clearly.

Textbooks and notebooks were wrapped in oil-cloth then, pulled together tightly with a strap, preferably a long one; you could fight with this bundle like a bludgeon. . . . This is where they fought, in the yard, it seemed large and spacious then. He hadn't thought that he'd return here so quickly, some seven years later. The war made it possible. Several people walked past him; he stared into their faces, no, he didn't know them.

Sasha ran up to his floor, but before he could ring the doorbell, the door flew open, his mother threw her arms around him, pressed herself close to his chest, tried to say through her sobbing that she had seen him walk into the courtyard.

"Mother, dear, calm down." Sasha kissed her on the head. "Everything's fine, everything's all right."

They walked into the room. His mother sank into a chair, and took his hands into her own. Her lips were trembling slightly.

"Mother, you've done enough crying, enough!"

He took a package out of his bag, putting stewed meat, bread, candy out on the table.

"My ration, now feed me, I haven't eaten anything yet today. . . ."

"Yes, yes, right now, right now, I've prepared everything."

"Give me a towel, and I'll wash my hands."

He walked over to the chest of drawers, where his photograph was in a glass frame. Somehow he didn't remember it, he'd never had such a large portrait.

"You don't recognize it?"

"No."

His mother got a small snapshot from the drawer — Sasha remembered this one. He was on the factory socceer team, the best in the district, and they were photographed after a socceer game.

Did he really have such a trusting, childlike face?

"We enlarged this snapshot," his mother said. "I wanted to have a large portrait of you."

Sasha's heart skipped a beat from this "we."

"The photographer made two photographs, Varya took the second one for herself, hung it on the wall, next to Stalin's portrait, remember? Nina was very orthodox."

"I wound up in good company." Sasha laughed. But he didn't inquire about Varya; possibly his mother would tell him something herself.

"Wash your hands," his mother reminded him, "and I'll serve dinner."

Everything had remained the same as it had been in childhood. The water gurgled in the pipes, the same peeling paint on the walls.

He returned to the room.

"I wanted to ask you, I rode past the Vakhtangov Theater. Was it bombed?"

"You didn't know? The actor Kuza died, do you remember him?"

"Of course. He was the head of the drama circle in our school."

"They say he was a relative of the Romanian king."

"I don't know, maybe. So the Germans deliberately targeted the Arbat?"

"They bombed the Arbat and also Gogolevsky Boulevard and the Bolshoi Theater."

She set out cold beet soup with sliced green cucumbers, little pancakes with meat, *kisel* pudding — everything that he loved as a child.

"Wow! You get this kind of stuff with ration cards?"

His mother did not answer, but sat at the table without taking her eyes off him.

"Can't look at me enough?"

She continued to say nothing, only looked at him. Her lips trembled again.

"Sashenka, what are your plans, when are you leaving?"

"Tomorrow morning."

"I let Vera and Polina know that you were coming, you have to visit with them, Sashenka, they're your aunts, you know, and they love you so much."

"I wanted to spend the evening with you."

"And I wanted it too, but they grieved so much that you didn't send for them in Butyrka Prison. I also let Nina Ivanovna know."

"Nina? She's here?"

"Yes, she's living in her old apartment. She comes by, asks about you. She called yesterday and that's when I told her, 'I just spoke with Sasha, he's coming tomorrow.'"

"And where's Max?"

"Max is at the front."

"Seeing Nina is simple, she's in this building, I can drop in to see her for a few minutes. But the aunts — why, that'll take the entire evening."

"They won't stay long. You can't be out on the streets at night, Vera has to be at work tomorrow, and Polina is doing defense work, cars pick them up at six in the morning and drive them."

"Very well," Sasha agreed, "let them come over. Where's father?"

She grew thoughtful, picking up crumbs with the tips of her fingers and pressing them into the table. She still had this habit.

"Father? He's in Moscow. He traded his room, lives in Zamoskvorechye, has a wife and a daughter; we got an official divorce, I gave him written consent and my passport, he filed everything himself officially. I don't know his address, but I have his telephone number, you can call him."

"I'll think about that."

He got up from the table, walked through the room, stopped near the bookcases, and looked back at his mother in bewilderment.

"How did Mikhail Yurevich's books get here?" He passed his finger along their spines. "Zhirmunsky, Tomashevsky, Tynyanov . . . literary and theatrical memoirs . . . Henri De Renier, Jules Romain, Proust, Hoffman . . ."

"It was all so strange. . . . Shortly before his death Mikhail Yurevich divided his books between you and Varya; he said that he was sick of living in the dust. We couldn't understand, but he insisted. Varya asked him if he was leaving Moscow. He answered: 'In a certain sense, yes.' And Varya, the kind soul, offered to help him pack his suitcase. 'I know how,' he said, 'to pack well.' "

"I was very attached to Mikhail Yurevich," said Sasha. "Why did he commit suicide?"

"There was a national census, they were required to hide the fact that six million people died, he didn't want to take part in it. That's what he told Varya. He was probably afraid of prison; he was afraid they would beat him, torture him. That's what we think."

She lowered her head and kept silent for a while.

"Tell me, Sasha, were you . . . ?"

He walked over to her and embraced her.

"No, I wasn't beaten or tortured. That began later."

There was a knock on the door, Galya the neighbor walked in, kissed Sasha, shed some tears.

"Well now," said Sasha, "this one's crying, too."

Galya had aged. In the past she had been a noisy neighbor, storming about the kitchen, but she was easy to placate and compassionate; she had stuffed a pack of cigarettes into his pocket when he was being taken away.

"You've changed," Galya sobbed, "you used to be so stylish, remember what they called you in the yard?"

"I remember." Sasha smiled.

" 'Sashka the fashion-plate' — that was your nickname."

"Where's Petya?" Sasha asked her about her son.

"I don't know where he is! I don't know. And I'm afraid I'll never know. He was in the army back before the war began: born in 1922, he was in Belorussia. Which means that he wound up right in the very center of hell. No letters, now news whatsoever."

"Don't despair, postal service with those units has been cut off, but the letter will get to you eventually."

"Where's it going to get to, Sashenka? they're already digging trenches on the outskirts of Moscow."

"The army is engaged in battles in the west, in breaking out of encirclement. You'll see, Petya will return, I'm telling you, I predict it."

"Thank you, Sashenka, from your lips to God's ear. May God grant you stay alive." Galya kissed him again. "They made you suffer, made Sofya Aleksandrovna suffer. And we just watched from the sidelines. Now the time has come for all the people to suffer."

"She's not a bad woman," Sofya Alexandrovna said when Galya left. "We had several misunderstandings, but everything worked out. You know, Sasha, people have now become kinder because of their grief."

Sasha suddenly smashed his fist on the table.

"Those sons of bitches! 'We won't surrender a single inch of our land' . . . 'Only on foreign territory' . . . 'Little bloodshed' . . . And the Germans are already in Smolensk."

"Will they really reach Moscow, Sasha?"

"I don't know. Maybe they won't make it here. Our great and brilliant one will lay out several million such Petyas, Vanyas, Grishas, what does he care? I couldn't look her in the eye. Her Petya is either dead or was taken prisoner. And to be captured has been declared treason."

"Sashenka, be careful, be more discreet, it's better not to speak about this . . . I'm glad that you're just a driver, that you're not responsible for anyone."

The doorbell rang in the hallway.

"Your aunts have arrived," Sofya Alexandrovna said.

It was them. The older one, Vera, still just as energetic and no-nonsense, hugged Sasha tightly, then pushed him away and looked him over. "What a brave little soldier!" She took a bottle of vodka out of her bag. "This occasion definitely calls for a drink!" And she had brought a gift, an imported Gillette safety razor and two packs of razor blades for it. "Do you know how to sharpen razor blades?"

"No."

"Give me a glass," she asked Sofya Alexandrovna, and took a razor from the packet without unwrapping it. "This way you'll understand how." She placed the razor on the inside edge of the glass, pressed it with two fingers, moved it along that edge. "Do just this for about five minutes, turn it over and do it again, it'll get sharp. You'll shave with one razor for three months, there are ten of them here, enough for thirty months."

Polina, the youngest of the sisters, quiet, full of smiles, brought Sasha a miniature book, the size of her palm, the short and longer poems of Pushkin.

"You love Pushkin, don't you, and this little book will fit into your pocket."

They sat down at the table, drank a little; his mother fussed over them, going out to the kitchen and returning, the aunts talked. Vera's daughter was a military physician, her son was in an artillery school, he'd be going to the front this year.... Polina's husband was a war correspondent, her son had just turned seventeen, but he was already registered for military service at the military commissariat.

"We're the only ones left, just the three sisters," Vera joked sadly, "the last reserve of the main command."

The aunts were glad, happy for Sasha — he had escaped from the bloody meat grinder, although it was true that he immediately wound up in another one, no less bloody, but everyone's fates were in this sense equalized; they say that our losses are counted in the millions, of course, the newspapers don't say anything about it.

"Thank God," said Vera, "at least we had a chance to see you, who knows whether we'll last until we see the others."

"Never mind, we'll meet at this table again."

Banal words, but he couldn't find any others.

"We'll overcome Hitler and begin a different life," Polina added.

Nina came by, stopped in the doorway, shed a few tears, embraced and kissed Sasha.

"Sit down, Ninochka," Sofya Alexandrovna called her.

Nina looked at the aunts.

"Did I come at the wrong time?"

"You came right on time." Sasha smiled. "You'll have a drink with us."

Nina pointed to the bottom of the vodka glass.

"This much."

The aunts stayed a little longer and then began to rush: it was a long way home, and tomorrow they had to be at work early. Sasha saw them off to the stairway, leaned over the bannister, watched as they left, waved, and they looked back and waved to him. He returned and sat down beside Nina.

"Where's your son?"

"I left him at his grandmother's."

Sasha told her about Lena, about Gleb.

"Now that's a sad story. What about Max and Varya?"

"Maxim is in the Far East organizing a division. Varya works in the military construction administration — they design defense structures around Moscow. She shuttles around the province, so I don't see her; sometimes we talk on the phone. I work in a school." She smiled. "I'm involved in patriotic training."

"In our school?"

"No, in a different neighborhood." She looked at him. "They'll destroy our generation, won't they, Sasha?"

"Some people will survive."

"I'm afraid that only Sharok will," Nina said sadly. "Sharok won't fight. And Vadim Marasevich won't. Incidentally, I met him recently, he's on the staff of some military journal, *Pogranichnik* [The Border Guard], I think, which means that he's sort of in the army, but he doesn't have to fight. And he's already a captain. Now Sharok and Marasevich, they're the ones who'll survive."

"Never mind, you and I will also live a little."

"Write to me, Sasha," Nina said.

"Without fail."

Finally he was alone with his mother. His mother made up a bed for him on the couch, but they stayed up for a long time and talked.

"I implore you, Sashenka, I know that you're not a coward, but you are proud and so you're often careless. You are thirty years old, but you essentially haven't lived, you've suffered. You have to take care of yourself; after the war everything will change."

"You think so."

"I'm sure of it." She looked back at the door, lowered her voice. " 'For the homeland,' 'For Stalin,' — you see, these are incantations, ritual. It was the same during the last war. 'For Mother Russia,' 'For the Tsar our little father.' And what did they do with the Tsar? After every war in Russia something always changed. After Sevastopol there was the reform of serfdom, after the Russo-Japanese war — the 1905 Revolution, after the Great War — the February Revolution."

"What kinds of changes are you expecting?"

"I don't know. I only know one thing: we've had enough of torturing the people! Russia has to become a normal nation."

"Along the Western model?"

"Yes, if you like."

"I'm afraid that your hopes will not be realized. The ideas of social justice advanced by the Revolution have become deeply rooted in the consciousness of the people. If we win, the people will seek a return to those Leninist times."

"Sashenka, forgive me, don't be hurt, I know your attitude toward Lenin, but don't idealize him. You were little then, while I lived during his regime, there were also plenty of executions, blood, cellars."

Sasha laughed.

"Well, I really didn't think that after years of separation we'd start discussing politics."

"No, Sashenka, to me this isn't politics, to me it's your fate. I pray to God that He preserves you. And that's why I'm thinking about what will happen after the war."

"Fine," said Sasha, "let's first drive Hitler out, and then we'll decide what to do. And now, Mama, I'm going to bed, I'm dead tired."

He undressed and got into bed; his mother kissed him and covered his sleeping body with a sheet.

❧ 15 ❧

SASHA and Military Technician Ovsyannikov drove a mobile workshop from Moscow: a hooded automobile with a small wagon hitched to it containing a lathe and a drilling machine, a workbench, vise, tool kit, blowtorch, compressor, and electric welding equipment. Ovsyannikov told everyone that they received such a great mobile repair shop because of Sasha — he had studied in the same Institute with the chief of the depot. But there was no time for talk. August was coming to an end. The schedules for organizing the battalion were not being met. A decree came out about the supplementary mobilization of men eligible for the draft born from 1880 to 1904; the battalion filled up with older drivers. Vasily Akimovich the mechanic was also drafted; he was appointed chief of the mobile workshop.

They were in a hurry to send off at least the first company. Ovsyannikov was transferred there as platoon commander, Sasha got moved with him as well, he helped fix cars together with the driver Protsenko, a sharp fellow: he could get everything, procure anything, he had family everywhere — at the supply depot and the technical service vehicle, and the gasoline installation. Yuldashev even wanted to use him in the supply area, but Berezovsky, the commander of the first company, objected; every driver had to be accounted for.

One day Berezovsky detained Sasha. There was a cubbyhole in the shop, where they sat down at an old office desk.

"Pankratov, I heard that you studied at the Transportation Institute and left in your fourth year. Is that true?"

"Yes, it is."

"I want to appoint you company technical assistant. This position will make it possible to recommend you for the rank of military technician. Do you have a document certifying your education?"

Sasha liked this man, he could be trusted. Nonetheless Sasha answered: "I don't have a document confirming my education."

Surprised, Berezovsky lifted his eyebrows, which were just as black as his mustache, while the hair on his head was quite streaked with gray.

"You can request it from the Institute; if you'd like, we can write them. Better still, we'll provide you with an official trip to Moscow, you can make it in a day."

"I won't go to Moscow, I won't request it. I'm a driver and that's what I'll remain."

For some time they looked straight into one another's eyes. Finally Berezovsky said: "You'll have with you an official request from the battalion: urgently issue documents necessary for a certificate. They don't have the right to refuse — it's a request by the War Department."

Apparently, he suspects something, he's probably also had a similar experience. At his age, a career military man should be at least a lieutenant colonel.

"Comrade Senior Lieutenant," said Sasha, "I've never served in the army. But I'm not sure that a private in the Red Army can be awarded a military rank against his will."

"During wartime, everything is possible," Berezovsky said harshly and changed the subject: "What vehicle would you prefer to receive — a one and a half tonner, a 'ZIS'?"

"A one and a half tonner."

"Choose one to your liking."

Sasha chose one that he liked, a 1940 model, practically new, from some quiet municipal establishment; it hadn't been banged up on country roads. It had a full set of tools, various spare parts, nuts and bolts, they hadn't even skimped on a winter insulating hood. You could see that it had been in good, caring hands.

Everyone in the company took care of his own vehicle; you couldn't survive at the front with a bad one. They demanded one thing or another from the commanders, so Ovsyannikov had to put up with a lot, but he was obliging, accommodating; old hands among the drivers pressured him, they knew how to coerce him and he would lose his nerve — he was young enough to be their son.

Sasha once told him: "Don't give in too much, they'll take advantage of you."

But Ovsyannikov lacked sufficient backbone. Besides, what could he really do? And the commanders of sections who were his subordinates were also powerless. Meshkov, the commander of Sasha's section, was an experienced driver, a sergeant, a good, solid guy, who had served in action, had two triangles on the collar tabs of his service shirt, who never raised his voice, whose favorite word was "Tranquility!" He good-naturedly advised the drivers: "Live by your wits, fellas, hustle, look at Protsenko, he gets everything for himself." He was respected, called by his name and patronymic: Yuri Ivanovich. Even Churakov, the biggest troublemaker of the officers in the company, did not pick fights with him.

Churakov was quarrelsome, dissatisfied with everything and everyone; short in stature and wide in the shoulder, he had a gloomy and distrustful look; he didn't speak, he growled: "I won't let anyone step on my toes." He took a dislike to Mitka Kuzin, a young collective farm driver, because of his inexperience, lack of skill, or maybe Mitka had simply said something to him in the wrong way. Churakov called him "Prune."

"You, Prune, how long have you been married?"

"I'm not married yet."

"Not married." Churakov pretended to be surprised, "Well, I'll be! But of course, you've slept with girls, haven't you?"

"Well now really, Comrade Churakov." Kuzin was embarrassed.

"Well what of it, it's a fact of life and you, Prune, are a fine-looking fellow. So tell me: how do you tell the difference between a young broad and an old one?"

"Well, how . . . Look at her face and you'll see."

"No, Prune! You have to check. A young one has breasts that stand up: if you put a pencil under them, it'll drop to the floor. An old one has tits that sag, so the pencil doesn't drop, understand, Prune? When you get married, make sure you have a pencil, you won't need anything else because you're so dumb, a prune is what you are!"

"Settle down," said Yuri Ivanovich Meshkov, "don't bother the man."

But Churakov couldn't settle down, and that's what tripped him up. He picked a fight because of a pump. And, as always, he began to curse so the entire garage could hear.

"What's eating you?" asked Baikov, a massive, arrogant driver who had chauffeured some provincial chief around in a passenger car before the war. He was well-fed, had a paunch and a smooth face, was lordly and sarcastic, and liked it when Churakov started fights. He also liked to take shots at people.

"What's eating me, I'll tell you," Churakov growled. "Someone switched pumps on me, the vermin! I had a new one, and this one," he shoved it under Baikov's nose, "this one, you see, the paint's peeled off it, it's all scratched, and doesn't pump worth a damn!"

"Fine, we'll get you a different pump," Baikov said, as if to calm him down, but actually he was teasing him. "It's a trifle. . . . Why are you getting upset?"

"I know which bastard took it, and I'm going to tear that stinker's head off!"

With these words Churakov walked toward Mikta Kuzin's car.

"Now, come on, pull up your front seat, Prune!"

"What is it? Comrade Churakov, why?" said Mitka, dumbfounded.

"Pull up your seat! I'm telling you!" Churakov roared.

Drivers started gathering around them.

Churakov pushed Mitka aside, opened the cab, lifted the seat a little, pulled out a pump, and raised it above his head. "Now! Do you see it? It's my pump!"

The pump really was new.

"And this one's yours!" Churakov threw the old pump on the floor and kicked it. "Pick it up, you bastard! I'll teach you not to steal!"

Sasha knew that Churakov had received a new set of tools, even the bag was new, he had been showing it to everyone, so that someone had in fact exchanged his pump. But it wasn't Mitka. Sasha had checked in Mitka's truck himself. It was a good truck. Sasha had even vacillated about which one to chose, the one he had taken or this one. That was why he remembered that it also had a new pump. And he said: "Comrade Churakov! I checked in Kuzin's vehicle. This is precisely the new pump that came with it."

Baikov interceded: "Even though they say you're an engineer, Pankratov, I can't believe that you remember which tools came in each vehicle. Maybe you can also recognize all the wrenches?"

Sitting in the next truck over was Guryanov, a serious peasant, a Party member who had been head of a garage, but was drafted into the army as a regular driver. Getting out of his cab, he remarked: "In cases like this, you have to report to the platoon commander, not act on your own and poke your nose into someone else's truck."

"It's more convenient for him," tossed in Nikolai Khalshin, who would join a conversation only when justice had to be defended.

Sasha liked him: he was conscientious, not a babbler, never asked Ovsyannikov for anything without good reason, wasn't hard to please regarding his vehicle, the only driver who addressed Sasha using the polite form of "you."

"Red, you shut up, Red!" roared Churakov at Nikolai. "And you!' he turned his head toward Guryanov. "You're used to ordering everyone around in your garage, but I'll manage without you. I'll take what's mine. Give me what's mine!"

"Now here comes the platoon commander," someone said.

Ovsyannikov came over.

"What's going on here?"

"What, what, nothing," snapped Churakov.

Ovsyannikov didn't even have a chance to say anything. Suddenly, for some unknown reason, Berezovsky, the company commander, appeared.

"Red Army soldier Churakov, why are you speaking with the platoon commander in that tone of voice?"

"I speak the way I know how to speak," Churakov growled, turning away.

"Stand at attention!" Berezovsky ordered.

Churakov looked at him confusedly; it seemed like he stood up a bit straighter.

"Put down the pump!"

Churakov put the pump down beside him.

"Arms at your sides!"

Churakov straightened his arms at his sides.

"Military Technician Ovsyannikov, explain what is going here."

"I saw that they were arguing for some reason, so I came over and asked what was going on. Well, then you heard what Red Army soldier Churakov replied."

"Permission to report, Comrade Senior Lieutenant," Baikov said firmly, "nothing in particular. The drivers are sorting out which pump belongs to whom, an ordinary dispute between drivers."

"Sort out the pump question," Berezovsky ordered Ovsyannikov, "and Red Army soldier Churakov will get three extra details out of turn for his rude behavior. I'm warning the staff: Everyone has to respect the Red Army fighter in his comrades. I will harshly punish breaches in discipline, disobeying commanders, rudeness. Don't forget that wartime laws are now in effect."

Churakov cleaned the garage for three shifts, walked around with a broom, cursed the drivers for throwing cleaning rags on the floor. No one paid any attention to him. They would soon be leaving, going to the front. No one knew where. Ovsyannikov secretly told Sasha that their company was being sent to the Bryansk region under the orders of the newly formed 50th Army. They would be issued rifles there.

The company got ready. They were in training during the day, working on their vehicles after lunch; each one laid in whatever supplies he could. A mobile movie theater came twice; they hung a screen on the wall and showed old films: the anti-Fascist *Professor Mamloch* and *Yakov Sverdlov*. When Sasha watched it, he thought: Sverdlov was lucky that he didn't live until 1937, otherwise Stalin would have executed him, too.

The day before their departure, training was canceled, they fueled their vehicles, lubricated them, did last-minute tightening and adjusting, the drivers were given overcoats, first aid kits, were told the number of their field post office. Quartermasters from the division to which the company had to deliver their freight arrived. They were demanding, these men on active duty.

At 7:00 P.M. formation was announced, they went to dinner, and even though many drank that evening, their mood was sad, peaceful.

The driver Ruslan Streltsov, a handsome brown-haired fellow with sad blue eyes, played on the bayan all evening. There was a bayan in every company, since you can take along anything you want in a vehicle. He played well. *"The burial mounds are sleeping, burned by the sun . . ."* He played Maxim's song: *"Where is that street, where is that house, where is that girl that I'm in love with . . ."* And the one about Zheleznyak: *"The partisan sailor Zheleznyak lay under the burial mound overgrown with weeds . . ."* All the melodies were sad. But then Streltsov himself rarely smiled. He was suffering — he had aspired to the air force, he was supposed to have been sent to aviation school, but his documents didn't arrive on time, and so they shoved him in the automotive battalion. He should have been flying in the sky.

Meshkov said good-naturedly: "You're making us sad, Streltsov, why don't you play something more lively?"

"If I had golden mountains and rivers full of wine, I'd give them all away for your loving gaze, and you alone would have power over me," Streltsov began. The song seemed more lively but it still sounded sad. Was it the particular fingering that made it sound that way? It's true what they say — "The accordion weeps."

Early in the morning on the next day they set off for the city. They loaded provisions, uniforms, fuel, lubricants. Ten vehicles with the most experienced drivers were sent off to the depot for ammunition. It was 3:00 P.M. before the company gathered at the designated point along the road out of Ryazan to the city of Mikhailov near the Stenkinsky collective farm. The battalion command, the mobile shop, and the field kitchen were waiting there.

They had lunch. The vehicles got into platoon formation along the edge of a forest. The drivers stood near their cabs. There were unharvested fields across the road, flocks of crows above them. There were no men in the village, there was no one to gather the harvest, it was perishing in the fields.

"Attention!" Berezovsky commanded and turned to Yuldashev. "Comrade Battalion Commander, the company is ready to march."

"Comrades Red Army soldiers," said Yuldashev, "defend our country with courage. Fulfill your duty to your country. Long live our Socialist fatherland. Hurrah!"

"Hurrah!" the company yelled out, not very simultaneously — they hadn't learned how yet.

Berezovsky summoned the platoon commanders, gave the order of march, speed, distance between the vehicles and platoons. The first stop was Zakharovo on the outskirts of the village.

The drivers got into their cabs, the motors started up.

The company set off southwest, to the city of Mikhailov in the Ryazan Oblast.

∾ 16 ∾

STALIN SHOWED THE COUNTRY how he planned to wage war.

Pavlov, the commander of the Western front, the same one whom Stalin had forbidden to occupy the field fortifications at the border two days before the war, was executed along with his staff. Dozens of generals and unit and formation commanders were executed. It was announced that "from now on commanders guilty of unauthorized retreat will be punished by execution. . . . Commanders who surrender will be considered intentional deserters, whose families are subject to arrest, while the families of Red Army soldiers who give themselves up as prisoners of war will be denied government benefits and aid. . . . All populated places in the rear of the German troops are to be destroyed and burned to the ground. . . . Detachments of volunteers for blowing up and burning of populated places are to be formed in every regiment. Outstanding daredevils are to recommended for government awards for courageous actions in destroying populated places."

However, in spite of Stalin's terrifying orders, the Germans advanced five hundred to six hundred kilometers in three weeks; the Soviet Union suffered nearly one million dead and wounded, and an equal number were taken prisoner. Smolensk fell on July 16. The road to Moscow was open. Hitler announced to the entire world that the Red Army was completely devastated, that the war would end within a few days with the complete triumph of German weaponry.

He made the announcement prematurely. It turned out that the Red Army was not completely devastated, and it defended every inch of land. The German army reached Smolensk exhausted. The shock tank corps had to be withdrawn to rest and were replaced with infantry sections. For the first time in all the years of the war, German troops had to go on defense.

The German military command viewed the situation in Smolensk as temporary. Autumn, the time of bad roads, was ahead; they had to assume an offensive more quickly and deliver a strike on Moscow. This would decide the outcome of the war. However, Hitler saw victories in the northwest and the south. To capture Leningrad, and unite with the Finns; capture Kiev, and embolden his southern allies, Romania, Hungary, and Italy; to seize the Ukraine, Donbass, and create a springboard for a jump into the Caucasus; to leave the Soviet Union without bread, coal, and oil. At the end of July, Hitler ordered preparations for an advance on Kiev, thus giving the Russians two months to prepare for the defense of Moscow.

On July 29, Zhukov delivered a report to Stalin.

The General Headquarters was situated on Kirov Street now, in a building from which one could quickly move during an air alert to the metro station Kirovskaya, which had been turned into a bomb shelter: it was closed to passengers, blocked off from the train track, and divided into several apartments, one of them for Comrade Stalin.

Zhukov would have been glad for an air alert — Stalin was easier to persuade in the bomb shelter. But the Germans were not bombing Moscow at that hour. Stalin was standing at the window in his office, with Molotov, Malenkov, and Beria sitting at the table as usual, something which Zhukov noted with annoyance — Stalin also became more accommodating one on one. But this trio was always hanging around his office.

Zhukov spread the map out on the table, reported on the situation. The German attack on Kiev could have catastrophic consequences: the troops on the Southwest front would be encircled. Stalin slowly paced around the office, at times he came over to the table and examined the map closely, then he sat down in front of it.

"What are you proposing?"

"We must immediately abandon the right bank of the Dnieper and organize the defense on the left bank."

Stalin lifted his heavy gaze up to Zhukov. "And what about Kiev?"

"Kiev will have to be abandoned."

Stalin got up, moved his chair back abruptly, walked around the room, sat down again, picked up a pencil. "Continue your report."

Zhukov indicated a point not far from Moscow.

"The Germans could use the Elninsky salient later on to attack Moscow. We must organize a counterstrike to eliminate this salient."

Stalin threw his pencil on the table.

"What counterstrikes, nothing of the sort, what kind of rubbish is this!"

He remained silent awhile, then suddenly and unexpectedly began to scream in a shrill voice: "How could you even think of surrendering Kiev to the enemy?"

"Comrade Stalin — " Zhukov's voice broke off. "If you consider that I'm capable of talking nonsense, then there's nothing here for me to do so . . . then, Comrade Stalin, . . . I request that you relieve me of my duties as Chief of the General Staff and send me to the front. I'll be of more use there, obviously. . . ."

Stalin turned away. "If that's how you put it! It doesn't matter, we can do without you. Go! I'll send for you when I need to. Take your papers with you!"

And he waved away the map that was on the table in front of him.

Zhukov left. Stalin began to pace around the office again.

Molotov was the first one to break the silence.

"No alternatives, no proposals, just surrender Kiev and that's it! . . . It's outrageous!"

"Khrushchev and Kirponos have been knocked out," said Beria; "they want to dig in on the left bank, it'll be easier for them there."

Stalin pressed the buzzer. The general on duty came in, and Stalin dictated a telegram to him: " 'Kiev. To Khrushchev. I'm warning you that if you take take a single step in the direction of withdrawing troops to the left bank of the Dnieper, a harsh punishment will befall all of you as cowards and traitors.' "

Stalin signed the telegram.

"Send it off right away."

And he began to walk around the office again. He didn't listen to what Molotov, Malenkov, and Beria said among themselves. He was thinking. They had abandoned Minsk, Riga, Vilnius, Lvov, Kishinev, Smolensk, now they want to abandon Kiev, and tomorrow they'll propose surrendering Leningrad. Each city that was surrendered was a blow to the heart of the people, each defeat weakened its will to resist, weakened its faith in its leader. And day after day the same reports in the newspapers: our troops have abandoned such-and-such a city. . . . How are the Soviet people supposed to read this?

Stalin extended a finger at Malenkov. "Propagandize the heroism of the Soviet people more. Reports about the heroic deeds our of Red Army soldiers and commanders have to predominate in the mass media. The Soviet people must know that we are smashing and will completely crush the Fascist swine. This has to be instilled in the people every day, every hour."

"Yes, sir, Comrade Stalin, I'll give the instructions," replied Malenkov and left the office.

The general on duty reported: "Comrade Voroshilov from Leningrad."

Stalin picked up the receiver. "Well, what news do you have?"

He listened silently, then said: "I'm going to dictate an order which concerns you. . . . Write," he ordered the general on duty: "They say that the German scoundrels are sending old men and women, women and children out in front of their troops. They say that there are soldiers among the Bolsheviks who find it impossible to use weapons against these kinds of people. If there are such soldiers among the Bolsheviks, they should be the first ones to be destroyed, because they are more dangerous than the German Fascists. My advice: Don't be sentimental and punch out the enemy and its accomplices, intentional and otherwise. Defeat the Germans and their accomplices, no matter who they are, mow down the enemy, whether they are intentional or unintentional enemies."

Stalin stopped dictating.

"Dispatch this off to all the commanders at the fronts."

Then he said into the receiver: "Did you hear what I said? Did you hear everything? Did you understand which Bolsheviks I have in mind? Yes, yes, exactly! Very good, that you understood."

He hung up and began to the walk around the office again. Klim is a fool, he distracted *him* from *his* main thought. . . . Why surrender Kiev? The best troops were gathered in the southwest, which was exactly where *he* expected the main strike, wasn't it? *He* was the one to forbid a retreat! And now the Chief of the General Staff is proposing a retreat! It was shameful! *He* didn't need a Chief of Staff like that!

Stalin pressed the buzzer, ordered the general on duty to call Zhukov in.

Zhukov appeared.

"Here's what, Comrade Zhukov," said Stalin. "We had a consultation and decided to relieve you of your duties as Chief of the General Staff. We're going to appoint Shaposhnikov to this position. And we'll use you in a practical capacity. You have experience commanding troops in a battle situation. You'll be a very useful man out in the field."

"Where are you sending me?"

"You reported on the operation near Elnya. That's what you should take on. Of course, you will remain the Deputy People's Commissar of Defense and on the staff of General Headquarters."

"Permission to leave, sir."

"Give the file to Shaposhnikov and be on your way."

After Zhukov was dismissed, no one dared to even mention the surrender of Kiev and the withdrawal of troops from the right bank of the Dnieper.

In a week Stalin declared himself Commander in Chief.

Zhukov, although dismissed from the high command, nonetheless was brave enough to send Stalin a telegram from Gzhatsk:

THE ENEMY HAS THROWN ALL ITS MOBILE STRIKE AND TANK UNITS TO THE SOUTH. THEIR PLAN: TO CRUSH THE ARMY OF THE SOUTHWEST FRONT WITH A STRIKE FROM THE REAR. A STRIKE TO THE ENEMY FLANK MUST BE DELIVERED AS SOON AS THEY BEGIN TO CARRY OUT THEIR PLAN.

This was the reply:

THE ADVANCE OF THE GERMANS IS POSSIBLE. IN ORDER TO PREVENT THIS, THE BRYANSK FRONT HEADED BY YEREMENKO HAS BEEN CREATED. OTHER MEASURES ARE ALSO BEING IMPLEMENTED. WE HOPE TO PREVENT THE GERMAN ADVANCE. STALIN. SHAPOSHNIKOV.

This telegram did not satisfy Zhukov and he called Shaposhnikov, who told him directly: "The Bryansk front will not be able to stop the probable strike. But in a conversation with Stalin, Yeremenko promised to rout the enemy."

This was true. Yeremenko came to see Stalin, behaved confidently, resourcefully answered questions about the reasons for our defeats.

With regard to Guderian's advance on Kiev he said: "I want to smash this son of a bitch Guderian and I will absolutely do so in the next few days."

Stalin talked with him in a friendly manner. After he left, he said: "Now he's the man we need in such a complex situation."

Yeremenko's conduct impressed *him*. He was firm, decisive, cunning in a Ukrainian way, but obedient. And Zhukov is obedient, too, but he turns his eyes away, shows that his obedience is forced. Zhukov's presence was *burdensome:* certain that he was superior to Stalin as a military leader, he doesn't realize that military strategy is primarily politics, about which he, Zhukov, understands nothing. *He* would not tolerate internal opposition in anyone else, but *he* tolerated it in Zhukov — Zhukov was the only person who inspired in *him* a feeling of reliability. And this was also oppressive — *he* had become accustomed to rely only on *himself.* Dismissing Zhukov removed this mental discomfort. Zhukov was necessary, but at a distance. Zhukov had a heavy hand, and like *himself* he didn't spare people, didn't count losses, he would carry out *his* assignments in the most complex sectors. Yeremenko would be here. He would destroy Guderian just as he promised, and then it will be possible to appoint him Chief of the General Staff.

Yeremenko did not destroy Guderian either in the next few days or those that followed. The Germans successfully advanced to the south. Yeremenko was wounded, and was brought to the hospital, to the Timiryazev Agricultural Academy building. Stalin visited him there, in this way showing that *he* still appreciated Yeremenko: it was only because he was wounded that Yeremenko could not fulfill his promise. *He* didn't misjudge people.

On September 11, Stalin issued the order to Kirponos: "Don't abandon Kiev, don't blow up the bridges."

Kiev fell within a week, on September 19, and 665,000 Soviet soldiers and officers were taken prisoner.

Kirponos and his staff died in the battle.

"He was a brave man," Stalin said about Kirponos, "the people are going to honor his memory."

However, Hitler, inspired by the victory, gave the order to attack Moscow. But he had lost two months, August and September, on the battles for Kiev. This loss turned out to be fatal.

17

BRITISH PRIME MINISTER Winston Churchill made a speech on London radio on the day Germany attacked the Soviet Union:

"In the last twenty-five years no one has been a more consistent foe of communism than I. I will not take back a single word I said about it. But it all pales before the sight unfolding before us now. . . . I see Russian soldiers standing on the threshold of their native land, protecting the fields that their fathers worked since time immemorial. . . . I see the gray obedient mass of the Hun soldiers. . . . I see German bombers in the sky. . . . I see a gang of villains planning, organizing. . . . We must speak out immediately. We are determined to destroy Hitler and all traces of the Nazi regime . . . Any man or state that is with Hitler is our enemy. Any man or state fighting against Nazism will receive our help. . . . The business of every Russian is the business of free people in every corner of the globe. Let us double our efforts and we will fight together as long as our strength and life last."

Two days later President Roosevelt of the United States made an announcement about support for the Soviet Union.

Litvinov had come in handy. *He* had done the right thing in saving his life.

And now Litvinov sat facing *him* again. Poskrebyshev brought in tea and pastries. He also brought in a small parcel and put it on the table next to the tray.

"What's this?"

"It's urgent from Leningrad, from Comrade Zhdanov."

"What's urgent about it?"

"I don't know. It says: 'Do not open, hand to Comrade Stalin personally.' "

"All right, I'll look at it. Later on."

Stalin went to the back room, brought back a bottle of cognac, splashed a bit in his tea, squeezed some lemon into it, then asked Litvinov with a look if he wanted some. Litvinov thanked him, and declined. In the same unhurried way Stalin capped the bottle, brought it back, returned, sat down at the table, stirred his glass with a little spoon, took a sip, looked at Litvinov. He had aged, become gray, but he was just as corpulent, solidly built, with the same imperturbable gaze behind his glasses: neither exultation nor reproach. Of his old comrades, of the friends of his youth, he was essentially the only one who remained, everyone had been exterminated — both those who were at *his* side and those who were at Litvinov's side. Litvinov himself, of course, expected to be arrested any day. And he didn't appeal to *him* once. He only babbled to his wife, but he did it intelligently, as if he were addressing Molotov; he was an old conspirator, an experienced one.

"Hitler attacked France first, that's true," Stalin unexpectedly began. "But why did he attack? Because he signed a nonaggression pact with us. Had we not signed the pact, Hitler would have attacked the Soviet Union as early as last year when we weren't ready for war. Now he's forced to support dozens of divisions in occupied Europe, whereas he would have attacked with all his forces then. And he would have been in Moscow by now. And we wouldn't be sitting here, you and I, we wouldn't be sipping our tea. What do you think, had Hitler attacked us last year with all his forces, moreover with France and England applauding, would we be drinking tea here?"

He looked heavily at Litvinov. What would he answer? Would he begin to argue? No, he wouldn't argue. He's a diplomat.

"Of course we wouldn't be drinking tea here," replied Litvinov.

Stalin took his eyes off him, stirred the tea in his glass, took a gulp, started speaking again.

"Hitler reached Smolensk and ran out of steam. He's marking time near Leningrad and Odessa; he'll be there for a long time. The Blitzkrieg has failed, this is obvious to the entire world. What we need from Churchill and Roosevelt is real help, not pretty words. I remember Churchill's words: the strangulation of Bolshevism is the main blessing for humanity. Weren't those his words?"

"Yes. But for him the primary enemy is now fascism. And he's already waging war with Germany. I think that for him the issue of assisting the Soviet Union is indisputable."

"Real assistance is a second front," said Stalin.

"Churchill will not open a second front until America enters the war."

"Won't Churchill betray us?"

"Of course he's afraid of a Soviet victory, but to his way of thinking this is a remote prospect. Right now he needs Hitler defeated."

Stalin finished his tea, set the glass aside.

"And what is Roosevelt like?"

"Roosevelt. . . . Religion, ethics, morality, and the like. But his attitude toward Hitler is clear. And you can depend on his assistance. America will enter the war in the near future. It will not tolerate Hitler's domination of Europe and Japan and Asia."

"Churchill, Roosevelt. . . . Who's stronger as a personality?"

"Roosevelt is milder."

Stalin rose. Litvinov also stood up.

"Well, then, Comrade Litvinov," said Stalin, "that's probably enough vacation, eh? Now is not the time to relax, Comrade Litvinov. We'll appoint you Molotov's deputy. If necessary, you'll go to America as ambassador."

Litvinov left.

Stalin extended his hand toward the buzzer. His eyes fell on the parcel from Zhdanov. He tore off the wax seal and opened it.

There were three German leaflets in the package. Stalin picked up the first one. The photograph of Yakov on it immediately caught his attention.

Stalin sank heavily into an armchair. His worst fears had come to pass: Yakov had been captured, his son was taken prisoner. The Germans were reporting this to all the Soviet people, to the entire Red Army. And they'll do whatever they want with Yakov, they'll force him to sign anything they want. Yakov was cheerful, taking a stroll in the woods with two Germans, looking into one of their faces, saying something. And under it were these words: "This is Yakov Dzhugashvili, Stalin's eldest son, commander of the battery of the howitzer artillery regiment of the 14th Armored Tank Division, who surrendered near Vitebsk along with thousands of other commanders and soldiers. . . . In order to confuse you, the commissars are telling you lies that the Germans are treating POWs badly. By his example, Stalin's own son has proven that this is a lie. He surrendered because any resistance to the German army is futile." And on the other side: "Pass for being taken prisoner. The bearer of this pass, not wishing the senseless bloodshed in the interests of kikes and commissars, is defecting to the German Armed Forces."

On another leaflet Yakov was photographed apparently in a camp or a collection point, in a military greatcoat, surrounded by Germans staring at him with curiosity. On the third one Yakov was reading something and smiling (the son of a bitch was smiling!), beside him sat a handsome, well-groomed German officer. And the caption: "Follow the example of Stalin's son! He surrendered. He's alive and feels perfectly fine. Why do you want to go to your death when even your leader's son has given himself up as a prisoner? Peace to your exhausted motherland! Stick your bayonet in the ground!"

On the back in Yakov's handwriting: "Dear father! I've been captured, I'm well, soon I'll be sent to one of the German camps for officers. I'm being well treated. I wish you good health. Regards to all. Yakov."

Stalin picked up the leaflets and put them in the package.

The son of a bitch! "I'm being well treated. . . ." The bastard! He disgraced his father, the army, stabbed his motherland in the back. Did they force him into it? Did they torture him? Possibly. But why did he give himself up? Why didn't he shoot himself? He had a weapon! He behaved like a coward! He was a coward!

He had never liked him, hadn't ever seen him until his dear little brother-in-law Alyosha Svanidze, the scum, brought him to Moscow. He brought him deliberately, in order to annoy *him*. . . . Silent, alien, sluggish, he had no pride; he got married, they had a girl who died, he got divorced, he attempted to shoot himself but he missed — he couldn't even shoot himself. He attempted suicide because of a girl, the son of a bitch, and now, *now* when it was a matter of his honor, he didn't want to shoot himself. Then he remarried, this time to a Jewish girl from Odessa, a dancer whose husband had left her — he couldn't find a modest Russian girl? A skirt turned out to be more important than his father's reputation. The son of a bitch! *His* own son gave himself up. "I'm being well treated!" The bastard! Well then, so much the worse for him. A sovereign cannot feel sentimental about his own children. Ivan the Terrible and Peter the Great killed their own sons, and they were right to do so.

Stalin pressed the buzzer, and asked Poskrebyshev, when he entered: "Who's waiting out there?"

Poskrebyshev placed a list in front of him with the names of the people waiting to see him.

Stalin noted on the list who should be allowed in to see him in what order, issued the order:

"Have Beria report at seven this evening."

Poskrebyshev, who knew his boss better than anyone else, warned everyone who was going into his office: "The boss is at the breaking point."

Beria reported at seven. Stalin was still talking with Shaposhnikov and Vassilevsky, and he silently handed Beria the package with the leaflets. Beria sat down and began to read them. Shaposhnikov and Vassilevsky gathered the maps from the desk and left.

"What do you say?" asked Stalin.

"The photographs are evidently genuine. This doesn't look like an actor who's been made up to look like Yakov," replied Beria.

"I can see for myself that it isn't an actor!" Stalin exploded. "Why did I get the leaflets from Zhdanov? Were the leaflets scattered near Leningrad?"

"No, they were scattered everywhere. We have them."

"Why didn't you report it to me?"

"I didn't know how to tell you about it, Comrade Stalin."

Stalin slammed his fist on the desk. "You were concealing it from me?"

"We were thinking over what steps could be taken before we reported it to you."

"And what did you decide?"

"We have to find out where Yakov is now. The Germans are undoubtedly guarding him carefully. He would be difficult to locate, given the mass transfer of POWs."

"And suppose you find him in a month or two, in a year?"

"Then we would try to arrange an escape."

Stalin stood up and walked around the office as he usually did.

An escape. . . . Thousands of our POWs could not escape, but Stalin's son managed to. Who would believe it? The people would say: Stalin arranged it with Hitler, rescued his little son. What kind of trust could the people have in Comrade Stalin after that?

He stopped in front of Beria.

"As soon as you find out where Yakov is, report to me immediately. We have to deprive the Germans of the opportunity of using his name to the detriment of our army, our nation."

Beria stood up.

"Put his wife in jail, in solitary," Stalin added.

"And his daughter?"

"Give her to Svetlana, she'll decide, maybe she'll take her to her grandparents."

❦ 18 ❦

AFTER A MONTH OF BLOODY BATTLES in the vicinity of Bryansk, the 50th Army broke out of encirclement on the east bank of the Oka river near Belev, having lost a considerable portion of its men and equipment. "The Katyushas," multiple rocket-launchers mounted on vehicles, shot their last volley at the enemy, then they had to be destroyed — they ran out of rockets and fuel. In early November under pressure from the enemy, the army withdrew again and consolidated itself on the Dubna-Plavsk line. The motor transport company under Senior Lieutenant Berezovsky's command was ordered to deliver the badly wounded to the rear, to the frontline evacuation hospital.

There were forty-two vehicles left; of the commanders, in addition to Berezovsky, there was only platoon commander Ovsyannikov. Berezovsky told Sasha: "You'll have to help, Pankratov. You can see, there's no sergeant-major, no political instructor, no platoon commanders. I've assigned Ovsyannikov to be second in command, but he won't be able to deal with the entire outfit. Take on the technical side. If they send me a technical assistant, I'll relieve you."

Berezovsky became completely emaciated, turned dark, he was shell-shocked and couldn't hear well, asked for things to be repeated; he clasped his quivering temple with his fingers.

Sasha's workload did not particularly increase. The technical vehicle was intact and so was Vassily Akimovich, the experienced mechanic. The drivers, even though experienced old hands, who had often come to Sasha for advice before, well, by now they considered him their superior. Sasha still had no rank, they called him either "engineer" or by his last name, Pankratov. And Nikolai Khalshin continued to address him using the polite form of "you."

They washed their vehicles, swept them out inside, put down straw, got as much canvas as they could, loaded the wounded, met at the designated place, filled their gas tanks, were issued food; the physician, medical attendant, and nurses got into the cabs and they drove off. Berezovsky was in the lead vehicle; Ovsyannikov, Sasha, and the technical vehicle brought up the rear.

Fog descended unexpectedly, the Germans stopped flying, and the motor transport company delivered the wounded to the evacuation hospital on the second day.

The rear areas of the front were situated in a small town, but you can't hide forty-two vehicles from the German Air Force, especially since the frontline outfits had their own vehicles. The company quartered itself in three neighboring villages, Ovsyannikov in one, Sasha in another, and Guryanov, the former head of a garage and Party member, in the third one.

Berezovsky stayed in town, waiting for instructions about where to go, what to transport. The driver Protsenko, the go-getter, was with him — spare parts, materials, fuel, lubricants, food had to be procured.

After the heavy September and October battles, after encirclement, breaking out of encirclement, looping around settlements, crossing rivers over hastily constructed, crumbling bridges; after the loss of more than half the company's men, retreating past burned villages, through destroyed cities, along roads clogged with refugees with children, collective farm carts, herds of cattle, wounded soldiers in bloody, blackened, and dusty bandages, the artillery, gasoline pumps, staff cars from headquarters; under constant bombing, when not everyone managed to jump out of their cabs, dash into a field, throw themselves on the ground, with carrying their dead comrades to their vehicles and digging their graves — after all of this, life in the quiet little village seemed like heaven.

Protsenko supplied them with tobacco and dry rations, and the villagers had their own potatoes, pickles, and cabbage. Piles of firewood lay in the neighboring woods, stockpiled from last year; the drivers delivered it to all the houses and stacked it — which meant that they also got some vodka. And there was a steambath. Life was a bowl of cherries. Only it didn't last long.

On the seventh day Protsenko drove Berezovsky over to Sasha's house, then drove on around the village to round up the drivers.

"I'm going to have a talk with the drivers at your place," Berezovsky said, "and you'll find me a place to spend the night."

"You can stay here, if you like; as you see, there are two beds."

Berezovsky took off his garrison cap and military overcoat and hung them on the hook on the door, then sat down on the edge of the bed, and lit a cigarette.

"I was over at Ovsyannikov's and Guryanov's. Their vehicles are ready. What about yours?"

"They're all ready to go."

After knocking the snow off their boots, the drivers came into the house and reported in. Berezovsky watched them silently.

Finally all of them were assembled.

Berezovsky put out his cigarette in a small dish.

"Sit down, whoever's standing. Only don't smoke, I've already smoked it up in here."

Some squatted near the wall, others remained standing.

"We're leaving tomorrow at six zero zero. I'll announce the loading station en route. We're not returning here. Any questions?"

"What about warm uniforms, Comrade Senior Lieutenant," asked Baikov. "It's actually winter out there."

"We'll get hats with ear flaps, felt boots, quilted trousers, and mittens at the designated station, and that's where we'll distribute them. Any other questions? No?" and he turned to Sasha.

"You want to add anything?"

"The engines have cooled down," said Sasha, "we ought to get buckets of hot water ready by morning. And also, don't forget your shovels, axes, towing cables in the huts."

"You can't clear up much with an iron shovel," Vassily Akimovich expressed concern, "you need wooden ones. It's simple: saw a handle lengthwise, wedge a piece of plywood in the saw cut, and nail it in. That's all there is to it."

"That's all there is to it," Churakov mimicked him, "and where do you get the plywood?"

"Come over, I'll give you some."

"Do you have much plywood?" asked Berezovsky.

"I have a few sheets," Vassily Akimovich replied evasively.

"Save it for the rest of the company. Any more questions? . . . And so I repeat: we leave at six zero zero. You're all free to go. Protsenko, bring my things in here."

The drivers left.

Protsenko returned with a small suitcase, carryall, and package. He explained that the package contained herring.

"Thank you, go. Pick me up tomorrow at five."

Berezovsky undid his belt, took it off, put his gun and holster under his pillow, undid the collar of his shirt, pulled off his boots, unwound his foot cloths.

"Is there some place to dry these?"

"Of course, give them to me."

"Order some hot water at the same time, and we'll drink some tea."

"Would you like something hot? I can have an omelette prepared."

"Boil some potatoes, if there are any, they go better with herring."

Sasha went to the kitchen, spread out the foot cloths on the stove, asked the landladies, two single old women, to put on the kettle and cook some potatoes. They began to bustle about. They were grateful to Sasha: not only had he brought them a load of wood, but he had sawed it and split it with his comrade; now they had fuel for the entire winter, they wouldn't freeze.

Sasha returned to the main room.

A thick aluminum water bottle wrapped in a wool cover stood on the table; it was vodka, of course. Berezovsky was cutting up a large fatty herring on spread-out newspaper.

"D'ya see the kind of herring people in the rear have — have you tried it?"

"I've had occasion to."

"My hands are dirty, get the can with bread and butter from my kitbag. While you're at it, cut some up."

The lamp, made of a flattened artillery case, was smoking. After Sasha trimmed the wick with scissors, the flame began to burn evenly.

The old women brought in glasses, forks, spoons, plates of pickles, sauerkraut, onions, and somewhat later, a cast-iron pot of hot potatoes covered with a towel.

"Enjoy it."

Berezovsky nodded at the water bottle. "Pour some, Pankratov." His fingers trembled when he picked up a glass. "The first one's supposed to be for victory."

They drank.

"That's good," Berezovsky shuddered.

He speared some herring with a fork, chewed it, raised his eyebrows.

"I haven't eaten herring like this in a long time. What do you think, Pankratov? Good?"

"Very," Sasha praised it.

Berezovsky took the towel off the cast-iron pot, the fragrant steam of potatoes hit them in the face. He served himself and Sasha potatoes, covered the pot with the towel again.

"So they don't get cold. Pour. When will we get another chance to drink together, Pankratov? Maybe after our victory. What do you think?"

"Maybe before then."

"Before the victory? Do you know the latest news from the front?"

"The Germans have taken the offensive again."

"Yes. Guderian's tanks are active on our front."

He held his temple with fingers, his elbows on the table, and looked at Sasha through his eyelashes.

"Now listen carefully, Pankratov. You're fulfilling the responsibilities of a technical assistant."

"I'm no technical assistant." Sasha grinned. "Nothing special, picking it up as I go along."

"You are, you are. And as a technical assistant, you have to know the mission. It is the following. The company has orders to pick up a shipment of winter uniforms, food, and arms. Now I'm going to show you the railroad flag-stop stations where we have to pick up the shipment."

Berezovsky took a map out of a map-case, spread it out on the bed.

"You see, here's the city of Mikhailov."

"Yes, I've been there."

"From Mikhailov the railroad line goes south, here's the section — Mikhailov's in the north, Pavelets in the south. Between them are the flag-stop stations where the train cars are *supposedly* waiting for us. But . . ." He slowly, distinctly, and meaningfully said: "Guderian's troops are occupying the city of Mikhailov, his mobile group is in Skopin."

"In Skopin?"

"This information is not in the communiqués from the Informburo, but the landlord of the apartment where I was staying called Skopin and the telephone operator told him: "The Germans are here. . . . They're drinking heavily. . . . They're seizing warm clothing from the towns-people. . . .' And they don't know about this at our rear headquarters. That's celebrated military reconnaissance for you. What's the meaning of this for you and us? Here's what: The Germans could have reached Skopin only via Pavelets. Which means that Pavelets is also occupied. Therefore, the entire section of the railroad line between Mikhailov and Pavelets is in German hands. Where are we going to pick up the shipment?"

"Why are we going there then?" asked Sasha.

"I asked the same question at headquarters. They told me: "There are no Germans in Skopin, those are local stories. German motorcyclists showed up in Mikhailov, but they were chased off. So drive over there and pick up your shipment.' Fine! Let's suppose we get there and pick up our load. Where are we supposed to go then? To the location of the 239th Infantry Division in the vicinity of Uzlovaya Station. Look where that is." He showed it on the map. "Do you see? It's to the north! But if Guderian's reached Mikhailov, that means that Uzlovaya is cut off. How are we going to get there? By air? At headquarters they told me: 'Uzlovaya is not cut off, we're in communication with them. Carry out the command's orders.' What prompted this order? Here's what. . . ."

He took a cigarette, used the oil lamp to light it, and continued:

"The 239th Division was transferred to the 50th Army. This division has to be supplied with warm uniforms, and the rest. How can this be done? Very simply. Our motor transport company also came from the 50th Army, so we have to go back to it. And also pick up the shipment for the 239th Division along the way. So they've taken cover behind us. Should anything come up, they'll present the documents: the motor transport company number X was directed . . . to train number . . . boxcars number . . . invoices number . . . You can't find fault with them. They sent everything off, dispatched all of it. . . . If it didn't get there, sorry, it's wartime. But we carried out the order. That's how it is, Pankratov. All I managed to squeeze out of these swine was five days' worth of food, three refills' worth of gasoline for each vehicle. They also gave me a nurse, whom I left with Ovsyannikov; you'll see, she's a child. They gave us twenty-three rifles for the entire company. We fought with our fists near Bryansk, now we're armed, every third person has a Mosin rifle, an 1891 to 1930 model. We'll beat them all!"

Berezovsky put the map in the map-case, poured some vodka, and drank without waiting for Sasha.

"That's the situation, Pankratov! We've been counting in the millions for a long time now, on the state level what's a paltry fifty people?" Squinting, he looked at Sasha. "*These* are the kind of people we have now, Pankratov. *Those* people are all gone. Poems were written about *those* people. . . ."

He held his temple with his hand, and declaimed in a toneless voice:

> *I watched those fearless warriors,*
> *as they into battle charged,*
> *How they did swallow, at the bitter end,*
> *Molten, red-hot lead.*

"Do you know who wrote these lines?"

"Utkin. 'On Esenin's Death.' "

"Right. Utkin. And so, Pankratov, I fought alongside those fearless ones, they're gone now. When *they* were with us, then Denikin, Kolchak, Yudenich, Wrangel, the Czechoslovaks, the Germans in the Ukraine, the French in Odessa, the English in Arkhangelsk, the Japanese in the Far East couldn't master the barefoot, naked, hungry, and unarmed Red Army! Now we're fighting just the Germans, and the Germans are already on the outskirts of Moscow. Do you know the writer Panait Istrati?"

"I read *Chira Chiralin*."

"He's a good writer, a Balkan Gorky. And so, he said about *them*: 'The golden stock of the Russian Revolution.' Where is this golden stock today? *These* people have come to replace them. *From the top to the bottom.* They're offering up Russia, they're driving people to their deaths."

Sasha remembered: Panait Istrati had called those who had opposed and fought against Stalin in the 1920s and who were annihilated by him in the 1930s "the golden stock of the Russian Revolution."

"You give the impression of being a career officer, Comrade Senior Lieutenant. Why is your rank so low?"

Berezovsky helped himself to some more potatoes, buttered them.

"Eat, while they're still hot. Have you noticed, Pankratov, that potatoes cooked in a cast-iron pot in a Russian stove have a completely different taste than potatoes cooked in Moscow on a gas stovetop? You're from Moscow, aren't you?"

Sasha laughed.

"I'm from Moscow, but I don't know which potatoes taste better."

"How long has it been since you left Moscow?" Berezovsky asked unexpectedly.

"A long time," Sasha replied curtly.

"That's what I thought," said Berezovsky, "and so, I'm answering your question. I fought in the Civil War, have been a Party member since 1919. A rare museum piece nowadays. I studied, became an engineer, worked at the Gorky Automobile Plant. When I got my certificate as a reserve company commander, I was given the rank of senior lieutenant and that's what my rank still is." He stood up. "Let's go to sleep, Pankratov, we have to leave early tomorrow. Let's lead people into their last, decisive battle. . . . I'll be leaving earlier, we'll meet in the village of Fofanovo, at Ovsyannikov's."

～ 19 ～

ON OCTOBER 2, Hitler's order was placed on Stalin's desk: "The prerequisite for the last enormous strike which must result in the destruction of the enemy even before winter sets in was finally created today. All the preparations, as much as was humanly possible, have been completed. The last decisive battle of this year begins today."

Half of the German Army that was massed in Russia moved in the direction of Moscow. The code name of the operation was "Typhoon." Oryol fell on October 3, Bryansk on the sixth, Vyazma on the seventh, where 600,000 soldiers and commanders were encircled, almost as many as were taken prisoner on the outskirts of Kiev in September.

On Stalin's order, newly formed and poorly trained units were thrown into battle. Unseasoned soldiers, who hadn't even managed to clearly understand how to hold a rifle, were driven into combat.

In those same days the Moscow newsreel shot the story: "The Flower of the Intelligentsia and Working Class Goes off to the Front." Faces without smiles, hair streaked with gray. Writers, artists, musicians, and actors, who had built the metro, who had signed up as volunteers in the divisions of the People's Volunteers Corps, lined up in columns, marching clumsily. The divisions of the People's Volunteers Corps were mowed down within several days.

On October 7 Zhukov flew to Moscow at Stalin's summons. After the successful operation that he led near Elna, he organized the defense of Leningrad and prevented the enemy from entering the city. Now, as head of the Western front, he had to defend Moscow.

Pale, pinched-looking, his eyes red from lack of sleep, Zhukov went to Stalin's apartment straight from the airport. Stalin had a cold and also looked bad; Molotov and Beria were in his office. With a nod, Stalin indicated an armchair to Zhukov.

"Will the Germans be able to repeat an attack on Leningrad in the near future?"

"I don't think so. They are strengthening the front edge of their defense. The tank and motorized troops have evidently been transferred to the Moscow sector."

"Assume command of the Western front, look into the situation, and call me."

Zhukov left.

Stalin rose from his armchair, walked around the office, stopped in front of Molotov and Beria, stared at them for a while.

"The enemy is at Moscow's doorstep, and we don't have enough forces to defend it. Kutuzov abandoned Moscow, but he won the war. Hitler has been fighting for over three months now, but he hasn't captured either Moscow or Leningrad or the Donbass. As you know, winter is fast upon us. The Russian winter! How are the Germans going to fight in their little military overcoats and garrison caps? Wouldn't Hitler prefer to end the war and keep what he's already conquered? The Baltic region, Belorussia, a part of the Ukraine — if need be, the entire Ukraine. A separate peace? Yes, a separate peace. Lenin wasn't afraid to conclude a separate peace with the Germans in 1918. Why should we be afraid to? Lenin understood that the Brest peace was a temporary one, and he was not mistaken: German imperialism was doomed. And we understand that German fascism is doomed and we'll get back what we give up now. Using your channels, find the way to immediately propose a peace treaty to Hitler."

This proposal was made to the German state through Stamenov, the Bulgarian ambassador. Hitler did not even respond to it; he had no doubts about capturing Moscow. At the beginning of the war he had issued an order: "The city must be occupied in such a way that not a single Russian soldier, not a single inhabitant — whether man, woman, or child — can leave it. The necessary preparations are going to be made to flood Moscow and its outlying areas with the aid of special constructions. An enormous sea must rise where Moscow stands today, a sea that will hide the capital city of the Russian people from the civilized world forever." Now, there wasn't any time to build these structures, and the new directive of the high command said: "The Führer has again decided that Moscow's capitulation should not be accepted. The city must be destroyed with artillery shelling and air attacks and the population must be made to flee before the city is captured. The more people that rush to the interior of Russia, the more chaos will take hold."

The Germans occupied Kaluga on October 13, Kalinin on the fourteenth, Maloyaroslavets and Mozhaisk on the eighteenth. But even two days before Mozhaisk capitulated, rumors spread around Moscow about German motorcyclists who had been seen on the outskirts of the city, on the Volokolamensk highway. Archives were burned in government offices. Train schedules were being revised at stations — government offices were being evacuated on a mass scale. The construction of an underground bunker for Comrade Stalin was begun in Kuibyshev. The apparat of the NKVD was also evacuated to the same place, Kuibyshev, and it took the most important people under investigation with it. But there weren't enough cars, and about three hundred of the top military command remained in the basements of Lubyanka. They were executed. Later, on October 28, the generals who had been brought to Kuibyshev were also executed: Loktionov. Rychagov, Shtern, Smushkevich, Savchenko. This was at a time when lieutenants were commanding regiments at the front.

A state of siege was declared in Moscow on October 20. Zhukov, the commander of the Western front, was placed in charge of the defense of the city. Soviet troops resisted fiercely. An entire battalion would be dying, but not a single soldier left his line. Tank drivers in tanks consumed by flames fought to their last shell and died. Soldiers with bundles of grenades threw themselves under German tanks and blew them up.

The Germans were stopped by the end of October. On November 7, there was a military parade on Red Square at which Stalin gave a speech addressing the fighters who were leaving for the front. This was his only brave deed during the war — a German airplane could have broken through into Moscow.

A sharp cold spell began in the middle of November, the temperature dropped to minus 10 degrees Centigrade. However, Berlin issued the order to make one more effort, to make the final assault, to capture Moscow; it was only fifty to sixty kilometers away!

∾ 20 ∾

BEREZOVSKY LEFT with Protsenko at five in the morning. Sasha started his own vehicle, warmed it up, said good-bye to the old women, and drove out onto the main road. It had gotten cold, the snow that had fallen the day before had become compacted, turned black in places; the road was good, hard.

Vehicles came out of the homestead yards. Sasha drove up to each one to find out whether everything was all right. Of course, Churakov did not make a wooden shovel.

"Where are we going?" asked Baikov.

"To the village of Fofanovo."

"And after that?"

"I don't know. The company commander will announce it."

"Do you know that Fritz is getting close to here?"

"The company commander will tell you everything."

The only car that didn't start was Mitka Kuzin's car; his battery had died.

"Turn the crank."

"Well, I've been turning and turning it. . . ."

"Run over to Vassily Akimovich's and get the 'collective farm one.'"

What they called the 'collective farm one' was a starting crank with a long handle that three people could turn at one time. Nikolai Khalshin, Yuri Ivanovich Meshkov, and Mitka took hold of the handle, Sasha got behind the wheel, the engine rumbled and started up.

"That's it," said Yuri Ivanovich, "the most important thing is tranquility. Kuzin, don't wear out your starter for nothing, you have a weak battery and you'll run it down, so use the crank."

Berezovsky's information turned out to be correct.

On the morning of November 18, Guderian's tank army broke through the defense of the Soviet troops south of Tula and, outflanking it, deployed an advance to the north, toward Moscow. The swamps, lakes, and rivers froze, the terrain became passable, it made movement easier for the German troops.

On November 24, Guderian's mechanized division occupied Mikhailov, its forward detachments reached Skopin. The enemy's reconnaissance scouts, security, and bivouac guard groups were roaming in the small area between Mikhailov and Skopin.

And the small railroad station that the motor transport company drove up to had also been bombed by the Germans: the railroad ties were pulled up, the rails were twisted into formless balls, charred and burned boxcars were strewn around the embankment. The station keeper said that they were empty cars, that there had been no shipments and, in general, not a single train had left Mikhailov after November 24, so that it was not likely that there was any freight at any other station. And since the Germans were in Mikhailov, there was no way to get to Uzlovaya now.

Berezovsky was thinking. The mission could not be carried out. Driving farther would mean condemning people to death. Returning without carrying out the order would mean he would be court-martialed, but his men would survive — they had obeyed his orders. They had to go back.

"Seems like there aren't any Germans in the neighboring villages," added the station keeper, "but their planes are flying."

And as if in confirmation of his words a "Rama," a German twin-engine reconnaissance airplane, appeared in the sky, flying very low, and then disappeared. Of course, the pilot had noticed the column of vehicles on the highway; they were going to swoop down and begin bombing. . . .

Half a kilometer away the forest was visible on the other side of the railroad track. They quickly drove over the railroad crossing, drove into a cleared area, piled trees near its entrance, and covered the vehicles with branches. And they did it just in time. Two German airplanes appeared, circled, but did not find their targets, and flew away.

In another half hour the noise of engines and the popping of motorcycles reached them. Taking cover behind trees, Berezovsky walked up to the road. Three German armored personnel carriers and five motorcycles with automatic gunners sitting in their sidecars appeared on it. They drove up to the railroad tracks, went upstairs to the station master's hut, and soon emerged from it with the station master; they put him in a sidecar and drove off toward Pavelets.

That meant that the Germans had also straddled this road, so they couldn't use it to return. The company moved forward along the cleared area, driving around tree stumps and over ditches.

Their mood was depressed. Memories of their encirclement and the deaths of their comrades were fresh in everybody's minds. But then at least they were a group, they were with the army, and now they were alone, fifty men with only twenty rifles among them. None of our troops were here; Fritz would advance from all sides, slaughter them all, strangle them all like kittens.

They drove to the end of the clearing, but did not drive out onto the highway. Berezovsky sent out scouts to the flag-stop halt. The scouts returned in the evening: there were no Germans there, but neither were there any boxcars.

It snowed, they had to get out of the forest. During the night they advanced with dimmed headlights toward the village of Khitrovanshchina; there was a road to Uzlovaya from there. They set up camp in the forest again and camouflaged themselves.

Berezovsky drove to the village and returned with two large cans of hot cabbage soup.

"Serve the soup in the mess-tins while it's hot, and then take the cans back to where we got them," Berezovsky ordered. He placed two men on patrol at the edge of the forest, called Ovsyannikov, Sasha, and Guryanov to Vassily Akimovich's mobile unit. Protsenko brought them bread and mess-tins of soup.

Berezovsky spread out the map on the workbench and showed them: "There's no way back. There are Germans in Uzlovaya and Mikhailov. That means we can't move either north or south, to say nothing of west. What are we going to do?"

"That leaves the east," said Sasha.

"We'll get to the railroad tracks. And then where do we go? Do you see the map? The only road east goes from Mikhailov, and the Germans are in Mikhailov."

"There is another road," said Sasha. "Here's the flag-stop station, and here's the village of Gryaznoye. Before the war a highway was being built here, a grading machine passed over it, but they didn't finish it, that's why it's not on any maps."

"Do people drive on it?"

"This I don't know."

The sound of an engine was heard. Ovsyannikov looked out the door.

"Streltsov's returning the cans to the village."

"But if people don't drive on the dirt road, it means it's covered with snow," said Berezovsky. "How will we find it?"

"There should be road markers. And they know about this dirt road in every village. Then there are ditches — we can find the road between them. Sand, stones, gravel were brought in, it's lying in piles along the sides of the road — they're also a sign. We have shovels."

Berezovsky measured the distance on the map.

"It's less than seventy kilometers."

"Two hours' drive," said Ovsyannikov.

"In these conditions, two nights, not two hours," Berezovsky objected.

Protsenko came in.

"Comrade Senior Lieutenant, there's a captain here with his men."

"Run! Whoever has a rifle, bring them all here!"

A captain and four Red Army soldiers with submachine guns, wearing hats with earflaps, sheepskin coats, and felt boots, were brought in.

"Your documents," Berezovsky demanded.

The captain unbuttoned his sheepskin and got some documents out and extended them to Berezovsky, casting a guarded look at the officers surrounding them.

"Let the soldiers get warm in the cabins," Berezovsky suggested, returning the documents, "and you, Comrade Captain, come with us to the mobile unit."

They returned to the mobile unit, where the captain took off his hat and his sheepskin coat. He had light brown hair and blue eyes; his round face, red from the cold, expressed annoyance.

"The motor transport company is headed to the position of the 239th Division," said Berezovsky, "and where are you headed?"

"You won't get through to the 239th Division." The captain took off the felt boot from his left foot, unwrapped the legging, took off his sock, and examined his foot, evidently he was looking for a sore spot. "The

239th Division is encircled, the 50th Army is cut off. Everything in the north is cut off."

"And how did you wind up here?"

"We dropped behind our unit. We're escaping south."

"Why south?"

"I've already told you," the captain impatiently answered, "the north is cut off and the Germans are advancing to the east, which means all that's left for us is to go south."

"What would you advise us?"

"You?" The captain shrugged his shoulders. "You won't get anywhere with vehicles."

"Leave them?"

"Even better equipment than this is destroyed when you break out of encirclement."

"We intend to make our way through to the east, to the city of Pronsk."

The captain frowned, became preoccupied with his legging.

"Movement along roads, especially with a column of vehicles, is out of the question, you'll be bombed within an hour." He began speaking with even more irritation and didactically: "Comrade Senior Lieutenant, you can break out of encirclement either as a powerful military unit, capable of engaging in battle, or in small groups of five or six people along trails in the forest. I, Comrade Senior Lieutenant, have broken out of encirclement several times and know: moving in the same direction as your enemy is certain death."

The captain stood up, put on his sheepskin coat and his hat, and saluted.

"God bless you, Comrades, I wish you luck!"

He climbed out of the road service vehicle, called his men. And suddenly a driver ran over yelling: "Comrade Senior Lieutenant, Fritz is bombing Streltsov!"

Everyone rushed to the edge of the woods.

Streltsov, having returned the soup cans to the village, was speeding along the road. A Messerschmitt flew over it very low. Streltsov stopped suddenly; the bomb fell and blew up in front of him. Streltsov drove around the hole and on ahead. The airplane circled around and flew toward him — you could see the pilot's helmeted head. Streltsov didn't stop this time, but drove even faster, and the bomb fell behind him.

While the German was turning for another approach, Streltsov drove into the woods not far from the company position.

"Great!" cried Ovsyannikov.

The captain said bitterly to Berezovsky, "You see, they chase after single vehicles, and you're planning to bring through an entire column."

And he left with his men.

Streltsov appeared, reported: The vehicle was all right. Berezovsky formed up the company, expressed gratitude to Streltsov for his courage and bravery, gave the order to prepare to leave, determined the march order, distance, and signaling, broke up the company into groups of five, and appointed senior commanders: he would be at the head of the column, Ovsyannikov in the middle, Sasha and Vassily Akimovich would bring up the rear in the technical vehicle. Tonya the nurse, the only one who was dressed in winter gear, handed out frostbite prevention ointment to each man and explained with childlike diligence how to use it.

Finally everything was ready.

It began to get dark. Berezovsky gave final instructions to Ovsyannikov and pulled out onto the road with Protsenko, drove a few meters, then suddenly stopped and got out of the cab.

Ovsyannikov ran over to him, turned around to the drivers, and yelled: "A flat tire!"

Sasha turned off his engine — who knows, it could be anything, what if he needs help?

But he didn't even make it out of his vehicle.

Everything happened instantly. Roaring, a Messerschmitt hedgehopped out of the woods and fired a long burst of machine gun fire.

Berezovsky and Ovsyannikov fell.

❧ 21 ❧

BEREZOVSKY LAY ON HIS BACK, his overcoat open, his service shirt bloody. One arm lay across his bloody face, the other, also bloodied, was flung to the side. They seated Ovsyannikov on the running board of a cab; he slumped against the door as Tonya bandaged his head, looking into his eyes.

"Easy, dear, easy, I'll be careful. . . ."

She glanced sideways at Sasha, who was standing near Berezovsky, and shook her head.

"It's all over."

Sasha and Guryanov lifted Berezovsky. Sasha removed his map-case and gun belt, and took the documents out of his service shirt pocket. His attention lingered on the photographs. A pretty-looking woman in a sleeveless frock was leaning her shoulder against Berezovsky, who was hugging two little girls in bathing suits. A summer day, a sandy beach.

They carried Ovsyannikov into the technical vehicle and Berezovsky into the woods.

They gouged the earth with crowbars, dug it out with shovels, taking turns; they were in a hurry to dig the grave before complete darkness fell. Yuri Ivanovich lit up the pit with a pocket flashlight and waved his hand — that's enough! They found two boards in the vehicle, they cut them down, nailed them together, laid the commander out on them, carefully lowered him down to the bottom on ropes, covered his body with canvas, threw earth over it, put an old "ZIS" outer tire on top of the grave, stuck a stake with a piece of plywood in the middle of it. It had a star and the inscription "Senior Lieutenant Berezovsky, M.S."

Vassily Akimovich and Guryanov called Sasha over.

"You are the technical assistant, which makes you the senior here. Give us the commander's last order."

The drivers fired a volley from their rifles, then stood near the little mound silently for a while. The wind buffeted the hems of their coats, the snow got under their collars.

Sasha suddenly realized that Berezovsky had a premonition about his death, that he had wanted to have his say before dying, which was why he was so frank the night before.

"The company commander's last order," said Sasha, "was to move east, to the city of Pronsk. We can't break through anywhere else. A road grader passed through there from Pronsk to the village of Gryaznoye before the war, so the road is hard. There are villages along the way, so there will be places to get warm. The commander gave us the marching orders. I'll ride in the lead vehicle because I know the way."

"The captain was heading south," said Baikov, "his men said."

"Yes, that's right, to the south, but they're on foot, they walked through the woods, but we need a road," Sasha replied.

"Messers are flying over the roads," Baikov insisted. "We should get out through the woods on foot also."

"And leave the vehicles for the Germans?" Khalshin objected.

"We can burn them, and then they won't get them." Baikov did not yield. "Streltsov took a drive and they shot at him; the company commander drove out and they killed him. How will we be able to break through in a column?"

"Streltsov drove during the daytime," said Sasha. "You saw how the commander died. It was an accident that the Messer caught him. The captain and his men had hats with earflaps, sheepskin coats, and felt boots, and we have garrison caps, overcoats, and boots. We'll freeze. Today is November 30, it's 22 degrees Centigrade, and tomorrow it's already December. I think it's wrong to abandon forty vehicles when we have a chance to get out. And that's why I'm driving out."

"You're dragging us to our deaths, Pankratov," said Churakov.

But he walked over to the column along with the rest of the drivers.

Protsenko's radiator turned out to have a hole in it. There was no time to weld it and they didn't have a new one. Protsenko moved his stuff to Sasha's vehicle and rode with him.

They drove about seven kilometers with difficulty, but without using their shovels, and drove out of the woods to an open place. The road was marked with telegraph poles, and despite the snowstorm, it became easier to drive. To the right, a burned-out village came into sight; it seemed uninhabited, but maybe the people were hiding in their cellars or somewhere else.

Rummaging around in his kit-bag, Protsenko pulled out a hat with earflaps, put it on, put his garrison cap away in the bag.

"Where'd you get it?" asked Sasha.

"I bought it in town near the hospital. I have another one — do you want it?"

He was lying, of course. He had begged for them at the clothing store.

"I don't need it," Sasha declined, "give it to Ovsyannikov, and when we get to the village, ask around, maybe they'll gather up some old hats."

The back window of the cab was covered with snow, you couldn't see a thing. Sasha put Protsenko behind the wheel, opened the cab door, stepped out on the running board and looked back. He could hardly make out the headlights through the shroud of the snowstorm. It seemed that five vehicles were driving along, but you couldn't see any farther and you couldn't stop; you had to lay down a driving lane.

"Close the door," said Protsenko, "you'll get the cab cold."

That was true. But still Sasha would open the door and look out. The snow fell more and more thickly, it stormed more strongly, but even with downed wires, the poles stood in their places showing where the road was.

They got to the flag-stop station at 3:00 A.M. It was empty, the railroad crossing-barrier was open, the signal hut was intact but also empty. The vehicles drove over the crossing. There were no lights, no houses, no people. And no telephone poles on the far side.

Where were they to go? Sasha knew that the village of Gryaznoye was very close to the railroad tracks, about two kilometers, no more, and if you stood with your back to the crossing, the village would be to your right. But where was the turnoff, how could you find it at night, especially during a snowstorm?

"Let's look around," said Sasha. "There has to be someone at the crossing-barrier."

Khalshin stumbled upon an earthen hut and called Sasha over. It was covered by snow but you could see steps going down and a chimney sticking up.

They knocked once, twice. A tall bony peasant came out in a sheep-skin coat and felt boots, a triple-flapped hat on his head. He turned out to be a trackman. There hadn't been any trains either from Mikhailov or Pavelets since November 24. However, he and his wife had no right to leave. It was their job.

"Have the Germans been here?"

"No, but we got their airplanes flying around here."

Sasha shifted from one foot to the other, his feet were frozen in his boots, and his ears were freezing, no matter how low he pulled his garrison cap down.

"Did you know that there was a road being built here before the war, a road grader passed through here?"

"How could I not know. That's what you're parked on right now."

Sasha looked around.

"There aren't any ditches or construction materials."

"They didn't dig any ditches here, they didn't bring in any materials, it was just the grader that came through, that's for sure."

"What about the road markers?"

"Maybe they fell down, you can see the kind of storm it is. Blinov Yakov Trofimovich lives in Gryaznoye, he's the road maintenance man, he's supposed to look after these markers."

"Where's the turn for Gryaznoye?"

"You go about two kilometers, and then take a right."

"Do people use the dirt road to Pronsk?"

"No, there's a road from Gryaznoye to Pronsk, it's a sled path. The dirt road is an open space; besides, people are used to the sled path, that's why when — "

"Fine, grandpa, get in and show us the way."

"Why should I show it to you when you just go two kilometers and take a right."

"That's what you'll show us. Get in, get in!"

"Wait a bit then, I put my sheepskin coat over my underwear, and stuck my bare feet into my felt boots. I'll get dressed and let my woman know."

Bending over, the custodian dove back into the earthen hut.

Lights flickered at the crossing. Streltsov's group of five had arrived. Sasha sent everyone with the conductor to the village, ordered them to leave one vehicle at the turn to show the remaining groups of five the road. He told Protsenko: you'll be the quartermaster; he himself stayed in Khalshin's one and a half tonner to wait for the rest of the vehicles.

"Be patient, Nikolai, as soon as the first vehicles approach, I'll send you to the village and get into another."

Khalshin sat silently. The collar of his coat was turned up, he was bundled nearly up to his eyes with a scarf, his garrison cap was pulled over his forehead, he was shifting his feet, which were freezing. And so were Sasha's, and his arms, too; he was chilled to the bone, even though he had put on a sweater under his service shirt and had wrapped a scarf around his neck.

Finally Baikov arrived with three vehicles, his was the fourth. Where was the fifth?

"Who the hell knows." Baikov was puzzled. "Zhuravlyov was last. He was lagging behind, and is evidently catching up."

Baikov was wearing a hat with earflaps and felt boots; he probably brought them from home, he laid things up in advance.

"Well now, did you see how many vehicles were behind you?" Sasha frowned.

"Now how could I see anything? You're riding with a driver, but I'm behind the wheel and I don't have eyes in the back of my head. Zhuravlyov won't get lost, he's not a little boy!"

"No one is obliged to pick up vehicles for you! You're responsible for your group of five. Maybe Zhuravlyov has lost his way. Be good enough to return and look for him."

"For sure," Baikov smirked, "I'm going to drive back in this storm. What a boss we have here, he's taking a break from his plow."

"You'll regret it."

"Don't try to frighten me, don't do it, I've seen far worse than you!"

Sasha put his hand on his holster.

"Are you going?"

Baikov looked at the holster, looked at Sasha, then walked over to his vehicle silently and drove off straight ahead, without turning around. What scum!

"Too bad you didn't shoot him, the creep," said Khalshin.

"Who'd drive his vehicle from here?" Sasha objected. But he felt his powerlessness. He was not a commander; no one was obliged to obey him. Fine, as long as he could get the column to Pronsk.

Dawn was beginning to break when Churakov drove up with his group of five.

"Have you run across Zhuravlyov?" Sasha asked.

"He's parked on the road, his ignition quit on him. Baikov abandoned him, the insect! I looked at it, fiddled with it, the coil has to be changed, mobile unit will come along and change it. It was Zhuravlyov who held us up — people started driving around him, and one vehicle drove into a ditch; we could hardly pull it out."

"The coil is not the point," said Sasha. "You didn't want to rescue Zhuravlyov — he's from Baikov's group of five, and you had a run-in with him. Both of you are shits!"

"Don't you call me names!" yelled Churakov, moving toward Sasha.

"Now, now, keep it down." Khalshin shielded Sasha. "I'll pop you so hard you won't be able to pick up your brains off the ground."

"Count them!" Churakov cried hysterically. "Count the vehicles! Do you see, five! These I'm responsible for. Don't hang anyone else's on me."

"Drive on!" Sasha waved him off.

It was completely light now, when Guryanov's and Yuri Ivanovich Meshkov's vehicles, with the mobile unit and Zhuravlyov's car, arrived.

"While Zhuravlyov was waiting for us, his radiator seized up, we had to warm it with the blowtorch," Guryanov explained, "that's what held us up."

Sasha asked Tonya how Ovsyannikov was.

"He's sleeping, thank God, I think we'll get him there."

"When you get to the village, find out if there's a hospital there."

Sasha was last to leave for the village of Gryaznoye. It was cold and gloomy, and snow fell continuously. Protsenko got into the cab and reported: the men had been fed and were resting, the village was large, the vehicles had dispersed among the streets and lanes, parked close to houses, near fences, they couldn't immediately be seen from the air, besides they were covered with snow.

Protsenko brought Sasha to his billet. It was a good, warm hut; the owners were an old couple, with their daughter-in-law and grandchildren. They greeted him politely, but you couldn't say in a very friendly way. This surprised Sasha — in other villages he had been treated more warmly.

Sasha took his boots off, placed his feet near the stove, warmed up a bit, changed his socks, ate his hosts' hot cabbage soup, and went off to see Blinov, the road maintenance man. He was sleepy, his head drooped, but he overcame it.

Blinov turned out to be a gloomy peasant, who said that the road-building materials had been brought as far as the village of Durnoye. They were on the sides of the road, maybe the road markers had fallen, since it had been blowing for three days. You could tell where the road was by the ditches, it was about ten kilometers from here to there.

"You'll come with us and show us the ditches," said Sasha.

"Why should I go?"

"Because you're the custodian, the road maintenance man."

"I worked in maintenance, that was indeed the case, but who needs my duties now? And I can't go anywhere — my spine won't bend. I have sciatica."

"You'll come, we'll wrap you in a sheepskin coat, seat you in the cab, you'll come!"

Blinov shot a stern sidelong glance at Sasha.

"When are you planning to leave?"

"By evening. We'll leave when it gets dark."

"Why wait?"

"The men haven't slept for two nights, they can't stand up on their feet."

"The road to the ditches has to be cleared during the day or we'll get lost in the field at night. Go to the collective farm chairman, Galina Ilinichna, ask for people with shovels, they'll clear it as much as possible, I'll show them."

❧ 22 ❧

GALINA ILINICHNA, chairman of the collective farm, a large middle-aged woman in a wool sweater with a medal pinned to it, frowned as she listened to Sasha.

"What local population? We have old men, women, children."

"In Moscow women are digging antitank trenches; it's tough for everyone."

"We know, we've heard about it, we've read about it." She smiled. "But as you know, they're digging trenches in Moscow so the enemy doesn't break through, and here we're supposed to clear the road so our defenders can run farther away from the enemy? Isn't that so?"

Stunned by this logic, "No" was the only response Sasha could think of.

"Now you, for example, where are your insignia? I don't know what you're supposed to have, cubes or triangles. Did you take them off, are you preparing to surrender?"

"I'm not the commander. The company commander was killed, the platoon leader was badly wounded, I've had to take command as a private. We're on our way to Pronsk to our division. And don't think that it was so easy for us to make our way through."

"That doesn't change things." She didn't yield. "The Germans are in Mikhailov, a stone's throw from here, they'll be here any day, whereas you're leaving, and to top it off, you want us to get the road smooth and ready for you. Why don't you take us with you? Why are you abandoning us here?"

"Fine! The vehicles are empty, get in them immediately, with shovels of course, you'll help clear the road. Come on, let's go, get ready!"

She sighed. "We don't have instructions to leave or drive the animals off. They can't be abandoned."

"No instructions . . . What about us? We're simple soldiers. That's how it is."

"Maybe that is how it is . . . but it hurts. Look where our fighting's got us. No enemy has set foot on these Ryazan lands since the days of the Tatars. And now it's invincible, unconquerable. . . . If you were advancing and not retreating, we'd be lining the road with floor matting." She fell silent. "All our women are busy now: at the dairy farm, the poultry farm. . . . All right, bring the vehicle round to the office, we'll round up whomever we can. Bring Blinov with you."

"Without fail. He's a mean one, by the way."

"What's he got to be happy about? Both of his sons were killed. We've only been fighting five months and he's already lost his sons."

They left in two vehicles. Sasha was at the wheel of the first one, with Blinov next to him. Khalshin drove the second one.

"Let's go, Nikolai," Sasha had told him, "give me a hand!"

They began to clear the road right after the turn. Blinov determined the direction by means of signs known only to him. He was dressed in a sheepskin coat and high felt boots; wherever he made a mark with his shovel, wherever he tramped down the middle of the dirt road with his feet, the girls shoveled away the snow from there, some to the right, some to the left, swapping places; they could hardly keep up with the old man, who was a fast walker. Sasha and Nikolai would also do some clearing, return to their vehicles, move them forward along the cleared road, come out of their cabs, take up their shovels again.

The girls stayed sullen, exchanging words among themselves from time to time; they avoided looking at Sasha and Nikolai. There was only one older peasant woman, her shawl crisscrossed over her fur coat, who said: "Your drivers are strong bucks — can't they clear the road themselves?"

"They haven't slept for two nights, and we're setting out on the road again tonight. If a driver falls asleep at the wheel, he'll wreck himself and the vehicle too."

"Most likely, he's been up with a woman for two nights, keeping her up too, and he gets up in the morning and looks terrific, but he falls asleep, the tender little thing, at the wheel!"

Nikolai replied without malice, somewhat lazily: "Depends on the woman. . . . You can't tear yourself away from some; with others — you turn over and sleep till morning. Especially if she can't shut up for a minute."

But Sasha didn't say a thing. There was the open field, the snow, the biting icy wind, the line of women leaning over their shovels, shifting from place to place. What could he explain to them? Say that they have to do their duty? They understood that themselves.

And he kept shoveling and shoveling snow, hoping to get warm from the work, but his feet still froze in his boots, his fingers froze in his wool gloves, his ears froze under his pulled-down garrison cap.

The same woman with the crisscrossed shawl worked alongside Sasha. She saw him pulling his cap over his ears, bringing his hands up to his mouth and blowing on his fingers. She said, either angrily or sympathetically: "You ought to sit in the cab, you'll catch cold in those little boots of yours."

Sasha smiled at her. "When we come to the ditches, we'll all go back to the village."

"I'll bring you a hat, mittens, felt boots, or you won't survive, handsome."

"Thank you for that," said Sasha.

The moon had risen when Blinov stopped.

"The ditches, here they are!"

Even though they were piled up with snow, the ditches were visible — in some places more, in some less — from both sides of the road.

"Where the ditches are covered with snow, feel it out with your shovels. About ten kilometers from here there are piles of materials on both sides of the road, and farther up from that, a bit to the side, there will be a village — Durnoye."

They cleared some more space, the vehicles turned around, the women got into them. Blinov got into the cab with Sasha, and they drove back to Gryaznoye along the cleared road. Sasha said good-bye to Blinov: "Thank you for everything, Yakov Trofimovich."

"All right, never mind. . . . From Durnoye to Pronsk count fifteen kilometers along the highway. At the fork there's a machine and tractor station, there are little huts, it's sort of a settlement. . . ."

"I'm familiar with those parts."

At his billet Sasha took off his overcoat and boots and tried to stretch his legs, and suddenly it hit him, he felt a fever, his head hurt and drooped, his back ached, and even though the hut was well heated, he shivered slightly. Had he really gotten ill? That was all he needed! He wasn't hungry, but he ate some hot cabbage soup, also some buckwheat groats which were hot, then slumped down on a bench near the stove, lost consciousness, and dozed off.

Sasha put Protsenko behind the wheel and napped in a corner of the cab, catching up on at least a little bit of sleep; everyone but he had slept during the day. His head was heavy, he still shivered, he couldn't get warm, even though he was wearing a hat with earflaps, felt boots, and mittens that the peasant woman had brought them. He had been dozing on the bench, so he didn't hear her come. He saw the hat, the boots, and mittens only when Protsenko woke him up and reported that everyone was ready, the engines were running. The felt boots turned out to be too big, and they slipped off his feet. The landlady said: "Those are Efrem's felt boots. Her Efrem was a huge man." She told her daughter-in-law: "Lyuba, give him your husband's, they seem to have the same build."

The drivers also had hats, a few had felt boots — the village folk had taken pity on them. Or maybe they thought: Better give them to our own boys than have the Germans wind up with them.

The vehicle stopped.

"The road has ended," said Protsenko.

Sasha got out of the cab. This was the place they had cleared up to, this was where they had turned around.

The full moon lit the snow-covered fields. Behind him car lights were visible — a long row which stretched back into the darkness. Sasha sent Protsenko along this row — everyone was to turn off their headlights and come forward with shovels.

Sasha ordered the metal workers, Shemyakin and Sidorov, to walk along the side of the road and feel out the ditches with their shovels; he himself went out in the middle of the road, like Blinov had, and stamped out a trail, sometimes marking it with a shovel. Khalshin Nikolai was behind him, and then the entire company in single file. Sasha was getting stuck in the snow, moving his feet was difficult — thank God, at least these felt boots fit him; he would have already lost those other ones,

Efrem's, a long time ago. He looked back, as the drivers moved along his trail. Finally the men stopped and began to shovel the snow.

"As soon as you finish this section," Sasha told Nikolai, "bring up your vehicles and continue following me."

Sasha was no longer walking, he was dragging himself. All he could see was the metalworkers and he knew that he needed to walk between them.... Then suddenly everything disappeared.... He opened his eyes; Shemyakin, the metalworker, was shaking him by his shoulder.

"Pankratov, you're walking in place. Did you fall asleep?"

"I don't know." He tried to smile, but his lips did not obey him. "Go on, Shemyakin, I'll catch up to you."

"Don't hurry, come to your senses a bit."

The vehicles pulled up and turned off their headlights. The line of people with shovels again stretched out following Sasha's trail.

And so on and on kilometer after kilometer. Sasha dragged himself, looked back. At times there was no one behind him, then cars would approach and stop. Sasha would again distance himself from them. He didn't know how much time had passed, he didn't want to take his mitten off to look at his watch, he only saw the snow-covered field lit up by the moon around him, the metalworkers to his right and left. And suddenly it seemed as if he caught a glimpse of a small hill on the side of the road.

"Get the snow off it," Sasha yelled to the metalworker.

So it was — a large pile of sand, and on the other side there was a pile of gravel.

Now they had landmarks, they didn't have to search for the road. Sasha and the metalworkers stuck their shovels in the snow, leaned on them as they waited for the column. The drivers brought up their vehicles. A murky dawn was already visible at the edge of the sky.

The drivers got out of their cabs and gathered around Sasha.

"How is Ovsyannikov?" he asked Vassily Akimovich.

"Still alive. He gains and loses consciousness. Tonya fears gangrene."

Sasha leaned toward the radiator of his vehicle, the first one in the column.

"Let's decide. The village of Durnoye is off to the side; if we have to shovel snow for another three kilometers, we'll lose time. Let's make a last dash and get to Pronsk, to the machine and tractor station. It's storming, which means that Fritz is not flying. We'll get there in a few hours and warm up there."

"The men are exhausted, and some have frostbite, Tonya's ointment didn't help a damn, we should go to the village," said Baikov, without looking at Sasha.

"No one in the village will help the frostbitten men, there's a hospital in Pronsk, and we'll get Ovsyannikov there, he's in a bad way."

"We have to go to Pronsk." Churakov supported Sasha. He took advantage of any situation, just to say something in opposition to Baikov.

"We've decided," Sasha concluded. "Fill up your tanks, and let's go."

While everyone went to get buckets, Churakov hung around Sasha. He asked sarcastically: "You really want to die for that little Armenian?"

"What little Armenian?" Sasha did not understand.

"That one." Churakov lifted his eyes upward.

"He's Georgian, not Armenian. And we're not fighting for him. We're defending the motherland."

"How politically conscious! We're defending the motherland. Look at yourself — you can't even stand on *crutches*. I just can't understand, why are you pushing so hard, in the name of what are you straining at the bit?"

"Churakov, are you an ex-convict? Suddenly you're using prison lingo!"

"I'm an ex-con! A political prisoner with burglary. Are you familiar with that statute?"

"All right, go get some gasoline, otherwise you'll be left without any."

"I won't. And you sit in your cab before I punch you out in the snow. We'll find the road without you."

~ 23 ~

THE LAST SECTION of the road turned out to be very difficult,
especially in the lower places. They shoveled the drifts and pushed the
vehicles. Sasha also came out of his cab with a shovel — everyone was
working and frostbitten and had colds. Tonya had no medicines, only
iodine and bandages — what's a cold at the front!

The blizzard blew without stopping, the wind drove the blizzard
low to the ground, burning their faces.

At noon they reached the most difficult spot, Sasha knew — a ravine
with steep slopes. There was a frozen stream at the bottom; they hadn't
had time to build a bridge before the war, they hadn't leveled the slopes.

They cleared for a long time. And they cleared far beyond the rise,
so the vehicles would not pile up together on the other side, so that
you could drive up the rise at a run. Not that you could pick up much
speed — everything was full of ruts. The engines strained and roared
as they made it up the steep slope, they got stuck, they had to be pushed,
carried out by hand, one vehicle lost its muffler, another had a flat tire,
engines died, and when Mitka Kuzin's vehicle died, he turned and
turned the crank, then weakened, leaned his head against the radiator,
and burst out crying.

"What a little baby," said Sasha.

Sasha ordered the vehicles up front to make their way through to
the settlement, find accommodations there, while he remained in the
ravine until the mobile unit — the last vehicle — made it up the grade.
Sasha rode in it to the settlement when it had already gotten dark.
Ovsyannikov, covered with coats and delirious, thrashed about in it. He
had to be driven to Pronsk to the hospital; if there was no hospital there,
then to the county hospital.

"Drive over with Tonya, Vassily Akimovich," he asked Sinel-shchikov. "Find out what we should do about the frostbitten men; we'll drive them over in the morning."

"You ought to go to the hospital yourself," said Tonya, "you have a fever, I can tell by your eyes, your lips are cracked with fever blisters, you're wheezing and hoarse."

"Then you should bring me something for my fever."

Nikolai and Protsenko brought Sasha to a hut — Churakov and Streltsov were already there. There were only ten huts in the settlement, so they put five men in each one.

And again, as soon as Sasha walked into the heated-up hut and took off his overcoat and his felt boots, he immediately began to shiver, his teeth chattered, his legs did not obey him, he had difficulty breathing, his head and back ached, everything swam before his eyes. It was hot, stuffy. There were men and young women in the hut, it was noisy, the table was set with glasses and plates with *zakuski*. Streltsov was finger-ing the buttons on his accordion, Sasha couldn't hear what he was play-ing — the ringing in his ears drowned it out. He sat on a bench with his eyes closed. But he did recognize Churakov's voice, as if he were yelling right into his ear: "We'll cure him right now."

Sasha opened his eyes.

Churakov extended a glass to him. "Down some firewater!"

"Dilute it with some water," said Nikolai.

"Doesn't have the same effect. . . . He'll wash it down with water. . . . Come on, Pankratov, gulp it down!"

Sasha lowered his head again.

"Help, fellas!" Churakov ordered.

Nikolai lifted Sasha's head, Churakov pushed the glass into his mouth.

"Wait, let me —"

Sasha took the glass with a shaking hand, drank it in a single gulp. It burned his throat, it burned everything inside. Nikolai had some water ready.

"Chase it right down!"

The burning sensation immediately went away, he felt better, but his head was spinning, his thoughts were getting confused. What kind of a party was this? There was alcohol and food. . . .

Nikolai pushed some sliced bacon and raw onion on his plate. Where

was all this from, what kind of a village was this? Ah, yes, it was a machine and tractor station, settlements. . . . How was Ovsyannikov? Did
they get him to the hospital alive? And if they suddenly brought him
back, what had to be done?

Sasha forced himself to nibble on something.

"Did you warm up?" asked Churakov.

Sasha nodded.

"We'll warm you up the right way. Do you have to use the john?"

Sasha shook his head in reply.

"Think again — we won't let you out at night."

Sasha shook his head again.

"Protsenko, where's his kit-bag? Take out some underwear, undress
him, fellas."

"I'll do it myself. . . ."

But Nikolai and Protsenko were already undressing Sasha.

"He's as wet as a mouse! Girls, give us a towel! Rub him down, fellas,"
Churakov ordered with drunk excitement. "Get up, Pankratov, get him
up on the stove, fellas!"

The stove was burning hot. Sasha jerked back.

"Hold him, don't let him go! Put up with it, Pankratov, you ordered
us around for a while, now obey our orders."

Sasha, completely weakened, fell down on his back; the ceiling was
low, he couldn't lift his head, Sasha stretched out his legs, stretched with
all his might, it seemed to make him feel better, it made his body burn
less. There was grain being dried on the stove, rye or wheat, and it was
hot, but it didn't burn as much. Nikolai held him down, while Protsenko
rubbed him down with a towel. Sasha became quiet, lay half-conscious.
Nikolai covered him with a sheepskin coat.

"Is he breathing?" asked Churakov from below.

"Yes."

"He'll come to, rub him down more often, let him lie there naked.
Don't let the women near him, he's not in the mood for them now, isn't
that right, Pankratov?"

Sasha didn't hear Churakov; there was ringing in his ears, and everything was in a fog. He stretched his legs and tried to pull the sheepskin
coat under him so he wasn't being burned so much, then he fell back
into sleep.

Sasha was certainly robust, if he could endure the night on a hot stove, especially after drinking alcohol. . . . He woke up in the morning, rubbed himself down with a towel, and felt an ease through his entire body; he only seemed to feel a pain in his chest and some discomfort near his shoulder blade.

"Don't go out to relieve yourself," Nikolai warned. "There's a bucket in the entry hall, the washbasin's in the kitchen."

Sasha threw his overcoat on, walked out into the entry hall, washed up, got dressed, pulled on his boots.

"Put your felt boots on," said Nikolai.

"I'm going to the military commissariat, I have to wear my uniform. Did Vassily Akimovich return?"

"He did. He left Ovsyannikov in the hospital. They're not taking in the frostbitten men — they don't have any beds. Tonya brought some medicine."

Sasha sat down on a bench. His head began to spin again, but the weakness was pleasant.

Protsenko and Churakov got up and were washing up.

"Where's Streltsov?" asked Sasha.

"You know where, with his fiancée."

"He's got a fiancée in every village."

Churakov and Protsenko also sat down at the table.

"Are you feeling better?" asked Churakov.

"Seems like I am."

"We could have steamed you in the steambath, beat you with a birch broom, but their bath wasn't heated up, so we warmed you up in another way. It's called 'folk medicine.' Are you going to have some grub?"

"I'll eat."

"That means you're well. You're hoarse, you cough, that will pass, you have fever blisters on your lips — that's good, the sickness is coming out. Take a few drops" — Churakov nodded at the bottle — "you'll get as right as rain."

"I can't. I have to go into town, to the military commissariat."

"Where are you going with a runny nose? Stay in bed a day. Guryanov and Sinelshchikov went to town — they're Party members," Churakov said with sarcastic politeness, "they'll do the reporting, the way it's supposed to be done. You'd better have a drink."

"I'm not going to drink and I advise you not to."

"Pardon me, according to the People's Commissar, a hundred-gram shot is legal."

The landlady put a large frying pan with eggs fried in bacon on the table.

"You're living well," said Sasha, "bacon, vodka . . . where do you get it?"

Churakov nodded at Protsenko.

"You must know, the chief of supplies is with us."

"I didn't know that he was so rich."

"Pankratov, you're a holy fool. That's why people obey you. The Russian reveres the holy fool, because he's a fool himself, and a holy fool is even dumber than he is. So Ivan the Fool likes it that there are people more foolish than himself."

"How am I so foolish?"

"You're a driver, aren't you? How can a driver with a *vehicle* be without vodka, without a piece of bacon? Ah! Think about it yourself."

The sound of a motor, loud voices, could be heard near the house. . . .

Nikolai pulled his hat on, threw on his overcoat, to go out to look, and came back. Baikov and four unfamiliar service men in sheepskin coats, two with guns on their belts — commanders, two with submachine guns on their chests — privates, came in after him. A major, a short fat man wearing glasses, immediately unbuttoned his sheepskin coat and stared at the drivers sitting at the table.

Baikov pointed to Sasha.

"This is our commander."

"Are you the company commander?" the major asked sternly.

"The company commander was killed."

"Who of the commanders is left?"

"Here, no one. The platoon commander, Military Technician Ovsyannikov, is in the hospital in Pronsk, he was wounded."

The major sat down on the bench, put his hat next to him, opened his sheepskin coat more.

"The commanders were killed, the privates survived."

"That's what happened."

"And who are you?"

"A driver, a Red Army soldier."

The major looked at Baikov.

"Who was in command of the company?"

Baikov pointed to him again.

"He was the one who was in command."

"I wasn't in command; I brought the company here because I know the road."

"He's the technical assistant," Nikolai intervened.

"Who appointed you technical assistant?"

"The technical assistant was killed near Bryansk. The company commander charged me with carrying out his responsibilities until a replacement was sent."

"Where's the order?"

"It was an oral command."

"You're telling me fascinating fairy tales!"

"Those are our ways, Comrade Major," Baikov pronounced in his solid, weighty bass voice. "The sarge in charge is the one with the gun."

"Shut up, you shit," Churakov yelled.

The major hit his fist on the table.

"What kind of an expression is that? Why are you butting in? Who asked you?"

"Why are you raising your fists at me?" Churakov snarled. "How dare you?"

"I'll show you what I dare, what I don't dare! I —"

"No," Sasha cut him off. "You don't have the right to wave your fists! And who are you, come to think of it, where are you from?"

"I'm the chief of the special section of the army."

Sasha hadn't seen *them* for a long time, somehow he hadn't run across them at the front, he hadn't met a single one yet! How much this major looked like that one, the one in Ufa who arrested Gleb. They all have the same face, the swine!

"You understand who I am? Now about you, who you are, we'll get to the bottom of that."

"Why look into it?" said Nikolai. "We're soldiers of the Red Army."

"Soldiers of the Red Army are fighting at the front," the major said didactically, and quickly asked Sasha: "Have you been here long?"

"We arrived in the settlement last night."

"We didn't sleep for two whole days," added Nikolai.

"Why aren't you in your uniform?" the major flew at him. "Where's the civilian hat from? Where did you get it?"

"Some people gave it to me."

" 'Some people!' To top it off they're also pillagers!" He shifted his eyes back to Sasha. "So you came to the village last night, now where are you headed?"

"To Pronsk, to the military commissariat."

"I can see how you're getting ready to go to the military commissariat. Drinking vodka in the morning, pillagers and drunkards!" He nodded to the lieutenant, who sat down at the table, pushed the glasses and plates aside, took out paper and a spillproof inkwell from his field pouch, and got ready to write.

Familiar questions: last name, first name, patronymic, year and place of birth, convictions . . .

"None," answered Sasha.

"Write that down: 'Says he has no convictions,' " the major ordered.

Again the sound of an engine, then the sound of it being turned off was heard nearby. The door opened, and a colonel walked in.

"Comrade Major! The commander demands that you immediately deliver the commander of the motor transport company to him."

"You can see, I'm conducting an interrogation."

"The order is to deliver him *immediately!*" the colonel repeated impatiently. "Don't waste any time, Major! Where's the commander of the motor transport company?"

The major pointed to Sasha: "They call this private the commander."

"Get dressed quickly!" the colonel ordered.

Sasha put on his belt; Berezovsky's gun hung on it.

"Whose personal weapon is that?" The major became guarded.

"The company commander's."

"Turn it in!"

Sasha took the holster with gun off the belt and put it on the table.

"Make a note of that," the major ordered the lieutenant, "a personal weapon without permission to carry it."

"Let's go, let's go!" the colonel rushed them.

Sasha put on his military coat.

"Why are you taking him alone? Take all of us," said Nikolai.

"We will when we need to," the major replied and walked out of the house after the colonel and Sasha.

24

IN THE MIDDLE of November, after a two-week respite, the Germans renewed their offensive. And although they reached the settlement of Krasnaya Polyana, twenty-seven kilometers from Moscow, Zhukov clearly saw that this offensive was doomed: the Germans were no longer standing up to the Red Army's retaliatory attacks. Moreover, they would not stand up to the general massed strike. Zhukov telephoned Stalin on November 29 and asked him to issue an order about a counteroffensive.

Stalin did not answer right away. Zhukov knew these pauses — he was having doubts.

"Are you sure that the enemy doesn't have large groupings in reserve?"

"I don't know. But its salients are becoming especially dangerous; they must be eliminated without fail."

That evening General Headquarters agreed to the counterattack. The headquarters of the Western front scheduled it for the morning of December 3. All the commanders of the armies confirmed their readiness except for the commander of the 10th Army.

As far back as October Stalin had asked Zhukov: "Will we hold on to Moscow? Tell me honestly, as a Communist!"

"We will, without a doubt. But we need two more armies and two hundred tanks."

They didn't give him the tanks, but Zhukov got two armies: the First Strike Army and the 10th Army. Vassily Ivanovich Kuznetsov, an experienced general, was in command of the First Strike Army. Zhukov stationed his army in the critical combat sector north of Moscow, near Yakhroma. Stalin appointed Golikov commander of the 10th Army.

Before the war Golikov was the chief of the Main Intelligence Directorate; a smart and cunning sycophant, he had no combat experience. The army was formed in the Volga region, and when Zhukov arrived he ordered it to be deployed south of Ryazan, where it would be in reserve. Now this reserve had to be put into action. In order to complete the encirclement of Moscow, Guderian's tanks were moving from south to north. While Guderian's army was stretched out, its right flank unprotected, a powerful blow had to be delivered to it. This was Golikov's task. And what do you know . . . Golikov sent a report: he could not mass the army earlier than December 5; he sent the report to Stalin — acting in his customary manner, while he was still the chief of the Intelligence Directorate, he had reported everything to Stalin personally, bypassing Zhukov, who was his direct superior at the time. He was not meeting the schedule for the attack and thinks furthermore that he will get special consideration here, too. He won't! This was not some office in the Kremlin!

Zhukov ordered Golikov summoned to front headquarters.

Golikov reported in Perkhushkovo on December 2. He walked in — he was solidly built, bald, youthful-looking — with his usual little smile on his round face. Zhukov had not been able to stomach this smile as far back as the General Staff days; it was usually on Golikov's face after he came back from Stalin's office. Golikov used to go to report to Stalin with two files. If Stalin was gloomy, he reported consoling information; if Stalin was in a generous mood, he told the truth. However, if Stalin didn't believe something, he instantly agreed with him — yes, you're right, Comrade Stalin, this is disinformation. . . .

Everyone was afraid of Stalin, and he, Zhukov, was too; he obeyed his orders, which were often absurd and harmful. But he also always reported his own position. And he never once told lies to please Stalin. Not everyone was able to get away with this. Three chiefs of Military Intelligence were executed before Golikov's time — Berzin, Uritsky, Proskurin — because their truthful information did not please Stalin. But they died honest Communists. Whereas Golikov was a disinformer! Zhukov had personally seen Sorge's telegram stating that Germany would attack the Soviet Union in the second half of June, with Golikov's instructions: "Add to the list of doubtful and disinformational reports." Information like that had been discarded three weeks before the war! How did Golikov dare become the head of intelligence without knowing anything about it? He had written on the "Barbarossa" plan that it was disinformation, intended to deceive the English. And all out of cowardice!

Now Stalin had given him an army. But here, too, Golikov continued to ignore his direct superiors and went directly to Stalin. Stalin couldn't care less about him. There were commanders of fronts begging Stalin for every single tank platoon, every battery, every squadron — he had taken everything into his hands, every trivial little thing, he wanted everyone to depend on him and him alone.

"If divisions were being sold in the market, I would buy you five or six of them, but, unfortunately they're not for sale." These were the words Stalin used in response to Timoshenko's request for one division. To Timoshenko! And here some little Golikov had come along!

"I received your report," Zhukov dryly said. "Why can't you attack?"

Golikov began in a roundabout way: "I left Moscow for the Penza region on October 26. They allotted me two-three months for the formation. . . ."

"Three months!" Zhukov laughed. "By that time the war might be over. Who set up this schedule?"

"The Chief Directorate of Formation," Golikov answered evasively, without naming names, "but on November 24 I received an order from Comrade Shaposhnikov to begin to advance and to mass near Ryazan."

"Why didn't you mass?"

"Transferring an army requires one hundred fifty-two troop transport trains. Only sixty-four arrived, forty-four are en route, and forty-four are still unloaded."

"Why didn't you get the train cars?"

"We telegraphed all the channels. You know the situation with railroad transport."

"The situation is the same for everyone. However, all the reserve armies arrived on schedule except for the 10th Army."

Golikov shrugged his shoulders — he had nothing to say in response to this argument.

"What is the troop readiness?" Zhukov asked with irritation.

"Sixty-five percent of the privates have not served in the army. They were trained with wooden shotguns, since there were no rifles. The majority of the forty-two regimental commanders completed parochial or village schools."

"I'm asking about the combat readiness of the divisions, not about the education of the commanders."

"Four of the eleven divisions are more or less capable of entering into combat. The rest are underarmed: there aren't enough rifles, heavy machine guns, Shpagin machine guns, mine-throwers; there are only forty-eight antitank guns, there are no tanks, heavy artillery, air cover; the divisions were supposed to receive warm uniforms today at the unloading stations — I don't know whether they have. There isn't even enough feed for the cavalry divisions. . . ."

Zhukov listened silently. All the armies were formed in this way, and everyone somehow managed to make the best of it. But this one complains. He couldn't get horse feed in the Volga area! He couldn't get hold of weapons at the factories of Gorky and Kuibyshev, he didn't have warm uniforms sewn there. Yes, the nation was not prepared for war. Wasn't Golikov himself responsible for this? He provided disinformation, assured us that Germany would not attack us!

"What is the numerical strength of the divisions?"

"Complete. There are eleven thousand men in each division."

"Now General Boldin of the 50th Army has six hundred to two thousand men in each division and they've been defending Tula for a month; they haven't surrendered it and they won't. That's how people are fighting now, Comrade General Lieutenant. They're fighting with whatever resources they have. If they don't have enough of them, they get them themselves."

"The 10th Army is carrying out the assigned mission." Golikov frowned.

"Let's hope so. What else?"

"Motor transport supply. The supply situation is only twelve percent. The divisions are disembarking in Ryazan and Ryazhsk and walking one hundred to one hundred fifty kilometers on foot along rural roads piled with snow."

"You should have gotten motor transport in the Povolzhye."

"Everything had been snapped up. Before we got there. There was only old junk left."

"You should have restored the old junk. No one is going to give us anything new. You have to understand the situation, Comrade General Lieutenant. . . . It's hard. But those who encountered the *unanticipated* enemy on June 22 at the border, they had it much harder. What do you think, General Lieutenant?"

Golikov understood the hint, but did not get embarrassed.

"Undoubtedly. But I'm responsible for the 10th Army now and must be ready to carry out the mission."

"No, General Lieutenant, we are also responsible for *those* who were left there. Show me the disposition of your troops."

As Golikov took a map out of his map-case and spread it on the table, he remarked: "We only have two maps with which to lead the army."

Sokolovsky, the Chief of Staff, walked in and exchanged handshakes with Golikov.

"Vassily Danilovich," said Zhukov, "the general lieutenant here is complaining that they don't have any maps."

"The maps were sent."

"And the things they requisitioned?"

"They provided two battalions of medium-size tanks, one artillery regiment, and two rank-and-file mortar battalions. The additional arming of personnel, companies, and battalions will take place at the unloading stations. We don't have anything else to give them at the moment."

"What about motor transport?" asked Golikov.

"There is none."

"We need a minimum of three or four motor battalions. I wrote to the General Staff about this."

"I request, General Lieutenant," Zhukov said sternly, "that you address your demands and requests to the front headquarters. If you want to appeal to the People's Commissar of Defense, please do, but do so through the front headquarters. That's the procedure in the army. No one is allowed to violate it."

Zhukov leaned over the map.

"Guderian is in Mikhailov, our headquarters is in Shilov. They've gotten far."

"We're transferring headquarters to Starozhilovo, near Pronsk."

"Show me the disposition of your divisions."

Golikov showed it to him. The army occupied a front that was 120 kilometers long: from Zaraisk almost to Skopin.

"How much time do you need to get to your headquarters?"

"Four-five hours to Ryazan, and another four-five from there."

"Get on your way. Tomorrow morning you'll *secretly* assemble the division commanders in some little village near Pronsk, and you will *personally* meet our authorized representative in Pronsk at 8:00 A.M."

~ 25 ~

T HE "AUTHORIZED REPRESENTATIVE" who came to the position of the 10th Army was Zhukov himself. He left at night accompanied by a guard of half a company and two armored cars.

No one besides Sokolovsky, the Chief of Staff, knew about his trip. The order was to answer calls from General Headquarters with: "He's among the troops." Stalin forbade commanders to travel to other fronts without his permission. He allowed them to move along their own fronts, but he was always unhappy about it, he didn't want commanders to stray far from their telephones.

Of course, Golikov could have been left to his own devices. Let Stalin admire his protégé. But Golikov's failure would mean the failure of the entire counterattack. Guderian would penetrate into the rear of the Western front, the German infantry would rush into this gap, and that would mean the fall of Moscow. But right now Guderian was easy prey: He had overstepped the mark, stretched out his army. A strike had to be delivered to the very foundation of their salient; it had to be encircled and destroyed. He would compel the 10th Army to deliver this strike. If necessary, he would issue an order this very day to execute negligent commanders, then the others would also feel their responsibility. When millions were dying, the lives of a few people were worth very little. This was Stalin's philosophy, but perhaps it was also the source of Stalin's power. Without his iron will, opposition to such an enemy would have been impossible. Stalin made many unforgivable mistakes that were very costly to the people. But they had no other leader. And you had to obey. And force lower level commanders to obey. This was the nation's only salvation.

This is what Zhukov turned over in his mind as he rode in the backseat of the car. His usual thoughts. Zhukov would doze, then wake up. He had spent many nights in this backseat, he had reflected on a great many things. He could no longer remember a night when he had slept normally, except during childhood, when he lived with his mother. The roof in their hut fell in from age, they moved to the barn, but sleeping was good there as well. From the age of twelve on, he had become accustomed to sleeping little. Their landlord, a furrier, had worked from 6:00 in the morning until 11:00 at night and slept on the floor right in his workshop. The rest of Zhukov's life — he was on horseback, in vehicles, on the road. If he managed to grab a few hours of sleep somewhere, that was lucky! And in Moscow at the General Staff, they stayed awake nights — Stalin left the Kremlin in the early hours of the morning, which was when they left for home as well.

Sometimes the cars would stop, the patrol scouts would report that the road was open. They would speed on ahead.

There was a bit of a delay right outside of Pronsk. It was still dark, but Zhukov woke up. The aide-de-camp reported: "There were vehicles found in this settlement, we weren't able to identify whose they are because of the darkness, we thought they were German, they turned out to be ours, seems to be a motor transport company."

"What division?"

"I don't know, Comrade Army General. We woke the drivers up, they're confused, they can't clearly say who is in command of the MT company."

"Stop in the settlement."

It was just beginning to dawn, but the vehicles were already visible, parked right up close to houses and barns, some in the yards; they seemed to have been camouflaged.

They drove on farther. About ten minutes later they stopped again. Golikov was waiting for them at the entrance to Pronsk. He wasn't surprised when he saw Zhukov, the old staff fox, who he knew would be arriving; he came over, reported: All the division commanders were gathered in Starozhil, it wasn't far, just south of Pronsk.

"What are these vehicles in the nearby settlement?"

"Vehicles?" Golikov was surprised. "There shouldn't be any vehicles here. Not a single division has been deployed here."

"There's an MT company there."

Golikov shrugged his shoulders.

"I have no idea."

"Did some division commander squirrel it away it? Maybe they're hiding them in other villages. Yet you indicate in your reports that there isn't any motor transport."

"These are not our vehicles — perhaps it's a wandering MT company."

"It's within the position of your army, and you're required to know. Investigate it and report to me. Are they hiding them? Concealing them? Who are they? On whose order? Are they deserters? From where? Who's their leader?"

Zhukov began the meeting in Starozhilov with these words:

"You indicate a lack of motor transport in your reports, but I just saw an MT company with my own eyes driving into Pronsk. Whose is it?"

Everyone was silent.

"Turns out it's nobody's." Zhukov frowned. "We'll get to the bottom of whose vehicles they are, and we'll harshly punish those who are concealing them. I'm warning you: Severe punishment awaits those guilty of the slightest falsehood in reports, for concealing arms and equipment. You had enough time for formation. Now you're on the front. We need combat-ready divisions here."

After a speech like this, the reports of the commanders sounded very different from Golikov's report. There were incomplete sets of this and that, it was desirable to receive them before the combat operations, but if not, we'll try to get them on the battlefield. But the morale of the soldiers was high, the mission of the command would be carried out.

Zhukov looked at his watch as he listened to the division commanders. It was half-past nine, time to return to Perkhushkovo. But this matter with the MT company had to be cleared up. If the division commander was hiding it, then he would be demoted to the rank of private; if it was a company of deserters, then the commander would be executed. It would be a good lesson for the entire 10th Army.

"What's happening with the MT company?" he asked Golikov.

"The NKVD officer is investigating it."

"Send a car for the MT company commander, let him report immediately."

Soon after that a fat major wearing glasses came into the room — it was the NKVD agent. A Red Army soldier with an exhausted face and wind-burned lips, in a military overcoat, cap, and boots, was led in after him. Zhukov looked at him, puzzled.

"I ordered the commander of the motor transport company to report."

The NKVD major saluted. "Permission to report, Comrade Army General. There were no commanders left in the company. Where they've disappeared to or what was done to them has not yet been established. The drivers pointed to this Red Army soldier as the one who was in command of them. He's the one I'm interrogating. There are a great many things still unclear, Comrade Army General."

Zhukov shifted his eyes to Sasha.

"Why aren't you reporting?"

Sasha lifted his palm to his cap, said something. His voice was hoarse, you couldn't make a word out.

"What, what?" Zhukov asked again with irritation.

"Red Army soldier Pankratov has been *delivered*," Sasha repeated.

Zhukov looked at him. No one had ever dared to reply to him in this way.

Sasha stood up to his stare. Would they shoot him? He didn't give a damn!

"Were you in command of the company?"

"I led the company to Pronsk."

"From where?"

"From the vicinity of the village of Khitrovanshchina, west of the railroad section Mikhailov-Pavelets."

"And where's the company commander?"

"He died during an aerial attack."

"That's it, that's it," the NKVD man intervened, "all the commanders are dead, all the drivers survived."

"Who gave you orders to lead the company?" Zhukov asked sternly.

Sasha looked around him with a hunted look. There were generals, colonels, sitting here, looking at him. They were well fed, wore diamond-shaped and triangular insignia. . . . They ought to be sent out there, into the snow, the ravine, to pull out the vehicles on their shoulders. . . . Strategic planners. . . . Look what they've brought the country to.... They've allowed Hitler to reach Moscow.... He ought to say everything he thinks about them....

"I'm asking, who ordered you to lead the company?!"

This one, too. The illustrious military leader — he was also *conducting an interrogation.*

"Well?" Zhukov raised his voice.

"The motherland ordered me, Comrade Army General," Sasha said hoarsely.

Everyone was silent. Both the generals and the colonels.

Zhukov did not stop staring at Sasha.

"Are you a member of the Party?"

"No, I'm not."

"How did you wind up in Pronsk?"

"The company was supposed to deliver some freight to Uzlovaya, in the rear areas of the 239th Division. On the way we met a captain with his men who said the the 239th Division was encircled. What were we to do? The German tanks were moving toward Mikhailov and Skopin. The only road for us was between Mikhailov and Skopin."

"There's actually a road there?"

"There's a dirt road."

Zhukov leaned over the map.

"There's nothing marked here."

"The road was being built before the war, it wasn't finished. They managed to grade it. Of course it's not on the map."

"And how did you know about the dirt road?"

"I worked on the construction of this road."

"Can you show me?"

Sasha leaned toward the map. A drop fell from his garrison cap, as the snow melted in the warmth.

"Permission to remove my headgear, otherwise I'll soak the map."

"Take it off."

Sasha stuffed his cap under his arm, leaned over the map

"Along these populated places: Durnoye, Gryaznoye, Malinki, Khitrovanshchina."

Zhukov moved the map toward the Chief of Staff.

"Transfer this to your map, run a reconnaissance check." He turned to Sasha. "What condition is the road in?"

"We cleared it with shovels. If a snowplow goes over it, it'll be easy to drive over."

"How long did it take you?"

"Two full days. At night. We were afraid of the air during the daytime."

"The nights are long now," Zhukov said thoughtfully. "Any losses?"

"There were no losses en route. But there's one wounded man, some frostbitten men. I request that they be given medical help." Sasha looked back at the NKVD agent. "Even though the civilian major called us criminals, criminals also have the right to medical help."

"Help will be granted," said Zhukov, "and do you know the name of the commander of the 239th Division?"

"I don't."

"Colonel Martirosyan!"

The Commander of the 239th Division, a young handsome Armenian, stood up.

"Colonel Martirosyan, is this your MT company?"

"Permission to report, Comrade Army General, a separate motor transport supply company was on its way to our position. However the division was already engaged in combat with the enemy's superior forces that had encircled it and, on November 27, after burying our heavy artillery guns, we broke through the encirclement and came here, near the vicinity of 'Bolshoye selo.' The MT company could not reach the encircled division. There are reasons to believe that this is the very same MT company."

"Well, are they, in your opinion?"

"Sounds that way, judging from the coincidence of circumstances, Comrade Army General. And if you would permit me to say —"

"Speak!"

"If you would permit me to say, Comrade Army General," Martirosyan repeated, "I consider the movement of this company to Pronsk, in the corridor between two attacking enemy tank columns, to be a courageous fulfillment of one's military duty."

"Really, that's what it turns out to be." Zhukov smiled. "Very well, sit down! Red Army soldier . . ."

"Pankratov," the NKVD man prompted.

"Pankratov . . . you know maps well. Where did you study?"

"In the Automotive Department of the Moscow Transportation Institute."

"That means you're an engineer. . . . And why are you a private?"

"It turned out that way."

"Do you have a document certifying your education? . . . Show it to me!"

Sasha unbottoned his military overcoat, got his folded certification from the pocket of his service shirt, and put it on the desk. There was nowhere to hide! The hell with them, let them find out. They wouldn't send him farther than the front.

Zhukov read the first page, turned it over. . . . Sasha did not take his eyes off him. . . . Now he'll get the line "Did not defend his degree project due to his arrest." He got to it! He lifted his gaze at Sasha. . . . He was looking at him. . . . Then he read again, looked again. . . .

"Where you a member of the Komsomol? Since when?"

"Since 1925."

Zhukov lowered his eyes to the certificate.

"There's an exam in military affairs indicated here."

"There was a pre-conscription training at the Institute."

Zhukov turned to Golikov.

"We don't have enough engineers, and here you've got them working as ordinary drivers."

Golikov could have said that he didn't know anything about this motor transport company and that this was the first time he had ever laid eyes on this driver. But he was an experienced bureaucrat and he understood — you can't raise any objections in a situation like this. Zhukov was right: It was a violation of order to use engineering cadres this way, and someone had to be reprimanded for the violation, it didn't matter who it was exactly.

Zhukov took Sasha's Red Army service record book, gave it to the Chief of Staff, and, looking at his certificate, dictated:

"Write down the additional facts: graduated the Automotive Transport Department in 1934. Certificate No. 186/34. . . . Did you write it down? Make up a certificate conferring the rank of military engineer, third class, I'll confirm it right now."

He gave the certificate back to Sasha.

"I congratulate you on receiving of the rank of military engineer, third class."

"Thank you, Comrade Army General."

"Work, fight, serve the Soviet Union!"

Sasha saluted. "Yes, sir, serve the Soviet Union!"

The morning of December 6, Soviet troops assumed a counteroffensive and, despite the bitter cold and deep snow, beat the enemy back to 150 to 200 kilometers from Moscow.

∽ 26 ∽

BRAVURA MUSIC blared from the radio, and there were reports every half hour about the swift progress of the German troops, about captured cities, airplanes shot down, and the hundreds of thousands of prisoners of war. "The Soviet troops are running away from us so fast we can barely keep up." The émigré newspapers rejoiced: "Our time has come." Merezhkovsky and Zinaida Hippius blessed the Germans as they went off on their "Crusade."

Germany would conquer Russia with the same lightning speed as it had the rest of Europe. What will happen to me? thought Sharok. Would Beria have time to destroy the documents of his organization? If he did not, then the Germans would discover behind their front lines, in Paris, there was a Mr. Privalov — Soviet spy. Even if the documents were destroyed, the Germans would capture NKVD people who would betray him to save their own skins. Either way, the noose awaited him.

What could he do? Turn himself in to the Germans? What would they need with him? Who was he? A spy abandoned in the West by the Soviets. He would try to come up with a justification. "I didn't work against Germany but against the White Guards émigrés." Who would listen or care?

Should he go to the British? What could he offer? Whom could he give them? Tretyakov? They didn't need Tretyakov or Sharok. They would hand over the feckless turncoat to the U.S.S.R. Here, a present from your faithful anti-Hitler allies.

Sharok was calmed down a bit by the way the Germans had been stopped outside Moscow. They didn't take it right away, and that gave the NKVD time to evacuate or destroy the documents. Mr. Privalov's cover would not be revealed so quickly. And if the Germans did win, it would not be as soon as some émigrés predicted. "The fiction of resistance," Boris Zaitsev insisted. Apparently, it wasn't a fiction.

All his life Sharok had feared the Soviet regime and believed in its indestructibility. And now he was gloating over its defeat. But if the regime were to fall, he would have to answer for his crimes. He was inextricably tied to the regime. It would be better if it remained.

In the meantime, he had to decide on the proper behavior. A young Russian émigré at a time like this could not be isolated from his fellow countrymen. In that sense Speigelglass and Eitingon had thought ahead — they had insisted he have a circle of good friends. They were not very rich, in fact rather poor, but real Russians, neighbors, habitués of the café where Sharok dropped in every evening and which was owned by a Russian. On Sundays Sharok saw them at the Church of the Intercession of the Virgin on rue de Lourmel, the parish of Father Dimitri Klepenin, very popular among the devout, and where Mother Maris Pilenko had opened a free kitchen for the poor and unemployed.

There were opponents of Hitler among the émigrés, but they kept silent and waited, and there were those who rejoiced, kissing and hugging at the news of every German victory. Sharok joined them. Not for hugs and kisses, but in order to safeguard his future. If the Germans won, he would have proven his loyalty even before victory. If the Russians won, he had done his duty as an intelligence officer — infiltrating the enemy camp.

The German authorities had closed down all existing émigré organizations and created a new, united one, loyal to Germany, called the Directorate of Affairs of Russian Émigrés in France. It was situated in a large building on rue de Galaner. They registered émigrés and published the Russian-language newspaper *Paris Herald,* which was run by someone called Yuri Zherebkov, a man with a swaying walk, who had been a professional dancer before the war. Sharok had attended some of his speeches. Pacing the stage, Zherebkov attacked "Soviet agents" who were trying to inflame falsely patriotic feelings among the émigrés.

"Follow the example of the millions of Russian soldiers who are forced to fight against their will in the Red Army!" Zherebkov exclaimed. "They do not resist the German attacks and at the first opportunity not only do they surrender to the enemy but also they express their willingness to fight against the Soviet regime with weapons in their hands, to free the homeland from the Stalinist and Bolshevist yoke."

Sharok attended other meetings arranged for the émigrés and he made acquaintances there, too. He shaved his mustache and beard so Tretyakov would not recognize him if they ran into each other. He was not worried about running into Vika, who had gone to London with her husband, one of General de Gaulle's closest aides. And then he stopped worrying about Tretyakov. The Germans arrested him as a Soviet agent. That meant they used the materials obtained by the French police when Plevitskaya confessed. He had done the right thing by breaking off with Tretyakov.

Tall, blue-eyed, with reddish blond hair, dressed in a decent suit, restrained and neat, Sharok made a good impression. But he was in no hurry to make a choice. The NTS — the National-Labor Union — was gaining strength. Young people added a parenthetical (NP) for New Generation to the name. They made their way into Germany from Yugoslavia and collaborated actively with the Germans. They recruited in the POW camps for "volunteers" to help in German auxiliary, guards, and police units, then they recruited for Vlasov's army, and for the national SS groups. The miserable POWs, whom Stalin had declared to be traitors, faced a dilemma — inevitable death in the camps or life serving the Germans. Many chose life. Sharok did not face the same dilemma. The NTS was also looking for people to work in the Eastern ministry, but work in the occupied territories of the U.S.S.R. in some regional administration in the sticks did not beckon Sharok. He kept thinking, postponing his decision, unable to make a decision. He realized one day that he had forgotten how to decide because people had been making decisions for him for a long time. And they decided for him this time, too.

A man walked alongside Sharok on the street in February 1942. Nothing special — a walking stick, a coat, and hat — but Sharok sensed danger in the way the man slowed his pace to match his own. Sharok moved away, looked up, and felt a chill — it was "Nikolai," the one who had come to Paris to liquidate Lev Sedov, Trotsky's son, the one who was a former boxer and who had astonished Sharok back then with his perfect French. Sharok knew what kind of "special tasks" Nikolai handled. He belonged to Yakov Serebryansky's group. But why was he here? Yakov Serebryansky and all of "Yasha's boys" had been shot long ago. "Nikolai" extended his hand and said in French, "Gérard Dural, or simply 'Monsieur Gérard.' "

They went into a café and sat in the corner. They ordered coffee. The café was empty and the owner was puttering about behind the bar.

"Why were you so taken aback? Weren't you expecting anyone?" "Nikolai" asked in French. They held their whole conversation in French.

The sense of danger did not abate. "Nikolai" could pull out a gun, shoot him and the proprietor, and vanish. "Nikolai" had not removed his hat and coat — he was ready to go. He had selected a spot opposite the window and the firmly shut door (it was February) and he had a good side view of the proprietor. He could do it in an instant.

Without taking his eyes from "Nikolai's" hands, Sharok replied, "I had heard that Serebryansky and his entire group had been arrested."

"Nikolai" had a sip of coffee, put down his cup, and looked at the door. Sharok kept his eyes on him and suddenly saw that his features were not in the least worn down. He had high cheekbones, like many boxers, a slightly flattened nose, and sharp eyes. Strange, Sharok had not noticed before.

"I was given ten years then," "Nikolai" said at last. "The others were shot. For some reason they dragged things out with Serebryansky. He was on death row waiting. And that saved him. The war started and the Boss asked our minister, 'Where's Serebryansky?'

" 'In prison, awaiting execution.'

"The Boss said, 'What nonsense!'

"Well, our people hurried to the cell, pulled out Yakov, and sent him to a sanatorium. Yezhov's bums had beaten his liver and kidneys pretty badly."

He had another sip of coffee. He kept the cup in his hands, thank God! "Yakov demanded that his group be returned to him, and I was the only one left. They destroyed a team like ours! That Yezhov ruined the service, that damned alcoholic pederast!"

He spoke very freely about "The Boss" — Comrade Stalin — and "our people" — Beria and Sudoplatov.... Why was that? Was he trying to lower his guard?

"Nikolai" chuckled. "You're watching my hands. Do you think I've come for you?"

"Why me?" Sharok said, laughing pointedly.

"And why me?" "Nikolai" said, narrowing his eyes.

"For no reason, naturally," Sharok hurried to say.

"But there is a reason for you, by the way."

"Nikolai, what are you talking about?" Sharok started to rise from his chair.

"I told you my name — Gérard."

"Excuse me, Gérard. I don't understand what you are trying to say."

"You ratted on me, didn't you?"

"Me? On you?"

"Yes, you ratted on me. In the Sedov case."

The memorandum that he wrote in Moscow. It flashed through Sharok's mind.

"I wrote what had happened. Only the facts, without any evaluation."

"No evaluation? 'He came, performed the action that resulted in making worthless a source of exceptionally important information' — that's not an evaluation?"

Damn it! He had worried about it then and hesitated whether or not to write it. Like a premonition.

"Nikolai" finished his coffee and put down the cup. "Let's not dwell on that. I am here to give you orders from the Center. Your task is to win the trust of émigrés who can recommend you to the Germans. The rest will be taken care of. The goal is to work as an interpreter in the Central Administration of the Concentration Camps in Oranienburg, near the Saxenhausen camp." He laughed. "There's a resort nearby called Saxenhausen, so that's what they named the camp. There are hundreds of thousands of our POWs in the camps and we must have information on them." He switched to German. "How's your language?"

"Pretty good. So you know German, too?"

"I speak French, German, English, and Spanish. In my day they took only people with languages."

He was stressing that he was a real Chekist, like the ones Yezhov destroyed, while Sharok was one of the new kind. Sharok swallowed the bitter pill and did not even let on that he got the dig, because this was a dangerous enemy. Naturally, "Nikolai" was lying. He did not need information on hundreds of thousands of prisoners. He did not deal in hundreds of thousands, but with individuals. His job was kidnapping and destroying. But that had nothing to do with Sharok. He was being told to gather information. He would gather information.

"While I am here, I am your contact," concluded "Nikolai." "I represent a Swiss commercial firm in Paris. When I leave, you will be contacted. The Center sees your assignment as top priority. They understand the difficulty, but they have great hopes and they will show their appreciation accordingly."

"With a bullet in the back of the head," Sharok thought.

27

ONE MARCH DAY Stalin asked Vassilevsky, "Have you brought your family back from evacuation?"

"Yes, Comrade Stalin."

"Where are they living?"

"I have been given an excellent apartment on Granovsky Street."

Stalin looked up at him. "On Granovsky? In the Fifth House of Soviets?"

"Yes, Comrade Stalin, that's what it used to be called."

"I know that house," Stalin said thoughtfully. "I have been there a few times. And where are your parents?"

"My mother is dead, and my father lives in Kineshma, with my older sister. Her husband and son are at the front."

"So, he left his parish?"

"He has, Comrade Stalin. My brothers and I help him and our sister."

"Good. And where do you rest when you have the chance?"

"At General Headquarters. There is a room off my office, and that's where I sleep."

"Don't you have a dacha?"

"No, Comrade Stalin."

A few days later Vassilevsky was given a dacha in the village of Volynsky on the bank of the Setun River, not far from Stalin's Blizhnyaya dacha. But Vassilevsky rarely went there, and when he did spend the night, he got up at dawn and left for work.

One day he was detained slightly. He had helped his wife in the garden and just as he was about to get in the car, Poskrebyshev called. "Comrade Stalin is looking for you."

Then he heard Stalin's voice on the phone. "Comrade Vassilevsky, you haven't had time to settle in yet, but you're already there too long. I'm afraid you'll move there permanently. Come here instantly."

Vassilevsky arrived after the meeting had begun. They were reviewing the plan of military actions for the summer of 1942.

"The Germans are demoralized by their defeat outside Moscow," Stalin said. "Now they want a breather to gather their strength. Can we give them that time? We cannot. Do we have the right to let them gather their strength? We do not."

Saposhnikov reminded him in cautiously couched terms that our forces were exhausted by the winter campaign and were not prepared to attack.

"We have to break the Germans quickly," Stalin said angrily. "Chase them without fail, chase, chase, chase them. And thereby guarantee the total defeat of the Germans in 1942. Who wants to speak?"

Everyone knew it was ridiculous to speak of the total defeat of the Germans this year. But no one wished to speak. Except for Zhukov.

"Without preparation and without reinforcing the troops with equipment and more men, it is impossible to attack," Zhukov said.

"We can't sit back with our arms crossed and wait for the Germans to strike first!" Stalin said with irritation. "We have to strike a few warning blows and get a feel for the enemy's preparedness."

Immediately, Timoshenko proposed striking such a blow in the direction of Kharkov. He was supported by Voroshilov. Zhukov tried to contradict them, but Stalin interrupted. "Just a minute, just a minute. . . . Where are we expecting the Germans to advance?" He looked around at all the men. "Where will the Germans advance this summer? There is one answer. They would definitely attack Moscow again. Why? Moscow is close. We have intercepted the order of Field Marshal Kluge to attack Moscow. The operation has the code name 'Kremlin.' We must prepare for it. But does this exclude powerful flank attacks to busy the Germans and weaken their attack on Moscow? No, it does not. On the contrary, it requires it. And where should such a blow first be struck? I think that Comrades Timoshenko and Voroshilov are correct. The proposal to attack Kharkov should be supported."

Vassilevsky could have told them that according to their intelligence information, the main thrust of the German attack would be to the south. But Vassilevsky was afraid of contradicting Stalin, and now, after being chastened for his lateness, he said nothing.

Instead, Zhukov spoke up. "Comrade Stalin, there is information that the Germans will attack to the south. Kluge's order can be considered disinformation. We cannot involve our troops in operations with a dubious conclusion —"

"Dubious?" Stalin interrupted. "Why dubious? Comrade Timoshenko, are you convinced of the operation's success?"

"Absolutely."

"Is that your personal opinion?"

"No. The leaders of the front believe that."

"You see how it is," chuckled Stalin. "The command at the front is convinced of success, but Comrade Zhukov has doubts. I think in this case the opinion of the front's commanders is better founded."

Leaving the office, Shaposhnikov said to Zhukov, "You shouldn't have argued. The question was already decided by the Supreme Commander."

"Then why was our opinion asked?"

"I don't know, dear fellow."

The invasion near Kharkov started on May 12. Within a week it became clear that it was hopeless. Vassilevsky, who was now acting chief of staff, suggested to Stalin that they stop the attack. But Stalin was not accustomed to changing his mind. The attack ended on May 29 in a disaster. Four Soviet armies were surrounded and 230,000 people were killed or captured. Generals Kostenko, Podlas, and Bobkin were killed in battle.

The year before, Stalin had miscalculated, expecting the Germans to attack to the south, and this year he miscalculated again, expecting them to attack Moscow. Capturing the Crimea and Sevastopol, forcing the Russians back beyond the Don River, the Germans headed for the Caucasus and Stalingrad.

On July 28, Stalin issued decree number 227.

"We have lost more than 70 million people. . . . Retreating farther means destroying ourselves and with us our homeland. Not a single step back! Form penalty battalions to direct middle and senior commanders there. Place them in difficult parts of the front to allow them to expiate their sins against their homeland with blood. . . . Form well-armed guard units and place them in the rear of unstable divisions and charge them to shoot panickers and cowards on the spot in cases of disorderly retreat."

This decree shackled the commanders' initiative, paralyzed maneuverability, and increased the meaningless losses. Executing the decree would doom the army to defeat. The Germans continued their forward drive, taking Maikop, Krasnodar, and Mozdok, reached the Terek River, and took almost all the mountain passes that led to the Transcaucasus. But they no longer had booty and prisoners. Despite Stalin's order, the Soviet troops fought a maneuvered war, did not allow themselves to be surrounded, and effectively moved away their units. It was only on a narrow part of the front that Paulus's army managed to reach the western outskirts of Stalingrad on August 23.

Stalin understood perfectly well. Hitler would take the entire south — Ukraine, the Caucasus, the Transcaucasus. But most important — Stalingrad! The Germans had the city in a vise and were pushing our troops up to the Volga. If Stalingrad fell, the Germans would have the main waterway of the European part of the Soviet Union. From Stalingrad they would turn north, enter the rearguard of Moscow, and in that way, catch the main forces of the Red Army.

The best army leaders were at Stalingrad. But they needed Zhukov there anyway. Zhukov was the only man who still inspired confidence. Vassilevsky knew what he was doing, but he was too soft for extreme situations. Extreme situations called for Zhukov. Of course, Zhukov's self-importance had grown because he was right — Hitler did not attack Moscow, as Comrade Stalin had expected, but the south, as Zhukov had predicted. This meant he was certain he was the strategist and not Comrade Stalin. Comrade Zhukov was not mistaken! When it came to Kharkov, perhaps he should not have listened to Voroshilov, the ass, who had lost the Finnish war. And he should not have listened to Timoshenko. This was the end of Timoshenko's career. But Zhukov should not feel too triumphant. Stalin would show Zhukov his place. His place was with the troops at the front. He can fight for success there. So let him go to Stalingrad. But first, Zhukov needed a pat on the back.

On August 26, Zhukov was called to Moscow from the headquarters of the Western front.

As usual, he found Molotov, Voroshilov, and Beria in Stalin's office.

Stalin invited Zhukov to the table. Tea and sandwiches were brought in.

"So, Hitler has decided to correct his mistake," Stalin said unexpectedly.

Zhukov regarded him uncomprehendingly.

Stalin pointed to the sandwiches. "Go on, eat. You must be hungry."

He got up and pacing the room, spoke. "What was Hitler's main strategic error last year? In not sending his main forces to Moscow, but in attacking in the south in order to get grain, metal, coal, and oil, and to bring in the nationalists of Ukraine, the Caucasus, and the Transcaucasus to his side. And now he is moving on Moscow from the west, north, and south. This is the strategy that we had expected. But when you are playing with a bad player, you never know which card he will play first. We thought Hitler would learn from his bitter experience, make the right move this year and attack Moscow. Moscow is close. But instead he decided to attack to the south. But what was right for last year is not right for this year. Once again Hitler, a desperate but not good player, tricked us. He has achieved some success and has reached Stalingrad. But this success is temporary. A bad strategist cannot have final success. Hitler must be deprived of his temporary success. We must stop him at Stalingrad just as we stopped him at Moscow."

Stalin approached Zhukov and said significantly, with a certain solemnity, "Comrade Zhukov! The State Defense Committee is appointing you Deputy Supreme Commander."

Zhukov stood at attention. "Thank you, Comrade Stalin."

"You must leave immediately for the Stalingrad region. The Germans must be defeated and chased away just the way you chased them out of Moscow last year."

Stalin offered him his hand. "Safe journey. I wish you success, Comrade Zhukov."

~ 28 ~

THE DEPARTMENT OF DEFENSE CONSTRUCTION, where Varya worked, was moved from Moscow to the Saratov region. If the Germans took Stalingrad, they would then turn north, and so defensive constructions were being erected along their presumed path.

The group's headquarters were set up in the village of Baidek, in the former republic of the Volga Germans. In August 1941 the republic had been liquidated and the Germans, possible collaborators with Hitler, were exiled to Siberia and Kazakhstan. But the old names of the villages and cities remained.

The stone and brick houses with outbuildings in the yards were roomy and comfortable. They were built to last, the way Germans built things. They were furnished with massive tables, benches, and beds, and unusual stoves, low and square, with both burners and ovens.

Evacuated Ukrainian kolkhoz farmers were living in them now, and they did not feel cozy in them.

"The Germans are in Stalingrad," Varya's landlady told her. "And when they reach here, what will they say to us? 'You've taken over German wealth and are getting rich on others' misfortune,' and they'll hang us all. And is it our fault? They ordered us to get rid of the kolkhoz cattle, so we did, and then they sent us here. And where else can we go, who else will take us?" She sighed bitterly.

Varya tried to comfort her — Hitler would not reach this far. She felt sorry for her new neighbors, but she felt even more sorry for the Volga Germans who had been forced out. What were the women, children, and old people guilty of? They had been shunted into cattle cars and taken to nowhere in the middle of the taiga. How many of them would die out there, and how many had died en route?

David Abramovich Telyaner, Varya's boss, also spoke of the Germans with sympathy. "They are law-abiding Russian citizens who settled the Volga. Before them, the steppes were filled with nodamic Nogias and Kazakhs. The Germans grew the famous Volga wheat, which was used to make bread for the Tsar's table, they grew tobacco and other crops. But still, they're considered foreigners — a foreign body — even though they've been here almost two centuries. After the war, if they have the chance, they'll all go back to Germany, I'm sure."

He regarded Varya with his intelligent and lively brown eyes as he moved on from the Germans to the Jews. "Jews are also outsiders, newcomers, and they interfere in everything. They are politicians, scholars, writers, philosophers, artists, you name it. Who could possibly like that? And so the indigenous nation tries to squeeze them out."

"But not here," Varya countered. "We have Jewish theaters and newspapers. At school and college, we were never divided into Jews and non-Jews."

David Abramovich raised a finger. "That was in other times, Varya, with other people and other ideas, which no longer exist. The Jews lived for centuries in Germany, they had German names, and Yiddish is basically German. And what was the result? Germany is trying to destroy them. However, it is impossible to destroy a nation. The Jews survived for two thousand years. History has intended for this nation to live. But live in its own country. They've taken care of other people's business for too long."

"Do you mean Palestine? The Jews will go there?"

"After what's happened, they will."

"Will you?"

"I'll try."

"But your wife is Russian."

"But her children are Jewish."

"Only half."

"People sometimes conceal their Jewishness — the mother is Russian, they are baptized or some other explanation. For me a Jew is anyone that Hitler would condemn to death for being Jewish. My children would be killed. Hitler would destroy the Slavs, too. He would destroy half the world's population. Fortunately, he won't win the war."

"Are you certain of that?"

"Absolutely. However, with our mess here, that victory is going to cost us dearly."

They thought along similar lines, but they did not discuss these things. A smart man, David Abramovich would smile kindly at Varya and say, "Save your worries. We have to do everything for the front, for the victory now. That evil is the greater one."

He was of medium height and heavyset. The military uniform did not fit him well. He had deep lines on his face, but his eyes were young and alive. "One of the best builders in Moscow," Igor Vladimirovich said about him.

Igor Vladimirovich was in charge of the technical department, and everything went through him — projects, drafts, plans. He had a phenomenal store of information and his decisions were impeccable. He made a pet of Varya because she loved her work and did it well. She had mastered the simple field fortifications instantly.

In October they built the main line of defense fifteen to twenty kilometers outside Moscow. Hundreds of thousands of Muscovites, mostly women, in rain and cold, under enemy air fire, in worn coats and jackets and mud-caked boots, dug trenches and communications lines, broke up the hard soil, burying concrete caps in the ground. Protected only by thin gloves and mittens, they ran barbed wire, and set heavy antitank installations made of railroad ties. They did not have enough shovels, pickaxes, or spades. Food was not delivered to them. But these women managed to build tens of thousands of meters of antitank trenches and moved millions of cubic meters of dirt.

Varya patrolled the highway. Concrete fell from trucks and women scraped with shovels to get the last bits.

"Next! Hurry it up, next!"

Varya checked, measured, signed off, and helped the women drag the heavy concrete loads. Would Germans actually trample Moscow soil? "We will not give up Moscow!" That was the first official propaganda Varya truly accepted. "We will not give up Moscow!" The streets were covered in barricades, sandbags, and antitank pilings wrapped in barbed wire. The Germans continually bombed the city, with air raids every night. Searchlight beams and tracer bullets crisscrossed the city sky, explosions illuminated it, and barrage balloons hung in the air like clouds.

Igor Vladimirovich headed the department and was his usual

demanding, precise, and punctual self. You could not hand in a messy blueprint or smeared copy. Telyaner, who did not pay attention to trifles, would say to Varya, "You know your husband. Do it more neatly."

Once, Igor Vladimirovich tried to transfer Varya to work that did not involve going to the front lines. She told him, "Igor, please, never do that. The fact that I am your wife should not give me any advantages."

He did not interefere in her work after that.

After the battle of Moscow ended, Igor Vladimirovich was transferred to the People's Commissariat of Defense, to the Main Directorate of the Corps of Engineers, and made a major general. Varya was pleased. She had not liked being the boss's wife. She did not accept any privileges. But still, there were very few women working with her who had been commissioned, yet she was in the very first, short list and made military technician, first grade. She had an engineering diploma and had worked in the department for a long time. Nevertheless, as far as her colleagues were concerned, she was the boss's wife. Now, she would be spared that.

And when Igor Vladimirovich told her the group was being moved to Saratov, but she would stay behind in Moscow, Varya refused. "No, Igor. I won't leave the department."

He was stunned. "Varya, it's the same work here. The only difference is that you will be at home, instead of living in filthy huts out there."

"That inconvenience applies to everyone."

He smiled. "Don't romanticize it, Varya. It's not the front lines, but the rear, far from the line of fire. And in the department, almost all the women work with their husbands. You'll be all alone in Saratov, defenseless. And besides, Varya, do you really want to leave me alone?"

She felt sorry for him, but she was determined to go. "I'm supposed to stay in Moscow because my husband holds a high post? I'm ashamed to act that way. I've worked for many years with those people. And I don't want to sit things out in Moscow. I wear a military uniform, you know."

"So do I."

"You are a national leader, and your place is in Moscow. I am a rank-and-file engineer, and I belong where the women are digging trenches."

He sat down next to her on the couch and pulled her toward him. "Varya, I'm afraid for you. I worry you'll say the wrong thing which could lead to trouble for you — court martial. I can't let you go on your own."

"I promise I won't talk to anyone about anything."

He got on his knees, embraced her legs, and put his head on her lap. "Varya, I beg you, please, I don't want to lose you."

She was touched by his despair and caressed his head. "All right. Get up."

He rose and automatically brushed the dust from his knees.

Varya shut her eyes. God! How could he think of his trousers at a time like this!

"No, Igor, I can't stay. I'd just be the general's wife, getting a general's food rations. I can't do that. Don't force me. I swear, I'll be careful, controlled, and cautious."

He accepted it. Varya left for Baidek. They traveled in freight cars equipped with shelf bunks, a dining car, and a medical service.

⌇ 29 ⌇

BAIDEK WAS FAR FROM THE FRONT. Even the German planes didn't fly that far. Varya worked for Telyaner and put together defensive fortification plans, which were built by field operations units, and closer to Stalingrad, by the Engineer Corps. Varya did not go out to the front lines, the way she had in Moscow.

It was basically a rear line, semicivilian department, but services, housing, and uniforms were strictly stratified — senior officers, middle and junior officers, hired help and rank-and-file. A leading engineer without rank lived in worse conditions than a nonworking member of the political section.

This caused friction, since it was a small village and everyone was living near one another. There were many women, including legal wives and illegal ones. All complaints went to Colonel Bredikhin, a boor and ignoramus who had replaced Igor Vladimirovich as head of the department. When he talked to subordinates, Bredikhin spoke in an angry pout and impatiently tapped his forefinger on the desk, demanding that they hurry it up.

The only person he treated as an equal was Varya as he tried to gain her favor. He insisted that she be treated well. Varya listened to his stupid jokes with a poker face. Bredikhin repulsed her and she found his attentions, his typical Party behavior, offensive. The fool did not notice, of course.

One day a panting messenger arrived at the department. "Comrade Military Technician First Rank, the colonel wants you."

Engineers from the field were sitting in Bredikhin's office, weary, in sweat-stained shirts and muddy boots. Bredikhin heard them out, his lip in a pout. He nodded at a chair, indicating that Varya should wait.

Varya sat, wondering why he had called for her, rather than Telyaner.

The telephone rang. Bredikhin picked it up and said in a hearty voice, "Yes. . . . Yes, sir."

He handed the receiver to Varya. It was Igor from Moscow.

"Varya, hello. It's me. Did you recognize me?"

"Of course. . . . Has something happened?"

"No, I just wanted to hear your voice. How are you?"

"I'm fine. Working. And you?"

"I'm fine, too, and working. And I miss you."

"Then, everything's all right. . . ."

"Aren't you glad I called?"

"I'm not alone here, Igor, do you understand? It's better to write."

"All right, darling. I kiss you."

"Kisses."

She hung up. "Thank you, Comrade Colonel."

She was ashamed before the weary engineers from the field. Bredikhin was rude to them and kind to her. She got calls from Moscow on the office telephone while they had to wait months for a letter from home.

When she got back to the department, she said to Telyaner, "My husband called from Moscow. You see what privileges we generals' wives have."

He understood what she was feeling. "He had a line and he managed to exchange a few words with his wife. In his place, I would have done the same."

Igor. . . . Why had she been so offended by his innocent dusting off of his trousers? Was it just the last drop in an accumulating well of suppressed irritation? He was decent, honest, and good, and he had saved her. He wrote frequently. And she replied irregularly, she couldn't find loving words, she had to struggle over every sentence. And whenever she thought about Moscow, she never thought about their apartment on Gorky Street. She thought of the Arbat, of her house, her room, the post office on the corner of Plotnikov Alley, where she sent off packages to Sasha, and how Sofya Alexandrovna and she put the packages together. She remembered the Arbat Cellar, where she had danced with Sasha, and she remembered their school in Krivoarbat Alley. When she did think about Igor, for some reason she kept picturing either the union meeting where Igor babbled in boilerplate or the Kanatik Restaurant, where he threatened in his high-pitched voice to send Klava to the police.

God, that was ages ago. Why did she still remember it? It was her fault. She didn't love him, she never had. And by marrying him, she had deceived him — and herself. She had only herself to blame. After all, they got along, they never argued, but she didn't want Igor to come here and she would never transfer to Moscow. And she probably would not go back to Igor after the war. . . . You can't live with someone you don't love, it's not honest. Igor was still in his thirties, handsome and famous. He would have a happy life without her. But she? Her second marriage, and another failure. She probably should not marry at all.

She shared a room with Dr. Irina Fedoseyevna — a military doctor and Party member. Irina Fedoseyevna was direct and categorical, but easy to live with and, what Varya particularly liked, not a gossip. She did not suck up to the bosses; she cared for patients in the same way no matter their rank, and was a tough boss herself. She told her nurses, "Girls, forget the whole idea of affairs! At war, husbands are temporary. Use Varvara as an example — no man dares come close to her."

"She has a husband in Moscow," the nurses countered.

"Husband, so what," Irina Fedoseyevna grumbled. "I got rid of my bum. I didn't even want alimony. I brought up my son alone. He's a doctor now, like me. So you have to depend on yourselves, not on some husband."

She told Varya she had adopted a Spanish girl in 1936, when her parents were killed in the bombing of Madrid. "She's a good girl. She's fifteen now. She's smart and works hard, the teachers are full of praise. So I've done my duty in proletarian solidarity."

She said it proudly, a sacred phrase. Lenin, Stalin — the names brought a severe and noble expression to her face. She had no doubts. Yes, there were problems, outrages, corruption, but it was the fault of bureaucrats and had nothing to do with Comrade Stalin, who would show them a thing or two if he heard about it. Because those bastards were compromising the Party and the state by their behavior.

She believed totally in victory over Hitler. It was guaranteed by Soviet power and the socialist structure.

"What would we be without the Soviet regime? My father was a village peasant, my mother an illiterate village woman. But I have a postgraduate degree. And who gave me that? The Soviet regime. The engineers and technicians in our department, where did they come from? From the people. The generals and other leaders were simple soldiers in the Red Army. Everything is the flesh of the people, and no Hitler can ever beat us."

Varya wanted to ask her where were the millions of peasants who died of hunger during collectivization, where were the heroes of the Civil War who were destroyed in 1937, and why were the Germans in Stalingrad? But remembering her promise to Igor, Varya kept quiet and marveled at how confused these people were, how their thinking was so skewed. Irina Fedoseyevna took in an orphan, the ordinary act of a decent, kind Russian woman, but she had to call it "proletarian solidarity." They were all like that.

In September the Department of Defense Construction was turned over to the newly created Don front and moved to Kamyshin. They were settled in a village on the road to Stalingrad. They spent the whole night packing papers, blueprints, and files. In the morning, trucks came, loaded it all up, and took them with their desks and chairs to the new place.

They were being moved by the motor unit. Varya kept looking at all the drivers, in case Sasha were among them. She had heard from Nina that he was now a military driver. Sasha was not there. And it would have been an incredible coincidence if he had been.

It was less than a hundred kilometers from their village to Stalingrad. The war was now very close. Varya went out to the trenches. She sometimes spent hours by the side of the road at a control point, waiting for a car to give her a ride. The roads were filled with crowds of refugees fleeing Stalingrad, wounded, in filthy, bloody bandages, some with crutches, others with just sticks. Going the other way were troops, artillery, trucks. Officers' cars swiftly passed the slower trucks. But they were stopped at the control points. Varya kept checking the faces of drivers, still hoping to see Sasha behind the wheel. Fires blazed on the horizon, and German planes bombed the road and the ships on the Volga. Our planes attacked theirs, and air battles could be observed every day. People would stop and look up into the sky, and when a Soviet plane hit an enemy plane, which fell to the ground in smoke, people shouted "Hurrah!" and soldiers tossed their caps in the air, and women clapped their hands, and Varya clapped her hands, too. Our pilots were heroes!

When a truck traveling in Varya's direction would stop, Varya would clamber into the back, with the freight and other people. Once she was in a truck with a barrel of gasoline, which kept rolling into the passengers who had to keep it steady with their feet. Sometimes she would spend the night on a cold, earthen floor, happy to get some barley soup and a piece of bread for supper.

She traveled with Telyaner to Zavarykino, to the headquarters of the engineering corps. The young and businesslike military engineers took decisions quickly and boldly. They were friendly and hospitable, and gave Telyaner a clear Plexiglas cigarette holder and Varya a dagger with the handle wrapped in red German wire.

"It's beautiful," Varya said, "but what do I need with a dagger?"

"It's a lady's dagger. You see how small it is," the engineer who made the gift explained.

"For self-defense," another added with a smile.

"In close combat," said a third, with a wink.

One day they were working on a defense plan. Svinkin, the head of fortifications work, young and tall, a head taller than Telyaner, and a colonel, was pleased. "Let's get the general's approval."

"But first my bosses must sign off on it," Telyaner said.

"Comrade Major," Svinkin countered. "By the time you take it back, get it signed, and send it here, and I take it to the general, and who knows if he'll be here then, a lot of time will pass. And we don't have time. The line must be erected quickly. Your signature is all we need. After all, this has been discussed in your office?"

"Of course, we discussed it with the chief engineer."

"Well then, let's go!"

They went off to see the head of the Engineering Corps — Alexei Ivanovich Proshlyakov, a polite forty-year-old general. They reported on the plan. Proshlyakov listened attentively, examined the blueprints, did not ask unnecessary questions, wrote "Approved" on top, and gave Varya a quick, lightning-fast, look. She was used to those looks and she put on a face of marked indifference.

As they were saying their good-byes, Svinkin added, "Your department is stagnating, why don't you transfer to our group? David

Abramovich will be a colonel in a year's time, and Varvara Sergeyevna will be a major. I'm serious."

They got back to their department. Telyaner went off to report to Bredikhin. He came back angry and threw the blueprints onto the table.

"What happened?" Varya asked.

"Our jerk is unhappy. How dare we go to Proshlyakov himself without Bredikhin?"

"But we didn't go to him, we were taken to him."

"I explained that, but he didn't want to hear it."

"Idiot!" Varya said.

"He's not an idiot. He wanted to meet with the general."

A messenger came soon after. "Comrade Miltiary Technician First Rank, the colonel wants to see you!"

"Go on," Telyaner said. "You'll be questioned as a witness."

Varya came into Bredikhin's office and he nodded her into a chair. "What happened there at front H.Q.?"

"Nothing. The plan was approved."

"Did you go to see General Proshlyakov?"

"Yes."

"I don't blame you, Varvara Sergeyevna. But Telyaner, how did he dare do that without department approval?"

"The plan had been discussed with the chief engineer."

"His signature is not on the plan. Neither is mine. How could he act over our heads?"

"Major Telyaner did not want to go to the general. But Colonel Svinkin demanded that the plan be approved immediately, so that he could send in his troops tomorrow. He took it to General Proshlyakov himself and led us with him."

"You . . . you're not to blame. But Telyaner . . . Telyaner . . . he should have refused to go to the general. But no, he had to be pushy." He shook his head and laughed bitterly. "What a nation! They'll get through the tiniest crack. Pushy, that's what they are!"

Varya stood up. "What did you say? You're an anti-Semite? A Nazi? A Fascist? How dare you!"

He rose from his chair, too. "Watch what you say. Do you think just because you're a general's wife, you can do what you want?"

"I do not wish to speak with you. I will not listen to you!"

"You will!" Bredikhin screamed. "I won't allow conspiracies!"

"You listen, Colonel," Varya said. "You are going to call the head of personnel right now and get me transferred to the Army Corps of Engineers. Tomorrow morning you will send a car to move me. If you want to avoid a scandal, we will part now."

The next day, Varya was given a paper that sent her to the Engineering Corps and her files, sealed. The colonel's personal car drove her to Zavarykino.

A week later Telyaner transferred to the Engineering Corps, too.

30

AND THERE WAS HEAVY FIGHTING in Stalingrad. The Germans were dropping thousands of demolition and incendiary bombs. Buildings toppled like enormous felled trees. Engulfed in flames, enveloped in smoke, and buried in ashes, the city lay in ruins. Soviet soldiers fought house to house.

Blazing waves of burning oil leaking from tankers covered the Volga. But the crossings destroyed by Germans planes were instantly replaced to deliver ammunition to the trenches. The artillery supported its soldiers from the eastern bank of the Volga, forcing the Germans underground.

On August 29, Zhukov flew into Kamushin, then drove forward and turned west. The units of the Stalingrad front were located in the fifty-kilometer interriver area between the Volga and the Don. Opposite them stood the German infantry, defending their communications to Stalingrad.

Scorched by the August sun, the Volga steppe was open to enemy artillery. Zhukov went to the headquarters of generals Malinovsky and Kazakov, and both were of the same opinion — attack in this location was impossible. Zhukov could see for himself. There was no way to break through to Stalingrad from here. He went farther west, to Kletskoi and Serafimovich, where the troops were holding on to the right bank of the Don. They were fighting Romanians, not Germans, here.

At the village of Orlovsky, he was met by the commander of the 21st Army, General Danilov, a good and thoughtful professional, who reported on the situation. The divisions of the 21st Army were holding the right bank of the Don River. The Romanians tried to attack, but were weak and were acting passively now. Of course, if the Germans won in Stalingrad, they would move north, and the Romanians would be fortified by German troops, well armed and experienced. They had to improve their defenses. It would not hurt to add personnel and arms. Like everyone else, Danilov was thinking in terms of defense. And while Zhukov did not disagree, he was thinking of something else. The 21st would have to be one of the main participants in the plan that was maturing in his mind and that he had not yet shared with anyone.

On the next day, Zhukov and Danilov went out to visit the troops. This was open ground, too, cut by ravines, but it was high ground. It presented a good vantage point to watch the enemy, to maneuver, and there was adequate brush for cover. Serafimovich had enough depth to concentrate the needed men, and near Kletskaya a bend in the Don River created good conditions for attacking the rear of the Romanian army. Of course, the roads were bad. But by November, much of the land would be frozen over and would be hard enough for the vehicles.

They returned to the farm in the evening. Over dinner, Danilov reported on the commanders of the divisions, regiments, and brigades. Zhukov knew some of the names, but he trusted Danilov's evaluations. Danilov requested promotions for two division commanders, Colonels Efimov and Kostin.

"Efimov," Zhukov said, "is an old war horse. It's time he made general. And I noticed Kostin in the Far East. He has a future, and he is a Hero of the Soviet Union. But he's young, only thirty. There are older men."

"He deserves the rank, and I would like to solidify his situation."

"Is it necessary?"

"You said it yourself, he's young."

Zhukov knew Maxim Kostin not only from the Far East. Max's parents were from the same village in Kaluga as Zhukov. And when Zhukov was a student in Moscow and his father came to visit from the village, he would stay with the Kostins on the Arbat. Kostin was the boiler man and his wife, Maxim's mother, was the elevator operator. Zhukov began visiting them as a boy, and in the 1920s it was as a commander of the Red Army that he came to the Arbat, to see his mother, who was staying with the Kostins. In the Far East he saw Lieutenant Maxim Kostin in the list and wondered if he was from the same family. He called him in and had a talk. They reminisced about the Protva

River, where they used to swim, and the Ogublyanka, where they fished. Kostin was impressive and he was a good soldier. And if Danilov felt he needed to be reinforced in his position, there must be a good reason.

"You take care of your things," Zhukov said, "and have Kostin come to see me."

"It will take time to find him and get him here."

"That's all right. I'll work for a few more hours."

Maxim left the minute he got orders to appear at headquarters. Zhukov was here, so he must be having a meeting with all the division commanders. It would be interesting to see Zhukov. After all, he had met him only that one time in the Far East when they discovered they came from the same village. Zhukov probably did not remember him, but Maxim was proud that the Chief of the Armed Forces, known the world over, was someone from his village.

Maxim's mother had told him about the Zhukov family. "Konstantin, the father, was an orphan who was adopted by the lonely grandmother. When he turned eight, she sent him to apprentice with a shoemaker, and then he worked as a shoemaker in Moscow. After Moscow, he came back to the village. When his wife died, he remarried at the age of fifty, to a widow from a neighboring village. Her name was Ustinya Artemyevna, and she wasn't young — thirty-five. So they were both marrying for the second time. And they had a son, Georgii, and another son, who died in infancy. They were poor. We didn't have any rich people in our village. There wasn't enough land, and it was feeble land, infertile. And who was in charge of farming there anyway? Women and older men. The younger men were all working in Moscow and Petersburg. Ustinya Artemyevna was an exceptional woman. She could lift huge, heavy sacks of grain that not every man could lift. She hauled freight from Maloyaroslavets — men's work, that is. She was a strong woman in every sense. Georgii took after her. He even looked like her."

That was what his mother told him then. This year she reported she had seen Ustinya Artemyevna. Zhukov had gotten her out before the Germans took the village.

Maxim was remembering these things as he headed for headquarters. But when he arrived, he learned there was no conference. Zhukov had called for him only.

"I haven't seen you in a long time. Sit down, tell me how things are. What's new at home?"

"Everything is fine at home. My mother is alive, my brothers are in the army, my wife is teaching in school, and my son is growing."

"How old is he?"

"Five."

"What's his name?"

"Ivan."

Zhukov regarded him with pleasure — young, broad-shouldered, with an open face. Soldiers liked commanders like that. They could see he was one of them, of peasant stock.

"Tell what happened in your division."

"In my division? Nothing. Everything is fine."

"Come on now, tell the truth. What did you report to the general?"

After a pause, Maxim said, "I did not report anything to him, Comrade General of the Army. Perhaps someone complained about me — I don't get along with the political officer. There is a conflict over every issue. The latest is a squad commander, who slapped a soldier, and I removed him from duty. The political officer was upset. 'Why did you do that without checking with me? The squad commander is a Communist, politically correct, morally solid.' And so on, and so forth. Naturally, he reported to the political section of the army about me."

"And what if he had a reason for slapping him? Maybe he was driven to it?"

"How can anyone hit a soldier in the Red Army? You can court-martial him, you can throw him out, if he's guilty. But you can't hit or humiliate a man."

"When I was a soldier, do you know how often the sergeant's whip struck me? I was in the cavalry then."

"That was the Tsarist army, Comrade General. . . ."

"And when I was an apprentice, the master smacked me hard, too."

Maxim tried to keep his voice calm. "I cannot permit hitting in my division. The Romanians whip their soldiers, and that's why they fight the way they do. We are the Red Army and every soldier must have self-respect and his commander must respect him, too."

"What a lecture I'm in for!" Zhukov chuckled. "I've been in the Red Army since the day it was created and I've been in the Party since 1919. When did you join the Party?"

"I joined in 1934, and I joined the Komsomol in 1925."

In the Komsomol since 1925. . . . That reminded Zhukov of something. . . . Yes, that driver in Starozhilove. . . .

"You're a feisty bunch! I met a fellow like you last year. He must have been your age. A driver. And he had his own line of talk. I was planning to have him shot and then instead I ended up promoting him. He's an engineer."

A driver, an engineer, and his age . . . Maxim stood up. "Comrade General, permission to ask a question?"

"Go ahead."

"Do you remember his name?"

"His name . . . ? No. . . ."

"Pankratov?"

"That's it! Pankratov. . . . What are you so agitated about? Did you know him?"

"He's a childhood friend, we grew up in the same building, we shared a desk at school. . . . But his fate —"

Zhukov interrupted. "Everyone has the same fate now. We must fight. Do you understand?"

"I understand, Comrade General!"

That was clear. There would be no talk of fates like that.

Zhukov was busy with his map. Without looking up, he said, "Your political officer will be replaced. But will you get along with the new one? Watch it."

↤ 31 ↦

ZHUKOV RECEIVED A TELEGRAM from Stalin on September 3 with the demand: "Attack the enemy immediately, procrastination is tantamount to a crime." Stalin telephoned Malenkov the next day and checked up on how his order was being carried out. Malenkov, who understood nothing about military affairs and monitored Zhukov for Stalin, became agitated when he heard the angry tone of Stalin's voice.

"The situation is extremely difficult, Comrade Stalin. German bombers are flying up to two thousand missions a day. The troops have taken the offensive several times, but have not been successful."

Stalin was dissatisfied and summoned Zhukov and Vassilevsky to Moscow.

"Why aren't you attacking?"

"The terrain near Stalingrad is not suitable for an attack," Zhukov reported. "It is open country, broken up by deep ravines, the enemy has good cover in them from our fire, and, on the contrary, having occupied commanding heights, adjusts its own fire well. We have to seek different solutions."

"I know the country around Stalingrad as well as you. What are the solutions?"

Poskrebyshev walked in.

"Comrade Stalin, it's Beria calling; he urgently requests that you come to the telephone."

Stalin picked up the receiver and listened to Beria; his face darkened. "Come over!"

He hung up the receiver, raised his eyes to Zhukov, and looked angrily at him.

"So what are the other solutions?"

"Comrade Vassilevsky and I have been thinking about them, we need another day."

"Fine, we'll meet here again tomorrow at nine in the evening."

Beria came with the report. Yakov had been found. He had spent the winter in Berlin, in the Hotel Adlom, in the custody of the Gestapo. Early in 1942 he was transferred to the officers' camp Oflag HS in Lübeck. His roommate was captain René Blum, the son of Leon Blum, the former Prime Minister of France.

"Blum? Were the Germans really interning Jews in officers' camps?"

"Yes. The most famous ones, as hostage for deals, as disinformation: people say that we're supposedly exterminating Jews, here's the Jew Blum for you, just look at him!"

"Very well, continue!"

"In Lübeck, the officers decided to give Yakov packages that they receive through the Red Cross."

"And Yakov is accepting them?"

"The packages are from the International Red Cross," Beria repeated.

"I understand that they're not personally from Hitler. But other officers of ours are not accepting these parcels, are they?"

"Almost all of our officers are being held in general camps, very few of them are in officers' camps. I don't know whether packages are shared with them, but I can find out."

Stalin said nothing.

"We have our people planted among the prisoners," Beria continued, "as far as I know, an escape is imminent."

"And where will he escape to?"

"The escape plan is being formulated," Beria replied cautiously.

They had found Yakov. They had transferred him from a Berlin hotel to a prisoner-of-war camp, which means that he refused to collaborate. Nevertheless the fronts were strewn with German leaflets: "Follow the example of Stalin's son!" While Yakov was still alive, the Germans would continue scattering them. But *he* had no time to think about this. Let Beria think about it.

Stalin rose.

"Escaping from captivity is an honorable way out for a Red Army commander."

He looked at Beria with his heavy gaze.

"Of course, he could be killed during an escape. Well then, such a fate is also an honorable way out for a Red Army commander."

The next day at 9:00 in the evening Zhukov and Vassilevsky spread out a map in front of Stalin. Zhukov reported:

"A narrow corridor connects Paulus's army with the main German forces. Romanians, Hungarians, and Italians are defending the north side of this corridor. They are poorly equipped and lack sufficient combat experience. There is a Romanian Army of similar caliber on the corridor's southern lines of communication. Our plan: A powerful group of troops is being built up outside Serafimovich and Kletskaya, which will deliver a rapid strike in the vicinity of Kalach, where it joins with a group that is delivering a strike from an area south of Stalingrad. Paulus's army will be surrounded. Simultaneously" — Zhukov showed on the map — "strikes are delivered in the west so that the Germans will not be able to relieve the blockade of their troops encircled in Stalingrad."

Stalin scrutinized the map.

"You're overreaching by a long shot. . . . Way the hell out, west of the Don. You should be closer to Stalingrad, at least along the eastern bank of the Don."

"That's impossible," Zhukov objected. "The German tanks from the Stalingrad area will turn west and counter our strikes."

"And do we have sufficient forces for such a large operation?"

"Right now we don't," said Vassilevky, "but we can provide sufficient forces and prepare it well."

Stalin threw his pencil on the map.

"And by November the Germans will capture Stalingrad and advance on Saratov!"

"Paulus's troops are exhausted and are in no position to capture the city," replied Zhukov. "Of course, our losses are also enormous, but in the next few days we'll throw new reserves into the city and save Stalingrad."

Poskrebyshev came in, as he had the day before, and reported that Yeremenko was calling from Stalingrad.

Stalin picked up the receiver, listened, said one word — "Fine" — hung up, and looked first at Zhukov, then at Vassilevsky, then at Zhukov again.

"You're saying: 'The enemy is exhausted.' But Yeremenko reports that the Germans are pulling up tank units to the city, that the city should expect another strike tomorrow. Both of you fly to Stalingrad at once — it has to be saved no matter what has to be done, now matter what the cost."

Vassilevsky rolled up the map and asked indecisively: "What about our plan?"

"We'll return to it again, there's plenty of time," Stalin replied impatiently. "Get out to the airport. Your flight leaves in an hour."

Fierce battles continued in the ruins of Stalingrad. But the Germans were not advancing. Soviet troops continued to repulse them with their former doggedness.

Meanwhile, Zhukov studied the situation in the Serafimovich and Kletskaya areas, and defined the plan for the counteroffensive with the army commanders more precisely; Vassilevsky did the same on the left flank. Stalin summoned them to Moscow from time to time, became thoroughly involved in the details, began to realize the immensity of the scheme, sought Shaposhnikov's advice, spread out the map on the desk, pored over it thoughtfully. During the Civil War *he* had spent many a month in Tsaritsyn, he was in charge of its defense, he sent trains full of grain to Moscow and Petrograd. That was why Tsaritsyn was renamed Stalingrad, in *his* honor. And Nadya was with him. But he stopped taking her on trips after that. She had caught a cold there. She was young then, a foolish girl, she kept recalling Nekrasov, "Come down to the Volga, whose moaning can be heard. . . ." And that's where she caught a cold, right there on the Volga riverbank.

Now *he* couldn't recognize a single street in Stalingrad, although they had shown *him* photographs and run a newsreel: there were ruins everywhere, bits of broken glass, bent tram rails. . . . He had read either in *Pravda* or the *Krasnaya zvezda*: an untouched four-story house stood amid the ruins in the center of town. It was the only one that survived intact. Three scouts led by a sergeant liberated it from the Germans. He forgot the sergeant's name. A simple Russian name beginning with an "L" or a "P." He asked Shaposhnikov, who had also forgotten it. He reported an hour later: the name was Pavlov. Another twenty soldiers had gotten through to Pavlov and assumed an all-around defense;

they mined the approaches, connected it with firing positions by means of underground communications trenches, and turned it into a strong defense point. It was holding out to this day.

"Publicize this through the press and the radio. Let the people know how its sons are fighting," Stalin ordered.

That was the order *he* issued, the journalists themselves would add the fact about the soldiers fighting like this in *Stalin's* city.

Stalin hung up the receiver, his eyes moved down to the map again, to the red arrows, directed from the north and south toward Kalach. He had come to believe in the success of the operation and, as was his custom, he began to rush everyone. New fronts were established, new armies were formed, infantry divisions and tank brigades were transferred, armies were fortified. At last Zhukov and Vassilevsky signed the final draft of the plan, and Stalin inscribed on top of it: "I approve."

"Comrade Stalin!" Zhukov addressed him right then and there. "We must immediately begin a diversionary attack near Moscow, in the vicinity of Vyazma and Rzhev, in order to prevent German troops from being transferred to help Paulus."

"Very well," said Stalin, "we'll think about it. . . ." He looked at Zhukov attentively. "We'll think about it. . . . That seems to be the right idea. . . . We'll think about it. . . . In the meantime, fly back, check on the readiness for attack."

On November 16, Zhukov reported that everything was ready. The attack was set for the morning of November 19.

Zhukov flew back to Moscow again. His report was confident and optimistic: The armies were ready for the offensive, there was no doubt about the operation's success.

"Well, then," said Stalin, "good, very good. Congratulations. And when the operation is completed successfully, we'll congratulate you once again."

"Thank you, Comrade Stalin!"

Stalin looked intently at him. . . .

"Comrade Zhukov! Last time you spoke about a diversionary strike near Rzhev and Vyazma."

"Yes, it's essential."

Stalin rose, brought a map from an adjacent table, placed it in front of Zhukov.

"Here, the General Staff officers have developed a plan, take a look at it."

Stalin paced around the room slowly, waiting for Zhukov to look over the plan.

"The idea is correct," Zhukov said finally. "The details have to be worked out."

"You see, we haven't been sitting around here idly either." Stalin smiled. "What do you think, Comrade Zhukov, who can be entrusted with this operation?"

"It's difficult to say offhand. We'll discuss it with Comrade Vassilevsky."

Stalin sat down in his armchair again and looked at Zhukov.

"And what if you take this operation on yourself? Everything's ready near Stalingrad. Comrade Vassilevsky is there, experienced people are in command of the fronts: Rokossovsky, Yeremenko, Vatutin. I think they'll manage with the forces they have. Moreover, you yourself reported: the preparedness is complete, success is guaranteed."

Zhukov looked aside. At the key decisive moment Stalin was dismissing him from the supervision of the operation that he had planned and prepared; he knows all its future participants, has studied the terrain, knows the condition of each division, has all the possible tactical maneuvers in his head. And now they're just dismissing him like that. Stalin doesn't want him, Zhukov, after his Moscow victory, to be the victor in the Stalingrad battle as well. Stalin's usual game . . .

"Why will this decision be the right one?" Stalin began speaking again. "Here's why: If we send a second-rate individual to eliminate the Rzhevsky salient, then the Germans will realize that this is just a diversionary maneuver. But if Zhukov himself carries out this operation, then they'll consider this offensive a serious one and will not only not throw over their troops to the south, but on the contrary, they'll pull them up here. And our task near Stalingrad will become easier."

Zhukov continued to say nothing.

Without taking his heavy stare off him, Stalin continued: "You will receive the same information that I receive. You will be able to give instructions, make proposals. You prepared the Stalingrad offensive, we are not planning to dismiss you from it. All instructions will be issued with both our signatures."

Stalin looked at Zhukov once more and concluded: "That's what we'll do."

"As you wish, Comrade Stalin!"

It had nothing to do with laurels. *He* didn't need laurels. But victory had to be embodied in one person. Zhukov is considered the victor of Moscow. Very well. A major military leader has to win *individual* battles. But to win a second battle, the pivotal one, the key one. . . . No, the Stalingrad victory has to be linked with Stalin's name.

One million one hundred three thousand Soviet soldiers moved into attack on November 19 from the north and on November 20 from the south. Nearly an equal number of German, Romanian, Italian, and Hungarian troops resisted them.

On November 23, both groups of Soviet troops joined together in Kalach and surrounded Paulus's army. Promising Paulus that he would relieve the blockade of his troops, Hitler forbade him to break out of encirclement. However, all the attempts to break the surrounding encirclement were unsuccessful.

Bloody battles were waged in the vast territory of the south of Russia all through the month of December. Soviet troops repulsed the Germans far to the west, beyond the Don River.

At the end of December, during a discussion of the plan to eliminate Paulus's army, Stalin said:

"One person has to direct the total defeat of the enemy."

It was a question of two candidates: Yeremenko, commander of the Stalingrad front, and Rokossovsky, commander of the Don front.

Stalin had already made his decision. He had not forgotten Yeremenko's self-confident drivel which the Soviet people had paid for with the catastrophe in the Kiev area. And let's not have him hoping for rehabilitation with a Stalingrad victory.

And there was another thing. *He* had a *special* attitude toward Rokossovsky, who reminded him of Tukhachevsky in some way. He was just as handsome, also of Polish background, the nobility most likely. It was true that his father had worked in Velikiye Luki as a locomotive engineer before the Revolution, but there were impoverished gentry working as locomotive engineers then as well. . . . But he wasn't alien like Tukhachevsky. He was arrested before the war, then freed.

He asked him about it one time. Rokossovsky confirmed it, yes, it had happened. *He* then remarked reproachfully:

"You certainly chose your time to be in prison."

Rokossovsky smiled — fine fellow, he had appreciated the joke. He proved his worth in war, and unlike Tukhachevsky, he was not conceited.

"Yeremenko proved himself very poor as commander of the Bryansk front," said Stalin. "He is immodest and boastful. The fronts must be joined and Rokossovsky must be appointed commander."

On January 10, Rokossovsky issued Paulus an ultimatum to surrender. Paulus declined. Soviet troops took the offensive and cut the German Army in two. The southern half capitulated on January 31, the northern one on February 2.

The Stalingrad battle lasted two hundred days. The Germans lost a quarter of their armed forces in Russia during this time. The halo of invincibility that Germany had acquired at the beginning of the Second World War, which had begun to fade during the winter of '41 near Moscow, definitively lost its luster.

For the Stalingrad victory Comrade Stalin was awarded the highest military rank: Marshal of the Soviet Union!

The mandatory epithet — greatest military leader of all times and peoples — was now added to his name.

❧ 32 ❧

AFTER THE COMPLETE DEFEAT of the enemy in the Volga and Don regions, Soviet troops repulsed it far to the west and liberated Rostov, Novocherkassk, Kursk, and Kharkov.

However, Golikov, the commander of the Voronezh front, overestimated his capabilities and did not pull back his units that broke out ahead — the Germans went into a counterattack and took back Kharkov and Belgorod.

Stalin summoned Zhukov to Moscow, asked him several formal questions about the state of affairs in the northwest where Zhukov had come from, and ordered him to fly out to the Kharkov area to correct the situation.

Stalin knew that Zhukov would take advantage of Golikov's blunders, would demand his dismissal, and that it would be impossible to refuse; that was why it was better to beat Zhukov to it and do it himself.

"We're transferring Golikov to a different job. Who do you suggest he be replaced with?"

"General Vatutin."

"A suitable candidate," Stalin agreed, "and that's what we'll do. Fly out."

Vatutin took charge of the Voronezh front, Golikov was appointed Deputy People's Commissar of Defense in charge of personnel. Zhukov was not surprised by this promotion — Stalin stuck up for his favorites. Well, the hell with him, Golikov. Let him sit in Moscow and shuffle papers.

The situation at the front was stabilizing, a calm settled in. Having wedged in deeply to the west, Soviet troops formed an enormous arc near Kursk. This salient could be used for strikes into the rear of

German groupings. But the German armies could also deliver powerful strikes from their flanks to the salient's foundation, surround it and
eliminate the troops massed there, and open the road to a new attack on
Moscow. It was clear to all participants that the impending battle would
be the major one of the '43 summer campaign, and possibly the decisive
one for the outcome of the war. The only question was: Who would
deliver the first strike?

The General Staff was considering the offensive, and as always what
Stalin wanted. However, Zhukov sent a report to Stalin on April 8 in
which he wrote: "I consider it inadvisable to have our troops launch an
attack in the next few days. It would be better if we exhaust the enemy
with our defense, knock out its tanks, and then, by launching a general
attack, finish off its main grouping."

Rokossovsky and Vatutin supported Zhukov.

It was a question of nerve: Whoever's nerve did not hold out would
rush to attack. Hitler's nerve broke. He stated in his order No. 6:

> I have decided to conduct the offensive "Citadel," the first offensive
> this year, as soon as weather conditions permit. This offensive is to be
> considered decisive. Victory in Kursk must serve as a torch for the en-
> tire world. . . . We must surround and destroy the enemy troops located in
> the Kursk area by means of a concentrated strike delivered strongly and
> quickly by the forces of one army from the Belgorod region and another
> one from the Orlov region.

Zhukov's nerve turned out to be steadier. His plan was accepted at
General Headquarters. But with a proviso to please Stalin: The defense
of the Kursk salient is premeditated, not forced. If the Germans don't
attack, we will.

The same day that Stalin signed the plan to defend the Kursk arc,
Beria arrived to see him with a report. Stalin understood by his anxious
face: Yakov!

Without sitting down, Beria said quietly: "Comrade Stalin, the difficult mission of informing you about Yakov's death has fallen to me."

Stalin nodded at a chair.

"Sit down, tell me."

Beria sat down, opened the file.

"Can't you do it without the papers?"

"There are German and English names here . . ."

"Fine, tell me. Tell me everything."

"At the end of 1942," Beria began the report, "Yakov was transferred to the Sachsenhausen camp, thirty kilometers from Berlin, and placed in barrack 'A' of the special section where the relatives of the leaders of enemy governments were interned. The barrack was spacious: a large common room, a dining room, two bathrooms and two bedrooms. One bedroom was for four Englishmen." Beria looked in the file. "Thomas Cushing —"

"I don't need their names," Stalin interrupted.

"Yakov and another Soviet prisoner of war, Vassily Kokorin, were in the other bedroom. He's passing himself off as Molotov's nephew."

"Does Molotov actually have a nephew?"

"No."

"Go on."

"Yakov was in a state of depression. He was interrogated for an entire year and a half: when he was captured, by the Gestapo, in prisons and camps. It must be said that Yakov Dzhugashvili behaved courageously, honorably."

"If he had wanted to behave honorably, he wouldn't have ended up a prisoner," remarked Stalin.

"I'm reporting on how he behaved as a prisoner."

"I know that he was a prisoner. Continue."

"The interminable interrogations exhausted him. And there was another circumstance. Yakov had been on good terms with other prisoners in all the previous camps, but in Sachsenhausen hostility between him and the Englishmen arose from the start. Why? Yakov was a calm person by nature, and the English also seem to be restrained."

"Every Englishman is a colonizer by nature." Stalin frowned. "For the English every person from the east is an Asian."

"You're right, Comrade Stalin. The Englishmen yelled about the fact that Yakov and Kokorin were slovenly, that they fouled up the bathroom and the like. . . . They accused Yakov of conducting Communist propaganda among them. They had daily arguments. On April 14, an argument led to a fight. . . . Yakov ran out of the barrack; the guard demanded that he return. Yakov refused, and then the guard shot him in the head and killed him. The guard's name is Konrad Harvich. Karl Jungling, the head of the guard, was present at the scene. After the murder, they threw Yakov's body on the electrified barbed wire in imitation of an escape attempt, even though it was simply murder. The Germans killed Yakov."

Stalin walked around his office silently, then, avoiding looking at Beria, he said: "We'll consider that through his death Yakov Dzhugashvili redeemed his guilt before his motherland. You can free his wife."

∾ 33 ∾

THE LULL IN THE KURSK ARC lasted nearly one hundred days. Both sides were getting ready; their forces were roughly the same (one million soldiers and officers). The troops of the Voronezh front were defending the south side of the Kursk arc; the Central front (formerly the Don front) troops, still commanded by Rokossovsky, defended its north side. This was where Varya served now, in the fortifications section of the 13th Army engineer troops headquarters. Her rank was engineer captain; she had four stars with one color stripe on her shoulder strap.

The Kursk Oblast had been occupied by the Germans twice; fierce battles had taken place here. Cities were destroyed, villages burned, only chimneys remained where there had once been houses. The engineer troops headquarters was located in a tiny village, and maybe that was why it was still intact. They lived in cramped quarters, but separate living quarters were found for Varya, the only woman — a little old sunken hut with windows nearly level with the ground.

"There's nothing else," the quartermaster said defensively, "and the owners sleep on the Russian-style oven, so they'll let you have the main room."

Varya went and looked at it. She said: "I like it."

Afinogen Gerasimovich, the landlord, turned out to be fifty-six years old. Varya thought he was older: he had a thin face lined with deep wrinkles, a piercing look beneath his bushy eyebrows, a beard streaked with gray, hands gnarled from overwork. He wore a threadbare jacket and patched pants stuffed into old felt boots with lined soles. He complained: "It's warm outside, but my feet feel cold."

He smoked some sort of trash, either grass or home-grown tobacco mixed with grass. Varya began to give him either the cigarettes or tobacco allotted to her in her rations.

"But you don't smoke." The chief of food supply expressed surprise.

"Now I've started."

Afinogen Gerasimovich, grateful for the tobacco, would roll up a homemade cigarette carefully so as not to drop a single crumb, and shake his head. "It's bad when you're hungry, but when there's not a speck of tobacco, that's death itself. You take a little drag of smoke and life seems easier. A Russian just can't do without tobacco."

"The Germans smoke, too," Varya remarked.

"They do indeed. Once you've stuffed yourself with food, you also have to delight in a little tobacco. Their cigarettes smell good. Some Germans, of course, smoke because of their nerves, because they are forced to be animals — burn, scorch, kill the young and the old and the children and the tiny infants. If your house is on fire and you want to put the fire out — the German will kill you right then and there — don't you dare save your property! We hid in cellars, he'd go rat-a-tat at your cellar or set your hut on fire, and you'd just have to stay in the cellar. And as for our people they captured, you just can't count up how many of them died from hunger and from various epidemics. They shot the sick and wounded, they took the healthy ones with them. . . . They'd be driving the hungry like cattle, but if you shoved them a piece of bread, the Germans would shoot both him and you. Did we ever expect this from them?"

He glanced over at Varya and corrected himself: "They're enemies for sure, but they're people you know, that's what we thought and figured. Would a Russian soldier ever kill an infant? But the Germans killed them."

He'd grow thoughtful, moisten his finger with spit, carefully extinguish his home-rolled cigarette, and put it in on a plate; he'd finish it later. . . .

"I fought in the Great War, we didn't lay a hand on the civilian population, oh no, it wasn't allowed. And the Germans didn't either. They were in the Ukraine in 1918, it's right here, next door. Would you look at the habit they've picked up now! They drive off the young to work in Germany. By what kind of right? Well, and our boys aren't fools either: 'Look at me, I have this itchy rash.' The physician looks at the guy and he really does have a rash on his entire body — on his arms, legs, chest, my ass, pardon the expression. But they don't take people with scabies, they're afraid. So people began to get infected from each other with these scabies on purpose, it's very contagious, the microbe, the scabies one, lives everywhere — there's dirt everywhere — there's been no soap since the very beginning of the war. And people got skinny, they get short of breath just getting from their ovens to benches, a weak person picks up all sorts of ailments. If one person gets it in a household, in a month the whole family's scratching, our whole village was scratching, except for me and my old lady, because we live alone and didn't permit familiarities. And we try to keep up cleanliness and neatness in our household."

It really was clean in the hut. And it smelled pleasant. It smelled of some sort of grass. The landlady dried it and placed it around in bunches; its aroma was mild and gentle.

"Can it be cured, this scabies?" Varya asked.

"Why cure it, so they can send you off to Germany to work? People smeared themselves with something just so it itched less — it itches like all get out — and as soon as the Germans were chased out, it dropped off by itself, meaning its time had come. That's what they've reduced the civilian population to. But in that war nothing like this happened. People were kinder, both the Russians and the Germans. After that war was when everything started. The Reds against the Whites, the Whites against the Reds. If you, for example, had the rank of bourgeois — it was against the wall for you; if you were a proletarian — the same thing — execution. And so people became vicious. . . . Now then, Mother," he addressed his wife, "throw some pine cones into the samovar fire, Varvara Sergeevna has brought us some tea."

The samovar was large and made of copper, with round company seals and awards stamped on it.

"We've saved this samovar through all the different regimes, see how many medals and awards it has won."

Afinogen Gerasimovich drank his tea, wheezed, continued the conversation.

"And when the Civil War ended, it seemed like everything quieted down. And then things got moving. They brought in electricity, it was called 'Ilyich's bulb' in honor of Comrade Lenin, Vladimir Ilyich, they started up a reading hut, opened up a school for kids in the morning and old folks in the evening. This was '*likbez*,' meaning the eradication of illiteracy. We lived all right, we lived in harmony. . . . Well, then in 1930," he looked at Varya, "everything went awry, people got vicious again, they broke everyone one after another, without distinction — the guilty, the innocent, whoever happened to be nearby. Now there's a war. Of course, as they say, 'Victory is with us,' this is actually so, but how we'll recover after the victory, this I can't actually predict."

"You think that agriculture will not recover?"

"Why won't it recover? The huts were burned down, but does it take a long time to build them? But who's going to live in those huts? There will be millions of people knocked out by the war. And whoever survives, it's not likely they'll return to the village. After the last war the soldier rushed home because he had been promised land. Now what's he going to come home to, what's he going to return to? Back to these workdays, to little marks in his work card? you can't feed a hungry stomach with those little marks. Back to our collective farm passportless state? don't run off anywhere, don't go either left or right. No, they won't come back to the village. When a machine breaks down at a factory, it can be replaced, but who can replace the peasant in the village? No one. So, actually villages won't recover for a long time. And without villages — it just isn't Russia anymore. Besides, to me it seems like there's no state, no government that can do without agriculture. So nowadays you can't figure what the conclusion and outcome are going to be, it's a mystery to everyone. There you have it, Varvara Sergeevna."

It wasn't clear what they lived on, how they survived. They planted potatoes and cabbage, you couldn't survive without them. "You won't be full, but you won't die of hunger." Evdokya Karpovna smiled and looked up suddenly at her husband with her faded eyes. Their poverty was habitual, long-standing, it was how the Russian peasant had lived from time immemorial. And their submission to fate was also centuries-old. When there was shooting nearby, Afinogen Gerasimovich wouldn't even turn his head; shooting was what war was about. He immediately recognized aircraft, and he would say "ours" or "Hitler is flying," but he didn't think about whether they would bomb the village, he had no control over the situation anyway.

Varya often rode out to the front. The 13th Army line was considered the most threatened sector. Four divisions occupied its assault echelon; its forward edge was mined. Tens of thousands of people dug trenches, communication trenches, antitank ditches, earthen huts and shelters night and day, just as they did around Moscow. "Earth is the infantryman's armor," Varya's commanding officer, Colonel Kolesnikov, would say. They equipped firing positions for antitank guns, hand and heavy machine guns, they adapted the banks of rivers and the slopes of ravines for defense, and repaired bridges and roads.

The summer was rainy, humid, and, on sunny days — hot. The soldiers on the forward edge area worked in their boots, but stripped to the waist, the village peasant women and girls wore white scarves, blouses, long skirts; they were barefoot, their feet yellow and brown from the mud that stuck to them. They would look up at the sky — was the German flying above . . . ?

When she left, Varya would collect her dry ration and leave it for her landlords, since she'd be fed at the division. Looking at a can of stewed meat, Afinogen Gerasimovich said:

"The Americans make a beautiful canned good. The Germans also had canned goods, there are lots of cans scattered around here, but they're not as attractive as these. As far as how they taste, they didn't treat us to any. You're just denying yourself, Varvara Sergeevna, that's not right, we'll *get by,* but you're young, you have to eat."

Varya would return, the rations would be untouched. She would sit down at the table with them, make them open the canned goods, cut up the meat, then they would eat and give praise.

"You care about us, Varvara Sergeevna, you're a kindhearted person," Afinogen Gerasimovich would say.

Evdokya Karpovna would then wash out the cans and put them on the stove: "You can see in them, like in a mirror, they're golden. . . ." She would look at Varya affectionately.

"You're also our golden one, so fine and attractive, is your husband also in the military?"

"He is."

"You don't have children; God willing, you will. In the last war women were only nurses, there weren't any woman officers like you in uniforms with guns. Aren't there enough men now?"

"That's been the custom since the Civil War," Afinogen Gerasimovich explained, "women were also commanders then. Do you remember we had a woman commissar here, she wore a leather jacket with a gun on her belt, she was Jewish or Armenian, she was energetic and fair-minded, she put an end to all sorts of disgraceful things, she wouldn't allow them."

"You take care of yourself," Evdokya Karpovna admonished Varya. "Don't go poking around where you shouldn't, for no reason at all."

"I won't." Varya laughed.

Once when she was going to headquarters she looked back. Evdokya Karpovna was standing at the entryway, making the sign of the cross after her. She just froze, with her arm up in the air, embarrassed — she hadn't expected Varya to turn around.

∾ 34 ∾

VARYA WOULD ALSO RIDE OUT to see Telyaner at the headquarters of the Central front in the Svoboda settlement. He was already a lieutenant colonel, but his uniform looked just as awkward on him. This had not been conspicuous before among the freshly hatched servicemen at the Directorate, but it drew attention among the fashionably dressed staff officers: coarse imitation leather boots (he wasn't able to get shiny calf ones), and his tunic didn't fit right. But Telyaner played an important role here, too: he organized the manufacture of reinforced concrete parts for defense structures, the parts were delivered to positions, all you had to do was assemble them.

Varya supervised the delivery of spare parts to the 13th Army and monitored their assembly. A day without surprises was rare: deliveries were delayed, parts came in incomplete sets. Varya would call around everywhere, first of all to Telyaner, and he helped her out of tight spots.

The line of the 13th Army was thirty-two kilometers, eight kilometers for each of the four divisions. There were another two divisions in the second zone, one of which Maxim commanded. His headquarters was located in a small woods near a village. When she drove out to the forward position, Varya would stay with him. She was a stone's throw from any of the divisions, and at the end of the day Varya would call him, and he would send a Jeep for her. Varya's commander, Colonel Kolesnikov, would jokingly ask: "Whom are you serving under, me or General Kostin?"

He knew that Varya was Kostin's sister-in-law, everyone knew it. Nonetheless, to avoid gossip, Maxim did not have Varya stay in his dugout overnight, an unoccupied earthen hut would be found for her; of course, it would be small and cramped, you couldn't walk around in it without lowering your head, but it was suitable for the night. Maxim was out among regiments all day, preparing troops for the impending battle, returning home to the division in the evening, gathering the staff personnel, assigning tasks, listening to reports. Varya came to some of these meetings. Maxim always spoke about business, simply, in a confiding manner, without raising his voice. This won people over.

Everyone would leave after the meetings — the chief of staff, the deputy commander of political affairs, the deputy of the rear units, other representatives who had come from the army or the front. Maxim also knew how to get along with the command.

Then they would have supper. Maxim's dugout was large, dry, comfortable. A small portable engine rumbled evenly and cozily nearby, to be turned off as soon as Maxim went to sleep. At dinner they spoke about their work, and Varya tried not to stay late. She'd say good-bye, go to her hut, and leave early in the morning for the line or to return to army headquarters.

When she managed to talk to Maxim one on one, Maxim let her know in a good-natured way, but firmly and clearly, that conversations on political subjects were inappropriate here, and Varya did not initiate them. They reminisced about Moscow, the Arbat, the house. Maxim would relate what Nina wrote, and praise Vanya — he was a smart boy. Once, he looked at her somewhat slyly and said: "I saw a certain person here not long ago. You'll never guess who."

"Who?"

"Sasha Pankratov."

"Sasha?" She took a breath. "Where did you see him?"

"He came here. He sat on the same bench you're sitting on."

Varya looked at him expectantly.

"He sat on this bench," Maxim repeated and smiled. "He's become a big boss now, he's inaccessible: he's in Front Headquarters!"

"Sofya Aleksandrovna told me that he had been drafted as a driver."

"That's right. He was a driver, distinguished himself in the battles of Moscow and was promoted to an officer's rank — Marshal Zhukov himself granted it to him *personally*, imagine that."

He was proud of Sasha and did not hide it.

"A guard engineer major, he serves in the Motor Transport Administration of our front. As I understand it, wherever it's tough, that's where they send him. Sasha is a good worker, he's experienced, knows how to get things done."

"Did you tell him that I'm here?"

"Of course. We talked about all our friends and acquaintances."

Max told Sasha during their first meeting that Varya was in the same army, in the headquarters of the engineer troops. He had sat facing him, shaking his head: "What a meeting! We haven't seen one another for ten years, ah!" He was deeply moved, old friendships don't fade, he even wanted to tell him about how Varya had brought the little boy to them in the Far East, they thought they would raise your kid, Sasha, along with hers. But he remembered Nina's words just in time: "I think that Varya only really loved Sasha." He decided it was better not to venture into such delicate subjects. Well, he did mention the fact that Varya was married, that they had visited them before the war on Gorky Street, the apartment was stylish and ostentatious, her husband was a famous architect, now a major general, they lived well. Sasha took all this in calmly, he didn't ask questions or try to get details, and Max was convinced that Varya's love was a matter of the distant past, it was all *childhood*. That was why he told Varya about his meeting with Sasha in such a calm way, only slyly winking, as if saying, As a young girl you were in love with Sasha, isn't that so?

But he caught Varya's reaction: "Did you tell him that I was here?" was not a casual question. Evidently women have deep feelings about their memories. Very well, they're adults, they'll sort it out. . . .

So then, Sasha was here. And he knows where she is. He drives around the front, he comes to their army, he can drop in to see her. Just to visit. After all, there was so much that connected them. What does it matter that she's married — couldn't they be friends? She didn't have any claims, she had reconciled herself to everything, if only she could see him alive. At the front, everyone tries to see people from his own region, even strangers, Muscovites seek out Muscovites, Leningraders other Leningraders; something connects them, possibly homesickness. Tell a sapper from Vologda that there's someone from Vologda in an adjacent company, and he'll rush right over to see him. And here they were with Sasha. . . . Today they're alive, tomorrow they're gone, it was such a terrible war, how could they not meet? if there was a chance, maybe the last chance. He could simply say: "Hello, Varya, I found out that you're here and I dropped in." And she would reply to him: "How wonderful, how marvelous, Max told me about you, I expected you to come." They would sit and talk for a while, he would leave, maybe for a long time, maybe they would never see each other again — it was war, yet nonetheless there would be relief, a clearing from this meeting, so much heaviness would be lifted from her soul.

But Sasha didn't come. Varya decided to go see him herself. And what was wrong with that? She was in the Front Headquarters and dropped in. "Hello, Sasha. . . ."

However by early June the principal construction work on the lines was completed, all the papers were all drawn up, so there was no reason to go to headquarters. Nonetheless Varya called Telyaner: let him summon her under some pretext. Telyaner happened not to be there. Colonel Svinkin answered the phone, said that Telyaner would be back in about three days, and asked if he could be of any assistance.

"No, thank you, nothing in particular," replied Varya. "I wanted to clarify some things with David Abramovich. Very well, I'll call in three days."

Varya didn't manage either to call or to see Telyaner, and so she didn't see Sasha.

June was very intense at the front. There were powerful aerial battles, General Headquarters warned about the possibility of a German attack on July 2, troops were brought to complete combat readiness, the headquarters staff of the engineer troops were ordered to stay put.

The German attack did not take place on July 2 and everything quieted down, but there was yet another reason why Varya couldn't drive over to see Telyaner.

The Fifteenth Division, which occupied the left flank of the 13th Army, transferred responsibility for a section of their sector to the 132nd Division, and the latter complained that some of the defensive structures it received were unsatisfactory. Such things were an ordinary occurrence at the front and normally were solved on location. However the 132nd Division was part of another army — the 70th Army — and it was situated at the junction of two armies, the most vulnerable spot for defense. The conflict acquired an interarmy character.

The issue hadn't arisen just now, a month had already gone by while arguments and negotiations between the divisions, then the armies, went on, and the order came from Front Headquarters: "Clarify, clear, report. Conclude within 5 days."

Varya's superior, Colonel Kolesnikov, called her in: Varya had supervised the work on the Fifteenth Division line, she had all the documentation. The convivial joker Kolesnikov did not joke this time. He held out the Front Headquarters order to Varya.

"Read this."

Varya read it, shrugged her shoulders:

"Our division had no complaints, suddenly our neighbors have them."

"My colleague Vitvinin did me a good turn. I'll be talking with him now."

Colonel Vitvinin was the chief of the engineer troops of the 70th Army, which was where the complaints were coming from.

The telephone rang. Kolesnikov picked up the receiver. Colonel Vitvinin was on the line. They talked without mentioning either the division numbers, the army numbers, or the location of the line, but Varya understood everything.

"Our representative will leave tomorrow, send yours," Kolesnikov concluded and hung up. "He's justifying himself, says that they went over his head to complain. We know these tricks. . . . And so, Varvara Sergeevna. . . . Both our cars are out today; take all the documents and drive out to Fifteenth Division headquarters, and from there go to the location with the division engineer — I'll let him know in advance. If anything is incomplete, it has to be fixed. I've also instructed the division engineer about this."

"None of what we did was incomplete," Varya objected.

"It's possible, it's possible. . . . But the conflict has to be settled, so you must bring back an attested statement with the signatures of their representatives. Don't haggle over who'll complete the work, whether we will or they will or we'll do it together — the important point is not to return without a document. I'm providing you with a car only to the Fifteenth Division's headquarters, from there you'll use one of their cars, and when you return to headquarters, call, and I'll send a car for you. If you find one coming this way, that would even be better."

Varya drove out to the division early in the morning on July 3. The usual road: military trucks, staff passenger cars, checkpoint places, our aircraft in the air. For some reason there weren't any German planes in sight. Afraid that Kolesnikov would not send a car for her return trip, Varya dropped in at Maxim's along the way in order to let him know beforehand that she might possibly need his help.

Maxim was standing near his dugout next to his "Jeep"; it departed.

When he found out where Varya was headed, he was displeased and said:

"Couldn't they have sent someone else besides you? Don't they any have male engineers there?"

"It's my sector."

"That's not important. The situation is dangerous. We were expecting an attack yesterday. It didn't take place, but it can happen at any moment."

"It's no use talking, Maxim, I'm here already. I'm just afraid that the command won't send a car out for me. If something comes up, send for me, and I'll be able to get back somehow."

" 'If something comes up,' " Maxim growled, "I'll send for you, of course."

"I'll say: Ivanova is calling, you'll understand that I'm at the Fifteenth Division headquarters, at the division engineer's, all right?"

"All right," said Maxim, "if I'm not here, call the Chief of Staff or Velizhanov, our division engineer, I'll let him know. How long are you going to be there?"

"I don't know. If we have to fix something, three to four days."

"Don't spend the night in the regiment, return to the division headquarters."

"I won't be in our territory, I'll be in the 132nd Division."

∾ 35 ∾

As SOON AS SASHA HEARD that Varya was serving in the 13th Army, he immediately went to see her. He didn't start thinking about what he would say to her. "I found out that you were here, and I came to see you." Everything that happened between them, or rather, that could have happened but didn't, all of that was past. The letters, the expectation of a meeting, jealousy, resentments — all of this vanished, dissolved in time, all that remained was what was young and joyous and what had happened ten years ago when he sat in their room and she, a schoolgirl, showed him how she wrote crib sheets on her knees. And her youthful unwillingness to compromise: "I'd expel all of them, the scum, all they do is look for people to ruin." And how she sang when her sister reproached her: *"Flower of the fragrant prairies, your laughter is more tender than a reed-pipe."* She was showing her character, the little squirt.

Maybe he would just say: "Forgive me for that telephone call from Kalinin, my life wasn't going too well then." However, it wasn't likely that he'd have to justify himself; *that time* for her had also passed. But it would probably be pleasant to meet someone from your youth, from your past, which seen from the present bloody time appeared beautiful and joyful no matter what. *"Wherever I wandered during the blossoming spring, your voice whispered to me that you were with me."* They danced to this in the Little Arbat Cellar. And she invited him to go to the skating rink with her. Going to the skating rink never happened, nothing they had planned then ever happened.

Varya happened not to be there, they told him at headquarters that she was out among the troops. Then for about two weeks Sasha had neither time nor an excuse to drive over to the 13th Army. In a short time the front was being supplied with nearly 100,000 boxcars and flat cars of artillery, tanks, ammununition, fuel, food supplies, and uniforms. For motor transport servicemen this meant tens of thousands of daily trips for long distances — the depth of the frontline rear areas was as much as 350 to 400 kilometers — under bombings, along damaged roads, on detours around destroyed bridges. There was a shortage of spare parts, rubber, and gasoline, but nevertheless — "Give me, give me!" No one wanted to hear any excuses.

Like other engineers in the administration, Sasha took in new vehicles, formed battalions and companies and mobile motor transport repair workshops, drove out to railroad lines; the concentration of vehicles attracted enemy aircraft, causing the drivers to push ahead, and Sasha had to bring them back into line. Sasha knew how; he had learned during his two years at the front, and they obeyed him.

And so he raced around in his captured Opel — he had picked it up near Stalingrad, repaired it, held on to it by hook or by crook — sometimes he was told that he had a right to a vehicle, sometimes he was told that he didn't. And he also held on to the driver, Nikolai Khalshin — he was the only one left from his original motor transport company. Ovsyannikov had died in Pronsk. Sasha grieved for this splendid fellow, who was just beginning to live. Churakov and Ruslan Streltsov were lost near Ukhnov. But Nikolai survived, and he was Sasha's driver as well as his orderly and special messenger, a loyal, reliable man.

When he was issued his certificate, Sasha had to fill out an application — there was no getting around it. And he had to include convictions in the application, there was no getting around it, but they didn't trouble him, didn't pester him. He wasn't the only one with convictions, and the NKVD behaved cautiously — people around them were armed. Quite possibly, Zhukov's name had an effect — he had personally promoted Sasha from private to officer.

It was the beginning of July before Sasha managed to get over to the 13th Army. New American trucks had arrived: Studebakers, Chevrolets, Dodges, the best drivers were reassigned to them. There were never enough drivers in the army, and permission was granted to get them from the penal battalions. This was a difficult procedure, but they needed drivers, and you could save at least a few people's lives.

Sasha arrived at the penal battalion in the 13th Army position with two lieutenants. They formed up the first company. Sasha gave the command: "Vehicle drivers, step forward!" The entire company stepped forward and froze. Sasha looked into the faces of these condemned men, who looked at him with supplication and hope: ending up in a vehicle was the only chance to save your life. Not guilty of anything, they were paying for the mistakes and failures of the commanders. In "reconnaissance by battle" they were put out ahead in open country, the enemy fired on them, killed all of them, but our side would locate and neutralize the enemy firing positions and then launch into a real attack. That was the pitiless practice of this war.

None of the penal soldiers had driver's licenses — "I lost it," "it got taken away when I was arrested," "I worked on a collective farm driving a tractor, had occasion to drive a truck." Two one and a half tonners were brought over. A penal soldier would sit down at the wheel, beside him sat the lieutenant who tested his driving. They selected seventeen men from the entire battalion, at least those could start up and drive around the circle.

They finished work at about 3:00 on July 4. Sasha turned over the selected drivers to the motor battalion and drove to the headquarters of the 13th Army engineer troops. Captain Ivanova was out among the troops again, they didn't say where she was exactly: he was an unfamiliar officer who had come on a personal matter, why should he know?

"I'm unlucky." Sasha smiled. "We were neighbors in Moscow." He hoped that the staff officers would cooperate. There are six divisions in an army; if they'd identify the number of the division she was visiting he'd find Varya more quickly. No, they wouldn't cooperate. Sasha drove to the nearest division, the one Maxim commanded. Maybe Varya was there, and if not, he would order his engineer to search for her, their meeting would be delayed for another few hours, that didn't matter, the important thing was to see her!

The day's heat cooled down. The evening was unexpectedly quiet, there were no aircraft, no shooting, it was as if there was no war. The sun was setting, long shadows fell on the road. There was a forest to the right, a hilly plain to the left, beyond it on the horizon were small groves of trees.

A young woman traffic controller at the checkpoint waved a yellow flag, stopped the car, asked for documents.

"Couldn't I pass without them?" Sasha asked jokingly.

"No, we need to follow regulations."

She was a splendid young woman wearing a forage cap, blue skirt, fine boots.

They drove on. The hills in the plain and the small grove were still visible. An enormous antitank ditch stretched along the grove. Illuminating rockets burst in the sky, two green ones, an orange one, a white, then again green — they were German rockets, the forward position was close by.

The aide-de-camp would not allow Sasha in to see Maxim.

"The general is having a meeting, you'll have to wait."

The telephone rang often, the aide-de-camp would write things down, sometimes he would connect the caller with Maxim. The monotonous voice of a radio operator could be heard in an adjacent room: "I'm Sokol, I'm Sokol, do you read me? Over. . . ."

Finally the door opened and three colonels walked out of Maxim's office: the Chief of Staff, the deputy of the rear area, the third, apparently, the deputy commander for political affairs. Sasha understood from their anxious faces that something had happened.

Maxim appeared and nodded dryly to Sasha: "Come in, Major!"

There was a map on the desk. Maxim sat down and invited Sasha to sit as well.

"What I'm going to tell you is not for general disclosure. In the Fifteenth Division zone scouts under Lieutenant Mileshkin's command have captured a German sapper by the name of Fermello. The Germans have cleared the minefields. This sapper revealed that the attack would start at 3:00 A.M. on July 5, which means tonight. I think it's serious. So wrap up your business here and return to your headquarters."

"I only have one concern: I have to see Varya. They told me that she was at a division, I thought maybe it was yours?"

Maxim was slow to reply.

"Varya was here yesterday and went to the Fifteenth Division, the same one where the German sapper was captured. There's some kind of squabble with the neighboring army over defense structures. She promised to call, and hasn't. Given the situation, they may not let her phone, since other conversations are more important. I ordered our engineer to find out where Varya is on my line. He reported: 'Departed to the disposition of the 132nd Division.' And as you know, she's not ours, she's

with the 70th Army." He nodded at the telephone. "An hour ago I spoke
with the commander of the Fifteenth Division and asked about Varya.
Not a very convenient time for such questions, you understand. But I
asked. He gave the same answer: she departed for the adjacent division
with a division engineer."

"Would you show me where she might be?"

Maxim showed him on the map.

"See, Krasnaya Zarya–Krasnyi Ugolok? That's the meeting point
between the flanks of our armies, where Varya and the engineers are
sorting things out. But, this is where, I think, the Germans will deliver
their strike. Apparently they're moving in the direction of Olkhovatka.
Are you planning to head over there?"

"Of course. Under these circumstances, for sure."

Maxim frowned. "You have to know where you're going. The front
is large, where are you going to look for her? And if the Germans launch
their attack, you'll get completely lost. You have to pinpoint where she
is. Go see our engineer, he'll help you — at least he has some means of
communication."

"Can I register an official duty trip with you?" asked Sasha.

"The aide-de-camp will arrange everything."

Velizhanov, the division engineer, a tall, handsome major of about
thirty, greeted Sasha courteously. There was friendliness and willingness to help in his blue eyes, but unfortunately, he couldn't tell him
anything new; he repeated what Sasha had already found out from
Maxim.

"Maybe she's returned to her own headquarters. Let's call."

He picked up the receiver, identified the number.

"Let's wait, they'll connect us now."

He smiled as he looked at Sasha. And Sasha couldn't decide: Was
this person friendly and courteous by nature or was it because Sasha
had come from the division commander? Of course he knew that
Varya was his relative, and he also knew who Varya's husband was:
his name was well known among engineer troops. But he feels awkward asking Major Pankratov how he's related to them — if a general issues an order, you carry it out and you don't ask questions.
And Sasha was also surprised by Velizhanov's dugout: it was cramped,
damp, and smelled of earth. Usually engineers built good shelters for
themselves.

Sasha was suppressing his anxiety with these trivial thoughts. Varya was at the forward position. How would she get out if the Germans launched the attack? No one would bother about her. He had to get through to Varya no matter what.

"Hello, hello . . . Aha . . . I understood you, that's clear, thank you." Velizhanov hung up the receiver and sighed.

"Varvara Sergeevna has not returned from her official duty trip. I think that you have to wait; everything will get clear by morning."

Sasha placed his map in front of him.

"Please show me the road to Krasnaya Zarya and Krasnyi Ugolok."

"You can get there by different routes."

Velizhanov penciled in several routes, marked the populated areas, put down his pencil, and looked at Sasha with a serious expression.

"I have to warn you, Major, that you won't find Varvara Sergeevna in Krasnaya Zarya or Krasnyi Ugolok. The troops have taken up their battle positions, everyone not involved in the battle has been sent away, and we don't know where Varvara Sergeevna has been sent. Looking for her along the frontline now is like looking for a needle in a haystack. And you won't get anywhere at night, you'll get lost, and if you turn on your headlights the Germans will fire on you. Besides, no one will allow you into the combat formations. You have to wait until morning, when the situation will be clearer, and at least the road will be visible."

Sasha left Velizhanov. The headquarters, hidden in the small woods, had quieted down. It was warm, the sky was scattered with stars. If the Germans were going to launch an attack, it was a good night for them to do it.

"Where are we going?" Nikolai asked the usual question.

"Look here, Nikolai, I have to go to the Fifteenth Division. It's not quiet at the forward edge. Since it's a *personal* matter, I don't have any right to risk your life, so I'll drive there alone."

Nikolai leaned toward the steering wheel on which his hands were folded and turned toward Sasha. "There's no question whatsoever about it. Wherever you go, I go."

"I've warned you. Now let's doze a little."

Nikolai stretched out on the front seat, Sasha on the back one. He loosened his belt two notches, moved his gun onto his stomach, turned over on his side, and fell asleep.

At 3:00 A.M. the thunder of artillery guns woke them. The gunfire was so loud that they couldn't hear one another.

The troops of the Central front conducted powerful counter-preparation fire, delaying the German attack by two and a half hours.

~ 36 ~

THE GERMANS launched the attack at 5:30 in the morning. The powerful "Tiger" tanks, low, with large turrets savagely thrusting out long-barreled guns, supported by artillery and aircraft, formed wedges inside of which smaller tanks and armored personal carriers drove. When they stopped, the infantry would dismount and charge into attack. The German bombers flew in groups of fifty to one hundred aircraft. Turning on their sirens, the Junkers dive-bombed the positions of the 13th and 70th armies. The explosions, the roar of the engines, the whistling of shrapnel, the bursts of shells, mines, and bombs deafened everything. People communicated by signals. Columns of smoke and fire obscured the sky.

At 3:00 A.M., when the artillery counterpreparation fire began, Major Velizhanov, running with other officers to Maxim's dugout, shouted to Sasha, "Now we'll find out what the situation is."

They had to wait a long time. Nikolai dozed with his hands on the wheel. Sasha paced back and forth, sometimes sitting on the seat without closing the car door. The noise of the battle was clearly audible, the glow of huge fires covered the horizon.

At 7:00 A.M. Maxim came out of the dugout, the Jeep immediately drove up to him out of the woods, and Maxim left. Almost all the other officers also left. Velizhanov appeared, called Sasha over, and spread a map out in front of him.

"Here's what the situation is, Major. In our army sector, the enemy has broken through to the Fifteenth Division and is moving in the direction of Olkhovatka. Their headquarters has been redeployed. The enemy is advancing on Krasnaya Zarya—Krasnyi Ugolok in the 70th Army sector, 132nd Division headquarters has also been redeployed.

We don't know where Varvara Sergeevna is. If the enemy breaks through to the second zone, then our division will go into combat today." He gave Sasha a significant look. "The general has already left for the command post."

"What do you advise?"

"If you go out in search now, you won't find her and you'll lose contact, no one will permit you to use a telephone or radio set. I advise you not to go anywhere; from here the situation is more visible and there's some kind of communication. We'll see how things develop."

A messenger came in. "Comrade Major, the Chief of Staff urgently requests you."

"Perhaps I'll find something out," said Velizhanov.

Sasha paced near his car. He was losing time, losing hours, but he would lose even more time if he moved blindly in the confusion of combat operations without knowing where Varya was. He had to wait; maybe Velizhanov would report something to him, some detail he could grab onto. And waiting for Velizhanov to appear, he impatiently watched the Chief of Staff's dugout.

Sasha felt thirsty, so he asked Nikolai for some water. Nikolai kept two cans in the car — one with gasoline, the other with water: "What if the radiator suddenly starts to leak, at least we won't be stuck." He poured Sasha a full cup.

Velizhanov finally came out, went down into the dugout with Sasha, and spread out the map again.

"The enemy is continuing to advance in the direction of Olkhovatka. The Fifteenth Division has retreated to the second zone. The 132nd Division is pulling back to the Degtyarnyi-Rudovo line." He showed it on the map. "Engineer Kochin of the Fifteenth Division isn't there yet, but they're expecting him. This gives us hope that perhaps Varvara Sergeevna is with him."

Sasha marked the villages that Velizhanov named on his map, and also copied all the rural, field, and forest roads from Velizhanov's large map.

"So you're still planning to go?" asked Velizhanov.

"Yes."

"Traveling along the front during combat . . ."

"Yes." Sasha extended his hand to him. "Thank you for your help."

"I wish you luck, and one more thing." He pointed to the map. "Do you see these small woods? If the Fifteenth Division headquarters has relocated, then it's to this place, this is where its reserve command point is. And if Major Kochin has returned, then it would be to these woods. Of course, it depends, but it's some sort of landmark for you. If you see Varvara Sergeevna, give her my regards." Velizhanov lifted his large blue eyes up to Sasha. "Pardon me, Major, for the indiscreet question: Is she a relative?"

"A sister," replied Sasha.

The artillery — both German and Soviet — was thundering at full blast, "Tigers" were firing, Junkers were already dropping bombs on the second zone of defense, Soviet fighters and tanks entered into combat. Sasha was stopped at rail crossing-barriers, his documents were checked, he was asked where he was going, he was detained for long periods. Sasha would present his written order for official duty travel with the registration that he was in Maxim's division, he called off the numbers of the motor transport battalions, stated where he was going, he knew their disposition well.

Finally Sasha got to the small woods that Velizhanov had shown him. Dugouts and earthen huts, unloaded staff cars, the signalers laying down cables, soldiers dashing around the woods, the bustle of a newly arrived headquarters — they didn't know whether they was settling in for long, maybe they would have to retreat further today; they didn't even ask for Sasha's documents. When he asked for Major Kochin, they pointed — he was sitting near a dugout, a corpulent middle-aged man, one of his arms in a sling, the other one moving over a map as he explained something to a lieutenant standing next to him. The lieutenant he had crossed-ax insignia on his shoulder straps, just like the major — they were engineers. Sasha walked over, introduced himself, asked if he was Major Kochin.

"Yes, I'm Kochin."

He was blinking, his eyelashes burned down to hairy stubs on his lids, his eyebrows were also burned; Kochin winced at the slighest movement, you could see that his hand and face hurt.

"Major Velikhanov sent me to you," said Sasha, "I'm looking for Engineer Captain Ivanova Varvara Sergeevna."

"Varvara Sergeevna was wounded," said Kochin, "a shrapnel wound in the right part of the chest, apparently the lung was grazed, she lost a lot of blood. I was able to get her to Rudovo, to the battalion medical aid post. The medical attendant considers her condition critical, but he promised to evacuate her to the regimental medical aid post today. Maybe they'll manage to save her."

Sasha stood without moving. He was too late to see Varya!

"We should drive her to the hospital, but on what?" Kochin continued. "I walked here from Rudovo."

He blinked his lashless eyelids; it was difficult to watch.

"Varvara Sergeevna became obstinate, got into a conflict with the commanding officers, refused to go to the division, spent the night in the regiment, and everything began at night. We were hit. At least there was a nurse right there. She bandaged it as best she could."

Sasha took the map out of his map-case, checked the route to Rudovo with Kochin. It was open country, but there were small groves and thickets along the way.

By evening Sasha reached the village of Rudovo. At one end of it, the battle was in progress, huts were on fire, shells thudded as they exploded, bombs fell with a piercing wail, mines exploded. At the other end of the village, the side Sasha had driven in from, two medical orderlies were bringing in the wounded on a large quilted blanket; others hobbled, leaning on their rifles. An elderly medical attendant and a nurse were bandaging them quickly, and either seating them or laying them into a cart.

Nikolai parked the car under a tree, Sasha walked over the medical attendant and asked whether engineer captain Ivanova was here.

"We're not taking names down, we don't have time," the medical attendant answered, continuing to bandage a wounded man, "but there is a woman officer here." He nodded toward the last hut. "She's in there, she's been bandaged."

Sasha walked into the hut. Varya was lying on the floor, on straw, her service shirt torn, her shoulder and chest bandaged, her eyes closed. Sasha got down on his knees and took her hand in his. Her hand was cold. . . . He was peering into her face and past her features distorted by pain, past her deathly paleness, past the ten years that had gone by — he saw the former Varya, a girl with full lips, blowing her bangs off her forehead. . . . He was on his knees, holding her hands in his, looking into her face, in despair because he couldn't tell whether she was breathing or not breathing, entreating fate that Varya open her eyes.

And Varya did open her eyes. Her gaze dim, she looked at Sasha, and her lips trembled in a weak smile.

"You came, Sasha. . . ."

And she closed her eyes again.

✌ 37 ✌

THE BATTLE WAS MOVING CLOSER. Shells and mines exploded in the middle of the street. The paramedic finished bandaging people and hurriedly helped the wounded into the last cart and ordered those who could stand to walk, holding on to the cart. He shouted, "Move on!" to the driver. As he put rolls of bandage, cotton wool, and iodine back into his bag, he said to Sasha, "I told the regiment that there is a badly wounded woman here, a captain, and that they should send a car to take her straight to the hospital. She won't survive being loaded in and out of vehicles and medical units. She had lost a lot of blood by the time they brought her here. But they haven't sent the car." He was having trouble closing his overstuffed bag. "Could you get her to the medical point or to the hospital?"

"Where are they?"

"Who knows where they are now? We're retreating, which means they're retreating, too. You'll find them. In Gremyache, in Fatezh. . . . Ask along the road. Put her on her back in the car, with something under her head. Drive carefully, watch the road."

The paramedic put the bag over his shoulder and ran after the cart.

Sasha and Nikolai carried Varya to the car using a blanket as a stretcher, laid her down on the backseat, and put a rolled-up overcoat under her head. Sitting on the floor, Sasha held her by the legs. Varya had not opened her eyes, and it sometimes seemed that her lids were trembling, a tremor crossed her face, but maybe he was just imagining it. When they moved her, she seemed to have moaned, but it was hard to tell in the noise of the artillery fire and the bombs.

They headed for Gremyache, and if the medical unit had left, they would go to Fatezh. The map showed a woods about six kilometers from Rudovo — that was a bit of cover, where they could stop, remove the back of the front seat, and make Varya a little more comfortable. Exploding shells raised black columns of smoke, high-explosive shells blew up just above the road in a burst of flames, and the roadbed was churned up and full of potholes. Sasha held Varya, to cushion the jolts from the road, and it felt like holding a corpse. He peered into her face, listened for her breathing. She was still alive, but Sasha knew that she would die.

The road was better through the woods, but behind them the battle raged, the explosions, shots, machine-gun rounds, and roar of the fighter planes rising in a single crescendo.

"Let's go about five kilometers and then stop —" Sasha did not finish. There was a bang up close and a sharp whistling sound, the sound of shrapnel, and then broken glass. The car shuddered to a stop. . . . Nikolai got out and opened the hood.

"Ruined."

The bullet that broke the windshield and side window had not touched Nikolai.

Sasha got out of the car and looked around. The sky was red with the burning fires all about them, and on the horizon to the left he saw low black boxes moving toward them — tanks!

"Hurry!" Sasha said.

They carried Varya on the blanket into the woods, and then came back for the coats, rifles, bags, and water. They took the shovel and ax, because they knew what lay ahead.

They carried Varya deeper into the woods. The treetops were torn by shells, and the ground was littered by rags, wine bottles, cans and cigarette packs, yellowed newspapers in German script — the Germans must have been here in the spring.

They moved on with Varya, deeper into the grove, and stopped by a large fallen tree with upended roots. The ground was flat and the green grass was clean. They lowered Varya to the ground and put the overcoat beneath her head. Sasha listened to her breathing, she was still breathing, and examined her bandages. There was no fresh bleeding. Nikolai poured water into a mug and raised her head. A quick shudder passed along her face. Sasha poured a few drops into her mouth, but she did not swallow. The water collected in the corner of her mouth.

"Better not," Nikolai said. "She might choke."

They lay down on the grass. The sun was setting and the land grew dark. It was dry, the way it had been all day, and they could smell the sun-baked aroma of wormwood. Nikolai made a small fire and boiled up some oatmeal. They ate. The smell of the porridge and the crackle of burning branches reminded Sasha of the fire in the taiga. None of his comrades from exile was left. They buried Kartsev in Boguchany, intractable Volodya Kvachadze naturally had been destroyed in the camps, and Soloveichik had died in the taiga. They were all gone. He was the only one who had lingered.

"Who is she to you, Comrade Major?" Nikolai asked.

Sasha was silent. He had told Velizhanov that she was his sister. He couldn't have said anything else, since Velizhanov knew whose wife she was.

"We were in love, and then we met ten years later. You see how we met."

It grew dark in the woods.

"Get some sleep," Nikolai offered. "I'll keep watch."

"No, you sleep, and then we'll switch. I'll wake you up. Take the overcoat!"

"Wear it, it'll be cold at night."

"Take it, I said. Don't worry, I won't freeze. As soon as it gets light, we'll move on."

Nikolai unfastened the belt of the coat, covered himself with it, and fell asleep.

Sasha bent over Varya again. She was still breathing. He took her hand, felt for a pulse, and found the weak beat. Maybe that was his own pulse that he felt in his fingers.

He had told Nikolai that they would move at dawn, but he knew that they would go nowhere. They could not get away from death. The thought did not frighten him. He did not want to live anymore — not a life without Varya. His past, his suffering, his wandering — it was all gone, and Varya was all that he had left. Sasha held her hand, looked into her face, and softly spoke her name. "Varya." Did she hear? She did not. She was silent.

The moon was not visible beyond the trees, but the light broke through the leaves, flickering on Varya's face, and it looked as if she were moving her lips, talking to herself. Sasha leaned closer. "Varya." She did not reply.

Why hadn't he asked her to visit when he was in Butyrka Prison? Why hadn't he said she was his fiancée? "How I'd like to know what you are doing now." Why hadn't he been able to say that to her? He was so horrible to her on the telephone from Kalinin. "Isn't there anything else you want to say to me, Sasha?" If he had told her then that he loved her and was waiting for her, maybe it would all have been different, maybe she would not be dying now. But he didn't tell her.

And still . . . her last words were for him. "You came, Sasha. . . ." She had been waiting for him. "You came, Sasha." He came and now he would not leave her.

Varya's face darkened as a cloud covered the moon. Sasha thought she was dead. He leaned toward her chest and listened for her heartbeat. He called her name again, and there was no answer.

Sasha walked a bit and then leaned against the fallen tree. The evening freshness had been replaced by a dry warmth. His mother was probably thinking about him. He felt sorry for his mother.

A touch roused Sasha out of his reverie. Nikolai.

"Comrade Major . . ." Nikolai nodded toward Varya.

Sasha walked over to Varya. He opened one eye, then the other. Varya was dead.

"It's over, Comrade Major," Nikolai said.

Sasha shut her eyes and emptied her pockets — her identification, her orders, a small notebook and pencil. He put it all in his pockets and folded her arms over her chest. He got up.

It was light, the cannons were roaring and bombs were bursting.

Sasha looked around for a free spot, picked up his shovel, and marked a rectangle for the grave. He told Nikolai, "Use the ax to chop through the roots."

Nikolai chopped, and Sasha followed along with the shovel, digging. They worked for an hour or two, getting about forty centimeters deep; they dug standing in the grave. Nikolai suddenly straightened and listened closely. He pulled Sasha by the sleeve behind the fallen tree, took out his rifle, and handed one to Sasha. Running from tree to tree, someone was moving toward them.

"Who goes there?" Sasha called.

"And who are you?"

"Soviets."

Two soldiers with rifles came out from the trees. When they were convinced that they were among their own, one soldier turned, put his fingers in his mouth, and whistled. Other soldiers came, a platoon, led by a boy lieutenant in a faded uniform. Sweat streamed down his dusty face. He saluted Sasha.

"Where are you from and where are you going?" Sasha asked.

The lieutenant waved his men on. "I'll catch up."

Their gear gently clinking, the men moved on into the trees.

The lieutenant looked at Varya on the ground, her arms folded, and at the grave. . . .

"We got out of encirclement and are headed for our assigned point."

"What unit?"

"Fifteenth Division. Six hundred seventy-sixth regiment. Commander Colonel Onuprienko."

"Nikolai, go with the lieutenant!" Sasha ordered.

"I won't leave without you, Comrade Major!" Nikolai responded.

"Obey orders!"

"Comrade Major!"

"Obey orders!" Sasha raised his voice.

"You shouldn't stay, either, Comrade Major," the lieutenant said. "The Germans are behind us. They'll fine-comb the woods."

"Nikolai! You'll report that I remained in the village of Rudovo."

"The enemy took Rudovo last night at nineteen hundred," the lieutenant said.

"Then, in the woods near Rudovo."

Nikolai gave Sasha a pleading look.

"Get going, hurry it up. Don't keep the lieutenant waiting," Sasha said.

Nikolai took his coat, rifle, and kit-bag.

"Leave the grenades."

Nikolai took three hand grenades, F-1s, they called them "Fenkas," and put them down near the fallen tree. He put his bag over his shoulder.

"What is your name, Lieutenant?" Sasha asked.

"Nikishev." The lieutenant shifted his feet, he was in a hurry to go.

"I am Pankratov. Please confirm in writing that I ordered Private Khalshin to return to the unit in your presence."

"Yes sir!" The lieutenant saluted. "Let's go, soldier!"

"Farewell, Comrade Major," Nikolai said, his voice catching.

"Farewell. Thank you for everything. Go!"

Sasha went on digging. The earth was full of roots, strong threads, like wire. The shovel couldn't get through some of them and he had to use the ax. His sweat-soaked shirt and trousers stuck to his body and his feet were burning. He took off his boots and set them down near the tree, next to his rifle, grenades, pistol, and water.

He went on digging. Large white clouds moved slowly in the sky, fires blazed on the horizon, cannons boomed, went still, and roared again.

Sasha stopped digging when the grave was waist-deep. He got out, cleared the dirt from the edge and dragged Varya over on the blanket. He jumped back in, lifted Varya, and lowered her into the grave. It was crowded, but he laid her out well, evenly, and covered her with the coat. He did not cover her face, he would use the cap for that. He kissed Varya on the lips — for the first time in his life. And the last.

He climbed out of the grave. He could hear shots and running, German words and curses, German orders.

Sasha got behind the fallen tree, put his automatic rifle on it, got his grenades and pistol ready. He saw dark-green uniforms in the bushes. They were moving in a chain, shooting just in case. And when three soldiers appeared before Sasha, he fired a round at them, and the Germans dove to the ground. Sasha tossed a grenade at them. He crouched just as it exploded — they wouldn't be getting up!

And then from all sides — front, right, and left — machine guns opened up. The soldiers were not visible, they were down low. The bullets hit the tree or landed beyond Sasha.

Sasha waited — they would get up and go forward. What else could they do? He was right. The bushes on the right moved, green uniforms appeared behind the trees. They were back. Sasha fired a round and threw a grenade. He turned to the left, saw a green uniform, and threw his last grenade. He picked up his gun but did not shoot. His head fell onto the tree. He was killed by fire from behind. They shot him in the back.

The Germans jumped up, red and sweaty, furious. They shot another round into Sasha's dead body, into the open grave. They ran on. . . .

The German advance was stopped on July 10. In five days they had managed to move only eleven kilometers. The Soviet troops moved into counterattack, and it turned into a general advance at the front that was two thousand kilometers long.

An old GAZ-AA pickup with the burial brigade stopped near the woods on the road leading to Rudovo. The unit was there, smoking in the back, waiting for the remaining two men of their group.

"I know those bums," the sergeant grumbled. "They're having themselves a drink in the bushes."

"What are you talking about?" countered an old soldier sitting in the corner of the truck. "Maybe they came across a killed general or colonel. Or maybe they decided to bury some rank and file."

"The division command buries people, not us," the sergeant cut him off. "Our work is to gather the documents. The instructions were read to you, weren't they?"

"Instructions are instructions, but people are people, even if they're dead."

"Stop philosophizing, you old bastard! We're advancing! In an advance, we don't lag behind. Do you understand?"

"We'll catch up."

The two men causing this argument were older men, like everyone in the unit. They had been walking through he woods and came across an open grave. In it, covered by a coat, was a woman officer, and not far by a tree was a dead major.

"Look, they took his boots."

"No, there they are, by the tree. He took them off himself. That means he was digging the grave himself. There's the shovel."

They turned Sasha over on his back and took our the documents.

"See, he had her papers, too. That means he was burying her, but didn't get a chance. Let's give them a decent burial."

"We'll be late and the sarge will yell."

"The hell with him!"

They put Sasha next to Varya. They shoveled dirt into the grave and stuck two sticks into the mound. They hung their uniform caps on the sticks.

"Let's take the boots, they're fine leather. Why let them go to waste?"

"We'll give them to the sergeant. That'll shut him up."

"Where the hell were you?" the sergeant demanded.

"There was a dead major, here are his boots. And a female captain, in a grave already. So we decided to cover them up, since the grave was dug and the shovel was there."

"Get in and give the documents to the clerk," the sergeant ordered. "Let's go!"

The truck started.

The clerk went through their papers and read out loud: "Pankratov Alexander Pavlovich, born 1911, and Ivanova Varvara Sergeevna, born 1917."

"How old were they then?" asked the old soldier who was half-asleep in the truck bed.

"Makes him thirty-two, and she was twenty-six."

"They were young," said the old soldier.

1991–1994